noah quince

A first novel by Caroline Wood, Undiscovered Authors Regional Fiction Winner.

noah quince

By
Caroline Wood

Cover Design, Text and Illustrations copyright © 2007 Caroline Wood

Original Cover Design by Tom Bunning Design

First edition published in Great Britain in 2007
by Discovered Authors

The right of Caroline Wood to be identified as the Author
of the Work has been asserted by her in accordance with
the Copyright, Designs and Patent Act 1988

A Discovered Authors Diamond

All rights reserved. No part of this publication may be reproduced, stored in a retrieval system, or transmitted, in any form or by any means without the prior written permission of the Author

All characters in this publication are fictitious and any resemblance to real persons, living or dead, is purely coincidental

ISBN 978 -1-905108-46-6

Printed in the UK by BookForce

BookForce UK's policy is to use papers that are natural, renewable and recyclable products and made from wood grown in sustainable forests where ever possible

BookForce UK Ltd.
50 Albemarle Street
London W1S 4BD
www.bookforce.co.uk
www.discoveredauthors.co.uk

With love and thanks
to A

one

Noah forced himself to enter the bright, confined space of the cupboard under his stairs. He stood perfectly still, holding his breath, his pointed shoulder blades set rigid, the flaky skin of his face stretched over his small, bony skull.

But nothing happened. Noah breathed. His thin neck loosened slightly. *All this time*, he thought, *I've been terrified of this bloody place. And there's nothing here.* Relieved, he sank to the floor. He admired his neat row of shoes, his box of candles, and his two identical black umbrellas. He looked up at his jackets, hanging above him, each zipped into a white plastic jacket of its own. Comforted by this order, Noah's knotted stomach began to untie.

Then he felt the hand on his head. It brushed his skull lightly. The fingers made stiff gestures through his fine tufts of hair. His throat constricted and made a dry click as he gulped down air. 'I knew it,' he said, 'I *knew* there was something in here.'

He crouched and, like a tortoise, tried to absorb his neck into his body. His head lost contact with the prying fingers, and he scuttled his folded, foetal shape out of the cupboard. Compelled to see the owner of the hand, Noah looked back through half-open eyes from the hall floor. And saw his jackets. The opaque plastic protectors swayed slightly.

He wailed his relief and shame. Tears diluted the strings of snot that wetted his papery skin. He wiped his face on his sleeves, and rocked himself from side to side on his small, scrawny bottom. Deep, rasping sobs shook the wire cage of his ribs.

'Stupid, stupid bastard' he said to himself. His stomach was still heavy with the meal he'd forced himself to eat before the cupboard ordeal. It threatened to travel upwards, reassemble itself in front of him on the hall carpet. Noah remembered his Mother's voice. 'Don't you make yourself sick again Noah Quince.'

There was a knock on the front door. Noah jolted backwards, grinding notches of his spine against the wall. 'Who the fuck?' he muttered through clenched teeth. 'I'm in no fit state …' The knock was repeated. Then louder, with the addition of a voice.

's'only me, Noel. Won't take two ticks, love.'

Noah's neighbour, Godfrey, peered through the letterbox. 'Noel, darlin', let me in a minute, I'm freezing me whatsit off out here.'

Noah knew protest would be futile, in the same way he knew correcting his name would be – he had tried so many times without the slightest effect. He'd given up years ago. He dragged a dry piece of sleeve across his face, pulled himself to his feet, and unlocked the door. Godfrey entered in synchrony with the opening door, his apron flapping in a chill breeze. He held a fluffy yellow duster in his hand, and smelled of furniture polish. In spite of his hunched posture, Godfrey was the taller of the two men. Noah nearly always found himself looking up his nose.

'Just popped round,' Godfrey said. 'Got cakes in the oven, and I'm in the middle of a big clean, so I can't stay long. Just wanted to check you're still all right for driving us to see the old boy this week, love?'

Noah groaned and covered his eyes with his hands. *After what I've just been through*, he thought. *And all he's worried about is going to see that worthless old bastard*. He'd forgotten about the visiting arrangements. Forgotten that Godfrey was still adjusting to driving again after a couple of weeks with his foot strapped up, that he'd twisted his ankle getting off a chair after cleaning his pelmets. Noah loathed the visits to their ancient, absent neighbour, now in a nursing home. He'd agreed to go only to stop Godfrey's relentless pleading. And because he thought Joseph Pepper would soon be dead.

'Oh go on, Noel. You know it's not too bad once we're there. Old Joey's always pleased to see us, bless him. *And* they always make us a nice cuppa. You give me a little toot tomorrow at six and I'll dash round with the flowers and the fairy cakes. I'm doing some nice iced ones for the girls at the home.'

Too weak to argue, Noah nodded and leaned against the hall wall. He knew from years of experience that the best way to get rid of Godfrey was to remain silent.

'Right, lovey, I'll be off then. Got to get them cakes finished. Then get on with me dusting. P'raps it'll get rid of the swelling. Bloody nuisance.' Godfrey patted his apron and hunched over further. His erection was permanent. A minor handicap he'd learned to live with.

Noah's feelings swayed from indifference to envy, depending on the functioning of his own sexual organ. He had become so familiar with the sight of Godfrey's bulging pinny that he no longer consciously registered it, and would probably only notice its absence.

'Right, I'll see you tomorrow then, duck,' Godfrey said. 'And don't wipe your nose on your sleeves, it's a bugger to get off in the wash.'

Noah submerged himself in a fragrant bath and lay motionless. His knobbled shoulders and skeletal knees broke the surface, like an insect set in aspic. His head throbbed with the day's events. *Should have waited to do the cupboard another time. I wasn't up to it after a day like today*, he thought. *But I've got to make sure its safe before she comes round. Don't want my little angel scared to death as soon as she sets foot in the place.*

He replayed in his mind the earlier telephone conversations with three women. All of them strangers. And how he had fallen in love with one of them the moment he'd heard her voice. *Wish I hadn't arranged to meet the other two*, he thought. *How was I supposed to know I'd find my angel on the last phone call? I can't get out of it now though. I'll just have to go through with it, get it over and done with. Then I'll be ready for my angel. Never thought this dating thing would be so easy. Should have tried it ages ago.*

Cheered by his plans to meet the love of his life, Noah climbed out of his cooling bath, dried himself and went to bed. He made a deliberate effort not to think of the hall cupboard. Or the cellar. Or the thin screeching noise his stairs sometimes made. But *not* thinking about the house fears had the same effect as focusing directly on them.

The jackets filled out. Became dead, bloodless torsos. The plastic that had scuffed across his head transformed again into lifeless fingers. He curled himself into a tight ball underneath his huge feather quilt and pushed fists against his screwed-up eyes. Pictures of dismembered bodies and piles of mummified hands danced against a pulsating red background.

Leave me alone, he thought. *Please, please just go away and leave me alone.*

two

By the time Noah arrived at work the next morning, he'd already spent several hours cleaning his house. Bleach and disinfectant smells were still strong on his hands. An empty stomach caused the light-headed, alert sensation he knew well. *Won't be anyone here for at least an hour*, he thought. *Give me a chance to get on without the wonder boys making their pathetic comments. Not that I give a toss.*

He spent a frenzied hour at his desk, disconnected from the memories of his house. He finished designs and plans that were not due until the end of the week, and placed them ready for collection in his out-tray with a smug and satisfied feeling. *All very well that lot taking the piss out of the way I look*, he thought, *but not one of them can turn out work like this. They wouldn't know a good graphics department if they bumped into one — be lost without the work I put out though, wouldn't they? They ought to try their fancy selling patter on the phones all day and see how well it works without my leaflets and brochures to back it up. Only so much you can say about waste disposal systems, after all. They're too busy hanging about by the coffee-machine half the bloody day, coming up with all their stupid wisecracks and pathetic jokes. Bunch of wasters.*

When Helen arrived, Noah was inspecting his face in a magnifying mirror. Helen gathered a pile of papers from her desk and backed out of their shared office, towards the photocopier. The sleeve of her latest charity shop outfit caught on the door handle. Her clothes pulled her back into the office.

'I can see what you had in mind, Hell, but it doesn't quite work, does it?' Noah said as he surveyed Helen's lopsided outfit.

'*Thank* you. And good morning to you too.' She sounded unusually irritable. 'Perhaps you could stop the personal grooming session now? You did say you wouldn't do it in here any more, Noah.'

She sighed deeply, tugged at the sleeve of her top, and then added. 'I'll bring some coffee after I've done these.' She held up the papers.

'Don't forget …'

'I know, don't forget your china mug,' she said. 'Hardly likely to forget, am I? What with you reminding me every single time I make a drink. I think I know by now that you don't like paper cups Noah, and I also know that you only use your very own personal china mug. The squeaky clean black and white striped one, with no chips on the rim and your name on the bottom. See? Can I go now?'

When Helen returned, Noah was concentrating on his distorted reflection as he plucked hairs from his nostrils with tweezers. His eyes watered. 'You wouldn't have a look at my neck, would you Hell?' he said, 'I can feel a lump, look just here …' He patted the back of his neck.

Helen pushed his hand out of the way, and peered down the neck of his crisp white shirt. 'Nothing there,' she said, 'well, nothing new anyway. The same old lumps and bumps as always. Why all the fuss today?'

About bloody time, Noah thought, and put his tweezers down. *Thought she'd never ask.* 'Obvious isn't it?' he said. 'Got to look my best. Can't go turning up with things festering and sprouting everywhere, can I?'

Helen dragged her chair next to Noah's, and put their coffees on his desk. She slid the mirror into his drawer. 'You really did it then? The personal ads thing – the lonely hearts and all that? I didn't think you'd …'

'What? Didn't think I'd have any luck? Didn't think there'd be anyone desperate enough to -'

Helen tapped his knee. 'Hold on, hold on, I didn't say that, did I?' She shook his bony leg. 'I just didn't think you'd go through with it, that's all. Come on, tell me all about it. When's it happening? This weekend?'

Noah brushed freshly-plucked nose hairs off his top lip. 'No, the one after. Got a week to prepare.' He reached down for his shiny leather briefcase. The joints of his elbow and wrist clicked as he heaved it up onto his lap. The folder he gave Helen was labelled *Find a Woman*.

Helen shook her head and smiled as she read through the detailed notes. 'Taking it all a bit casually as usual, I see,' she said. 'This is so you, Noah. It's all here – their adverts, the dates and times you spoke to them – which by the way was last night and you never said a word to me about that – where and when you'll be meeting them. And this bit – I love this bit – you've even given them marks out of ten.'

Noah snatched the folder away. 'If you're going to laugh …' He stood up, both his knees clicked. 'There's no point doing something if you don't do it properly, is there? Just because *you* don't mind things being slapdash and shoddy …'

'Oh, thanks very much. Another subtle dig at my clothes, I suppose?' Helen adjusted the neck of her green and black striped top. 'Or are you saying my work's shoddy now as well?'

Noah shook his head. 'No, not your work. It's just that, I thought you'd be really pleased for me, Hell. Especially about Angela.' He twisted the fine hair above his left ear.

Helen sighed deeply. She put her hands on Noah's bony shoulders and pressed for him to sit down again. 'I am pleased for you. Sort of. It's just the way you've gone about it. It's a bit … well, different I suppose. But that's okay. Don't go building your hopes up too much though. I don't want you to get hurt, Noah.' She stroked the back of his hand. 'And you don't *know* her name's Angela. She never told you her name, did she? It's all there in your folder.'

'No, but I know she is an angel though, I could tell that just by her voice, so it's a good name for now. I'm in *love*, Hell. I don't really care about the other two, but I'm in love with Angela and I can't wait to see what she looks like.'

Helen gave a resigned shrug. 'Just be careful, Noah.'

three

'Think he'll like them whasnames, duck, them coronations?' Godfrey said. 'I had a devil of a time making me mind up what ones to get. They come in all colours these days, don't they? D'you know, I've even seen blue ones in the big supermarket. Blue! Course, you can't beat the proper colours, can you? Red ones, pink ones, and them lovely half-caste ones. You know, Noel, they're sort of orange with a red frill round the edges. Or white with a pink frill. Whas your favourites, duck?'

'Blue.' Noah sounded sullen, like a moody teenager. He glanced sideways at Godfrey in the passenger seat, the large bunch of flowers on his lap. *Just what I wanted*, he thought. *An in-depth discussion on the finer qualities of carnations.*

'Oh, Noel, you're pulling my do dah, you are ... my leg. You don't really like them blue ones do you? They're all syn ... all, you know, they don't look real, do they?'

Noah sighed, peered in the rear-view mirror. 'To tell you the absolute truth, I don't care if I never see another bloody carnation in my entire life. Of any colour. Actually. Now, can we make sure we're not there more than twenty minutes tonight? I've got a lot to do at home.'

'We can't go rushing off like that though, Noel. What will Joey think? Poor old thing – he looks forward to these visits all week long. Matron told me he does.' Godfrey turned the bunch of flowers round so the pale lemon blooms faced away from Noah. He patted the tissue paper protectively. 'You know he likes a bit of company. And *he* 'preciates flowers, even if you don't.'

Noah blew a short huff sound though his nose. 'How can you tell?' he said. 'He's got no idea we're there most of the time. And when's the last time he said thanks for the flowers? You've taken him so many bunches it looks like a bloody florist's shop in there. The old bastard's not interested. I don't know why you bother.'

'Noel, you mustn't talk about Joey like that. You don't know him like I do. He might not say much but I reckon it cheers him up, having some nice flowers by his bed. Gives him something to look at. And anyway, the ones they take out of 'is room get shared out between the other old ducks in there. It don't do no harm, having a bit of colour round the place, does it?'

Noah shook his head dismissively. 'Like I said, I don't want to be there long.' He leaned away from Godfrey who, as was his custom on these car journeys, had edged closer to the driver's seat.

'If you say so, duck,' Godfrey said. 'Just remember though, we'll be old and lonely one day. And we'll want someone to come and spend a bit of time with us then, won't we?' He patted Noah's leg.

Christ, he makes it sound as if we'll be sitting side by side in some stinking nursing home together – holding bloody hands if he's got anything to do with it.

'You won't find me in a place like that,' Noah said.

Godfrey patted his leg again. 'Oh, don't you be so sure, Noel. You never know what's round the do-dah ... the corner. You take my old Mum. Very independent she was. Never a day's illness in her life. Did all her washing and cooking; still doing mine, she was, when she was eighty. She never wanted to go in that place, that nursing home. Fought like cat and mouse over it, we did. But in the end, she had to. I couldn't look after her no more, not after she had that last whasname ... that stroke.

'She was too heavy for me, see. And she used to call out and get herself all worked up. Wanted to get up the stairs, wanted to give the house a good old clean and all sorts. And would she listen? "Mum," I used to say, "Mum, you can't go getting the carpet sweeper out at your age. Let me do it. I'll give it a good old going over, you know I will."

And she knew I didn't like it dirty any more than she did. But it's not the same is it, someone else doing your chores? I used to try and let her help me. Put the feather duster in her hand – she couldn't hold it – and sort of squeeze her fingers round it, then we'd do a bit of dusting together. Her in her wheelchair, me leaning over her, and we'd do a bit of cleaning and that made her happy, see? Only if I didn't let her help, she could get really whasname, you know, really stroppy, bless her. She'd try and waggle her finger at me. And I used to pretend to smack it. "You can put that away," I'd say to her. "You can put that away right now, young lady. We'll have none of that sort of behaviour in here." And she'd laugh. You could tell – she couldn't move her face but I could see it in her eyes. She was happy. And eat – oh, Noel, she loved her food. Packed it away, she did. Course, she used to be a lovely cook in her time, the dinners she put in front of me every day, I can't tell you. So when she couldn't manage any more, I did all the cooking. That was the highlight of her day, that and the telly. We'd have our dinner about half-twelve, then Mum'd have a little doze while I got on with the washing up. Then I'd wake her up with a nice cuppa and a slice of cake, and she'd want the telly on for the afternoon. Used to sit there glued to it, we did. All them quiz shows and gardening programmes and as for the cooking shows, she used to make rude noises, you know, like do-dahs ... raspberries. That was her way of saying they didn't know what they was talking about. Oh, we did have a good time duck, me and my old Mum.'

The bunch of flowers on Godfrey's lap rose up as he struggled to pull a handkerchief from his pocket. He dabbed his eyes. 'And she used to like a nice bunch of flowers as well. Not too often – she'd tell me off if I bought them too regular. Waste of money she said it was. But if it was her birthday or a special treat, she loved a vase of flowers, she did – all whasnamed, you know, all arranged nice, so she could sit and look at them.' He patted the tissue paper again. 'Just like poor old Joey.'

Jesus, thought Noah, *if that's all there is to look forward to – staring at a vase of half-dead flowers from the petrol station for hours on end, I think I'll drive into the next bloody lorry we see.* He was moved though, in spite of himself, by Godfrey's story of life with his elderly Mother. *I couldn't do it. All that feeding and toilet business and getting them dressed ...* He shuddered.

'Whas up, duck? You cold? Here, turn the thingy up.' Godfrey leaned forward, started fiddling with the switches on the dashboard. Hot air blasted through the vents at full speed, sounding like a hairdryer. 'That'll warm you up, love,' Godfrey shouted over the noise.

Noah snapped the switch off. 'What the bloody hell you doing? Did I say I was cold? Just leave things alone.'

'Only trying to help, Noel. You've got your driving to think about, haven't you? I just thought I'd —'

Noah cut in. 'Well don't. Okay?' *Must have driven his Mother mad, all that interfering and anticipating, trying to guess her next move. Bet she wanted to kill him. I couldn't stand it, I know I couldn't. Don't know what's worse – wiping dribble off somebody's chin, pulling socks over their scrabbly old yellow toenails, or being the helpless one; having someone else decide what side to part your hair or how much you should eat.* He shuddered again, then shot a quick look of warning at Godfrey, who gave a cheerful grin in return. 'So how long did you, er, take care of your Mother?'

'Not all that long, duck – she'd just turned ninety-one when she had to go in that nursing home place. Did everything herself right up till she was eighty. Then, when she couldn't do that no more, I took over. "You're staying here with me, Mum," I told her. "We'll manage." And we did, Noel. We didn't want her going in no home. Not right, is it? People want to be in their own home, don't they? Not locked away in some insti... you know, one of them affirmary places. So, we got on with it, just the two of us. Kept her lovely, I did, Noel. She always looked nice. They used to say down the club she went to how nice she looked; always paying her whasnames ... confidents, they were. Had her hair done once a fortnight as well; they had a girl used to come to the club and do it. Then when she couldn't get out no more, I used to do it for her meself.' He sighed, dabbed at his eyes with the hanky again. 'Course, that didn't last long, and she had to go in that nursing home place after all.

'Only ninety-one as well, bless her. And she still had all her marbles and everything. We just couldn't carry on, you know, what with the stairs and her wheelchair and me lifting her and them chest affections she kept getting. Broke my heart it did, Noel, when they came and took her away. "Mum," I said, "don't worry; we'll have it all cosy for you in no time at that hotel" – that's what we called it, the hotel. "And then you can come back here and we'll carry on just the same. Me and you."' He wiped his eyes again. 'But she never did come home, poor old soul. And I didn't half miss her. Mind you, I used to go up there, to the hotel, every day. Couldn't get rid of me, they couldn't. I was doing cooking, cleaning, singing to the old dears, feeding them, all sorts. We used to have such a laugh, duck'

'But you took care of your Mother for over *ten* years before she went there?' Noah said. *Christ, what a life*, he thought.

'If only it could have been longer, Noel. I'd have given anything to keep her at home with me.'

'But what about, I mean, didn't you ever have … What about your own life? Didn't you have someone, you know, a relationship or something?' *God, there must have been some old queen or other that he used to get together with.*

Godfrey laughed. He flapped the hanky, folded it up and slipped it in his jacket pocket. 'Oh no, duck. I'm one of them whasnames … a conformed bachelor. Never got married or anything like that. Oh no, nothing like that, never bin interested, Noel. No, it was always just me and my old Mum, bless her.' He laughed again and slapped the top of Noah's arm with the back of his hand. 'Fancy you thinking I was a married man. Just goes to show, don't it duck? We never really know about people, do we?'

You're right there, thought Noah. *You are absolutely right*. He gave a weak smile, just a twitch at the sides of his mouth. 'No,' he said, 'I don't suppose we do.' *What's he talking about, never been married? Course he's never been fucking married. He's as camp as a tent site. He's about as likely to get married as I* … he stopped himself, gripped the steering wheel hard. He felt angry that he had allowed himself to engage with Godfrey, and that the discussion had gone this far. *I didn't even want to know about his bloody private life*, he thought. *Not about his Mother, not any of it.* He wanted to blame Godfrey, accuse him, but that would mean further discussion. The sense of something shared between the two men had already brought Noah great discomfort. The confessional quality of the talk in his car made him uneasy. 'Nearly there,' he said sharply, pushing the indicator. 'Better shut up and start looking for a parking place.'

During the visit to Joseph Pepper, Noah watched Godfrey. Saw how he chatted to the nursing staff, made a point of saying hello and how are you to the residents they passed on their way to Joseph's room. When Godfrey sat next to the old man's bed, holding his hand, telling him news from the neighbourhood, Noah stood in the corner of the room. Waiting to leave. *What does he get out of this? And how can he sit there like that, with* him*? He knows more than he's saying about Joseph fucking Pepper, I know he does. So how can he do this week after week?* He tapped the toe of his shoe on the floor to interrupt the muttered, one-way conversation. 'Time's getting on,' he said.

'All right, duck. Be right there.' Godfrey stroked the back of Joseph Pepper's large white hand, which lay on the pale blue blanket covering his chest. The old man stared at Godfrey, no expression on his face. 'See you next week, duck,' Godfrey said to him. 'I'll bring you some more of them fairy cakes, you like them don't you?' There was no response.

Noah watched from the corner, his arms folded. The distaste he always felt for these visits made him eager to leave. But something else was present. For all his loathing of Joseph Pepper, his dismissal of Godfrey's kindness, Noah felt excluded. There was no way for him to access this world of giving and generosity - this connectedness. Although he had no wish to be part of what he saw, he still felt left out in the cold. A baby on a doorstep.

'Come on,' he said. 'I've had enough.'

four

'Thought he looked a bit better tonight, didn't you Noel?' Godfrey fussed with the seat belt, twisting awkwardly beside Noah.

'How can you possibly tell?' said Noah. 'He never looks any different to me. If anything I'd say he looked a bit greyer round the gills than usual.' He looked at Godfrey then quickly back at the road. 'What are you doing?'

'This do-dah, duck. I can't get it across me … can't get it done up, see.'

Noah sighed and shook his head. 'Don't yank at it like that. Just pull it slowly. It's not exactly difficult, is it?' He studied the car in front of him, edging forward even though it hadn't moved. *Come on, come on, what are we waiting for here?*

'Well, you should of let me get meself sorted out before you drove off like that, duck,' Godfrey said. 'I can't do it on the move.' He continued to pull at the seat belt.
'Well, we're not moving now are we? Thanks to this idiot in front here. Think he wants to set up home at this bloody junction. Just pull it down smoothly, don't snatch at it like that.' Noah glared at Godfrey who persisted with his heavy-handed attempts. 'Oh, for God's sake.' Noah heaved the handbrake on, snapped his own seat belt undone and leaned across Godfrey. His fingers fumbling to find the seat belt behind Godfrey's shoulder, and holding his head back to avoid any contact. 'Here,' he said, 'it's quite simple. All you have to do is …' And he eased the wide black webbing from its restraining mechanism, pulled it over Godfrey's beige zipped jacket, then twisted himself back into his the driver's seat. He looked down at Godfrey's bulging lap. 'I'm not bloody clicking it in for you as well,' he said.

Godfrey had started to giggle. He was shaking as he took the seat belt off Noah. 'Oh gawd, Noel, what a do-dah ... a pavlova. Never had to have meself strapped in before.' He bent forward to fix the belt into place, laughing all the time. A car hooter sounded from behind. Godfrey threw his head back and laughed harder.

'Yes, yes, all right,' Noah said, looking in the mirror. The car in front had gone and he was holding up a small queue of seven or eight others. 'No need to have a fucking heart attack is there?' His hurried, un-coordinated movements to drive off made the car stall. 'Fuck,' he said, and slapped the steering wheel. 'That bastard behind better not start again or ...' He turned the ignition and pulled away. Too fast but smoothly.

Godfrey had his hand over his mouth, trying to stifle more laughter.

'This is your bloody fault, you know that don't you?' Noah said. 'Buggering about with that bloody seat belt.'

'Sorry, duck,' Godfrey said, 'you've got to see the funny side though, haven't you, ay? You strapping me in and all that.' He clapped his hands, still laughing. 'Oh, deary me.'

Noah held the steering wheel tight, his arms tense with the effort. 'I'm not just talking about that; it's the whole thing. Dragging me along to see that old bastard week after week; the flowers and bloody fairy cakes – all of it.'

'You don't mean that, Noel, I know you don't. You like to see how the poor old boy's getting on, don't you? After all, he's lived next door to you donkey's whasnames.' All signs of laughter had left Godfrey.

'But he hasn't,' Noah said. 'He's never lived there, not really, not since I've been there. Nearly seven years I've lived there now, and right at the beginning he was in and out of different places for months at a time. I hardly ever saw him. Just used to see the ambulance outside. Or all the home helps and meals-on-fucking-wheels people that used to turn up one after the other would just stop arriving. Then they'd come knocking on my door, asking where the old man was. How was I supposed to know where he was? Poking their bloody noses in like that. And then he got put in this place and that was it. His house has stood empty for years. I don't know why it hasn't been sold. The garden's a fucking disgrace. If they're not careful, there'll be squatters in there or something. And just to make it all extra special, you go on and on about visiting him. "He hasn't got no one else", "It's not far", "It won't take long", and on and on.'

'I didn't know you thought of it like that, duck.' Godfrey sounded shocked. 'If you don't want to go no more, you've only got to say.'

'I never wanted to go in the first place. It was you – going on and on, knocking on the door every five minutes, waiting for me to come home from work – you made me go. And apart from all that, there's something you're not telling me about that old bastard, I know there is.' Noah wound down his window, leaned his face sideways into the breeze. *If I hadn't listened to him, we wouldn't have been going through these weekly bloody nightmares.* He glanced at the passenger seat. 'Well?' Godfrey was hunched now, and seemed to have slid down in the car seat. His arms were folded over his bulky jacket. When Noah looked at him out of the corner of his eye, Godfrey reminded him of an old pillow, the feathers all sunk to the bottom.

'Old Joey was living there a long time before me and Mum arrived, and that was back in, oh let me think now ... must have been —'

'Never mind the date, just get on with it.' Noah sighed.

'Anyway, he lived there on his own. Used to run 'is own shop and everything, he did. Butchers it was, duck. Mum used to go there for all our meat. Lovely sausages he used to do. Famous for 'em, he was. Always had a queue in 'is shop of a Saturday morning. I can see it now. There'd be old Mrs Whasname ... Mrs Plum with the bad leg, and Gladys Evans who had that funny son —'

Noah cut in again. 'Don't do a list of his regulars, for God's sake, we'll be home soon.'

'All right, duck, it just takes you back, doesn't it? Anyway, that was Joey's shop, and then he'd do odd jobs as well – you know, he was the local do-dah ... jack-of-all-shapes. Anyone had a bit of mending wanted doing; Joey was the one to do it. Turn 'is hand to anything, he could. Bit of plumbing, bit of plastering, all sorts, he did. You name it duck, he used to do it. In and out of people's houses all round the street, he was.' Godfrey paused. He eased himself up higher in the seat, looking ahead as he spoke. 'Not my old Mum, though. She wouldn't have him in. Always pleasant to him in the street or over the garden fence, see. But she didn't want him coming in doing no jobs in her house. I remember saying to her when we had that damp patch in the whasname … down in the cellar. "Why don't you get Joe Pepper in, Mum; he'll sort it out." I said. "Oh, we all know what sort of sorting out he gets up to, don't we?" she said. And that was that, Noel, she wouldn't say no more about it. Got the man from Winch's Builders in. Did a nice job as well, he did.'

'So is that it, then?' Noah said. 'All the mutterings and rumours about Joseph Pepper, the way people go quiet if he's mentioned, like he never existed or something, all that's down to the fact that your Mother wouldn't have him in the house?'

'No duck, don't be daft. It was shortly after that when he … well, he went off for a while. Nobody knew what was up or anything. His shop shut down in the end. And he'd left jobs half done – the Dickson's were left with no toilet seat for over a fortnight. Had to get someone else in the end to finish it off, they did. Gone a good few months, he was. And people talk, don't they? Said he was wrapped up in that nasty business with them little boys what went missing. Never found 'em neither, they didn't. Those poor families, they must have never got over it.' Godfrey sniffed.

Noah's driving had become automatic as he listened to the story about Joseph Pepper. He had no recollection of the many gear changes, or left and right turns he had made to get them to the entrance to their road. Now, as he waited to turn right, he became more alert to his surroundings. *Thank Christ we're back. I need to get out of here. Need to think.* He could feel the beginning of a headache. 'Right,' he said as he stopped the car outside his house. 'Another fascinating journey.'

Godfrey remained where he was, the seat belt still across his chest, the bulge in his lap concealed by his slumped position. 'You mustn't go making your mind up about old Joey, just because of what I said. He came back in the end. And he lived there for years after that. Course, he wasn't never the same no more. Kept hisself to hisself, he did. Let the place go a bit. But no one never knew what really happened, see? So it's not fair of you to, you know, to send him to Colchester or nothing like that, is it duck? Me and Mum used to argue about it. It's the only thing we ever had a cross whasname about, duck. "You can't go judging someone unless you know they did something wrong," I used to say. And she'd get all uppity with me; start on about how there's no smoke without matches and everything. In the end we stopped talking about it. So did everyone, eventual, like. I mean, what could you say? There weren't no proof or nothing duck. And you can't hang a man when he's down, that's what I say. So it all died down in the end. That's why I didn't say nothing about it to you, Noel. Didn't want you to think the worse of him. He's just an old man who needs a bit of company, that's all.'

He undid the seat belt and sat looking ahead. Both men were silent for a long while. Then Godfrey opened the door and hauled himself awkwardly out of the car. 'Coming in for a cuppa, duck?' he said cheerfully before he shut the car door. Noah shook his head.

Later that evening Noah scrubbed his body in a hot bath. He carried out the ritual with speed and indignation, his nostrils flared and his mouth stretched tight over his teeth. *What a waste of fucking time*, he thought. *That old bastard hasn't got a clue who we are or anything. Just sitting there like a zombie all the time. And I knew there was something about him. I've always thought he was … I just knew there was something.* He scrubbed furiously at his arms. *Him with the apron is going to have to take his bloody fairy cakes on his own now I've got Angela.* He scrubbed his concave chest with a stiff nailbrush. His thin skin reddened. 'That place stinks,' he said as he scrubbed harder. 'Just like everyone in it, just like that fucking old butcher.' He scowled at his heap of discarded clothes on the bathroom floor. 'I'm sick of coming back smelling like them. Like cabbage and piss,' he said.

five

The arrival of the weekend was marked as Noah crossed out Friday on his kitchen calendar. His weekday shirts were half-way through their Saturday wash. Monday and Tuesday would be on his washing line before most of his neighbours had made their first cup of tea. He wanted to avoid being spotted through the trellis as he pegged out his colour-coded laundry. *None of that, 'Nice day to get your knickers dry,' from him with the apron*, he thought. He had transferred his shoe collection from the cupboard under the stairs to the cellar, where they waited in a tidy row for their weekly polish. *I'll do them later*, he thought.

He broke his no-breakfast rule, and forced himself to eat a poached egg on a thin slice of toast, trimmed into an exact circle. He followed this with a cup of weak tea, and patted his full, uncomfortable stomach. 'Got to eat something, I suppose. Keep my strength up. The Mother-parent would be proud of me. Interfering old busybody.' He rattled the washing machine door. Its safety latch seemed to take forever to release. Noah pulled harder, until veins stood out on his forehead. 'Come on, you bastard, just open will you?' He clenched his teeth. A purple lump throbbed on his jaw.

Noah stabbed pegs onto his shirts; hanging them in the same sequence that he wore them. He took his white cotton underpants to hang on the indoor washing line, in his tidy garden shed. *I'll have to get some new ones*, he thought. *Can't let Angela see these, she'll think they belong to a little boy. A fucking choirboy, by the look of them*. He slapped the nearest pair of tiny, brilliant-white Y-fronts.

With his *Find a Woman* folder on the sitting room floor, Noah sat cross-legged and began to go through the painstaking details. He made notes in the margins. He ticked and underlined with a pencil, like a teacher marking homework. Occasionally he stopped for a few seconds to rub his stomach, which still felt bloated. He imagined the egg, suspended in manila-coloured fluid inside him. In his Mother's voice he said, 'Don't you go making yourself sick, Noah Quince.'

He paid extra attention to the section on Angela, used a new pencil for the notes in her margins, and highlighted most of the carefully handwritten text in fluorescent pink. *Look at this bit*, he thought, tapping the page with his long bony finger. *She sounds like an angel. A bit shy, a bit nervous. Not one of those big-mouthed women, all brash and independent. Ten out of ten. Twenty out of ten, even.*

He returned to the beginning of the Angela section and read it aloud. He forgot about his full stomach. And became aware instead of his penis. 'Slim,' he said, 'like me.' His breathing had become shallow. 'Average height – that means she should be shorter than me. Pale complexion. Not attached.' Noah unzipped his Saturday jeans, untangled himself from his clothing and allowed a disproportionately large penis to bounce and sway in front of him. 'Been a long time since I've had to fiddle about with you,' he said, watching the penis as if it had nothing to do with him. 'Looks like I'll have to sort you out.'

On his knees, he shuffled to the back of the sofa, tugged until there was enough space for him to fit behind it. Then, trapped between the wall and the taut fabric, Noah released his physical tension. There was no emotional satisfaction from his miserable masturbation. Tears spurted uncontrollably from him as he experienced the familiar mixture of sexual release, forbidden behaviour and loneliness. He pushed away his disappointment by making the same promise to himself that he'd been making since childhood. The same promise that followed every morose masturbatory lapse. That it would never happen again.

I need to get outside for a while, Noah thought. *Have a bit of a break. This lonely-hearts thing is hard work.* He sat on the back doorstep, his eyes closed against the bright sunshine. Gold sparks exploded behind his eyelids as he heard Godfrey call from his garden. ''ere, Noel, love, your flies are wide open. You'll get your whatsit sunburnt if you're not careful. Do 'em up, darlin', or put some suntan lotion on it.'

Noah looked down and saw startling white cotton in his lap. He clenched his fists, jumped to his feet and stamped back into his kitchen, slamming the door behind him. 'Fuck off, fuck off, *fuck off*' he spat and spluttered.

The telephone rang. Noah banged his hand on the worktop. *That'll be the Mother-parent, doing her weekly fucking check. "Have you eaten your fruit, Noah?"* In the hall, he snatched up the receiver. 'Yes?' he said.

'Hi, it's Crystal. Any chance we could change the plans a bit?'

Annoyed at the interruption, Noah drew his lips back into a scowl and said, 'Wrong number.' He slapped the phone down. 'Stupid bitch' he said as the phone started ringing again.

The same voice spoke. 'It's me, Crystal. We talked before, yeah? The dating stuff? I'm the poet, black hair, likes cats, yeah? I —'

Noah interrupted. '*Sorry.* Yes, Crystal. Sorry. I do remember. Of course I do. Didn't er ... you know, didn't recognise your voice.' *And she never said she liked cats before either*, he thought. *Stinking bloody things.*

'I was wondering if you could make it tonight instead?' Crystal said. 'You know, same place and that but, like, tonight, yeah? Only, I've got to be somewhere else next —'

'No,' Noah said, too quickly. 'I mean, sorry, but I can't do that.' *It's all arranged*, he thought. *She can't go fucking about with things now. I've got to get myself prepared and everything.* 'So you won't be able to make it next week, then?' he said. *This could be it; this could be the answer to the problem. I won't have to meet her after all.*

'Not on the Saturday. I can do it on the Sunday, yeah? If that's cool with you?'

No, it's not bloody cool with me, he thought. *She sounds like a bloody hippy or something. That's when I'm meeting Angela. I'm not changing that for anyone or anything. Don't even want to bother with this one now anyway.*

'That won't be ...' he said.

'Well, what about tomorrow, then?' Crystal said. 'Can't really do this stuff on the phone, you know? I mean, you have to get the vibes and body language, don't you?'

Noah pressed the back of his neck, picked off a crust of skin. 'I suppose you do …' he said, and thought, *How do I get out of this?*

'So you'll be there, yeah? The Cherry Tree, yeah? Tomorrow, at what time did we say, four, yeah?'

'Three. Actually. We said three o'clock. I've got it written down,' Noah said.

'No problem. See you there then, yeah?'

Noah took a deep breath. *I've got to say something, tell her I don't want to go through with it, tell her I can't make it, that I've met someone else.* He breathed in deeply again. 'Well actually …' But the line was dead. Crystal had gone.

Exhausted, Noah slumped down to the hall floor and leaned against his heavy wooden pew. He rubbed his forehead. A fine dust of skin sprinkled his jeans. A series of long yawns prised his jaws wide apart, with small snapping noises. *Won't have this kind of trouble with Angela, won't have to think up excuses not to meet her. And I bet she won't try to mess about with the arrangements and everything, like this Crystal person.* He yawned again, and stretched. The sole of his shoe pushed against the cupboard door, which clicked fully shut. Noah jumped, his whole body seized with fear. 'No.' The word came out in a jagged spasm, the second involuntary eruption from his body that day.

six

Noah took his shirts off the line. Thursday – his pale blue shirt – had a streak of bird droppings on the left sleeve, a thick chalky exclamation mark. At the back of his mind, Noah heard his Mother say that it brought good luck. He rolled the shirt carefully. *Need all the luck I can get*, he thought, and decided not to re-wash it.

'Looks like the seagulls have had a field day with your washing, Noel.' Godfrey was peering through his trellis. He looked more hunched than usual.

Probably been waiting for me to come out again so he's got someone to talk to, Noah thought. He made an effort to be civil. He lifted a hand and called across Joseph Pepper's garden, 'No harm done.'

'Oh, I don't know so much, love,' Godfrey said. 'It's full of germs, is bird's muck. You don't want to go getting that on your skin, Noel. Not before you've given it a good old soak in whasname … disaffectant.' Godfrey climbed on his plastic chair to look over the fence. He pressed himself against the trellis. The rubber gloves in his apron pocket poked through one gap and the outline of his erection through another. 'You've been a busy bee, getting that lot all washed and dried. Tell you what, you come round and have a cuppa, while I iron them smart shirts of yours. I'm good at getting the creases straight.'

You might be, but you're not getting my creases straight, Noah thought, horrified at the idea. He forced a smile. *Get him off the subject otherwise he'll go on and on about it.* 'No,' he said, then added, 'er, thanks though. I've got some reading to do.'

'I could come round there and do it, duck, only I've got something in the oven, so I'll have to keep popping back.'

Noah made his hands into fists. *I'm not having him round here.*

Nosing and poking about. But I do need to know more about Joseph bloody Pepper though. 'Look, I'll come round to you, all right? But I'm not staying long,' Noah said.

The warm smell of baking wafted through Godfrey's open front door. Noah was surprised to discover that he was hungry, and that the smell was so inviting. His stomach growled softly as he entered Godfrey's clean, homely kitchen.

'Just got to finish these while me water comes to the boil,' Godfrey said over his shoulder. 'Sit yourself down, duck.' He gathered up a conical white bag, plump with icing, and raised it above a wire rack of small cakes in pleated paper cases.

Noah sat down and tapped his fingers impatiently on Godfrey's kitchen table. *All he's got to worry about is what colour icing he's going to put on his fucking cakes*, he thought. *How would he like it if his hall cupboard* … Noah bit the inside of his cheek, to stop his thoughts developing. He stared at Godfrey's rounded back to distract himself. Then he noticed the icing bag again. *Looks like part of a leg,* he thought. *A pudgy little thigh, filled with liquefied fat. The sort of thing they do experiments on. The sort of thing seeping into the floor of my cellar.* He gripped the edge of the table, which moved slightly and scraped on the floor.

'Nearly done, Noel,' Godfrey said. 'Just got to do me balls.' He placed a tiny silver ball on six of the cakes. He turned to Noah and sighed. 'There, all done. They're for old Olive Fitch. You know, round the corner; goes out in her nightgown and bare feet? Anyway, she used to do a lot of baking years ago. Always taking cakes round to the neighbours, she was. You could bank on it with Olive. If it was a Monday, it was baking day and she'd turn up on the doorstep with a lovely sponge or an apple thingy, or something nice she'd made. Course, she's a bit whasname now. A bit do-lally. So I pop her a few nice little cakes round, then I sit with her for a bit of company, and pick the balls off while she makes the tea – don't want to choke the poor old bugger. Just makes 'em look nice though, don't it duck?' He made tea and carried it to the table. 'You all right, Noel? You've gone quiet as a whasname.'

Noah rubbed his forehead and stood up. 'I've got to go,' he said. He saw the icing bag, now flat and empty on the worktop, and turned his head away. 'I was going to ask you about *him*, that old bastard Joseph Pepper, but another time. I've really got to go.'

'Don't be daft, Noel, you've only just got here. I've got a bread puddin' in the oven, and a Battenburg that I've done as a bit of a celebration. Come on, you carry that tea tray out and we'll have this in the garden. I'll check me oven. Then I'll bring us a few little nibbles to go with our tea.'

A gnome grinned up at Noah in Godfrey's garden. It held a fishing rod, and had a little red pouch for its bait. *Can see why he chose that one*, Noah thought. *Looks just like him.* He sipped tea from the gleaming blue and white teacup and held the saucer on his knee. The tea calmed him. The cakes on Godfrey's garden table made Noah think of Helen at work. *She'd love all this sticky, sickly goo. She'd wolf the lot down in one go if she was here.*

'Right duck, now what do you fancy?' Godfrey said. 'There's them whasname cakes ... butterflies. Or there's almond tarts, and that one in the middle – that's a new recipe out of me magazine. It's called Apricot Dream. Have a bit Noel, see what you think.' He sliced through layers of puff pastry and syrupy filling, and handed Noah a plate.

'I'm not keen on sweet things. Actually,' Noah said. He turned the plate round in front of him, examining the puffy creation from all angles, annoyed to hear his stomach growl again. He broke off a corner of the pastry and placed it on his tongue, which darted back into his mouth like a lizard's. Unexpectedly, he liked the taste. He bit greedily into the crumbling portion, taking larger mouthfuls.

'That's it duck, you get stuck in,' Godfrey said as he took a huge bite of his own slice of Apricot Dream. Crumbs fell onto his yellow gingham apron, which bulged cheerfully in the centre of his lap. 'You don't have to watch your waistline like me, do you Noel? Nothing there to watch, is there duck?'

Noah felt light-headed as he posted the last wedge of cake

between his thin, sticky lips and then wiped them with his clean hanky. He reached out to accept the butterfly cake Godfrey offered. *I haven't done any of my usual Saturday chores*, he thought. *Haven't wound the clocks, spoken to the Mother-parent, been down the cellar to polish my shoes, or thrown the fruit away.* He bit the wings off the cake. *But I don't care. Things are different now. I'm in love.* He laughed as he removed the case from the body of the cake.

'What's tickled you then love?' Godfrey said, brushing crumbs off his uneven lap.

'Oh, nothing,' Noah said. *Just the butterflies in my stomach.*

Godfrey shrugged and poured more tea. 'You said you was going to ask about old Joey. And you mustn't call him names like that, Noel. He's an old man, it's not nice to talk about him like that, whatever he's supposed to have done.'

Noah put his plate on the table and leaned forward. 'What do you mean – supposed to have done? From what you told me, there's no suppose about it, is there?' Noah's heart was racing, his hands felt hot.

'I just told you what was said at the time, duck. But people say all sorts, don't they, ay? You can't believe everything you hear though, Noel. All the time I lived next door to Joey, he never did me no harm.' Godfrey pushed the refilled teacup towards Noah. 'Drink up, duck.'

'Never mind the bloody tea. I want to know more about Joseph Pepper.' Godfrey folded his arms and sighed. Noah stared at him, waiting.

'You know what they always say, duck. You shouldn't never listen to no whasnames … no rumours. And I reckon that's true —'

Noah pushed his chair back suddenly, knocking over Godfrey's gnome. 'I'm not interested in what they say, whoever *they* are. All I want to know is what happened. All of it, I mean. It's a simple question. I think you know more than you've said about what went on. Just exactly what did Joseph fucking Pepper do?'

Godfrey scurried round to pick up his gnome. He looked up at Noah and said, 'Now you stop that bad language, Noel.' He stood the gnome up and tapped its head. 'There, still in one piece. Now, I don't know why you've gone and got such a do-dah … such a bees' nest in your hat Noel, but I told you all about what went on, didn't I? The other day? There used to be talk there did, like I said. And it was just talk, mind you – nothing else. Talk about him taking a liking to little kiddies. Little boys and all that sort of thing. It wasn't nice, I can tell you Noel. And the poor old bugger even had a brick through his window once.'

'Oh, and you say he didn't do anything wrong.' Noah's face was taut with anger. A small flake of pastry was stuck to his chin. 'I'm going home now, I've had more than enough of this.' He gestured at the plates and tea things.

Godfrey grabbed Noah's arm. 'Hang on a minute duck. Don't go storming off in a grump. Just hang on a bit longer while I go and check on me do-dah… me Battenburg.' He scuttled away, flapping crumb confetti to the ground.

Noah stood in the garden, his fists clenched in tight balls. *I always knew there was something. Just knew it. But why my house? What's Joseph Pepper got to do with my house?* He sat down again on Godfrey's plastic garden chair. His thin limbs were heavy, and he felt deeply tired. Gradually, his shoulders began to relax. Noah closed his eyes and made himself think about Angela. His sugar–coated mouth tipped upwards in a small smile. He took another butterfly cake and pushed it, whole, into his mouth. He sucked the moisture from the cake until it stuck to the roof of his mouth. *Used to do this when I was a boy,* he thought. *Mashed potato moulded to the shape of my mouth for hours while she sat there waiting for me to swallow. A real battle of wills. And I won. In the end, I always won. I could wait longer than her before giving up. She didn't have the same willpower. She'd slap the back of my head and say go on then, get off to bed if you're not going to eat that. And I'd bend my head forward, open wide and out it would plop. A dentist's impression of the inside of my mouth, all ridges and teeth marks and covered in a shiny film of saliva. Disgusting.* Noah heard his Mother's voice. 'You'll sit there until you've eaten all that dinner, Noah Quince.' He shook his head defiantly. 'You think so?' he said, and spotted Godfrey out of the corner of his eye. Still with the cake in his mouth, he sat and watched Godfrey approach. *Look out, Mr Gnome, here comes the hunchback,* he thought.

'All done, duck. Come out nicely as well it has, even if I do say so meself.' Godfrey patted Noah's shoulder as he passed his chair. 'What's come out nicely?' Noah said. He felt highly irritated. *Don't want him treating me like we're best friends,* he thought.

Godfrey picked up a knife. 'The Battenburg, duck. I've done it to match me new front room. Same colours as me soft furnishings. Just as a little, you know, a little treat.' He poured more tea and carried on. 'Come and have a little peep, Noel. Looks a right picture, it does.'

Yes, I bet it does. Just like a bloody cake, thought Noah. He moved his chair. 'No. I've had too much already,' he said, 'I'm off now.'

'All right then, Noel. Come back and have a bit of Battenburg with me tomorrow though, won't you? I'll show you me new colour scheme then. Lovely, it is. All pink and yellow.'

Well, there's a fucking surprise, thought Noah.

seven

The telephone was ringing as Noah opened his front door – his Mother was making her regular Saturday call. Every week she asked him the same questions and every week Noah gave the same resentful replies.

'They've got a special offer in Cluster's this week, Noah,' she said. 'Bananas half price and grapefruit three for the price of two. You really should stock up. You know you don't eat enough fruit and veg. Or anything else, come to that.'

Oh, God, not again, thought Noah. He gritted his teeth and said, 'I eat exactly the right amount, thanks very much.'

'You forget, Noah, that I've had years of trying to get enough food inside you to make sure the local authorities didn't accuse me of neglect and-'

Noah cut in, 'Yes, all right, all right. I don't think they're going to threaten to send a forty-seven year old man to a children's home for not eating his potatoes though, do you?' He poked his tongue out as far as he could, just like he had done when he was a child, behind his Mother's back.

'You can make fun if you like, but it's not natural – you being so thin. I don't know where you get it from,' his Mother said.

Well, not from you, that's for sure, Noah thought. *Or the Father-parent. Both padded out like a couple of armchairs. Even that stinking bloody dog's fat.* 'Oh well,' he said, 'some of us are just lucky, I suppose.'

'But I still think —'

Noah interrupted again. 'Got to go. Speak to you next week. Bye.' He put the phone down before his Mother could say anything else. *Bloody interfering old goat*, he thought. *Eat this, eat that, don't forget to buy some fruit. Blah blah blah. Why's everyone so obsessed with eating?*

Godfrey, Hell, the bloody Mother-parent, they're always trying to stuff food down me. He imagined flakes of Apricot Dream and sections of butterfly cake mingled together in his distended stomach, and saw the image of a brick being thrown through Joseph Pepper's window. He ran upstairs, knelt in front of his sparkling white toilet bowl, pushed two fingers to the back of his throat and made himself sick. In his Mother's voice, he said, 'I've told you before, Noah Quince, if you go bringing up your dinner, I'll make you eat it all again.' He flushed the toilet.

Noah eased himself onto his bed. He lay on his back and stared at the ceiling. His body was tense, his nails dug into his palms. *Just need a bit of a rest, then I'll get on with things. Got to keep the place in order for when Angela comes. Want her to feel at home.* He yawned, and became aware of a distant sound. He strained to hear more clearly. A steady, thudding noise made his temples throb. *The cupboard,* he thought. He held his breath and listened. The sound continued. It was muffled, far away. 'It's not the cupboard. It's the cellar,' he said, and made fast, jerky movements to get under the quilt, then pulled it over his head. The noise faded. Noah fell asleep.

He dreamt of the cellar, of himself sitting cross-legged, cleaning his shoes – one of his usual Saturday jobs. But he was not polishing the shoes. Instead he was filling them with thick white plaster, which he squeezed out of Godfrey's icing bag. When he'd finished, he leaned back, stretched his legs out straight. His foot reached the cellar wall. But it didn't stop. The wall was not solid. Noah's foot sank into something soft and cold. It had the consistency of marshmallow but the smell of mushrooms, damp and musty. Without looking Noah knew that his foot had embedded itself into the decayed body of a young boy. 'This one's been walled up,' he said. 'Done a good job with the plastering as well.' He pulled his foot out of the soft, sucking wall and pushed himself up off the floor. He tried to run to the stairs, but his dream made him move in slow motion. When he finally reached the first step, Noah looked back. The shoes were behind him. They were heavy now, with the chalky plaster setting inside them, and they dragged themselves along, their laces trailing. Noah heard his Mother telling him not to drag his feet. 'You'll scuff the leather,' she said. Noah heaved himself up the cellar stairs. He heard the shoes bumping and kicking against the faded, grey wood of the first step. Like battery toys, they toppled and repositioned themselves to bang repeatedly into the same obstacle. *They can't get upstairs.* He laughed. *The bastards can't get up the stairs.* His legs felt suddenly very warm. Then they cooled quickly. 'Oh no,' he wailed. 'I've pissed myself. I've wet my bloody trousers.'

At five on Sunday morning, Noah hung out his washed sheets and the clothes he had slept in. He gave his body the same scouring he performed after visits to Joseph Pepper. 'Not cabbage this time,' he said. 'Just piss.' He scrubbed at the thin, sore skin on his chest, back, buttocks and legs, then rinsed himself again and again with hot water. 'It was all that tea. That's what did it. He shouldn't have made me drink so much bloody tea in his garden. Or eat all that disgusting sweet stuff.' He refused to think about the dream.

Still wearing his bathrobe, Noah cleaned his house for the rest of the morning, vacuuming pristine carpets and polishing gleaming surfaces. His rubber gloves squeaked against the glass case of his grandfather clock as he rubbed it with a cloth. 'I'm not going to wind it yet,' he said. 'Not going to wind any of them until Angela comes.' He stood back and admired the tall wooden case, the pendulum perfectly still inside. He gave the glass a final polish. *Once she's settled in, it will be time to start the clocks again,* he thought. *Time to start our life together. Got to get this other one out of the way first though, this poet person. Then it'll just be me and Angela. She'll make the clocks tick again.*

He sat on the sofa and let his bathrobe fall open. He looked down at his penis, soft and puckered in his lap. 'Come on, you,' he said, 'we've got work to do.' Still wearing his yellow rubber gloves, he pulled the damp foreskin and twiddled his wiry pubic hair. His penis remained limp. 'This wouldn't be any good if Angela was here. I mean, Sunday morning, breakfast in bed, then …' he stopped pulling, watched as his penis curled back into itself. 'No good if I can't even get my stick up, is it?' He tied the oversized bathrobe around himself.

A knock at the door made him clutch his bathrobe tighter across his chest. Noah could hear Godfrey humming the theme from an advert. He opened the door and peered through a slit of daylight. 'I'm busy at the moment. Actually,' he said, and tried to close the door.

Godfrey pressed his face close to Noah's and laughed. 'You're telling me porkies, Noel. You've still got your nightie on.' Noah gritted his teeth, forced a smile. 'Been up ages, just not dressed yet,' he said. *Not that it's any of your fucking business*, he thought.

'Well, never mind, duck. I've only come to remind you about the Battenburg. See you at one, love.'

As Godfrey stepped back to leave, Noah saw the bulge in his apron. *What's the point of him having that all the time? He never uses it. It's me that needs my stick in working order, not him.* Noah scowled at Godfrey's hunched back before he closed the door. His mood darkened as he thought of the meeting with the poet. He was angry with himself. Wished he'd been more assertive when she had rang to alter the arrangements. *I don't even want to meet the bloody woman now*, he thought. *But I've got to go to all the bother of getting ready and driving over there on a Sunday afternoon.* He got dressed with an escalating feeling of spite, which clamped his jaws tight and made his neck stiff. Angry red bumps and festering spots stood out on his face and neck. *Why did I get myself into this? Why didn't I just tell her I'm not fucking interested? That I'm already spoken for.*

eight

Noah knocked on Godfrey's door at one o'clock. *If he thinks I'm eating that awful pink and bloody yellow cake, he's got a surprise coming. I'm not staying more than ten minutes either. Got to get myself over to the other side of town for the bloody poet person.*

Godfrey opened the door and stood back to let Noah in. His apron was striped, blue and white, and he had a clean white tea-towel over his left shoulder. 'Oh, you're right on time, Noel. Come on in, duck. Everything's ready.' Godfrey patted Noah on the shoulder as he followed him into the kitchen. 'Now,' he said, 'you close your eyes, lovey, and I'll lead you in. Then it'll be a surprise.' He reached out to take Noah's hand.

Noah snatched his hand away. 'I'm not pissing about with all that sort of rubbish. Can't we just get this over and done with? Come on, show me this new lick of paint you're so impressed with.'

'Oh, you're such a spoil-sport, you are, Noel,' Godfrey said. He pulled the tea-towel off his shoulder and pretended to swipe Noah's legs with it. 'Come on through then. Have a look at me new parlour.'

Noah saw the Battenburg as soon as he entered the room. It was in the centre of the dining table, raised up on a glass cake-stand, a lace doily decorated the edge. And there was more – the table was covered with an array of party food. Small triangular sandwiches, sausages on sticks, cheese cubes, bowls of crisps, fairy cakes, and a bottle of pink sparkling wine.

'What d'you think then, duck?' Godfrey nudged Noah's arm.

Noah stepped away. 'Well, there's a bit much, isn't there? You expecting a bloody coach-load or something?'

Godfrey laughed. 'No, the *room*. Silly sod. What do you think of me new colour scheme? Look, new curtains, new cushions. And everything matches.'

Noah looked round the pastel, ice-cream-coloured room. *It's actually not too bad*, he thought. *At least he hasn't gone too over the top with the pink. And it's all immaculately clean.* 'Hmm, nice and clean anyway.' he said.

'I thought you'd like it, duck.' Godfrey smiled broadly. He picked up the wine. 'Come on; let's have a little drink.' He popped the cork. 'Oohhh, watch out Noel, or it'll have your eye out,' he said, and giggled.

Christ, all this excitement for a few coats of paint and a pair of cheap curtains, Noah thought. But he took the glass and sipped at the frothy pink wine. 'I mustn't have too much of this,' he said. 'I've got to go out later.'

'What, on a Sunday? You never go out on a Sunday, Noel. What you up to then, you do-dah … dark horse?' Godfrey held out two plates of sandwiches. 'Egg and cress or cheese, love?' he said.

Noah took one of the tiny triangles and nibbled the edge while Godfrey continued to describe the fillings and toppings of the food he'd prepared. Noah's stomach tightened as the list went on. His mouth puckered in reaction to the display of so much food and he took large gulps of the fizzing wine to take his mind off it.

Godfrey held plate after plate under Noah's nose, to see what would tempt him. 'Come on Noelly, eat up. And tell Auntie what you're up to this afternoon.'

Noah's neck muscles were taut. He clamped his fingers hard on the plate. *He just can't mind his own fucking business, can he?* he thought. 'Look, it's just some woman. I'm going to meet a woman, all right? Now will you just shut up?'

'Gordon do-dah,' said Godfrey. He sat down and patted the chair next to him. 'Come and tell me all about it.'

Noah sat down. He took another mouthful of the wine and held his glass out for more. 'Look, it's nothing really. I'm just going to meet this woman, have a cup of coffee and that's it.' A noiseless burp popped at the back of his throat. He put his hand over his mouth.

'Excuse me,' he said. He felt the urge to laugh, but managed to stop himself.

Godfrey patted Noah's knee. 'Better out than in, that's what I always say, duck.'

Hope he doesn't say that about his stick, Noah thought. This time he couldn't prevent his laughter. He drank some more wine. 'I'm only going because I said I would. I don't even want to really,' he said.

'Well who is she then, Noel, this woman you're spending the afternoon with?' Godfrey brushed a wilted cress stalk off his apron, and dropped a handful of Iced Gems onto Noah's plate. They rattled.

Noah was reminded of a cheap toy he'd had, from a Christmas cracker. He had sat absorbed in concentration, tipping and angling the circular, plastic-covered card to make four metal beads settle in four dents at the same time. His Father, ordinarily silent and aloof, suddenly exploded, furious about the barely audible clicking sound. 'Can't you do something more useful than make that bloody irritating noise hour after hour?' He slapped down his newspaper and left the room. No further communication took place between them until his Father was enraged enough by Noah to speak again.

Noah tipped his glass back and finished the wine. 'I'm not spending the fucking afternoon with her. I'll only be there an hour. And *she's* not the one I want, either. I wish I hadn't said I'd go. She made me say I would. I tried to get out of it … well I was going to try but she'd gone. Then it was too late and I couldn't get out of it. All I want is to get it over and done with, out of the way.' He rubbed his forehead.

Godfrey stood up. 'There's another bottle of that whasname in the fridge. That champagne, whatever you call it. I'll go and get it for us duck. You wait there. And help yourself to something to eat, Noel.'

Fizzing sounds whispered past Noah's ear as Godfrey poured him more sparkling wine. He shook his head and held the glass upright. *Must have nodded off for a second*, he thought. He could feel Godfrey's bulging apron pressing against his upper arm. He leaned against it, still feeling sleepy. *Like a pillow*, he thought. Then he remembered his impending meeting with the poet. *I don't want to do it*, he thought. *I really don't want to go.* Tears filled his eyes, spilled down his dry face. 'I'm frightened,' he mumbled into Godfrey's blue and white apron.

'Silly sod, you don't want to be scared of that, Noel. Believe me, duck, it's nothing but a nuisance, it really is. I'll chop it off one of these days, you see if I don't. Gets on my whasname ... wick.'

Noah grinned and rolled his head slowly. The ice cream walls swayed as he moved. He could feel Godfrey's thick rubbery erection cushioning his head. 'Not this,' he said, 'I don't mean *this*.' He patted Godfrey's apron. 'I mean this woman I've got to go and meet. She's scary. I'm frightened of her and I haven't even met her yet.' He started to cry again. 'Anyway, it's Angela that I'm in love with.'

Godfrey took a large clean hanky out of his pocket, shook it open and gave it to Noah. 'Here, have a blow, love. A good old cry will do the whasname of good. The powder of good.' He stroked Noah's head.

'Where's your clock?' Noah asked Godfrey. 'I've got to be there at three.'

'I'll go and have a look; it's in the kitchen. I'm not like you with clocks everywhere. Don't know why you want all them anyway, duck. You must be forever going at them with a feather duster.'

Godfrey came back with a glass of cold water for Noah. 'Whoopsy daisy,' he said as Noah grabbed at the air several times before he took hold of the glass. He watched Noah drink the water, then he said, 'Now, is what I think we ought to do, Noel, is get you over to meet this young madam. Explain you don't want to get up to any funny business because you've already got yourself a nice young lady – your Angela – and then come back here and finish off our little tea party. How about that?'

Noah nodded. His head was spinning. He felt an overwhelming sense of gratitude towards Godfrey.

When they reached The Cherry Tree café, Godfrey bumped the kerb several times as he tried to park the car.

'Bloody hell, be careful.' Noah said. 'I already feel sick, thanks very much.'

'Sorry, duck. It's me foot, I can't feel the pedals properly. It's still a bit whasname … a bit tender. Still, never mind, we're here now. Want me to come in with you?' He started to fumble with his seat belt.

'No. Of course I bloody don't. I can sort this out on my own.' Noah got out of the car and made his way unsteadily to the entrance of the café, which was above a shop. With his palms flat against the glossy red walls to guide him, he went up the narrow stairs. *Hope she hasn't turned up. Please don't be here*, he thought.

nine

A tall, young waiter greeted Noah.

'Table for one, is it?' he said.

'Two, actually,' Noah said. He swayed slightly. 'I'm supposed to be meeting someone, and …' He looked round the café, leaned closer to the young man. 'And I'm looking for the lavatory.'

The waiter smiled. 'I don't think the management approve of that sort of meeting,' he said. 'I can get you a coffee though – I'll put it on table six, okay?' He smiled again. 'Oh, and the gents is through there.' He pointed towards the far end of the café.

Smartarse, thought Noah. Once he had emptied his bladder, he felt better. He splashed his face with cold water and smiled at himself in the mirror. 'Oh fuck, look what I've done,' he said to his reflection. Dark smudges of water were seeping into his trousers, through to his thighs. 'She'll think I've pissed myself. Again.'

In the reflection, a cubicle door opened behind him, and Noah saw a woman. She was dressed in black. She stared at her own image as she tugged a large make-up case out of her sagging shoulder bag. He watched as she wiped at her scarlet lipstick. She glanced casually sideways and saw Noah looking at her. He sniggered.

'I think you're in the wrong one,' he said, wobbling slightly as she continued to stare at him.

'No,' she said. 'You are.'

A cup of cappuccino waited for him on table six. Noah sat down quickly and stared at the pale foamy surface of the drink. *I don't want this*, he thought. *I just want to go*. He looked out of the window and saw Godfrey's car, waiting below. *He's been good to me today. His heart's in the right place. And his stick.* He laughed to himself.

The chair facing him was pulled away from the table with a loud scrape. The woman from the toilet sat down.

'Yeah, I thought it was funny as well,' she said. 'I'm Crystal. You Noah, yeah?'

'Oh God,' he said. 'I'm really sorry. They should put proper signs on the doors.'

Crystal shook her head. 'Well, the sign I went for was definitely a triangle with arms and legs. Least it was when I went in anyway – maybe they changed it just to trick you? Anyway, it doesn't bother me. All ends up in the same place, right?'

Noah was not sure if she was joking or if this was some sort of poetic statement. His mind was still bleary from the pink wine. He couldn't think what to say. 'Mmmm, yes probably.'

The poet opened the flap of her huge bag and began rummaging inside. She extracted a scratched metal tin and a large brass lighter, and started to roll a cigarette.

'I mean, shit's shit, you know?' she said and lit her cigarette. She pushed her hand through her greasy black hair, leaving it in thick messy clumps.

Noah smiled nervously and said, 'Er, yes, I suppose it is'. He wanted to call through the window for Godfrey to come and get him. 'I didn't think you smoked,' he said. *God, this just keeps getting worse.*

'Yeah well, like, I don't. Not really,' Crystal said. 'Just the odd one now and then. All got our props and crutches to get us through, you know? Any chance of a coffee, talking of props?'

Noah pushed his cup towards her. 'You can have this one, I haven't touched it. I don't really fancy it now.'

'Whatever,' Crystal said. The cigarette dangled from her lower lip. She played with the drink, dipped her chipped fingernails in the froth and sucked them. Finally she slurped the coffee, a reverse cappuccino machine. Red smudges glistened around the rim of the cup. She replaced her thin cigarette and lit the end. Smoke mingled with the moist food-tainted atmosphere.

Noah felt his stomach churn. The poet was grubby. Her layers of black clothes were stained and spattered, her hair was untidy, and her red fingernails were too long, packed with germs and dirt. Worst of all, she hadn't washed her hands. *I saw her in the Ladies*, he thought, *and she didn't so much as run the tips of her fingers under the tap.* 'I need fresh air,' Noah said, standing up.

'Cool with me. Where d'you want to go?' Stale perfume surrounded her as she moved.

Noah fought the swell of nausea in his throat. He gritted his teeth. 'Got to get outside,' he said. 'You stay here.' He hurried to the top of the stairs, trying not to breathe the thick warm air. Three stairs down, he pressed his forehead against the cold surface of the red wall and swallowed hard. *I could sue her under the Trades Description Act*, he thought. *She's not my type, nothing like it, not in a million years. Getting me to traipse all the way out here on a Sunday and then turning up like something the cat dragged in. And she bloody smokes. And she didn't wash her hands. If that's poets you can keep them.* He inhaled the cool air circulating in the stairwell. 'I'll tell her,' he said. 'I'll go back up there and put her straight, it'll only get harder the longer I wait.' He sniggered at his unintentional rhyme. 'Perhaps I should write her a poem, get the waiter to take it over.' He laughed again. His forehead knocked against the wall.

Two women darkened the space at the top of the stairs. They hesitated before coming down. Noah flattened himself to the wall and indicated there was room for them to pass. They did so in silence. At the bottom, one of them said, 'Weirdo.'

Noah snapped. 'They don't know what I've been through, fucking cheek,' he said. 'If anyone's a weirdo, it's her upstairs with three layers of clothes and big black boots under her tatty old skirt. And all sorts of diseases on her filthy hands.'

He stamped back up the stairs and made his way to the poet's table. She was huddled over the empty coffee cup, fiddling with a tangle of earrings, which dangled from several holes around her right ear.

'Hi,' she said, when she finally noticed Noah's return. 'Got your head back together, yeah?'

Noah sat down opposite her and apologised for keeping her waiting.

'No problem,' she said, 'I was just like, chilling out, and seeing what came into my head, you know?'

'What did?' he asked. *Not that I give a shit*, he thought. *Why am I even asking?*

'Oh, this and that, just stuff really, nothing heavy,' she said. 'But I did sort of wonder about what you were doing here. I mean, you seemed a bit uptight. I tune into other people's vibes really easily, you know? If you want to go, it's no big deal, yeah? Just say.'

Noah couldn't believe his luck. Or his reaction. He wanted to thank her for letting him off the hook, then turn and run. Instead, he shook his head in kind denial, leaned half an inch closer to the table. 'No, no, nothing like that,' he said. 'I just felt a bit off-colour.' *What the fuck am I saying?* Panic simmered inside him.

Crystal stopped fiddling with her earrings, shrugged her shoulders and gave a weak smile. 'Like I say, 's'up to you.'

I don't even fucking like her, he thought. *Why am I trying to spare her feelings?* 'What about another coffee?' he said, feeling his heart sink at the idea of more strained conversation.

'I'm easy,' she shrugged again. 'I could sit here all day, just, you know, drifting.'

Noah tightened his jaw. 'Ha. Yes. Well, we all like to relax, don't we? The thing is, I'm going to have to make a move soon – I've got some work to do for tomorrow. But there's time for a cup of coffee, then I'm afraid I'll have to be off. Do you write much poetry?' He knew he was talking too much. His thoughts whirled. *Why don't I just shut up?*

'On and off, you know, now and then. When it comes along really.'

Noah nodded. *What's she talking about? I haven't got a clue what this woman is saying. And I don't care either.*

'Look, I'll get the coffee,' he said. 'Then we can get this out of the way. I mean – then we can be on our way. I'm sure you've got things to do as well.'

'Nothing planned, no.'

'Right, good. Let's get a move on then,' Noah said, rubbing his hands together briskly. He twisted his neck sharply to look for the gaunt waiter, caught sight of a different one at the periphery of his vision and made an impatient beckoning gesture. He turned back to Crystal, drummed his fingers on the table. 'So what sort of poetry do you write?' he said, watching her bored face for signs of a reply but she was looking over his shoulder. *The waiter must be waiting*, Noah thought. *At last.*

'Two coffees,' he said, still looking at Crystal. *Make it snappy, on the double, quick as you like, not too hot, and get a fucking move on,* he thought as he turned to the waiter hovering by his shoulder. It was Godfrey.

'You all right duck? You've bin such a long time. Not ill, are you?'

Noah stiffened, touched his temple. 'Of course I'm not ill,' he said. Embarrassment mingled with relief. Noah had the urge to grab Godfrey's hand and run. At the same time he wanted Godfrey to disappear. His brain was still slow, and before he could think what to say, Godfrey had dragged out a chair. *Oh fuck, it's not supposed to be like this. Surely this can't really be happening,* Noah thought.

Godfrey settled himself and held out his hand to Crystal. 'Hello love, I'm Godfrey, Noel's friend next door but one. He's told me all about you.' Then he turned to Noah and slapped his arm. 'Have you told her yet?'

'Told me what?' Crystal asked, looking from Noah to Godfrey with only a trace of curiosity.

'It's er … it's just something I wanted to mention. Nothing important really. I can bring it up another time. Actually I'll phone you.' Noah's hand crept back to his temple. His fingers twisted the wispy hair.

Crystal and Godfrey began talking at the same time. Godfrey's - 'She's sitting right in front of you, tell her now, you prune,' overlapped Crystal's 'Whatever's cool with you.'

Noah stood up. 'Er look, we – I mean, *I've* got to go. Thanks for the coffee, I mean, you know ... whatever. I'll be in touch.' He pushed past Godfrey's chair and headed for the stairs. Then he paused. 'Come *on,*' he said.

Godfrey had hunched further over the table. He patted Crystal's hand. Noah cringed. He watched the back of Godfrey's head and listened to his neighbour's account of his romantic situation.

'See, what it is, lovey,' Godfrey said, 'is that young Noel has gone and got hisself in a bit of a muddle. He's got someone already, duck. Deeply in whasname, they are. In love. So he can't go making arrangements with you or we'll have fur flying all over the place. You understand, don't you duck?'

Noah clenched his fists. *Why on earth did I involve him in this?*

Crystal looked at Godfrey for a while. Then she said, 'I got you. And it's like, fine with me. We're all fluid, you know? I mean, if he's bi, that's no big deal from where I'm coming from. But if the two of you have got this heavy thing going, well ... you know, two's company and all that. He should have said before.'

'Whatever you say, duck,' Godfrey said. 'I'm just glad we've got things straight. He's been in a right old state about it.'

Noah groaned. *Now she's going to think I'm homosexual.*

'I hope your Angela's a bit nicer turned out than that, her hair was —'

Noah cut him off. 'Thanks a lot,' he said. He pulled at the car door handle. 'Hurry up and open this fucking thing. I want to get out of here.'

'Oi, what's up with you?' Godfrey said. 'I thought you'd be full of the joys of do-dah now, with her off your hands. Come on, love, let's get back to our party.'

Noah glared at Godfrey as the car pulled away, scraping against the kerb. Nausea filled him again. 'She thinks we're together – I mean, *you and me,* she thinks you're my ... you know, my *friend.*'

Godfrey squeezed Noah's knee. 'Well I am, you daft bugger.'

Noah snapped his knees tightly together and brushed where Godfrey had touched him. 'Look, thanks to you, that scruffy cow thinks I'm incapable of having proper, normal relationships with females, and that I can only manage with the likes of you. God knows what she'll think. She might even write a poem about me.' He crossed his arms furiously over his chest, sat in mouldering silence for a few minutes. Then he fell deeply asleep.

'That's it, darlin',' Godfrey said quietly, 'you have a nice little snooze.'

ten

A fluffy, turquoise blanket covered Noah when he woke. The light had changed. He was under Godfrey's car shelter, its yellow roof giving everything the glow of sweet wrappers. He tried to open the car door. It was locked.

'Oh God, what's he up to now? – I bet he's going through my things, nosing about. I'll bloody kill him,' Noah slammed his fist on the car hooter.

Godfrey appeared at his back door. 'You all right, Noel? What on earth's happened?'

Noah wound down the window. 'You've locked me in the fucking car, that's what's happened.'

Godfrey laughed and rushed to the side of the car. 'You've pressed the thingy down, duck, that's all. What would I want to lock you in for?' He pointed at Noah's elbow on the release button. 'You were dead to the world when we got back so I let you sleep. You look like you could do with a nice hot drink, love. Come on in, you're the colour of milk.'

The tea was already made. Godfrey poured it, bustled around his kitchen, and chatted happily to Noah. 'You shouldn't of bibbed that hooter, Noel. Not at this time of the evening,' he said. 'We'll have the neighbours complaining. Mind you most of them are either deaf, dead, or been put away so I don't suppose it did much harm.'

Noah sat in sullen silence. He felt cold and shaky. Eventually he said, 'What d'you mean? About the neighbours being dead?'

As Godfrey sat down, Noah caught a glimpse of his lumpy lap but quickly averted his gaze. 'Oh, you know, duck. They're all getting on a bit, aren't they? There's been quite a few pop off in my time. I reckon Olive Fitch'll be next. Poor old dear. There's nothing of her, even with all them fairy cakes she eats.' He sighed.

Noah thought he could see tears in Godfrey's eyes.

'Then, of course, there was all that whasname … all that scandal I told you about. All that what you was on about the other day, duck. You know, about poor old Joey and them little boys what went missing. Years ago that was, but they never did find 'em. They must have ended up somewhere, mustn't they, Noel? 'Spect they're dead and buried somewhere or other. Sends shivers down me whasname …, that does. True or not.'

Shivers ran down Noah's own spine. He thought of his cupboard, his cellar, and all the frightening corners in his house. *I don't want to hear this, not now*, he thought. Although part of him knew already, without hearing it from Godfrey. Part of him had always known. There was something – an atmospheric tension, a minute vibration, too slight to pick up consciously. But something was … what? Wrong? Different? Present? *Don't know, don't know*, he thought. *But there's something in my house. I can feel it*.

He drank some tea, felt hot liquid slice through the stale coating in his mouth. He wanted to stay in Godfrey's safe kitchen, and accepted the offer of toast. *Anything to avoid going home*. He muttered an ungrateful thank you for Godfrey's help at the café.

'If I spoke out of turn, Noel, I do beg your pardon. Only it pays to get things clear, that's what I always say.'

Noah shrugged, gave a weak smile. 'It's not important. I didn't like her anyway. She didn't wash her hands.'

Both men grimaced.

Noah let the chatter wash over him. He glanced at Godfrey's blossom pink apron, ignoring the bulge. He felt warmed and comforted by the continuous cups of tea, and even ate more cake and biscuits. *He did me a favour with that poet. Even if he did mess it up. I owe it to him to sit here for a while. Be rude not to. If he ever takes the fucking hint to let me stay, that is.*

'Why don't you get your head down here tonight, duck?' Godfrey said. 'You look fit to drop right there on the table. I've always got my box-room ready.'

Bloody hell, he's finally got the message. Thought I'd have to get a loud hailer. Noah made feeble noises about not wanting to impose. But he knew when to stop. He yawned several times, rubbed his eyes, and finally gave a heavy shrug to indicate his lack of resistance to the kind offer.

Godfrey's rose-filled box-room enclosed Noah in a pink, nocturnal garden. The wallpaper was covered with large pink roses. The sheets smelt sweet as he sank into the bed. He could see every clean, floral corner. There were no recesses or shadows. He felt himself slide into sleep. From an ornate shelf, Godfrey's bald teddy bear, a toy rabbit wearing a tutu, and three knitted mice in red trousers kept watch through the night. Noah barely moved.

The moment he woke, the room felt familiar and safe. His neck was loose and flexible, his shoulders relaxed. He could tell by the light and the quietness of the street that it was early but he'd had enough sleep. He got dressed in yesterday's clothes that were neatly folded on the back of a chair. On the landing, Noah could hear the sound of a bath being filled. Floral-scented steam hung in the air. The bathroom door opened as Noah crept past.

'Who's an early whasname then? Early bird?' Godfrey said, as he emerged from the steam. 'I was on me way down to cook you breakfast, duck. You go back to bed if you like, have a bit more shut-eye.'

Noah shook his head and continued towards the stairs. He forced a thin smile. 'I really couldn't eat a thing, honestly. Thanks for letting me stay. I've stripped the bed. Must get off, I've got to get to work.'

Godfrey followed him down the stairs, his dressing gown flapping round his damp legs. Noah didn't want to argue, and tried to get to the front door without further conversation.

Godfrey's bare feet padded faster down the stairs. 'Hold your horses, Noel,' he said. 'Its only half-five, you've got plenty of time. Have a bit of brekkie. To start you off proper for the day.'

Noah looked back at Godfrey, still halfway up the stairs. His gnarled toes hung over the carpeted edge. Hair clung like fine seaweed to the white skin of his legs. His erection was huge and pointed. It almost parted the maroon fabric of his dressing gown like a puppet trying to find the gap in the curtains and make an entrance to the stage.

'I said *no*,' Noah said. 'No thank you. Bye.'

After a quick bath, Noah ironed his white, Monday shirt. It was still warm when he put it on. With his eyes closed, he reached inside the hall cupboard for one of his jackets, and then closed the door carefully. *It's not the right one*, he thought as he unzipped his Wednesday jacket from its protector. *But it'll have to do*. He wore his suede, weekend shoes, which were still next to the front door. The smell of fabric conditioner surrounded him as he drove to work. He felt full of energy after his sleep. But memories of the previous few hours nagged at him. *What was I thinking of? Sleeping in someone else's bed, using his toilet … It was that bloody poet woman. Must have upset me more than I realised. Be all right this time next week, after me and Angela have got together.*

'Good weekend?' Helen asked him the moment she arrived. She struggled to remove a tight jacket, which skinned the cardigan from her shoulders as she peeled it off.

Noah had been waiting for her arrival, had paced the empty office, unable to concentrate on his work. He twitched and fiddled with his hair. 'Where have you *been?* I've been going fucking mental here,' he said.

Helen was separating the cardigan from the jacket. She turned it the right way out again and put it back on. The matted pink shape ended too high above the gathered-in waist of her voluminous pleated trousers.

'You look like an egg timer,' Noah said.

'Thanks for that. I can always rely on you for a bit of a boost at the start of the week. Didn't have a good weekend, then?' She wrapped the cardigan across her chest and folded her arms.

Noah perched on the edge of a desk, nudged a chair towards her with his foot. He twisted his legs round each other like pipe cleaners. 'Fucking disaster. Actually,' he said.

Helen sat down. 'Go on then,' she said. 'I'm all ears. But no more rude remarks about my appearance.'

Noah took a deep breath. 'You shouldn't be so touchy about it. I'm only telling you for your own good, trying to help. Anyway, that's not important. Wait till you hear what happened to me.' He was still telling Helen about his meeting at The Cherry Tree when other workers started to arrive. Muted greetings were exchanged between colleagues but no one spoke to Noah. And because she was with him, no one spoke to Helen either. Occasional bursts of laughter came from the group gathered at the coffee machine.

'Look, why don't you come round one night?' Noah said. 'I'll cook you a meal. There's something else I need to talk to you about as well, Hell.'

Helen smiled. 'Blimey,' she said. 'I'm honoured. Thank you, that'll be great.' She touched his arm and added, 'It probably wasn't as bad as you think, you know – at the weekend. And anyway, there's still the other two to meet. Perhaps you'll be more relaxed and everything.'

'I'm only interested in Angela,' he said. 'She's the one I'm in love with.'

'Well, you never know, Noah. You just can't tell what someone feels. Not until you give them a chance. What about this other woman – the one who scored five out of ten? What's her name?'

'Esther.' He looked towards the coffee machine and scowled. 'But she's not the one, Hell. I know she's not.'

'No,' Helen said quietly. She walked to the window, opened the blinds. 'No she isn't.'

eleven

'You'll want some more of this,' Noah said as he cut another wide triangle of cheesecake, eased it off the cake-slice and onto Helen's plate. 'Obviously.' He put the cake slice down, wiped his hands on a napkin.

Helen dug her spoon into the dense creamy pudding. 'You don't have to make it sound like a foregone conclusion. I do sometimes refuse seconds, you know. Not often, but it has been known.'

Yes, when it's physically impossible to poke another crumb of food in, I bet, Noah thought. He watched Helen eat the cheesecake. She placed each spoonful in her mouth with great precision and care, closing her lips over the spoon. Then, for a few seconds, she sat with her eyes shut before pulling out the spoon ready to dig for more. 'You may as well finish that off. Actually. I won't eat it. And it will only go to waste, as my bloody Mother is always telling me.'

Helen shook her head, the spoon just leaving her mouth. 'I couldn't eat any more, Noah. Really.'

'Who are you kidding?' he said. 'I've seen you devour a whole packet of doughnuts on your own, don't forget.'

'Thanks for that, Noah.' She kicked his leg under the table. 'I hadn't had a three-course meal then though, had I? As delicious as this is, I honestly cannot manage any more. Put it in your fridge and eat it tomorrow.'

Noah shook his head, pulled a face. 'God, no. I can't eat that bloody stuff; I'd never get up again. I got it for you. You can take it home when you go.'

'Deal,' Helen said. She scraped the last traces of cheesecake off her plate and sat back in her chair. 'Phew, I'm stuffed. That was a fantastic meal, Noah. Thanks for the invite, it was a really nice surprise. For someone who doesn't eat much, you certainly know how to cook.' She rubbed her stomach.

Noah looked away. 'Well, it's not difficult, is it? Just have to follow a plan, do things step by step.' He stood up, started clearing the plates and bowls. 'You go and sit in the other room, I'll just get this sorted out.' *If she can move with all that food inside her.*

'Let me help with the washing up.' Helen stood and joined in with clearing the table, scraping leftovers and clanking cutlery onto plates.

'No. No, leave that,' Noah said, holding her wrist. 'You just ... well, just go and have a sit down while I do this. I ... well, I'll be quicker on my own.'

Helen laughed. 'Yeah, I get the message. Bugger off Helen; Noah wants to sort out his expensive crockery on his own. He doesn't want you breaking anything. Am I right?'

Noah nodded. 'It's not just that. I prefer it, that's all. It's what I'm used to.' He carried the plates to the kitchen. *Don't want it all ending up chipped and cracked like hers,* he thought.

Working his way methodically through the washing up – glasses followed by side plates followed by dinner plates – Noah listened for house noises. He heard nothing. *Typical*, he thought, *got myself all ready to tell her about the house and what happens? Bugger all. If she could hear it.*

He left the dishes to drain, poured bleach down the sink. He pulled off his rubber gloves and slapped them down on the worktop. *She's going to think I'm mad anyway. Unless she hears it for herself. Then she'd understand.* He hesitated in the kitchen before walking past the hall cupboard. *I can't stand much more of this,* he thought. *There's something, I know there is. And I've got to get it sorted out before Angela comes round.*

When he joined Helen in the sitting room, she looked relaxed, sitting on his sofa with the newspaper spread out next to her.

She scanned the pages lazily. 'Says in here that we're all living longer. There'll be more people over the age of sixty than —'

'Helen, can I talk to you?' Noah said before he lost his nerve.

'Course,' she said, smiling. 'About the women?'

Noah sat down on the empty sofa opposite Helen, leaned forward and rubbed his eyes, pressing into the sockets with the heels of his hands. After a while, he sat back and sighed. Then he spoke quickly. 'No, it's about my, er this … it's about this house. I keep thinking there's something, well something going on. No, that's not it; it's not just me thinking … there *is* something going on. I know there is. I don't know what, but, well, something isn't right.' *Go on then*, he thought, *laugh.*

Helen folded the paper shut and put it on the floor. 'What sort of thing do you mean?' she said gently.

'Oh, God, I don't know. It's not easy to explain. I wanted you to hear it for yourself, but of course it's not going to do it tonight, is it? Making me look like a lying bastard. But I'm not, Hell, I …' He drew his knees up and hugged them in front of him. 'I'm just so sick of it; feels like I'm living in some sort of, I don't know, an experiment or something.'

Helen leaned forward. 'An experiment? How do you mean? I don't think I know what — '

Noah interrupted. 'No, of course you don't. Why should you? You don't live here, do you?' He spoke impatiently, a stressed teacher to a slow-learning pupil. 'Look, it's as if there's these two houses, right? Identical. Inside one of them it's, well, it's just normal. Safe, ordinary, a normal house with everything just how you'd expect it to be. But the other one, that's full of … well, it's different. Looks the same but it's got this feel about it – makes you on edge, like you don't know what's coming next. And things aren't right, somehow. Just like they're doing this experiment to see … I don't know, to see how the different houses make you behave or something.' He watched Helen for a reaction.

She stared at him, waiting for more.

'And it's not just the fact that *I* keep hearing it either – what about when Angela comes here? What on earth will she think?' He paused. 'Not making any fucking sense at all, am I?' He pushed his forehead against his knees. *Christ, I sound like a complete lunatic. How do you tell someone something like this?*

'But who's doing an experiment?' Helen said. The smile she gave Noah changed to a frown.

'Oh look, forget about the bloody experiment bit will you? That was just a way of … I was trying to describe … oh never mind.' Frustration gnawed at him, made him twitchy and irritable. 'In fact, forget about the whole thing, okay? Just forget I mentioned it.' He couldn't sit still, his fingers darting to his temples, twisting his hair, his feet tapping frantically against each other, his jaw clenching.

'Oh, come on Noah, give me a chance here. I'm trying to understand. I got a bit confused, that's all. I might be a bit slow but I am listening. Please, carry on.'

Noah didn't move. He could sense Helen watching him from the other sofa. Neither of them spoke for a while.

'Well, whenever you do want to talk, I'm always ready to listen,' she said. 'You know that, Noah.'

Her words pierced his irritation, which was quickly replaced by sadness and self-pity. He sighed heavily, felt tired and close to tears. 'You don't know what it's like, Hell,' he said. 'You just go home and everything's always the same. *You* don't have to wonder what will be in *your* hall cupboard, do you? *You* don't hear thudding noises coming from *your* cellar in the middle of the fucking night, do you? And I know you haven't got a cellar so you don't have to come back with that one —'

'Wasn't going to, Noah. I'm not that bad am I? Can be sensitive sometimes, you know. Well I try to be anyway. But are you saying that you *do*? You do hear noises? I mean that must be … well, really scary. But you have checked for what it might be, haven't you? I mean things, you know, like plumbing and pipes and —'

'No, it's not that sort of … it's got nothing to do with the bloody plumbing. There's all these noises – the stairs and the cellar and everything – and sometimes it just happens, for no reason. Then other times, there's nothing and it's all okay. And the cupboard under the stairs, when I put my shoes in there, or go to get a jacket, there's this … I don't know, sometimes there's this feeling of someone being in there. As if you can hear breathing or … but you can't really hear it, it's sort of, how can I describe it? Sort of below the surface, in the walls or something. And I never know if it'll be there or not. I can go and get a jacket and it's fine. I just get the jacket and that's that, nothing happens. Except I'm so wound up expecting it to happen … but then another time, there's been, well … I've seen things, felt things in there. I know what you're thinking. Noah's gone all neurotic, too much time on his own, got himself a bit worked up and all that …' He shuffled himself backwards against the cushions, tucked his legs closer to his body. *Wish I'd never started this*, he thought.

Helen moved to the edge of her sofa, held out her hand. Noah did not take it so she touched his right foot for a moment before sitting back again. 'I don't think that, Noah, none of it. But I do think you sound really upset.' She waited. 'Could it be that you've got something on your mind, perhaps, and it's, you know … maybe it's making you hear things, or —?'

'Oh, brilliant. Thanks a fucking bunch, Hell. Now you're saying I'm mad, is that it? You're saying I'm off my trolley just because I've got problems in the house? "Noah's hearing voices", is that it? "Noah's having hallucinations and getting … I don't know, getting out of touch with reality." Is that your diagnosis then?'

Helen was shaking her head while Noah spoke. 'No. I'm not saying anything like that. Not at all. All I'm wondering is, if there's something playing on your mind, well, it can cause all sorts of strange things, can't it? I mean, I'm not the most stable person in the world myself sometimes, none of us are. Not all the time. We all have things that can throw us off balance. Make us feel unsure, a bit, well, you know …'

'Mad?'

'Yeah, all right then. Mad. And I'm talking about everyone. Anyone. Not just you. Just normal madness.'

Noah leaned his head back, stretched his neck. It made a small clicking sound. Postponed tiredness caught up with him; a huge yawn took him over, forcing his jaws wide apart. *Don't want to be on my own tonight*, he thought. *Mad or not, I don't want to be here on my own.* 'Hell?'

he said. She raised her eyebrows in response. 'Will you stay?'

twelve

Helen accepted every offer of tea Noah made during the rest of the evening.

He carried each cup and saucer in on a tray, a spoon clinking against his best china. He sipped water from a thick-bottomed tumbler, watching Helen as she drained her third cup of tea.

'Okay, okay, I'll stay,' she said. 'If you're sure it's what you want. But don't blame me if you regret this in the morning.' She stood up and stretched, her arms held towards the ceiling of Noah's sitting room. Her top parted company with the waistband of her trousers exposing a band of dimpled, rubbery white flesh.

Looks like a dumpling, thought Noah. *But I still don't want her to go. Don't want to be on my own in this house.* He yawned and bent down to collect the cups off the floor. Quietness seeped into the house like a mist under the doors – the whole street was still and silent, with neighbours long since gone to bed; anything that moved did so on padded feet. No traffic had passed for a couple of hours. 'I'll just wash these up,' Noah said, his voice low.

'Leave them till the morning. It's ever so late.' Helen also spoke in a whisper. She looked at Noah and smiled. 'Yeah, I know, wasting my breath – you never leave washing up till the morning, do you? Not normal, if you ask me. Washing up can take over your life, if you let it, you know.' She slumped back onto the sofa and cradled a cushion.

Noah placed the cups on his tray, making a small chinking sound, and carried it towards the door. Then he stopped. *Can't go out there,* he thought. *I can't go past that cupboard, not now.* His feet frozen to the spot, he stood and gripped the tray, making his wrists ache. He looked over at Helen for help, but said nothing. She sat with her eyes closed, the cushion held to her chest.

'Hell,' he said in a whisper. She didn't move. 'Hell, can you just …' Still there was no response. 'Hell, wake up, I need a hand here,' he said, almost shouting.

Helen jumped, her arms automatically clasping the cushion tighter.

'What?' she said. 'God, what's wrong?' She looked as if she'd been wakened from a deep sleep instead of half a minute in a light doze. She tried to stand but lacked the momentum to lever herself up from the sofa. Rubbing her eyes, she looked at Noah. 'What is it?'

'Can you take this for me?' Noah nodded at the tray. 'I can't go out there, Hell. I really can't.'

Helen forced herself up. 'Tell you what; I'll come with you,' she said. 'Go on, you go first and I'll be right here behind you. It's only going to get worse if you don't face it.' She stood behind him and put her hand on his back. 'Come on, let's get the cups washed up.' She spoke gently and pushed her hand harder against him.

Noah resisted, but as Helen pushed he was forced to move forward. He cleared his throat and walked briskly past the hall cupboard and into the kitchen, where he washed and dried the cups in silence. Then he wrung out the dishcloth and started wiping the work surfaces. In the harsh fluorescent light of the kitchen he felt awkward, embarrassed. How could there be anything to fear in such clean, bright domestic surroundings? *I must seem such a prat – what does she think of me?* He bunched up the cloth and wiped harder and faster at the surfaces. He wouldn't look at Helen, and kept his head down, fixed on the job of cleaning.

'You going to do a full spring-clean now, or what?' Helen said. She stood near the door. 'Only it's half-past two in the morning – a little bit late for housework, even for you, don't you think?'

Noah carried on, his hand clamped over the cloth and his arm making small circular movements as he rubbed at the clean worktops with more force.

Helen stopped him by placing her hand over his. 'Come on,

Noah,' she said. 'We're both knackered. Leave this now and we can get to bed. I mean *you* can get to bed. And so can I.' She sounded flustered. 'You know what I mean – getting myself tied up in knots here. Just go to bed, Hmm?'

What, just to lie there for hours wide awake? he thought 'Yes, you go up. I'll just finish this,' he said, still refusing to look at her.

'Do you want me to go home, is that what's bothering you? I can easily get in my car – it's only out the front here – and be home in twenty minutes, less probably. I don't mind —'

'No' Noah shouted and slapped the dishcloth down on the gleaming stainless steel draining board. He saw Helen flinch but she stood her ground next to him. He took a deep breath and spoke carefully. 'No, I mean, it'd be stupid to go home now – you might as well stay. The spare room's ready and everything. I've put some pyjamas in there for you. It's all clean. You know where everything is, don't you?' *I don't want to be on my own. Really don't want her to go. I need her here.* 'Anyway,' he said, pushing past her and snapping the kitchen light off, 'I've finished now.'

He held open the door to the spare room and Helen looked inside. 'Pyjamas on the bed for you,' he said. 'Don't know if they'll fit you – they might be too small.'

'You cheeky sod,' she said, playfully slapping his chest with the back of her hand. 'But thanks. You didn't have to, I'd have been happy to sleep in my clothes, it's only going to be a few hours now isn't it?' She stepped into the room and sat on the bed.

Probably wouldn't notice the difference if she did sleep in them, he thought. 'They've never been worn, the pyjamas – Christmas circa 1985, I think. From one of the parents' siblings, I expect. I wouldn't be seen dead in them. Actually. Been in the drawer for ages.'

'Oh cheers,' Helen's face erupted in a huge yawn. 'God, I am so tired,' she said.

'Yes, me too.' *If only,* he thought. *I can't see me getting any sleep for the next few hours. Don't want to lie there staring into the bloody darkness. And listening.* 'Oh well, goodnight and all that. And no snoring, if you please – my room's only next door.'

'I don't snore, as it happens.' Helen's voice was muffled by her top, which she had started to pull over her head.

Noah closed the door.

Noah lay in the middle of his large bed. Although his body felt limp with tiredness, his mind was racing. *Stupid bastard, getting in a state like this. I manage all the rest of the time on my own. Why did I have to make her stay tonight? Just couldn't let her go – don't know what I'd have done if she'd left me here all on my own. But what difference does it make? Now she's sound asleep, I might as well be on my own anyway. And what if there are noises – the usual – in the cupboard or from the fucking cellar? Then what? Do I go and wake her up like a little kid? Mummy, I'm scared of the dark. Mummy there's someone in the cupboard. I don't want to go in the cupboard ... Oh, that would go down well, wouldn't it? That would just about make her mind up that I'm heading for the fucking loony bin.*

He heard his Mother's voice in his head. 'I'll have to lock you in the cupboard under the stairs again if you don't do as you're told, Noah.' He pushed his palms into his eyes. *Christ, where did that come from? I haven't thought of that for years – forgot she used to do that. Well, I thought I had. That was her favourite punishment, fully sanctioned and approved by the bastard Father-parent, of course. But I never cried, never asked to be let out or anything. Just sat there. Waiting. He must have really hated that.*

He stared into the darkness of his room, tried to make out the shapes of furniture, the lines of the window and door. But he could see nothing other than the dense, felty black. It was too early for light – the darkest, slowest part of the day, when the weak and the frail stop holding onto life. *It's just like the cupboard, when I was a boy. So dark you couldn't tell what time it was – or how long you'd been in there.* Unwanted memories of being in that small dark place swamped him – the physical sensation of sitting on the cold floor, his arms clasped in a tight band, holding his knees to his chest, trying not to brush against anything in the dark. And all the time, listening. Listening for his Mother's approaching footsteps and the click of the lock being undone. 'Out you come,' she would say, her lips thin and tight. 'And perhaps you'll think twice before you misbehave again.'

He curled himself into a ball. *I don't want to think about this. I don't want any of this. I just want to go to bed like everyone else does, fall asleep, wake up and go for a piss, go back to sleep and moan in the morning when the alarm goes off. That's all I want — just the normal boredom, the normal misery of ordinary existence. Instead, I get this fucking rubbish spilling all over the place. Like shit coming back up out of a blocked toilet. Up it comes, swelling and rising and swirling until it gets to the edge, and you think it's going to stop just in time, think it's going to sink back down and disappear. But it doesn't, it just creeps over the edge and down the sides. And then it's too late, suddenly it's all over the fucking place, spreading, staining whatever it touches.* A deep moan surged up his throat like vomit and he wailed into the mattress. *I don't want this. I don't want to keep thinking all the time. Want to stop. I just want it to stop. Please make it stop.*

Just before four in the morning, Noah pushed open the door to the spare room. He watched Helen's shape rise and fall in the spare bed. Every few breaths, she let out a high-pitched sound, almost a whistle, like a heavy sigh at something annoying her. Noah crept into the room, his bare feet making dents in the hardly used, stiff carpet pile. He hovered over Helen's sleeping form, uncertain how he got there, but not wanting to leave the comforting sound of her breathing. *She looks different asleep*, he thought. *Smaller. And young. Like a little girl.*

In slow motion, he lifted the edge of the quilt, then held it between his fingers, waiting to see if Helen would stir. She didn't. He inched his body closer to the bed, held the corner of the quilt up higher, then lowered himself and perched on the edge of the bed, supporting most of his weight with his legs. Hardly daring to breathe and with his eyes squeezed shut, Noah held this painful position until his legs started to shake. As he finally let himself sit fully on the bed, Helen turned over to face away from him. *Oh God, she's going to think I'm …* He struggled to finish the thought, expecting Helen to sit up at any moment and spit accusations at him … *think I'm doing something.* But Helen settled into a new rhythm of breathing, sounding less annoyed, and continued to sleep.

Noah gradually insinuated himself into the space behind her. He gripped the mattress firmly, determined to maintain the thin slice of space between his body and Helen's. A ridge of stitched fabric running round the edge dug into his ribs and hip. Humid heat escaped from the bed, past Noah's taut face. The smell of the new pyjamas mixed with the smell of Helen's hair, stale sweat, the faint aroma of old perfume, and some underlying smell that he couldn't identify. *Hope she's had a bath in the last week.* He shuddered at the thought, then mentally told himself off. *Got to stop thinking all the time – that's what starts all the problems. Just ignore things, let them go; don't get so wrapped up in thinking all the bloody time.* He relaxed his muscles a fraction, his neck easing slightly into the strip of pillow left by Helen, and closed his eyes. *But she does smell though – there's that ... odour. That femaleness.* He listened to Helen's steady breathing, the broken pattern of her occasional whistling sigh, and eventually his breathing deepened into a pattern of its own. The muggy warmth of the bed thawed his rigid body and his thoughts finally lay dormant.

'Let me go. Noah. Let me go.'

He heard the words but didn't move, in a hinterland somewhere higher than sleep but beneath wakefulness. And then he snapped his eyes open and was awake – shockingly, horribly awake. Reality crashed hard against him. 'I ...' He shook his head. His arms were clamped around Helen's middle. The one she was laying on had gone numb.

Helen half sat up and patted his hand, 'It's all right, I didn't mean to make you jump – I just need the loo, so if you could ...'

Again, she patted the back of his hand pressing against her stomach. He felt her soft, warm belly wobble and vibrate under his palm, and snatched his hand away. He manoeuvred himself onto his other side so she couldn't see his face. He felt the bed judder with her movements and then the springy shift of the mattress when she stood up. He stared at a strip of weak light on the wall and listened to the floor creaking as Helen walked across the landing to the bathroom.

What the fuck am I doing? I should have pissed off back to my own bed before she woke up. Tears of shame sprouted from the corners of his tightly-closed eyes.

'Sorry about that,' Helen said. 'I thought I could get out without waking you, but …'

Noah felt the bed shake as Helen climbed back in beside him. He stared at the strip of light on the wall.

'You should have … well, why didn't you just say?'

'I told you – I didn't want to wake you up, but in the end, I just had to, you know, just had to go. You wouldn't want me wetting the bed or anything, would you? You might never ask me to stay again.' She snuggled down under the quilt.

Noah could feel the coolness she'd brought back from the bathroom being reheated by the warmth trapped in the bed. He grimaced at her words, and hooked his fingers over the edge of the mattress, holding himself away from Helen's body. 'Do you have to? Say things like that?' He thought of a childhood dream and the humiliation that had followed it.

In his long-ago dream, Noah had been swimming across the local pond, something he had never done in real life – only the big boys, the unruly, unruled boys ever swam across the pond – and he could feel the soft, slimy leaves of pond weeds against his legs. His bare arms pushed out in front of him, just below the surface of the clear cold water; his skin pale green, shining. He felt at ease, happy – alone in the middle of the pond, treading water, his legs escaping again and again the slippery grasp of waving plants.

Then the water became warm, warmer – like a shaft of sunlight had penetrated the cold and heated this one spot. And in the split second before he woke, Noah smiled.

As he surfaced abruptly from the dream, the smile still on his face, he knew that he had wet the bed. Was still wetting the bed. Warm urine flowed down his thighs, caught in the hollows behind his knees and seeped away into the sheet. He sat up. Tore back the blankets. Saw his crinkled, sodden pyjamas, stuck to his legs. And still he couldn't stop the flow of urine. His confused head told him it was all right. He was in the pond. No one would know. His eyes told him the terrible truth. He had pissed the bed. Pissed gallons and gallons into the bed.

Staring at his legs, he began to sob, great heaving gulps that hurt his chest but made no sound. And when the stream of urine finally stopped, he kneeled on the bed, trying to straddle the yellow pool in his mattress, and peeled off his wet pyjama trousers, by then cold against his skin. He pulled the bottom sheet off his bed, rolled it with the pyjama trousers and crept to the bathroom. Twisting the cold wet fabric over the basin, he wrung out as much as he could, then went silently back to his bedroom. And spent the rest of the night in terror that his disgusting behaviour would be found out.

For hours, he flapped the sheet in huge silent billows. His arms ached; his head throbbed with physical and emotional exhaustion. When it started to get light, Noah went to the airing cupboard on the landing and took out an old towel that his Mother used for tearing up into cleaning rags. He put it on his mattress and placed the damp sheet over the towel. In the dim light of his room everything looked normal, and although still damp to the touch, the sheet gave no visible clues of what had happened. Noah sat on the floor, in the corner of his room, listening for the sounds of his parents waking up.

When he heard his Father's cough, Noah tugged the damp, smelly pyjama trousers back on and stood next to his bed. When the door opened, he acted the part of having just got out of bed. He stretched and yawned and rubbed his eyes, willing his Father not to come in. His shoulders slumped in relief when his Father shouted for him to 'get moving in there' without actually coming into the room. But it was a short respite from reality for Noah. Inevitably, his accident was discovered.

His Mother noticed the smell and, bustling her way into his room as if he didn't exist, went straight to his bed, pulled the sheet off and stood looking at the towel with its damp oval stain. The sense of shame, of stupidity that he could have concealed what he'd done, of being so out of control and so ... dirty, was unbearable for Noah. His knees buckled, he sank to the floor and crouched with his hands over his head.

The shouting, mockery and harsh, angry voices of his parents seemed to come from a distance. He heard his Mother yanking and pulling at the bedclothes, his Father heaving the mattress off the bed, and caught odd words as they ranted and cursed at him, 'vile; disgusting; baby; pathetic; can't do anything right,' but somehow, Noah managed to disconnect himself from the intensity of their anger. Instead, he was engulfed by his own self-loathing.

Folded into an angular foetus on his bedroom floor, while his parents cleared away his shameful mess, Noah dug his fingernails into the pale mauve skin of his ankles. Each time he felt the skin pierce and the wetness of blood on his fingers, he moved to the next piece of thin, tender young skin.

'You gone back to sleep on that side?' Noah jumped slightly at the sound of Helen's voice.

'I'm wide awake. Actually. Just ... just thinking. Wish you didn't have to lower the tone, going on about, well, about what you said.'

Helen laughed. 'What, about wetting the bed? It was just a joke. I *haven't* wet the bed, if that's what you're worried about – come and check if you want to.'

'God, no thank you,' Noah said. *How the fuck do I get out of here? I don't want to look at her. Don't want her to look at me. I don't know why I came in here in the first place. Must have been ... don't know, must have been upset or something.*

For a long time, neither of them spoke. Helen was restless; every time she moved, the bed shook and bounced. Noah clung to his edge of the mattress, his body rigid, his mood resentful. *For Christ's sake*, he thought whenever she moved, *can't she keep still for at least two bloody minutes? Or nod off. That would give me a chance to get out of here, go and have a shower, go out even – and when I get back she'd be gone ...*

Finally, Helen sat up. 'You want me to go, don't you? You're uncomfortable, with me here … you and me like this, aren't you?'

Still facing the far wall, Noah closed his eyes and took a deep breath. 'Well, we can't stay here forever, can we? I mean, you've got to get home, haven't you? Got to get ready for work and everything.'

'Well, I wasn't thinking of forever,' she said. 'But it's not even six yet – not the sort of time I'm usually awake. Don't know about you but it still feels like the middle of the night to me. But I know you'd rather I wasn't here. So I'll be off, okay?' She sounded cheerful although Noah thought he could pick out an undercurrent of sharpness in her voice. 'I did wonder last night, well, if you'd regret this. I was perfectly happy to go home you know.'

'Oh well, never mind, you'll be home soon, won't you?' *Go*, he thought, *please just go. This is fucking painful*.

Helen swung her legs round, sat with her feet on the floor.

Noah felt his back cooling where she had lifted up the quilt. He heard her sigh and waited for her to stand up, but she sighed again and stayed where she was, on her edge of the bed while he held onto his.

'This doesn't feel very nice, Noah,' Helen said. 'Like you can't wait to get rid of me. Or that I've done something wrong. It's not as if … well, I didn't ask to stay here. And I certainly didn't ask you to … well, you know, to —'

'All right, all right,' he said, 'you don't have to rub it in, do you? I must have walked in my sleep or something, that's all. I was as surprised as you when I woke up with … in here. And now you want to go and make a big thing of it. Why can't we just —?'

'What? Why can't we just what, Noah? Ignore it? Pretend it hasn't happened? Lay here all awkward trying to work out what the other one is thinking and what we ought to say? Or not say? Only that doesn't feel right to me. And no, I don't want to make a big thing of it – it doesn't have to be a big thing. But it does feel strange to me – you know, not mentioning it and me feeling like the unwelcome guest and all that. I wasn't surprised when I woke up and you were here – I was half awake when you came in. And it's okay, you know – I don't mind.'

Noah felt himself flush. His shoulders tensed into harder knots. 'So why didn't you say something then? Wake me up or something? Why did you let me make such a fool of myself?' He could feel Helen moving again – feel her feet back in the bed and her weight shifting as she twisted her body round to face him. *I don't want this*, he thought.

'Make a fool of yourself?' she said. 'Is that what you think? Is it foolish to want comfort? Is it?' She jabbed his back with her fingers. 'Is is foolish to try and find a bit of warmth for once in your life? Do you really think it makes you a fool?'

'I told you, I must have been sleepwalking. I ...'

'Oh come on Noah – at least give me credit for some intelligence – we both know you weren't bloody sleepwalking.' She rubbed his shoulder, her voice softened, 'Come on, turn over, look at me. I'm real, you know. I'm here, in your bed. With you. And you wanted that. All night you wanted that. You held onto me so tightly that I could hardly breathe. When I tried to get away, you just gripped harder and harder. Once you even said "No" and held me tighter still. I thought it would be easier for you if I just disappeared in the night – I knew you wouldn't like it when you woke up. I knew how difficult it would be for you to have such a big reminder that you'd asked me to stay – and you did ask me – so I tried to leave in the middle of the night. And like I said – you wouldn't let go of me. You held me, Noah, you held me very tight. And do you know what?' She rubbed his shoulder again. 'It's okay.'

Noah remained on his side, his face turned towards the far wall. His eyes pricked with the threat of tears. *Shit. Oh shit, I know she's right.* He wanted to bury his head under the pillow, make himself invisible, rewind time back to the previous night and tell Helen to go home. 'It's not okay,' he said, in a whisper.

Helen leaned over him. Her stale, beddy smell surrounded him. She pulled him over onto his back.

Noah kept his eyes closed.

'It is okay, Noah,' she said. 'Everything is still okay. I'm here. You're here. The world didn't stop. The sky didn't fall down. And you don't owe me anything. You haven't signed your soul over to me, you know, just because you held me in the middle of the night. A cup of tea would be good, but that's up to you.' She laughed.

Noah pulled himself onto his side again. 'I told you, it's not okay,' he said. Tears fell from his tightly-shut eyes.

Helen got out of the bed. 'All right,' she said, her voice sounded weary. 'If that's how you want it …'

He heard her get dressed quickly.

'Bye, Noah,' she said as she left.

thirteen

For hours after Helen left, Noah stayed in the spare bed. He barely moved. As if his body had shut down, he lay in a paused state, like a video film waiting to play again. He stared at the wall, disinterested in the changing light and shadows, and oblivious to the noises from outside. His head was numb. His mind kept emptying – the opposite of thinking; thoughts drifted away, could not be pinned down, inspected, turned over and over. Whatever entered his head simply faded like an unfinished sentence, the ending left hanging, the beginning forgotten. Dry-eyed, small and still, he gazed without focus at the wall of his spare bedroom until the alarm call of his bladder brought back an awareness of himself again, and broke the spell of his trance.

Programmed to respond, he got up automatically and went to the bathroom. His neck and shoulders ached. His mouth was sour and dry. He filled the basin with cold water and took a deep breath before dipping his face in to wake himself up. But he couldn't do it – and stopped with his nose just above the surface of the water. 'Fuck that,' he said, his voice thick from lack of use. *Why should I dunk my head in there?* He pulled out the plug and watched the clean water sink away. 'Could do without a shock like that. Actually.' Instead, he ran the hot tap, cupped water in his hands and patted each side of his face, then dabbed it dry with a towel. He refused to look in the mirror. Refused to think.

In his own bedroom, Noah pulled on his clothes and opened the curtains. Reluctantly, he looked at the alarm clock beside his crumpled, unmade bed, afraid that it would show an afternoon time, something to be ashamed of. 'Half-eleven, that's all. Nothing wrong with that. Not as if I've stayed in bed all day. And anyway, I don't do it very often, have a lie-in.' Talking to himself, he sounded like an amateur actor rehearsing his lines, and found it impossible to shake off the acute sense of self-consciousness that came from his determined effort to erase the night with Helen. 'Better have something to eat, I suppose,' he said in the same false tone. 'Even if it is too late for breakfast. And then I ought to ring work,' he told himself, the idea instantly forgotten.

In the kitchen, he filled the kettle and waited for it to come to the boil. He stood a white china cup on the worktop. He looked at the row of tins containing his selection of teas, chose Darjeeling and placed the threaded tea bag in his cup. 'This is all I want. Actually.' He rubbed his stomach, savoured the empty sensation, the tight concave flesh under his hand. He stood and watched the kettle, heard the water start to bubble then move more violently as it built up to boiling point; saw steam begin to curl its way out of the spout, then push out with more force. And he heard the kettle click itself off; the water gradually calm, saw the steam disappear.

 He didn't move. Didn't lift the kettle or fill his cup. He simply stood looking at the shiny chrome surface of the kettle as it lost its heat, rage and power. *I wish she hadn't gone. I wish she was still here. I want her here with me now.* He leaned against the worktop, his spine pressing painfully into the edge. *It's not as if it would have hurt her to stay a bit longer – we could have had a bit of breakfast or something. Not that I've got enough food in the house to feed her...* He smiled momentarily, then his face fell back into its expression of sadness, all pretence of nonchalance gone. His back hurt where the worktop was digging in so he turned round and propped himself on his elbows. His distorted reflection stared back at him from the gleaming, cooled kettle. *Jesus, there's one reason why she didn't stay. Frightened her away.* His face looked longer, thinner, sunken, his eyes deep hollows of shadow. The area below his sharp cheekbones was more gaunt, exaggerated by the kettle's curved surface. His nose was huge and comically red, his mouth too large for his face. *I look like some sort of mutant deep-sea fish, one of those things they want to sell with chips now the greedy fuckers have eaten all the cod*. He pushed the kettle to the back of the worktop, knocking his white cup and dry tea bag. It tipped, threatened to fall over then rattled itself back into place.

Noah snatched up the cup, sure that he would follow through the action and hurl it across the room. But he stopped himself and stood holding the cup too tightly, heard the clean white surface squeak under his twisting fingers. *I made her go. I made her. As good as told her to fuck off.* He lifted the cup to his mouth. It felt cold against his lips. *I sent her away.* He rolled the rim of the thin china teacup from one corner of his mouth to the other, never letting it stay long enough to pick up any trace of warmth from his pale, dry skin. *And I don't even know why*. A stifled cry hurt his chest, made him choke and cough.

'I sent her away. And I don't know why,' he said, his voice weak and cracked.

With the cup clasped in both hands, Noah cleared his throat, waited for his breathing to calm, and lifted it to his mouth again. He placed his teeth on either side of the delicate china. Heard the tiny chinking sounds as he tapped them against the cup. Then he bit down very carefully and very hard. His teeth strong on the thin edge of the cup, where the china was almost transparent. He liked the brittle, cracking sensation, the easy way it broke, splintering between his teeth. And the shards, not quite separating from each other, not straight away – they stuck together momentarily, as if trying to maintain the shape of the cup they had formed until now – and then collapsed; slowly imploding, smooth and jagged edges crisscrossing each other on their way to different resting sites.

Noah picked the cup handle off the front of his shirt, where it had caught on a button. He placed it with great care on the work surface and bent to get his dustpan and brush from the cupboard under the sink. Kneeling, he swept up the broken pieces of china, wondering vaguely why there were so many. *It wasn't that big,* he thought. *This looks like enough to make two cups*. A drop of blood fell onto the lid of his pale blue plastic dustpan. It made a cartoon splash shape before it trickled to the floor. Noah wiped his wrist across his mouth. A sharp sliver of china, half embedded in his bottom lip, was snagged out by the action and he swept it from the flaky skin on the back of his wrist. His lip bled freely now and Noah hung his head over the kitchen sink to stop the blood going on the floor.

As the blood dripped into his sink, Noah turned the cold tap on full and blasted it away. When the bleeding stopped, he scrubbed the sink and worktops. With the kitchen restored to its pristine state and bleach fumes filling the ground floor of the house, Noah rang Helen. The phone rang five times. Noah felt relieved that there was no answer – however much he wanted to speak to her, it would be easier not to.

When Helen suddenly answered the phone, Noah was thrown. *What do I say?* he thought.

'Hello ... who is it?' Helen said.

'Hell ... I ... I don't know what to say,' he said.

'Oh, hello Noah.'

He twisted his hair. 'It's a bit ... I just thought, you know, thought I'd give you a ring and ...' *This was a bad idea. I haven't got a clue what to say.* His mind was blank; he felt panicky. He could hear distant office sounds – ringing telephones, muffled voices. His fingers fiddled nervously with the hair at his temple, then with the cut on his lower lip. It stung when he touched it, but he couldn't stop.

'Oh right, okay. So?' Helen said.

She could at least help me out here. She knows I'm struggling. 'What are you up to then? Is it busy there?' *Shit, what did I say that for?* He held his hand over his eyes, embarrassed.

There was a long pause before Helen spoke again. 'Noah, if you really rang to ask what I'm up to today, I can tell you. I could have told you before I left this morning. But anyway, it's not very interesting, won't take long and will probably bore you rigid. But if you really did ring to ask me —'

Noah interrupted. 'Okay. All right.' He sighed, started again. 'Okay. That's not why I rang. It was ... it was about ...' *Christ, help me out here*, he thought. *She usually does.* He took a deep breath. 'You know, last night.'

'Last night,' Helen said back to him.

Noah snapped. 'Look, why are you making this so bloody hard for me?'

'Am I? You don't want to think about that a bit and change your mind, do you? I mean, after all, you made the phone call, Noah. You got all awkward this morning. You wanted me to evaporate into thin air and disappear as soon as I woke you up —'

'No,' he said, his voice raised. 'No, I didn't want that. I didn't. Really, Hell, I didn't.' At last, he started to cry, the tears that wouldn't come while he'd lain for hours like a coma patient on the bed where he had held Helen so tight.

Then Helen did help him; comforted him. As she always did. 'Oh look, come on. Don't get upset, Noah. I didn't mean to be, you know, so sharp with you. But ... well, it's because I was a bit upset. You know, about this morning and everything. I just wanted you to realise, that's all, that it's all right to show your feelings sometimes.'

What, so some bastard can laugh at you? Noah sniffed, tried to stop his tears. He swallowed several times before he felt calm enough to speak. 'That's all right for you to say,' he said.

'Why is it? What d'you mean? We're all the same, aren't we? We all get scared and lonely. We all want to be loved, feel safe. We all need someone. Don't we? All I'm saying, Noah, is – if you don't open up, let people in, well, it's not going to happen the other way round is it?'

Noah dragged his hand wearily across his face, rubbed his eyes. 'Everyone likes you though, Hell. You're ... you know, easy to get on with, and all that.' He felt tired. 'I'm not ... I don't ... well, it's not easy to trust anyone, is it? I mean, how do you know you won't get, you know, won't get ...'

Helen helped him again. 'Won't get hurt?'

'Mmmm.' he nodded. She'd hit the nail on the head like she had so many times. Even though he knew she couldn't see him, he nodded again, feeling understood. 'Yes, hurt,' he said. 'How do you know you won't get hurt?'

'You don't. Just have to take that chance. Like everyone else.'

'Yes, but I'm not everyone else, am I, Hell? I'm an ugly, skinny little fuck, with bad skin, not enough hair, and look like I belong in the seven bloody dwarfs.' *Don't try and spin me all that rubbish about how we're all the same,* he thought. *She hasn't had the life I've had.*

'Don't do that to yourself, Noah,' Helen said. She sounded angry. 'Don't talk about yourself like that.'

Why not? he thought. *Other people do. Even my parents have always treated me like a freak. It's all right for her, I bet her Mummy and Daddy are sweetness and bloody light.*

Helen continued. 'If you started by liking yourself a little bit —'

Noah interrupted. 'Thanks for the advice, but it's not all that easy when you've been brought up to believe you're some sort of failure, some sort of outcast, can't do anything right. You wouldn't know about things like that though would you? I suppose your family is one of those happy ever after ones. Well, mine isn't. Actually.'

There was silence for a long time. Eventually Helen spoke. 'My dad died when I was four,' she said. 'I don't really remember him.' She sighed deeply. 'And my Mum … my Mum's been ill for years. Mental health problems – she's got bipolar disorder – you know, manic depression. Life's never the same for long, I suppose that's one thing I can say.'

'Oh fuck. I'm sorry, Hell. I … I didn't know.'

'Well, you couldn't, could you?' She waited for a while. Noah could hear her breathing. 'You never see anyone else. Only yourself.' She put the phone down.

Noah stood with his mouth open, ready to speak but not knowing what he had been about to say.

fourteen

The days passed in proper order. Noah wore the right shirts on the right days. He took special treats for their afternoon tea – a tried and tested way of keeping Helen happy – and watched as she wolfed down the wafer thin biscuits and delicate chocolates. Neither of them mentioned their night together or Noah's next meeting in his Find a Woman project.

At home, Noah occupied himself by cleaning the house. He stayed away from the cellar and the hall cupboard. He kept his Wednesday jacket on the back of the chair, and his shoes next to the front door. He checked the telephone every time he passed through the hall. His Mother left two cheerful messages. He erased them.

On Friday, Helen asked him if he was excited about the weekend, about his planned meetings with the women. Noah snorted for a reply, and Helen went off to inspect the local charity shops during her lunch break. When she came back, Noah was staring in his magnifying mirror.

'Put it away.' Helen marched into their office and stood over him with her hands on her hips. She was wearing a stone-coloured linen dress, ironed too dry and bumpy with creases. When she stood still, it was almost the right size. But as she bent to grab the mirror, it rasped against the lining and had to be twisted and tugged back into place. 'Before you say anything, I don't want to know what you think of my dress, thank you. All I'm interested in at the moment is getting you to stop picking and poking at your face. You'll make it all red and puffy.'

Noah pushed the mirror away. 'Okay, you're probably right, but will you have a look for me, Hell? Just to see if …'

Helen put the mirror in Noah's drawer and banged it shut.

'Look, just stop this,' she said. 'I'm not your bloody Mother. If you want someone to do all your personal bits and pieces, why don't you ask this bloody wonder woman? Your so-called bloody angel.' She walked out, leaving the office door open.

Noah heard an explosion of laughter from across the corridor.

Half an hour later, Helen came back. She patted his thin, sharp shoulders. 'Suppose this means I *am* your bloody Mother,' she said. 'Sorry I got annoyed. There's something … well, I've got something, you know, on my mind.'

Noah looked at Helen, 'Still love me?' he said.

'Course,' she said, and added, 'you have a lovely time – I hope it all goes … well, I hope it's what you want. And I look forward to hearing all about it.'

They left work together. Helen hugged Noah briefly again in the street before they went their separate ways. As she stepped back from the embrace, she hesitated as if about to speak. Noah felt his heartbeat quicken. *Don't*, he thought. *Please don't say anything about the night you stayed. I can't cope with that now.*

Noah decided to have a quiet Friday evening to prepare himself for the meetings ahead. The house was cleaned and ready. There was nothing to do except enjoy the evening. He opened his mail, scanned it quickly and then screwed it into a ball. There was a knock at the door. It was Godfrey. Noah's jaw tightened. 'I've only just got in the bloody door,' he muttered.

'I know you have, love,' Godfrey said. 'I've been looking out for you, wanted to catch you in case you were off out. It's Joey. Poor old bugger's taken a turn for the worse. We'll have to go and see him, Noel. He might not last much longer.'

'What d'you expect me to do about it?' Noah screwed the paper ball tighter. The sharp edges stuck into his hand.

'Oh come on, duck; you know he loves to see us. It'll cheer him up. When they rang earlier they said he was going on about the lovely young boys in his street – that's us, he means. The only ones who bother with the poor old sod.' Godfrey rolled the edge of his apron against his trouser leg.

Noah threw the paper across the room, squeezed his way out of the half-open door and dug Godfrey in the back. 'Come on then, let's get on with it,' he said. 'We'll go in *my* car. And I'm not sitting there all night, waiting for him to breathe his last breath. Understand?'

Joseph Pepper was breathing noisily but evenly when they arrived at his bedside. He showed no sign of recognition when he opened his eyes, and seemed to drift in and out of a shallow sleep.

'Christ, how long do we have to stay in this stinking bloody place? What a way to spend Friday night.' Noah said.

'Shush, he'll hear you, Noel. Look, have a couple of these. The old boy don't want 'em.' Godfrey held out a tin of iced fairy cakes.

Noah pushed it away. He stood up and paced the room, grinding his teeth.

Godfrey beckoned him back to the bed. ''ere, Noel, come and have a listen. What's he saying, duck? Can you hear?'

Joseph's grey lips were twitching and trembling. His large bony hands fluttered on the sheet. Noah leaned closer. An antiseptic smell surrounded the old man. The hollow of his cheek was rough with a silver patch of stubble. His lips were dry and cracked, with no colour.

'Well, he's not telling us where he's buried the bloody treasure, that's for sure,' Noah said. He backed away from the bed.

Godfrey stroked Joseph Pepper's arm and said softly, 'What's up, love, what you trying to tell us? Ay?'

Noah looked at his watch. 'All he's doing is rambling, as usual. Let's get out of here.'

Joseph opened his eyes and looked round the small room. 'Where are they?' he said. 'The lovely boys – where have they put them?' His gruff, croaking voice was barely audible. His breath smelled like sour milk.

Godfrey patted the old man's hand, 'Don't you worry, Joe. Your lovely boys are right here beside you, aren't we, Noel?'

Noah sneered. *Speak for yourself.*

Joseph rolled his head from side to side. 'Don't want anyone to take my lovely boys. I've got them safe. Nice and safe, my lovely …' The old man breathed out slowly; a slight whistle came from the back of his throat.

'He's gone, Noel. The poor old boy's gone, bless him,' Godfrey said. He wiped at the tears that were dripping into his lap.

After the drive back, silent except for Godfrey's gentle sobbing, Noah couldn't wait to get indoors. 'Look, you'll be all right. Have an early night or something,' he said as Godfrey heaved himself out of the car, a soggy hanky in one hand and his tin of cakes in the other. Noah reached across and pulled the passenger door shut while Godfrey still stood on the pavement outside his house. *And stop that bloody blubbing*, he thought.

'That's the last time I'll have to come home stinking like an incontinent old half-wit, thank God.' Noah laughed and pushed himself up out of the warm suds in his bath. Dry, warm and clean, he padded downstairs.

The hall cupboard was open. A boy of about ten swayed lifelessly between the coats and jackets. He was suspended by the neck, his pale head a heavy lump, flopped onto his shoulder. Noah screamed. He ran back to the bathroom, locked the door, crouched on the damp floor and bit the back of his hand until it bled. Too frightened to leave the bathroom, he curled up on the floor and stayed there all night, jolting in and out of sleep.

fifteen

'I've got to talk to someone. I can't go through with this without talking to someone first.' Noah twisted his hair while he paced in circles round his sitting room floor. 'And I'm not going round *his.*' *He'll want to have cosy chats and force mountains of cake down my throat. I haven't got time for all that. Got to meet this Esther person later today. But I do need to talk. Not that he'd know what I was on about even if I did go round there. Never had a relationship in his life. Not unless you count the years he spent doing his Mother's hair.* He picked a speck of fluff off the carpet, pinched it hard between his fingers and then, not knowing what to do with it, put it in his pocket. 'Where's Hell when I need her?'

He shouldered his way through the door, making it swing back and hit the sitting room wall. 'Fuck' he said, scowling. And then pushed the door deliberately so that its handle hit the wall again, hard. Noah spoke in his Mother's voice, 'You'll ruin the paintwork with behaviour like that, Noah.' *Well, what does that matter in the scale of things? When I've got all this going on* and *some sort of evil spirit haunting my house? She wouldn't even listen if I tried to tell her — not that I ever would. Gave up trying to talk to the Mother-parent a long time ago.* 'I've got to go on a course for work, Mother.'

'Oh, that reminds me, Noah, the people next door are going away for a week — a coach trip — and they've asked us to go in and water the plants, pick the post up. You know, that sort of thing.'

'I'm having these awful dreams, Mother.'

'Oh, did I tell you we've bought a new bed? Your Father wasn't sleeping well and we have had that bed a long time, they don't last forever do they? Anyway this new one's taking a bit of getting used to. Of course, it's a lot firmer for a start ...'

'I saw a dead boy hanging in the cupboard under my stairs, Mother.'

'Isn't it awful about that poor young boy in the newspapers. Missing for over a week, wasn't he? I mean, you stop having much hope by then don't you?'

Noah grabbed his phone for the fourth time in half an hour and dialled Helen's number again. *She knows she's the only person I can talk to. Where is she? She never goes out; the only life she's got is going to work. That and spending hours in bloody charity shops rummaging through other people's cast-offs. Bet that's where she is now. First thing Saturday morning, sorting her way through heaps of limp old clothes, all with that stale, musty, sweat-stained, matted-together sort of smell.* He shuddered at the thought. *Surprised Hell doesn't smell like that herself. That's one good thing I suppose, at least she's clean. Well, cleanish.*

He tried her number again. Again there was no reply. The ringing tone went on and on in Noah's ear, like an insect caught in a jar. *Just another three rings then that's it,* he thought, *just a few more – she's probably in the bath, garden, just coming through the door now.* But Helen didn't answer. Noah put the phone down with exaggerated care. His anger pulsed at his temples. His jaw ached from grinding his teeth.

'Right, I'm going round there then. She'll probably be back by the time I get there. With another carrier bag full of her latest old rags, I bet. Don't know why she keeps doing it.' *And a couple of extra large doughnuts for her afternoon snack.*

Noah drove to Helen's house through the clogged and chaotic Saturday morning traffic. Cars were filled with families, boisterous children in the back, their arms and legs everywhere. Or worse; children turned to face out of the rear window, smiling, waving over and over again. Or just staring – that stare children give strangers when they know their parents can't see them. Cold, almost menacing. And buses packed with Saturday shoppers, in search of shoes or dresses or coats. Or just a way to fill up some of their time, wandering in the hypnotic haze of too-bright shops, caught by the glare of new things crying out to be taken home. Things that became mundane once removed from their calculated surroundings.

The drivers in wrong lanes, the ones distracted by crowded cars filled with animated passengers; the ones slow to respond to traffic lights – they all fed Noah's tense, impatient and irritable mood. 'Wake up, for fuck's sake,' he shouted, the tendons on his neck as taut as tent ropes. 'Never mind yakking to the person next to you – let's try looking at the fucking road, shall we?'

When he arrived at Helen's house, Noah was rigid in his seat, his hands clamped to the steering wheel, his neck stiff and aching. His head throbbed with tight bands of pain across his forehead and at the base of his skull. His fingers shook slightly as he fumbled to release his seat belt. *All this just because she decides to go out for once in a blue moon.*

But Helen wasn't out. Noah pressed her doorbell, waited less than ten seconds before pressing it again, and then started to walk back to his car. He heard the door open and turned back to see Helen looking at him through a narrow gap. Her eyes looked startled though her face was blank and pale.

'Noah?'

'Who else does it look like?' He stepped closer to the door, expecting her to open it. 'Been ringing and ringing you. Where've you been? I need to talk to you.'

Helen stayed where she was, a white face in the gap of her barely open door. 'Oh, it was you ringing,' she said.

Noah edged forward again. 'Yes it was me. Who else is it likely to be? Are you going to let me in or what?' He tapped his fingers on the wall next to Helen's door. 'I mean, I haven't driven all the way over here to stand on the doorstep – traffic was fucking awful as well.'

Helen remained in the same position. 'I didn't know you were coming,' she said quietly.

'No, well it's a bit difficult to make an appointment with someone when they don't answer the bloody phone. Actually.' Noah rubbed the back of his head; the pain gripped his skull tighter. He winced.

'You don't have to make appointments, Noah,' Helen said. 'Are you all right?' She spoke slowly. Her face was puffy and somehow set.

It looked heavy and had a sickly sheen.

'No,' he said. 'No I'm not if you're really interested. Got three headaches all at the same time. Actually.' He rubbed his head again. 'You just got up or what?' *If it's beauty sleep, it's not bloody working. She looks twice her age with a face like that.*

Helen drew in a long breath, opened the door and stood to one side to let Noah in. 'You'd better come in,' she said in a slow, flat voice. 'Things are … well, in a bit of a mess, I'm afraid.' In slow motion, she closed the front door behind Noah. 'I've, well, I've had a bit of a rough night. Would you like something to drink?' As she asked this, Helen jerked her hand up and clamped it over her mouth. It was the fastest movement she had made since Noah arrived.

He was about to reply but Helen rushed upstairs, her baggy grey cardigan flapping out behind her. 'Make it myself then, shall I?' he called after her, and then turned towards Helen's small kitchen. 'Jesus Christ,' he said, 'what the fuck's happened in here?'

'That's the mess I told you about,' Helen stood behind Noah in the kitchen. 'The one I didn't particularly want you to see.' She had thumped her way downstairs.

The sound made Noah imagine her with callipers or wearing huge steel toe-capped boots that made her legs too heavy to control. Now she stood behind him and he could smell the scent of soap, something fresh and tangy. It cut through the mixture of cloying aromas in her kitchen. 'What is it?' Noah gestured with both hands at the work surfaces, the floor, and the top of the oven.

'It's food,' Helen said.

'I can see it's food. I mean …' Noah shook his head, rubbed his hands together, 'I mean, how did it get like this? What happened? Why's it all such a … well such a huge bloody mess in here?' He turned to look at Helen, saw that her face was still deathly pale, her expression just as flat.

'Oh, it's not just in here. The other room doesn't look too pretty either, I'm afraid,' she said. She wouldn't look at Noah, and stared past him. Tears slipped down her white face. She stood very still and cried without making a sound.

'But how did it get like this, Hell? You been a bit lax with the housework, or had a party, or what?' Noah looked round the kitchen. Cupboard doors were open, the contents spilling out. An empty cereal packet lay on its side on the floor. Next to it were three opened jars. *Looks like one of them used to have lemon curd in it, and that other one was definitely peanut butter*, thought Noah, shuddering inside. *Fuck knows what the red gunge is on the other one – looks like clots of blood round the top.* An empty bag from a loaf of bread and what appeared to be the wrappers from several packets of biscuits formed a loose heap in the corner near the fridge.

'Don't look at it.' Helen sobbed. 'Please don't look.'

'Hard not to – there's rubbish all over the place. I never thought you were … I mean I know you don't mind things a bit, well you know … but it's never been like this before.' Noah brushed at his chest unconsciously.

Helen pushed her hair off her face and stood with her hand on top of her head. She looked utterly drained. 'I know, I know, you thought I was a lazy bitch who lived in a bit of a pigsty.' She attempted a laugh, but it was flat and humourless. 'Nothing like this though, Hmm? And actually it hasn't been like this for a while. Things just, I don't know, just got out of control last night. Don't know why. Nothing's changed. Well, not really.' As she spoke, tears made wet lines over her cheeks and dripped into the fuzz of her grey cardigan. Her mouth twisted and trembled with her effort to make it form words. 'You'd better go Noah. I um …' She cleared her throat, tried to smile. 'I need to get things tidied up here. Get myself, you know, sorted out.'

Noah turned to face Helen. Something crunched under his shoes as he moved. He lifted his arms away from his sides, shrugged and let them fall again. 'But …' He shook his head slowly. 'What about all this fucking mess though, Hell? I just don't understand what … well, why, I mean, I don't know how you could —'

Helen interrupted. 'You don't know how I could what, Noah? Be so greedy? Be such a slut? Make such a disgusting mess? Get so bloody far out of bloody control? What? What don't you know?

Because do you know what? Neither do I.' She pushed a lank strand of hair away from her puffy, wet face. It flopped back and hung in front of her eyes. Her shoulders drooped. She looked somehow propped-up from inside, like a scarecrow that wants to collapse off its weather-beaten frame. 'I didn't exactly plan to get in this kind of …' she made a gesture with her hand toward the work surface, her pointing finger lost inside the cardigan's long, wavy sleeve, 'this kind of chaos. I suppose that is the right word, isn't it? Chaos?'

Noah looked at the food-strewn display. *Yes*, he thought, *chaos is exactly the right word. Like a horror film version of the teddy bears' fucking picnic.* 'Er, I, yeah, I suppose you could say that – I don't know.' *She must have been up half the night to make this sort of 'chaos.' I feel sick just looking at it, just being in the same room. Not to mention wading through toasted fucking wheat flakes or whatever it is all over the floor.* He noticed an open tin of cocoa, a spoon sticking out of the middle; brown dust scattered everywhere, some of it gone sticky and dark where it had got damp. A torn bag of raisins, the remainder of its contents spilled out and spread like shrivelled rabbit droppings among the muddle of other foods. And icing sugar. Was it icing sugar? Or flour? It lay in a drift near the kettle, a snowy mound contrasting with the garish spread of other ingredients. *Looks like some demented cook has been let on the loose in here. Him with the apron would have a field day with all this. He'd have his mop and bucket out in a flash. It's such a mess – none of it even goes together. Condensed milk and breadsticks; mint sauce and chocolate spread, for Christ's sake. And what was in that big packet?* He craned his neck to see. *Oh God, ready-made meringues. And she's eaten the lot.*

Helen tugged weakly at Noah's arm. 'Don't,' she said. 'Please don't look at it. I really do want you to go. I'm very tired.'

'Yeah. Yeah, all right.' Noah brushed his arm. 'I did want to talk to you. Actually. I came over specially, but …' He folded his arms tight across his chest.

'I'm sorry Noah,' Helen said. 'I can't do it now. I really can't.'

Noah backed towards the hall, treading carefully. He felt something soft under his right foot and lifted his leg behind him to see what he had squashed. A small lump of uncooked pastry was stuck to the sole of his shoe. Grey and greasy, it looked like an oversized blob of chewing gum picked up from a pavement. *Fuck's sake*, he thought, his jaw clamped tight. 'If you'd answered your phone ... well, never mind,' he said. 'I don't suppose the traffic will be as bad on the way back. Hope not anyway.' He picked the empty cereal box up off the floor and scraped the pastry off his shoe. 'What shall I do with this?' He waved the box awkwardly.

Helen shrugged and closed her eyes. 'I don't care.'

Noah dropped the box on the floor. 'Right. Bye then.'

Helen didn't reply. He left her standing in the middle of her kitchen.

sixteen

'At least the dents have come out of my face,' Noah said to the reflection in his rear-view mirror. 'She won't see a thing. Not that Hell noticed them this morning anyway.' He ached from his night spent sleeping on the bathroom floor. And now, with the shock of finding Helen so immersed in misery of her own that she would offer him none of her usual support, Noah felt muddled and anxious. He parked in the space furthest away from the pub entrance. He was forty minutes early. 'If I see some ugly bitch go in there with a crossword puzzle tucked under her arm, I'm off,' he said to the slice of creased forehead in his mirror.

Two women arrived in separate cars, each of them wearing a white top. 'This Esther person said she'd be wearing a white top. How am I supposed to know which one is her?' He drummed his fingers on the steering wheel. 'Still, they didn't have crossword books with them.' He waited another five minutes. Then he locked his car. As he entered the pub, someone near the bar finished telling a joke. A small crowd laughed. Noah twisted his hair, looked round the room. A woman was looking at him, an expectant smile on her face. She patted a magazine lying on the table. Noah nodded and made his way towards her.

'Can I help you with four down?' he asked.

'Ssorry?' said the woman, still smiling at Noah.

He tapped the folded magazine on the table. 'The crossword – do you want a hand with the clues?' He sighed. 'Never mind, never mind – just a joke. I'm Noah, by the way. And you must be … er, Esther? Like a drink?'

'Mmm, yess pleasse,' she said, nodding. 'If you're having one. That would be nice. Thank you.' She smiled at him.

Noah looked at her from the bar while he waited for two glasses of mineral water. *She's a bit bulky*, he thought. *Big mammaries. At least she's washed her hair, though. That white top doesn't do her any favours. Too tight. But her face isn't too bad, if only she'd stop doing that stupid grin. And that bloody lisping voice is going to get on my nerves pretty quickly. Definitely not keen on those mammaries. All that wobbling. Still, this isn't going to take long.*

Esther lifted her shoulders in a huge smile and raised her glass. 'Here's to uss,' she said. 'I've been looking forward to this all week. Can't believe we're finally here.' She gulped down half her glass of water. 'I've hardly sslept, wondering what you'd be like and everything.' As she spoke, she stared directly at Noah.

'Er, so have you had a busy week at work?' he asked. *Bloody hell, she's a bit intense. I'm not hanging about here for long.*

'Well, we did have someone leave this week,' she said. 'We all clubbed together to buy him a nice present and gave him a bit of a ssend off. Got him a lovely carriage clock, we did.'

'Retirement, was it?'

'Ssorry?' Esther looked puzzled. She gave another huge smile – her shoulders raised up high to join in with her upturned mouth and stared at Noah.

'Well, the clock …' Noah said. *Christ*, he thought. *She's so dense.*

'Oh no, nothing like that.' She touched Noah's arm. 'He'd just got to stop working because of cancer.'

Oh, he's going to get a lot of fucking use out of a clock then, isn't he? He can sit and watch his last few months ticking away. 'Oh. Right,' he said. He stood up. 'Do you want another?' He held the empty glasses out. *If she says 'another what?' I'm leaving.*

'So, have you done this a lot?' Noah said as he sat down with the drinks.

Esther lifted her glass and mouthed the word cheers. 'Done what?' She smiled her huge smile again, her shoulders lifted up to her ears.

Looks like a cushion, thought Noah. '*This*,' he said. 'This soul mates thing. Have you done much of it?'

'Oh, no, you're my first, Noah,' she said. 'I had some other messages, but I only wanted to meet you. We got on ssso well on the phone.' She smiled again, patted Noah's arm.

He moved it away, sat on his hand. 'Er, it's a funny old business though, isn't it?' He hooked his ankle round the chair leg. 'I mean, meeting up with complete strangers and all that. Not knowing how it'll turn out, wondering if you'll even like them, or if they'll make you feel like running away.'

Esther leaned forward. 'I knew it wouldn't be like that for uss. I put my faith in the Lord's judgement.'

Noah sipped his water; his fingers gripped the glass tightly. *Oh fuck, here we go*, he thought. 'I'm not … well, I mean, I'm not religious or anything like that,' he said.

'Aaah, that doesn't matter,' she said. 'He loves you just the ssame. I mean, He's brought you here today, hasn't he?'

You're lucky I'm here at all, Noah thought. *Nothing to do with God either. It was four wheels, a gear stick and a steering wheel that got me here today, you dense bloody cow. And I nearly didn't come anyway, after all the upset I had with Hell this morning.* He sat on his hands, aware of Esther's constant scrutiny. *I'm not going to keep struggling to find something to say,* he thought. *She doesn't understand a word I come out with anyway.*

Esther finished her drink. She laid her hand on Noah's knee, and whispered, 'Shall we go, then?'

'Yes it's probably best. I was thinking the same thing myself. Actually.' Noah sighed with relief.

Esther did her shoulder smile. 'Where?' She stared at Noah, followed his eyes as he looked round the pub.

He fiddled with the hair at his temple. 'Oh right. Er, I don't really know, I didn't think …' He clenched his jaw. *Don't want to be stuck with her all fucking afternoon*, he thought.

Esther smuggled her arm through Noah's, gave it a squeeze. 'Why don't we go for a little walk?' she said. 'We could have a proper chat, get to know each other even better.' She fixed her eyes on his.

Noah looked down to escape the intensity of her gaze. He was met by the white mounds of her breasts, and looked up again into

Esther's grinning face. He twitched his mouth in response.

'Ready?' she said.

They walked to the nearby park. Esther tripped and stumbled in her attempt to keep eye contact with Noah as she walked beside him.

Look where you're going, you clumsy bitch, Noah thought. He leaned away from her and looked straight ahead.

Esther remained cheerful and talkative. She touched his arm, his hand and his shoulder, again and again, and seemed oblivious to his sullen mood.

Noah clenched his jaw. *It's not right, coming here with her. This is where I'm meeting Angela tomorrow. Who does she think she is – barging her way into people's special places —?*

Esther interrupted Noah's thoughts. 'Fancy a little ssit down?' she said. 'Be nice, wouldn't it?' She pulled him towards a slatted wooden bench. Someone had carved *Fuck off* along the back – an anonymous memorial seat. Noah echoed the sentiments in his head. But he sat down.

Esther was on him immediately. Her heavy arm weighted his shoulder down. Her padded thigh wedged against him, and her thick fingers poked at the bones and tendons of his face, to turn it towards her. Noah managed only to say, 'I don't thi ...' before Esther closed in with wet, smiling kisses. She kept her eyes open and continued to stare at Noah.

'I'm glad that happened, aren't you?' she said when she'd let him go.

Christ, thought Noah, *she makes it sound like a fucking accident*. He wiped his mouth with the back of his hand. 'I'm not sure,' he said. 'A bit surprised. Actually.'

She gripped his knee, felt along his leg. 'Who's a sshy little thing then?' she said.

'It's not that. I'm just, er, well, we don't really know each other, and ...'

'S'nice that you're a bit sshy,' she said, and grabbed Noah's hand. 'Oh, what have you done?' She stroked the red bite mark. 'It looks all sore, you poor thing. Here let me kisss it better.'

'No.' Noah stood up, jerked his hand away. 'This isn't right. I can't do this,' he said.

'You're right, Noah, it's a bit public, isn't it? Come on, we can go to my house. You'll be more relaxed there. And I can look after your poor hand.' She grinned. 'Feed you up a bit as well, you're all bone and gristle aren't you?'

'No, I don't think so,' Noah said. He smoothed his clothes.

'Aaah, you're so ssweet. All nervy and everything, aren't you?' She plumped her shoulders up into a smile. 'What if we leave it till tomorrow then? Pick up where we left off? S'pect it's all a bit new for both of uss.'

Noah walked briskly back to the pub, his arms folded tightly across his chest. Esther stumbled along beside him. She fell off the same low-heeled shoe twice in her attempt to keep up with him. *Like a bloody puppy*, thought Noah. *All she needs is a tail to wag*. When they reached the car park, Noah unlocked his car, and angled the door in front of him. 'Look, it's not your fault,' he said. 'But I just don't think this is for me. I've got to go. I think you left your crossword puzzle in the pub.' He slammed the car door and drove away. He could see Esther waving in his mirror. 'Bet she's still fucking grinning,' he said to himself.

Noah pressed the button on his answer-machine as soon as he got home. Esther's lisping words filled the hall.

'Just wanted to say thank you for ssuch a lovely time. Hope you enjoyed it as well, Noah. I hope you got home all right. Sspeak to you soon. Bye for now.'

'Bloody dense cow. What more do I have to do to spell it out?' Noah jabbed at the erase button. 'I didn't think this dating lark was going to be such a pain, what with dirty poets and clingy fat women all over the place. Didn't want to be mauled about like that on a fucking park bench. Angela won't be like that. *She'll* know how to behave.'

seventeen

'No, I won't be there,' Noah said, 'you know I don't like anything like that. All that polite waffle with people you don't even know.'

His Mother's voice was patient but determined. 'Now, don't be silly Noah, this is your family we're talking about. Of course you know them.'

Noah sneered at the receiver. *Yeah and a right bunch of nonentities they are. Why would anyone in their right mind want to spend time with a crowd of village fucking idiots and boring small-minded pond-life like that?* 'Exactly,' he said.

'What do you mean? We thought it would be nice to get everyone together. Have a chance to catch up with news and see each other. After all, none of us are getting any younger. We don't want to be one of those families that only see each other at weddings and funerals, do we?'

Even that would be too often. Actually, he thought.

His Mother continued. 'Anyway, it's all arranged. You've got to come, Noah. I've done a lot of the organising myself. Booked the hall and all that.'

Oh, I bet you have, you interfering old goat. Bet the bloody tablecloths had to match the curtains and there'll be place-names telling everyone where to sit, and proper napkins and paper flags stuck in the food with jolly little descriptions. Just in case someone has never seen a cheese sandwich with the crust cut off before. Oh and there won't be any fucking alcohol either. Oh no, we don't want anything like that, do we? 'No, count me out,' he said, 'I'm not interested.'

'I've already told everyone that you'll be there. How's it going to look if you don't turn up? All your cousins will be there. And some of them live miles away but they're still coming. And their children, of course.'

Here we go – the 'I don't suppose I'll ever have grandchildren' lecture. 'Oh, that really makes me want to turn up, that does Mother – a load of little brats tearing round a community centre, going wild and screaming all day. Not quite my idea of a good time, believe it or not. Like I said, it's not my sort of thing. Won't be there, I'm afraid. Bye.' He put the phone down, kept his hand hovering over it and picked it up immediately when his Mother rang back. She carried on as if there had been no interruption, a slight edge in her voice this time.

'Noah, all I'm asking you to do is come along for a few hours and spend some time with the family. That really isn't too much to ask is it? And it's not in the community centre, by the way. I've hired a function room in that hotel. What's it called now? Park Lodge, that's it. All very nice – the girl on reception had a lovely smart uniform on. It means some of the cousins can stay overnight instead of driving all that way back. Especially the ones with children – they won't want to be travelling late in the evening. I always used to insist on getting you home in time for your proper bedtime. It's not good to go messing about with routine for the little ones.'

Noah stared at the ceiling and sighed as he listened. *Jesus, anyone would think I was still in nappies the way she goes on.* 'Aren't we getting off the point a bit here? The way I see it is this; you are organising some sort of ghastly family reunion. I don't want to be part of it. End of story.' He tapped his foot against the hall pew to emphasise his words. *Now will you get it into your obstinate head, goat woman?*

'Grandma Quince will be there, Noah. She's nearly ninety. You might not … well, you know, we never know when we'll see her again do we? Come just for her. You are the eldest grandchild after all.' Her voice sounded thick, as if she might cry.

Noah thought of his Grandmother. How she used to give him a yellow duster with orange stitching round the edge, and show him how to open the tin of beeswax polish by twisting the little lever on the side. He'd never forgotten the scent of that polish – warm and sweet – a deep yellow smell, just like its colour. Then he would rub the wax into the arms of the old leather sofa while his Grandmother hummed along to the radio and banged dust out of the cushions. Round and round, he would rub the hard wax into the cracked leather, making it cloudy and dull. 'Leave it to seep in, love,' his Grandmother would say. And later, his favourite bit – with a clean duster, he would buff away at the arms until they shone. And all the time that lovely thick smell surrounded him. His Mother's voice cut into his thoughts.

'She used to spoil you something rotten.'

'No she didn't. Me and Grandma just got on really well.' *And you were jealous*, thought Noah, *because you and I didn't, never have*.

'Well, I don't know about that, Noah. She always let you get away with things too much for my liking. I know she meant well, but it's one thing to be a doting Grandmother when you only get to see the best bib and tucker behaviour. It's a very different story when you have to contend with the other side of things. Like I did with you, Noah. She didn't have to pick you up, stiff as an ironing board, and carry you up to your bedroom after one of your mealtime tantrums. Or watch your every move to make sure you didn't poke your fingers down your throat to make yourself sick. And she didn't have the worry like I did of you not eating for days on end, and —'

Noah kicked the pew. 'Hold on, hold on. We're supposed to be talking about this bloody family get-together here, not going over the details of my unhappy childhood.'

'What do you mean, "unhappy"? We gave you everything we could afford. You wanted for nothing when you were a child. Your Father worked his —'

'His fingers to the bone?' Noah said. 'I think you've mentioned that once or twice before, you know. But let's get back to the point here. About this bloody party thing. God knows why you want to do it, but if it means some sort of peace and quiet, I'll come, all right?' Noah put the phone down. His Mother did not ring back.

Grandma Quince, he thought, *she always had a soft spot for me. She's a dear old thing. Not that I've seen her for ages. Be nice to see her for a while, but as for the rest of them ... I won't be hanging about long.*

Later in the evening, Noah had another phone call from his Mother. The family reunion had been cancelled. Her sister-in-law, Bunty, with whom she had never got on, had invited some long-lost and estranged members of the family without consultation.

'Without a word to me,' Noah's Mother kept saying. This news had spread through phone lines like a virus to the core of family already invited and booked to stay at the hotel after the party. One by one they had rang to make their excuses. 'Well, I can't blame them but it's all such a shame. All that planning. And I've had a cake made. Bunty had no place in this. She shouldn't have interfered. She's always been the same. I don't know how her poor husband puts up with it.'

That's probably why the gormless bastard married her in the first place. He's always been the type that needs organising – bet he can't even choose what colour socks to wear without her telling him. She is a bossy cow though. 'Oh well,' he said, 'perhaps this will teach her a lesson. She's poked her nose in – yet again – and now the whole thing's off. Serves her right.'

'Yes, but Noah, it's such a shame for everyone else. I know they'll all be disappointed.'

Not if they've got any fucking sense they won't, he thought. *But then again, most of them haven't.* 'Never mind, they'll get over it won't they? Now, I've really got to go – I've got some ironing I need to do ready for tomorrow. And clocks to wind.' *Not that you'd be interested*, he thought, and put the phone down. He bunched his small hand into a fist and punched the air of his hallway. 'Brilliant.' The movement toppled him slightly off balance and he fell against the cupboard door, knocking his shoulder. *There's nothing in there, nothing in there, nothing, nothing, nothing.* Palpitations made his chest judder, his breathing was erratic, but he moved away with a controlled calm and slowness. He forced a smile that felt both tight and theatrical, and walked away from the cupboard. *Nothing, nothing at all*. His tiny body flooded with adrenalin, Noah went to wind his clocks ready for tomorrow and to iron the clothes he would wear to meet Angela.

eighteen

Early on Sunday morning, Noah's Mother rang to tell him the family party would be going ahead after all. 'I spent hours on the telephone yesterday, Noah – hours. I spoke to the people at the hotel, they've been very understanding about all this … well, all this muddle.'

'I haven't got time for this,' Noah said, 'I'm meeting —'

His Mother interrupted. 'The good news is that they've managed to fit us in. Because there's only a small group of us now, they've offered to bring our booking forward. Isn't that nice of them?'

Noah tapped his fingers against his leg. 'Yes, yes, Mother, very nice. But what's any of this got to do with me?' He sighed. 'First you're having this bloody party, then it's all off, now you're saying it's back on again. When you get it sorted out once and for all, let me know. Until then, I really don't care.'

'But it is sorted, dear. That's what I'm trying to tell you. The hotel people have been very helpful. They've had a cancellation at short notice, and say we can use that function room instead. A daughter calling off an engagement party, I think it was. Imagine all the work that family must have put —'

'Never mind all that. What the bloody hell are you on about?'

'Well, it means we can have the room today, Noah. Isn't that good?'

'No.' he said. 'Absolutely not. Not, not, not.'

'Noah, you said you would come. Now, it's all arranged – I've checked with your aunt and uncle and they can make it. Your Father and I can, of course, and Grandma, well, she won't mind when it is. That just leaves you, Noah.'

'And I've just told you, Mother' he said, 'the answer is no. I've already got plans. Important plans.' He tapped his leg rapidly again with his twitching fingers. *If you think I'm changing one second of my plans with Angela ...*

His Mother cleared her throat. 'Now listen to me, Noah,' her voice had the contrived calm of masked impatience. 'I have moved heaven and earth to organise this party. You said you would come along just to see Grandma Quince. I expect you to be there.' She cleared her throat again, then added, '*She* expects you to be there. You don't want to disappoint an old lady of her age, now do you?'

Oh here we go, let's use fucking blackmail, he thought. 'Don't try and bring poor old Grandma into this, she's probably forgotten everything about it. And in case you can't remember, I never wanted to come to the bloody thing in the first place. I only said I would because —'

His Mother interrupted. 'Yes, you said you'd be there for Grandma. Well, she's going to be very upset this evening when her favourite grandson isn't there and —'

Noah cut in. 'I can't make it. I'm doing something, I told you. I didn't know you were going to change things like this, did I? You can't go telling Grandma that I wouldn't come, that's not fair.'

There was silence for a while. Then his Mother said, 'I just can't believe you would be so ... well, that you'd let us all down like this, Noah. The whole family ... it's just, well, I don't know what to say. Really I don't.'

'You mean you can't stand it that I'm not doing what *you* want. And anyway, what do you mean the whole family – how many of them are actually going to be there?'

'Six. There'll be six of us. With you there.'

Noah laughed. 'Oh for God's sake, Mother. Why are you bothering? What sort of bloody party will that be? Six!' He laughed again. 'Well, you'd better make it five. Now, I really must be going.'

'And what if your Grandma dies?' his Mother said, 'What then?'

'What, from all the excitement? Don't think that'll happen, do you, Mother? Not with five of you sitting there staring at each other.' *What did she have to say that for? I don't want that. What if she did die? Then it would be all my bloody fault. Grandma Quince always used to make a special fuss of me. She used to let me help her with the polishing ...*

'Well, I'm just saying she's not going to be around forever, is she? And it would mean such a lot to her if you were there this evening. Just think about it, Noah, at least think it over.'

Oh, how much more of this? Why not go all out and threaten to throw yourself under a bus as well? he thought. *Not that that would be much good as blackmail.* He kicked the pew. 'You said this evening?'

'Oh good, you'll be there then? I'll be off now and start getting things —'

Noah cut in, angry. 'Hang on, hang on. I didn't say that did I? All I said was ... well, what time this evening?'

'Well, late afternoon, early evening, Noah. We don't want anything too late do we? Not for Grandma, not at her age —'

'So what time?' He sighed loudly.

'Half past four. Until about eightish I thought, although the hotel people said we can have the room until nine. But that should be quite long enough for everyone to have a chat and —'

Noah interrupted. 'I'll see what I can do,' he said. 'But I'm not promising anything. Now, I'm busy. Bye.' He put the phone down. *Fucking wonderful, just what I needed – a family fucking reunion on the same day I'm meeting my angel. And if Angela wants to go somewhere for the evening ... if she wants us to spend the night together ... they'll just have to have their fucking party without me.*

Later that morning, Noah met his angel. She looked just as he'd imagined her. Her shiny hair and pale skin seemed to glow. There was a hint of something – nervousness? - around her mouth, but that was to be expected. *She's shy like me*, Noah thought as he looked at her, his heart pounding.

She was sitting at a small table near the birdcages in pets corner, as they had arranged. A mynah bird wolf-whistled repeatedly. Noah introduced himself and asked if he could sit down. The loud whistle made them both smile.

'I'm Grace. Hello.' She looked surprised, alarmed even, as she held out her hand.

Perhaps she didn't expect me to turn up, thought Noah. Her hand was white and slender. Noah felt the bones of her fingers fit neatly against his own. The dark red bite mark on his hand looked worse next to her white skin. He said her name inside his head, in time with the whistling bird. *Her name's Grace. It's not really Angela.*

'I was going to wear a carnation,' Noah said. *A blue one* – the thought flashed through his mind and he fought to prevent hysterical laughter.

Grace smiled. 'But everyone does that, so I still wouldn't have known which one was you.'

Noah laughed then. Too much and too loud. He squeezed his knees tightly together under the table to make himself stop. *She's gorgeous*, he thought. *Just like I imagined her. That lovely smile, that lovely blue dress, her shiny brown hair. Perfect, she's just perfect.* 'Would you like to go and see the birds, the other animals?' he asked.

'Okay, yes. I haven't been here for ages.'

Great, Noah thought. *She wasn't here yesterday, then.* He stood up and hovered behind her chair. *She smells lovely*, he thought as she straightened herself next to him. 'Oh, you're …' Noah said. He changed what he'd been about to say, clumsily. 'You're er … you're not a regular visitor here then?' His thoughts raced. *You're too tall. You're taller than me – you're not meant to be taller than me. Oh, Angela, you weren't supposed to be tall. I mean Grace. Grace not Angela. But not tall. Oh, not tall.*

The aviaries were filled with bright, darting finches, squawking budgerigars, parakeets and canaries. Noah and Grace walked slowly past the wire netting, pointed to various birds, pretended to read the information on small white boards. Noah kept a space between them, which made him more nervous and jittery, as he tried to anticipate her movements and keep enough distance not to be measured. 'Why don't we sit down again?' he said.

They found a table on the terrace of the park café. Noah went inside to buy a pot of tea and some scones. He looked at Grace from his place in the queue. *The more we have to eat and drink, the longer we can sit here.* The idea of eating made him feel uneasy. *Maybe she'll be like Hell and eat the lot on her own. I can just sit and watch.* He strained to see her feet. *Perhaps she's wearing high heels*, he thought. But he couldn't see from the café.

Grace poured the tea. She was careful and poised, surrounded by an air of calm, which helped Noah to relax. He cut his scone into small pieces, not wanting to risk the collapse of a whole one as he bit into it. He drank the tea in small sips. *I can even eat with her*, he thought. 'Well, this is nice' he said, and immediately thought he sounded like Esther.

'Yes ... yes, I suppose it is.' Grace put her hands in her lap. 'I must admit though, I nearly didn't come,' she said, looking at her hands.

'Oh,' Noah said. 'Is that because you've already met the other men, then?' He pictured a queue of tall men, each one better looking than the last. He reached for the hair at his temple, and then stopped himself.

Grace shook her head. 'It's just that I thought I'd given myself enough time. Now I'm not so sure. Emotions are funny things, aren't they? Things can come to the surface and surprise you.' She spoke softly and looked uncomfortable.

'Do you mean ...? You *do* mean there's someone else, don't you?' Noah was trembling. *She can't, she can't do this*.

Grace nodded and looked at the table. 'Yes. There was someone else.'

'Was?' *Oh, God, don't frighten me like that, Angela.*

Grace nodded again. She smiled, more to herself than at Noah.

He dug his fingernails into the palms of his hands, each one a fist under his armpits. *Oh, don't leave it there, Angela, please tell me what's what*, he begged her inside his head. Then he made the correction, *Grace not Angela*.

'There *was* someone very special,' she said. 'We were together for years. Then he met another woman. It was all very sudden, a real shock, and it took me a long time to get over it. Well, I'm not sure I have yet. I certainly haven't felt ready to meet anyone else.' She poured more tea and seemed distant.

'Not ready until now,' Noah said. He saw the expression on her face again – an awkward look of discomfort. Distaste even. *She must be remembering him – how he let her down. What a bastard he was …*

'I think it might be too soon,' she said. She flicked her long shiny hair over her shoulder, and smiled sadly at Noah.

'But it could help, couldn't it?' Noah said. 'I mean … it might, well, it might help you to move on and forget all about …' He shuffled in his chair. 'I mean, you wouldn't have to be on your own any more. I know what it's like. We could help each other …'

'So you've lost someone too?' Grace said this softly.

'Er, yes.' he said, 'Yes, I do know what it's like, you know, to be on your own.' *For longer than you could imagine, my angel. But it doesn't have to be like that now we've found each other.*

'I'm sorry,' Grace said. She took a deep breath. 'But I'm really not sure what I'm doing here.' She sat in silence for a while, looking down at her hands. 'Have I said too much?' she asked after the long pause. 'It's just that I prefer to be honest. I thought it best to put you in the picture. And I'm hopeless at small talk.'

'No you're not. Honestly, if you'd heard some of the conversations …' Noah bit his lip. 'I mean, no, of course you haven't said too much. I'm glad you're being honest. It's important.' He twitched his feet as he spoke. *But please don't say you don't want me*, he thought.

'It's just that I don't like game playing.' She scattered crumbs for the sparrows that hopped around under the tables. 'Have you met many other women like this?'

'No. No, nobody else. Only you.' *Well, it's true in a way. The others didn't count.*

'Oh.' Grace gave him the strange look again.

'What about you?' Noah asked. 'You said you'd had loads of messages, have you met them all yet?'

'Not loads exactly.' Grace smiled. 'I did have a few. I haven't made arrangements with anyone else. I suppose you could say I'm very cautious about all this. I take one step forward and then run backwards as fast as I can …' She smiled briefly before her expression changed to the one Noah had seen before. Curiosity? Surprise? Or more like a wince? As if she'd tasted something unpleasant but was trying, perhaps through politeness, to conceal this.

'You've got a very expressive face.' Noah hadn't meant to say it. He quickly added, 'Hope you don't mind me saying.'

'No, that's ... that's all right.' Grace bowed her head. When she looked at him again, Noah saw the same fleeting wince. Then her face changed back to the open, kind expression he wanted to look at forever.

'More tea, or a cold drink? Something else to eat?' *Anything at all, just say the word*, Noah thought.

'Oh I couldn't, thanks. I've drank nearly a pot full already.' Grace lifted the stainless steel lid. 'I'm a bit of a tea addict at the best of times.'

'Oh, me too. Nothing wrong with that, nothing at all,' Noah said. 'Please, let me get us another one.'

Grace shook her head. 'Actually, I think I'll make a move soon.'

Noah felt his heart thud. 'Oh, right. Yes. Right. Er ... do you, I mean, do you really have to?'

'Well, I ...' She put the cups and plates on the tray. 'It's just that I'm not used to this. It all feels a bit strange, to be honest.' She smiled. 'For you as well, I imagine?'

Feels absolutely bloody perfect to me, Noah thought. 'Look,' he said, 'what if we walk for a bit? Or we could just sit here and carry on talking? Get used to each other. We could go back and see the birds again, see the baby rabbits? Have more tea. *Not* have more tea ...' He curled his toes inside his shoes until they hurt. *Just don't go.*

Grace laughed. She held up her palms in surrender. 'Okay, okay,' she said, 'a short walk in the park, then.'

As they passed the *Fuck off* bench, Noah tried to nonchalantly catch Grace's hand. His bony fingers missed her hand and brushed the cornflower blue of her dress. Grace looked down sharply, apologised as if she had nudged into him. Noah also said he was sorry. 'Thought I saw a wasp,' he said. He pushed his hands deep in his pockets. He watched her shape out of the corner of his eye. Tried to see their shadows side by side to gauge the difference in height. *Maybe it's not as obvious as it seems*, he thought. *Probably not much in it — fractions, that's all. And anyway, lots of men have tall wives.* He checked her feet again. Her shoes were flat. *Why d'you have to be the tall one, Angela?* 'Just my luck.' He coughed as he realised he'd spoken aloud.

'What is?' she asked.

'Oh, nothing. No, nothing. Just thinking.'

'Let's go back to my house,' he said. 'We can sit down. I mean we can sit and talk, listen to music. Just, you know, sit …' Noah crossed his fingers behind his back. *Please, please say yes, Angela.*

'Oh, I couldn't. I really couldn't.' She sped up her pace.

Noah bit his lip. *Now she thinks I'm trying to get her clothes off. All I want, my angel, is to take care of you. To stroke your hair. Make you see there's no need to look for anyone else.* He sighed deeply. *And, if we sit down, she might stop thinking about how tall she is.* 'I didn't mean it to sound …' He stopped walking. 'I just thought, well, all these meetings in parks and everything, it's a bit, well, public, isn't it?' He was close to tears. To stop himself crying, he bit the inside of his lip until it bled.

'I thought this was your first time,' she said.

'Oh, it is. Yes, it is my first time. I was just, er, just saying. Ha ha.' His forced, false laugh lingered in the space between them. Noah couldn't stop hearing it. To himself, he repeated the word *Fuck*.

Grace stopped suddenly. She heaved a huge sigh. 'All right,' she said, 'why not? I can't keep hiding away. And it's not as if we … not as if you're … well, it's just a cup of tea and a chat isn't it? Both in the same boat and all that. Yes, I will come and have another cup of tea with you. There, I've said it.'

'What … now? At mine?' The thin coppery taste of blood spread through Noah's mouth. *Jesus fucking Christ. This is a dream, a dream come true.*

Grace smiled. 'Unless you've changed your mind?'

'No. Oh, no,' Noah said. His jaws ached with the effort of suppressing a manic grin. 'I do need a pi … er, I must find the loo though.'

Grace nodded. 'Me too. All that tea. 'They're just there, look, by the café.'

Noah wanted to run, but he walked stiffly to the brick cubicle. His penis was swollen and semi-rigid and when he tried to pee, the urine came in hot little bursts and trickles which increased the sensation of urgency. 'Not now,' he said, 'Come on, I just need a piss.' His penis grew harder in his hand. His bladder ached. To cancel the growing erection, he thought of his hall cupboard, the cellar, the creaking stairs. The dead boy hanging in the dark space between his jackets. A spiralled rope of hot urine spurted against the porcelain bowl. Noah sighed. 'That's better. Thought I was going to explode. I'll have to try and keep my stick under control. Don't want to give Angela the wrong idea.' He flicked his shrivelled foreskin, washed his hands and went outside.

nineteen

The smell of furniture polish filled the hall as Noah pushed open his front door. He pressed himself flat against it and gestured for Grace to come in. As he stood on the threshold, a sudden impulse to slam the door and run back down the path surged through him. He gripped the brass door handle.

'Are you coming in as well?' Grace smiled.

'Course,' he said, making an unexpected snorting noise as he laughed. *Perfect,* he thought, *I finally get her into my house then start doing pig impressions*. He scratched nervously at his temple.

He nudged the sitting-room door open with his foot. A clock whirred ready to chime, and Grace hesitated on the threshold.

'Oh, you've got a grandfather clock.' As she said it, other chiming clocks joined in from all over the house, seconds and fractions of seconds apart. 'Oh, how …' She looked confused, had that same wincing, flinching expression. 'How unusual.'

'Just a bit of an interest,' Noah said. He waved his hand dismissively at his treasured, expensive collection, then spun on his heel and headed for the kitchen. 'I'll get that tea. Stay there.' *Christ, she's here. Angela is actually here, with me, in my house.*

The white tray held an arrangement of fine white china, which rattled slightly as Noah carried it through the hall. The red light was flashing on his answer machine. *Not today, thank you*, he thought, and paused to tug the telephone cable from its socket.

Grace admired the room, the framed maps, Noah's choice of colours, and then she returned to the clocks, which seemed to fascinate her. 'How long does it take to wind them all?' she said. 'And clean them?'

'Oh, not too long. I usually do it on a Saturday morning.' *Yes of course you do, Noah,* he thought. *Shouldn't that be more like ten o'clock on the dot, every bloody Saturday? Except they haven't been ticking for a while. Not until yesterday – waiting for you to come along, my angel.* 'They're a bit of a nuisance. Actually,' he said.' *Don't want her to think I'm obsessed with them.* 'I might get rid of them, if ... you know, if I need to. Some of them anyway.'

'Oh.' She sipped her tea and looked round the room. She seemed awkward now, lost for something to say.

Noah felt panic constricting his throat as he searched for ways to engage her in conversation. His mind was blank. 'More tea?' was all he could manage.

'I think I've had enough to last me a lifetime, thanks.' She gave a weak laugh, and added, 'I really must go now.'

'No.' It came out too sharp and Noah saw Grace flinch. He added softly, 'I mean, I've only just got you here. Please don't rush off straight away.' Then his shoulders slumped. 'But if you must ...'

Grace stood. She seemed taller than ever. The aura of calm that had surrounded her at the café was gone. Now she was agitated. She fiddled with the folds of her dress and strands of her hair. She sat back down and drew in a deep breath.

'Look, I really don't think I can do this,' she said. 'It's nothing to do with you. I just don't feel ready to be, well, you know, getting to know someone else. No offence or anything, but this just doesn't feel right to me. I'm sorry. And anyway, I'm not really over ... over him.'

'Look, just give it time. There's no hurry,' Noah said. 'I do understand. It must be difficult. But I can help. I'm a good listener. So if you want to talk ...'

Grace shook her head. 'No, I don't want to talk about it. But thanks,' she said.

For the next two and a half hours Grace talked almost non-stop, making Noah feel as if he had unknowingly cast some magic spell over her. Noah didn't dare move in case the spell broke. She sat on Noah's floor, leaning against the sofa. He sat behind her, cradling his pointed knees and an enormous, uncomfortable erection. Grace's long legs stretched out on the carpet where Noah had sorted through his *Find a Woman* folder. Her voice filled the room. At times she sounded full of happiness as she recounted her great love story. Other times, there were cracks in her voice from the still painful loss.

She's not talking to me, Noah thought. *She's talking to herself. I may as well not be here.* He said nothing, but made the occasional soothing sounds of someone listening intently. Then he asked, 'What's his name, this man?'

'Bri.' She said it with great tenderness, as if trying to wake a sleeping infant.

Noah snorted, turned it into a cough. *Bri*, he scoffed silently behind her back. *What sort of name is that, for fuck's sake?*

'Of course, it's Brian really,' Grace resumed her outpouring into the empty space in front of her. 'But he's always been known as Bri.'

Among other things, I bet. Noah's erection deflated like an old party balloon. The withered skin sank back into itself as he listened to tales of the brilliant Bri. 'But you're getting on with your own life now aren't you, Angela?' he said.

Her back stiffened. She was silent. Noah pulled the toes of his left foot towards him so hard they made tiny cracking sounds.

'I think it's time to go,' Grace said in a flat voice. She rose swiftly and effortlessly from the floor. She wouldn't look at Noah as she placed her cup on the tray and made her way to the door.

'No, no, please don't. We were getting on ... You were talking to me. I mean you *really* talked to me. Don't go just because I —'

Grace interrupted, 'Because you what? Got my name wrong?'

'I'm really sorry. It just, well, just slipped out. I —'

Grace cut in again. 'Doesn't matter,' she said. 'It's best that I just go. Let's leave it at that.'

Noah stood in the doorway. He placed one hand on the frame. The other went automatically to his temple. He fingered the hair above his ear then slid his hand to the back of his neck. A collection of small bumps just below his collar provided distraction – a Braille message for his fingers to read. His narrow chest throbbed with the pounding of his heart. 'There isn't anyone else,' he said.

Grace had distanced herself. She had become a polite stranger. 'You needn't explain things to me. It's none of my business. Please, I'd like to go now.' She stared at Noah's arm across the doorway.

'Look, it's what I called you, that's all. You know, before we met. I called you Angela, just to myself.' His knees felt weak as he spoke, his stomach churned. 'I mean, I didn't know your name or anything and I just … called you Angela. I'm sorry.'

Grace put her hand over her mouth. She shook her head. Her eyes filled with tears. 'Oh no,' she mumbled through her hand, 'I'm going to cry. Oh God, how stupid, I'm sorry.' She waved her hand quickly in front of her face and opened her eyes wide but the tears slipped down her smooth white cheeks.

Noah felt tears of his own damming up behind his eyes, but he swallowed hard. 'Look, sit down. I didn't mean to upset you. I, oh … I only want to make you happy.'

Grace sat on the arm of the sofa, near the door. She searched for a tissue in her bag, dabbed at her eyes and nose, took a deep breath and looked up at Noah. She looked lost, tired. Maybe even afraid. He ached to hold her. *I've fucked things up enough already,* he thought. *Best if I just leave her alone.*

'How embarrassing, I feel such an idiot,' Grace said.

'Don't be silly. You've had a tough time. And today's probably been a bit emotional for you,' he said. *And for me.*

Grace nodded. Her lips quivered and she started to cry again. Her words came out in jagged gasps between her sobs. 'That's just it, you see, I really miss him – Bri, I mean – and talking about him like that … well, it just brought it all back. I don't know what I was thinking of, putting that advert in. I've been on edge about today ever since we spoke. I suppose I forced myself to come.'

Noah wanted to block out what she was saying, wanted to put his hands over his ears or hide under his quilt. *But you're here now, my angel. I'll look after you. You'll see.* 'Come on; don't think too much, you'll get upset again. Don't want that, do we? What about a nice cup of tea?' He struggled to stop himself crying.

Grace laughed. Her face was wet and blotchy but the laugh was real. 'My God, how much tea d'you think we've got through today?' she said.

'Who cares?' Noah said, and headed for the kitchen.

She seemed exhausted, too tired to move. Too tired to talk. The room was still as they sat and drank the best tea they'd had all day. It was strong and hot, and soothed Noah's ragged nerves. He watched over Grace's shoulder as thin curls of steam rose and disappeared. She sipped hypnotically. *Can't believe she's still here*, he thought. *Can't believe I got away with it. Got to be really careful now. Can't lose her, mustn't lose her.* 'Do you always sit on the floor?' he said.

'Oh, it used to drive Bri mad,' she said. There was a smile in her voice.

'Well, *I* don't mind at all. I think it's really nice.' *This Bri sounds like a total arsehole, the more I hear about him.*

'Oh, he didn't really mind. Just used to joke about why did we spend so much money on furniture when all I ever did was sit on the carpet. He ...'

'Go on, keep talking,' Noah said, hoping that she would talk about anything other than Bri.

'No, I mustn't keep on about him. Don't want to get all upset again. I spend nearly all my waking hours thinking of him as it is. Got to get used to the fact that he's gone.'

Wish you spent all your time thinking of me, Ang ... Grace, he thought. And on an impulse, he stretched his hand out flat and placed it gently on the top of her head. She remained very still. He let his hand stay where it was, barely touching her hair, for several seconds. He could feel her heat in his palm. He moved in slow motion, stroked the length of her shiny brown hair with the lightness of spider's threads. The smell of her clean hair filled his nostrils. *I love you, Angela. I'll always love you.* 'You like this,' he said and stroked her hair again.

'Makes me feel sleepy. It's what Bri used to do.'

Noah clenched his fist behind her head. The tendons in his neck stood out like wires. His dry, creased face looked older than ever, and his scowling expression emphasised the sharpness of his features – the pointed bones underlying his pitted, flaking skin. *Why's it always Bri? Bri this and Bri fucking that. What about me?* He carried on stroking her hair, but something of his anger must have been transmitted through his touch.

Grace pulled away, made a joke of the contact she had allowed. 'Hope you didn't find too many grey hairs.' She stood up. 'This time I really *am* going to go. If I can just use your loo, please?'

Noah told her where it was. He made himself busy with the tea things, all the time thinking of her upstairs. In his bathroom. Using his soap, his towel, his mirror.

'Well … I don't really know what to say,' Grace said. 'It's been quite a day, hasn't it?' She stood in front of the hall cupboard, her bag over her shoulder.

'Oh, it has,' Noah said. 'Thank you so much. I'm so happy you talked to me. There's lots more to say – next time.' *We've got plans to make, my angel.*

'You've been very kind, putting up with my weeping and wailing and everything. I'm still embarrassed, but it *has* helped – been like talking to a brother. Or a kind uncle. Neither of which I have, so thank you. I'll, er … I'll be off then.' She put her hand on the front door catch.

Noah's hand landed on top of hers at the same moment.

Grace pulled away as if it she'd been stung. 'Oops, sorry,' she said, stepping outside. 'Bye, then.' And she was gone.

twenty

Noah picked up the tablet of white soap. It was wet and felt slimy, with froth still on the surface. He looked at the white towel, folded neatly on its rail, and saw the flattened, damp area where Grace had dried her hands. He brushed his fingers over it softly, then picked it up and held it to his face, breathed in deeply. He clutched the soap and towel in the crook of his left elbow. With the fingers of his right hand, he traced a sweeping arc around the toilet seat. 'She sat here,' he said. 'Her naked *flesh* – here on my toilet.' He spoke in a rasping whisper, catching his breath between words. He bent down quickly, piled the damp towel by his feet and balanced the soap on top of it. He clawed and tugged at his trousers, unzipped them and pushed the loose fabric down to his hips, where it fell unhindered to the floor.

'Come on, let's give you a good wash,' he said, levering his thick penis out of his little white cotton underpants. Slowly, Noah ran the soap along the length of his stiff and throbbing penis. Then, he put his hand under the tap, cupped a trickle of water and started to rub the soap into a lather.

'That's it,' he said, 'let's get you nice and clean. A nice clean stick for Angela.' His hand slid faster over his purple, foam-covered penis. Soap bubbles burst and squelched as he masturbated harder. Before he sank to his knees, to spurt his own hot moistness into the folded towel, Noah caught sight of his reflection in the bathroom mirror. His teeth were bared, his lips pulled back and his nostrils flared in a fierce grimace.

'No, no, no,' he called out as he buckled with the spasm of his orgasm. As his semen spat against the towel, Noah was already sobbing. He watched as the warm fluid seeped into the fluffy white background. 'I can't help it,' he cried, 'I don't *want* to look like this.

How could she ever love *me*?'

twenty-one

Noah drove into the thinly-gravelled car park of the Park Lodge Hotel. He saw his parents' car, and deliberately avoided the space next to it. When he got out of his car, he saw their dog, the fat Labrador, panting on the back seat. *Could really do without this,* he thought. He scowled at the dog as he walked past his parent's gleaming car, fighting the urge to thump the roof. *Don't suppose the bloody thing would bark anyway – too fat and lazy to bother.*

A young man at the reception desk lifted his head as Noah pushed open the heavy glass door. The man raised his eyebrows and stared at Noah. He did not smile but kept his gaze fixed on Noah's face. 'Can I help you, sir?' he said. As he spoke, his eyes travelled over Noah – his face and hair, his neck and chest – inspecting him closely.

Yes, you can stop fucking staring for a start, Noah thought. 'Probably,' he said, 'I'm with the Quince party.'

The man continued to stare at Noah, his expression unchanged. 'Yes, let me see,' he consulted a book in front of him. 'That'll be in the Fuchsia Room, sir. Just through to your left here.' He held out his arm to show the way, still studying Noah's face.

'Thanks.' *And take your fucking goggle eyes off me. Weirdo*. He followed the direction he'd been shown. 'Fuchsia Room,' he muttered. *Got ideas above their station, haven't they? It's not exactly the Grand Hotel is it?* He spotted a sign for the gent's toilet and went in, hesitating as he pushed the door open. *Don't want to bump into the dreaded aunty in here, do I?* He checked the sign again and went in.

As Noah was about to unlock his cubicle door and wash his hands, he heard the door swish open over the plush corporate carpet. *Who's that going to be?* He stood perfectly still and listened. *Hope it's not that weirdo from reception. Don't trust him. Or some fucking woman who'll start screaming as soon as I come out.* There were no audible clues. Noah listened harder. *I'm not coming out until they've gone. They can think what they like, I'm staying in here until it's all clear again.* There was a cough and the sound of someone entering the cubicle next to Noah's. *Wonder if I can get out, wash my hands and get away before he comes out of there? Or she. Knowing my bloody luck.* He twisted the hair at his temple.

There was a flush of water from next door. *That was quick. Now come on, get a move on and get out of here. I don't want to spend the whole evening in the toilet, even if it would be better than this bloody farce of a party.*

'Noah? Is that you in there?' It was his Father's voice. 'What on earth are you doing?'

'What do you think I'm doing?' *Christ almighty, only he would ask such a stupid fucking question.*

'It's just that you've been in there a hell of a time. I saw you come in. You are all right aren't you? Don't want me to get your Mother or anything?' There was a sarcastic edge to his Father's voice.

Bastard, thought Noah. 'Think I can just about manage. Actually.' *Piss off back to the party, and mind your own business.* He waited, standing perfectly still in the cubicle until he heard his Father leave.

Noah pushed open the wooden door to the Fuchsia Room and peered inside. The room was large and bright. It felt cooler than the corridor and reception area. A small group of people were seated at the far end, except for his Father, who stood looking directly towards him.

'Ah, here he is,' said his Father, looking at his watch, checking it against the clock on the wall.

Noah's Mother waved her hand to beckon him in. 'Come on, Noah, we were starting to worry that you weren't coming.' She patted a chair next to her.

'Said I'd be here if I could,' Noah said, 'I'm only a few minutes late.' *For God's sake, what the fuck does it matter? There's only six of us here anyway. The whole bloody thing's a fiasco – what a comedown after spending the day with Angela. They don't know how lucky they are that I'm here at all. If she hadn't had to get away, I'd still be sitting behind her, my hand on her hair.* His stomach made fluttering movements at the still-vivid memory.

His Father coughed. 'I told you; he was lurking about in the gents. You know what he's like.' He looked at Noah and shook his head slightly.

'Er, excuse me,' Noah said. 'I wasn't lurking anywhere. Actually. I was just in the gents. It is permitted isn't it?'

His Mother stood up. 'Yes, all right you two. Come on now, let's all make a start on the food.' She smoothed the sides of her pale lavender dress and patted her hair. 'There's plenty to go round, something for everyone, so do, please, help yourselves. Now, Noah what would you like?'

'I think I can manage to help myself as well, Mother.' He could see his Father shaking his head. *Bastard.* 'But I think I'll just have a chat with Grandma first, if that's all right.' *Rather talk to her than those other two bloody half-wits.* He took a quick look at his uncle and aunt, Maurice and Flick, short for Felicity. *Oh, look at them. Same as ever. Him with his slip-on shoes and that stinking pipe, and her with her frumpy pleated skirt and handbag over her arm. She's had that skirt since I was a kid. She has got a fancy top on though – straight from the market if I'm not mistaken – that'll do her for a few Christmases to come. What on earth would Angela think of this unsophisticated bunch? I never want her to meet my family, not one of them.* Flick was looking in Noah's direction and gave him a cautious nod. Noah put his hand up in reply then turned sharply away. *Don't want to get stuck with her.* He sat down next to his Grandmother and put his hand on her forearm. 'Hello Grandma.'

The old lady drew herself up in her chair and smiled. She looked like a small bird, frail and tiny. Her clothes looked too big and she seemed a long way inside the too-dark navy blue jacket she wore. There were pearls at her neck, a brooch on one lapel and fabric flowers on the other.

'Now, which one are you, dear?' she said to Noah, taking his hand and patting it. Her loose, dry skin was icy cold.

'I'm Noah, Grandma.' He leaned towards her. She smelled of

something vaguely medical; menthol or eucalyptus.

His Grandmother sat and thought for a while, her head on one side. Her lips quivered and her hands moved in fluttery little spasms. 'Yes,' she said, 'little Noah. And how are you getting on at school, dear?'

'I, er ... I'll go and get some food, Grandma. Actually.' He fiddled with his hair and went to join the others at the long table of food.

Noah's Mother was organising the small group, putting sandwiches on plates and describing the fillings of various quiches. 'Well,' she said, 'it's all got to go. I had enough trouble getting them to change the order to a smaller buffet. We don't want leftovers, do we?'

'Is that all they've given us then, Mother, leftovers?' Noah said.

His Mother was about to answer – she had her patient, explaining expression ready, but instead his Father spun round to Noah.

'Now listen you. None of your clever little quips, understand? Your Mother has gone to a lot of effort to arrange things here. And with no help from anyone. The last thing she needs is snide comments from you.' He turned back to the table and picked up three triangular sandwiches. He slapped them onto his plate to close the matter.

'It was just a joke, for fu ... for God's sake,' Noah said. *Why did I come? I knew it would be like this. That bastard, he won't leave off, will he?*

Noah's Mother sighed. Then she took the sandwiches off her husband's plate and put them on her own. 'You can't eat those, Norman', she said. 'They've got cucumber in – you know it gives you terrible indigestion.' She picked up some cheese sandwiches. 'Here, have these.'

Noah watched with a sinking feeling. He felt trapped, although the narrowing of his Father's eyes as his food was organised for him did bring some satisfaction. *Now who's being looked after by Mummy then?* The five of them selected their food in silence. Noah's Mother watched carefully as each sausage, celery stick or vol-au-vent was lifted timidly from the table.

Noah sat next to his Grandmother again with his sparsely-filled plate balanced on his knee. His Mother had brought the old lady's food – a huge mound of sandwiches, scotch eggs and cheeses.

'I can't eat all this, Brenda,' his Grandmother said, her dentures seeming to move independently of her mouth. But she bent over the plate and ploughed through the food without saying another word. When she'd finished, she held the empty plate out for Noah. 'Very nice, dear. Did Brenda make it all herself?'

'No, Grandma, the hotel people did it.' *Poor old thing doesn't know where she is. Bet she'd rather be at home as well. They shouldn't have dragged her here just for this.* He looked at her fine silvery hair, cut in a short, manly style, and her face with its deep creases and folds. Noticed again the tremor around her mouth and the way her hands waved and jolted. And he thought of all the times she'd given him the tin of polish and the duster and how he'd been so proud of himself, making the leather shine. *Dear old thing.* 'You all right, Grandma?' he asked.

'No,' she said fiercely. 'I'm bloody freezing.'

Noah's Father stood up and coughed. He tapped a fork against his plate and coughed again. 'I'd just like to say a few words, everyone. I'll keep it short.'

Noah put his hands in his pockets and made fists. *Piece of shit*, he thought, *why the fuck do we want a speech from him?*

'Yes, it's really just to thank you all for coming and to say how happy we are to see you all here this afternoon. As you all know, there were a few last-minute changes to the schedule – and Brenda coped admirably with that, I think you'll all agree. And the good thing is – it means there's a lot more food for us.' He laughed.

'No, dear, I made sure they only catered for the six of us,' Noah's Mother said.

His Father narrowed his eyes and coughed loudly. 'A joke,' he said. 'That was a joke, Brenda. But thank you for spoiling it.'

Noah squeezed his fists tighter. 'Oh come on, there's only the handful of us here – do we really need an after-dinner speech?' He could feel his neck tightening and his heart beating faster. *That bastard always has to take centre stage, even with this pathetic fucking turnout. Suppose we'll have to listen to the speech he'd got ready for the whole bloody gathering now.* 'Can't we just – well, I don't know, just leave people to chat or something?' *And bugger off out of here as soon as possible. Let me get back to thinking about Angela. All the plans we need to make.*

His Father smiled too sweetly. 'Oh, of course, I knew you'd have something to say. The voice of wisdom, ladies and gentlemen. And what would you recommend, then? That we all sit here in silence, not mark the occasion? Or would you like everyone to do it your way – sit with a lump of unchewed bread in their mouths for hours, then spit it out and go home to bed? Is that what you want? Perhaps we could all wait here until the food goes mouldy? Just sit and look at it? Is that what you think we should do? Because you're the bloody expert, aren't you?' His face was flushed, his eyes dark slits.

Noah's Mother rubbed her husband's shoulder. 'He's not like that now, Norman,' she said, trying to smile. 'He eats properly now.' She smoothed the sides of her dress again and patted her hair. 'Anyway, let's see if we can get some tea made. And there's a cake still to come.' She looked at her husband, rubbed his shoulder again, then clapped her hands. 'Right, I'll go and sort out the tea.' She headed for the door then stopped and looked back at her husband. 'Norman, dear, why don't you go and see if Duncan's all right in the car?'

That's right, get rid of the bastard, thought Noah.

The cake was wheeled in on a stainless steel trolley. A second trolley, rattling with cups and saucers and a large pot of tea was parked next to it, in front of the table of food. Noah's Mother clapped, staring at Flick until she self-consciously joined in. 'Well, look at that – haven't they done a lovely job?'

Everyone nodded and stared at the huge square cake. It was covered in white fondant icing, with *Family Reunion* in rose pink piped across the top and a pink ribbon round the sides. Noah thought of Godfrey's icing bag and looked away. *Fucking size of it – what are we supposed to do with all that? I already feel like I'm going to explode with all the rubbish I've had to eat to keep the old goat off my back. A trip to the toilet is in order sooner rather than later I think. Get rid of all this junk. I've eaten enough for one of Hell's mega-binges. Well nearly. She'd be in her element here. Why is everyone so bloody keyed-up about food? Angela won't be, I know she won't.*

'Was Duncan all right?' Noah's Mother said. 'We're just going to cut the cake if you want to say a few words, dear.' She stood poised with a knife, waiting for her husband to make his way to the trolley. The other guests admired the cake.

His Father coughed. 'Yes, he was fine. *He* never gives us any trouble does he?' He glared at Noah. 'You go ahead and cut the cake. I shan't say anything else in case it upsets anyone.'

I'm not taking the bait that easily, Noah thought. *Don't want to give the bastard the satisfaction. Wish that useless lump of a dog would go for him. Take a big chunk out of his leg. That'd give him something to think about.* He stood with his arms crossed, waiting for the big ceremony to take place; his stomach felt bloated and made faint gurgling sounds. *Oh no, it looks like the Mother-parent is going to make a bloody speech now.* He groaned and his uncle Maurice, standing to his left, shot him a stern look, then turned quickly away. Without looking back at Noah, he said quietly, 'Your Mother has put a lot of hard work into this. And she's been badly let down by certain people. We all owe her a bit of appreciation, in my opinion.' Then he clapped his hands and in a raised voice said, 'Speech, speech.' The others joined in. Noah's Mother made feeble attempts to pretend she really had nothing worth saying but soon gave in to the insistent calls of her small band of supporters. Their voices echoed around the almost empty Fuchsia Room, giving the proceedings an even more pathetic and downbeat feel.

'Well, just a few words, then.' Noah's Mother lay the knife down, smoothed the sides of her dress several times, and smiled at her husband. 'I'd like to start by thanking you all for coming along and making the day such an enjoyable one. Please do all carry on topping your plates up – there's a lot still to be eaten, as you can see. I … well, I know you're all aware that there have been a few changes to what we had planned. One or two people couldn't – well, they couldn't manage to join us here today. So … well, that's just left the six of us here – and a very select group we are too, I think.' She laughed. Obediently, the others joined in. 'Anyway, I hope you've all had a nice time, and please do enjoy the rest of the evening.' She picked up the knife and plunged it into one end of the large white cake. 'Now, will you all have some tea and cake?'

'Tea'll be cold if we don't get a move on,' said Noah's Grandmother. 'And I could do with something hot to drink to warm me up a bit.' She hunched her shoulders and shivered inside her voluminous navy blue jacket, rubbing her quivering hands together.

'Not cold are you, Mum?' Noah's Father asked. There was a trace of mockery in his voice, as if he was daring the old lady to admit to a personal weakness.

Noah rubbed his own hands together. 'It's not exactly hot in here, is it?' he said. 'Not really enough of us to create much heat.'

'You just can't resist it, can you?' his Father said. He stared at Noah, his eyes hard and cold.

'Resist what? I'm just saying it's not very warm in here. Is it?' *Get off my fucking back*, he thought.

'You're determined to rub it in aren't you? Little digs here and there, not a thought for your poor Mother's feelings. Perhaps it's not as warm as you'd like it in here. And perhaps there aren't that many of us. But do you have to keep harping on about it?' Colour rose to his Father's face again, his cheeks blotched with red.

'I'm not harping on about anything,' Noah said. 'Actually.'

His Mother continued with her cake cutting, tipping slabs of dark fruitcake with thick white crusts of icing onto small plates. 'Come on now, you two. Come and have some of this lovely cake. And Noah, get your Grandma a cup of tea.' She patted her hair again and passed a plate to Flick, who gave it to straight to Maurice. They ate mechanically, standing next to the tea trolley.

'It is cold though, Brenda. I've been chilled to the bone since we got here,' Noah's Grandmother said, her cup quivering in her hand – a minor earthquake visible in the ripples on the surface of her tea. Noah's Mother pushed the cake trolley calmly to one side and repeated her dress smoothing routine.

'Excuse me,' she said, her voice rather stilted, and headed towards the door. Flick watched her go, cake moving automatically from fingers to mouth. She looked at Maurice who busied himself with his own cake and wouldn't meet her eyes.

Noah's Grandmother drank her tea in one go and gave him the empty cup. Then she started on her cake, losing crumbs, dried fruit and pieces of icing into the gaping, rigid opening of her jacket. She ate it quickly and held out the plate for Noah. He put it underneath his own plate, still with an untouched slice of cake and placed them both back on the trolley. His Grandmother sat down again. She had turned the collar of her jacket up and looked like a small Hollywood gangster from an old black and white film. Noah smiled to himself. *This has got to be over soon, surely?* 'Grandma,' he said, 'do you remember when you used to let me polish the big leather sofa?' He could smell the beeswax again. His Grandmother cupped her ear and pulled a face to show she hadn't heard. He said it again, loud in the silence of the party.

'I haven't got a leather sofa,' his Grandmother said.

'No, years ago, Grandma, remember? You used to give me a duster and tin of polish, and we used to have the radio on.' He was talking too loud. *How could she forget?*

His Father gave a mocking smile, 'Did you wear a little pinny as well? Keep your nice little clothes clean? Trust you to remember housework.' He made a snorting sound.

Oh, fuck off, Noah thought, his head pulsing with a tight band of pain.

'Nice armchair, I've got. Lovely deep plum sort of colour. Not leather though,' his Grandmother said.

His Mother pushed through the door and walked back across the floor beaming a smile at everyone. 'Everything all right? Good,' she said. It was clear that she had been crying. Her eyes were pink, her skin powdery. She patted her hair and made herself busy with the teapot. Noah's Father banged his plate down, the crust of icing rattled.

'That's it,' he said. 'I've had just about enough of this.'

'Well leave it, dear,' Noah's Mother said. 'You don't like icing anyway, do —'

'Not the bloody icing. I'm not talking about icing. I'm talking about him.' He pointed at Noah. His face was deep red now and his forehead was shiny with sweat. 'He's been determined to spoil things from the moment he got here. Like he always does. Can't help but ruin things, can he? And now he's upset you – well, that's it. I've had enough.'

Oh for fuck's sake, Noah thought. 'How exactly did I upset anyone?'

Flick and Maurice drank their tea, paying great attention to the bottom of their cups. His Grandmother was lost inside the tent of her jacket.

'Well? What am I supposed to have done? Actually?' He could feel his shoulders tensing.

'Actually,' his Father said, 'actually, you've complained and sniped and hung about with that bloody sour expression on your face ever since you got here. That's what you've done. And now, you've reduced your Mother to tears. It's not good enough for you that she's gone to all the trouble of organising this, is it? Or that she had to practically beg you to come along – "Let him stay where he is" I told her – or that most of the family decided to pull out at the last minute. None of that is enough to keep you happy, is it? Oh no, you have to go one step further and stand there glowering and looking down your nose at it the whole time. And as for hanging about in the toilet … what if it hadn't been me come in there? You just … I don't know, words fail me. You think of no-one but yourself, do you?' His face was twisted with anger.

Noah clenched his teeth, his jaw throbbing from the force. *You absolute bastard*. 'I was not hanging about in the toilet,' he said. 'If you really want to know, I was trying to decide whether to come in or not. I didn't exactly relish the idea of this bloody charade, believe it or not. I didn't want to come in the first place, but I didn't ask Mother to "beg" me, as you put it.' He twisted the hair at his temple. 'And it wouldn't exactly be my first choice to spend the afternoon with a distant aunt and uncle who I haven't seen since I was a teenager – none of us knows what to say to each other. I *did* want to see Grandma, but now I'm not sure she even knows who I am. And I certainly didn't want to be in a hotel bloody function room meant for fifty-odd people with only six of us rattling round trying to pretend we're all having a lovely time, being force-fed party sandwiches and cheese on sticks by my Mother. So yes, you might be right about all of that.' He let out a deep sigh.

'But do you know the worst part of it? The worst part was the prospect of spending time with you. I know you can't stand me. And I'm pretty sure you know I can't stand you either. And that to me seems like the end of the story. But no, we have to go through the motions of getting together just for the sake of form. Just for the sake of what everyone will think. Don't we? Well, I'll tell you what everyone thinks, shall I?' He stepped closer to his Father, his head jutting forward, his mouth distorted with rage. 'They all think what an oddball I am – the strange one of the family. I know they do. They all give me a wide berth and look at me out of the corners of their eyes. I don't mind, I'm used to it by now.' He fought to control his top lip, which drew back tightly over his upper teeth in a snarl as he spat out the words. 'But what about you? What do they think of you? I'll tell you that as well, shall I? They think you're the bee's knees. Hard-working, long-suffering, and with that weird bloody kid you had to bring up, poor you. Oh, you're a real pillar of the fucking community, you are, aren't you? – sorry Grandma – but they don't know you like I do, do they, Dad? They don't know the vindictive, bullying, cold-as-stone person you really are, do they?' He stretched out his right arm, his fingertips almost touching his Father.

'Ladies and gentlemen, let me introduce Norman, my Father – the man who helped make me what I am today. The man who disapproved of my every move, my very existence in fact, and who took every chance to show it. The man who humiliated me by standing me in a washing-up bowl when I was eight years old, to wash me.'

'Tell them why. Go on, tell them why I had to,' his Father spluttered.

'Because I'd shit myself, is that what you mean, Dad? Yes, you're right, I did shit myself. And do you know why? Because I was so fucking frightened – sorry again, Grandma – so frightened of you that I couldn't ask to go to the toilet. Christmas Eve, it was, and we were waiting to collect Mother after she finished work at the shop. You were in one of your silent, black moods. I remember looking up at the dark blue sky and it was covered with stars, millions and millions of tiny glittering stars. And I needed to go to the toilet. I could feel it getting more and more urgent. And I tried to will it away by looking at the stars. It was cold and dark and I was too frightened to ask. So I just held on. And then I couldn't hold on anymore and it took me over. I stood next to you, shivering, and knew I was shitting in my pants. And I started to cry. You shook me. Kept asking what on earth was up with me. Shook me roughly. I wouldn't say anything. Just cried harder and harder. Then you must have realised, I suppose – must have caught the smell. You just kept calling me filthy. Dirty. You great big baby.' Noah paused to catch his breath. His heart was pounding.

'You yanked me by the arm, drove us home and stood me in that bowl. And all the time you cleaned me up, you swore at me. Called me disgusting. Called me vile. Told me I should never have been born. And there were flaky, disintegrating pieces of shit floating round my ankles. I wanted to die. I was eight years old and I wanted to die right there and then. And when Mother finally came home there was a huge row because she'd had to get the bus, and it was all my fault. You even showed her – you showed her the foul water in the washing up bowl, outside the back door in the garden.' He paused again, screwed his eyes up so he wouldn't cry. 'So, there you have it ladies and gentlemen, the touching story of a boy and his Father sharing an intimate moment from the past. And rest assured, there were many more just like it.'

Noah's Father stood totally still, his face drained of colour. He looked like a statue. Nothing happened. No one moved or spoke for what seemed like hours. The Fuchsia Room had turned into a still-life picture. The only sound Noah could hear was his own heart thumping, and the white-noise of blood racing in his ears. He felt lightheaded; his knees were weak as if they might buckle. But he also felt a sense of elation, and an enormous feeling of relief. *Like being sick*, he thought. Distressing, unstoppable, uncontrollable – and then the calm, the release and the nothing-can-be-as-bad-as-this-ever-again sensation.

Flick moved first. She cleared her throat and turned to Noah's Mother. 'I'll give you a hand with the clearing up, Brenda,' she said. 'It won't take long with the two of us.'

Noah's Mother patted her hair and nodded. They both started to slide food from plate to plate, making a pile of the cleared ones.

'Not too bad, is it?' Noah's Mother said. 'I thought there'd be a lot more than this left at the end. Still, it won't go to waste – you'll take some with you, won't you? – be handy for Maurice's sandwiches.' Both women made an effort to laugh and the Fuchsia Room was restored to party mode.

Noah stood rooted to the spot and watched as Maurice held open a black bin-liner for the women to empty rubbish into. They chatted and laughed together. He looked across at his Grandmother. She was asleep inside her navy blue jacket. Noah's Father walked out of the room, unnoticed by the busy workers clearing the table. They also ignored Noah as he stood there, in shock at what he had, at last, said. *Well*, he thought, *that must be that then*. Finally, Noah lifted his heavy feet and left the Fuchsia Room. His Mother called out her goodbye, a strained effort to sound cheerful made her voice quaver. No one else even looked up.

In the car park, Noah walked past his parents' car – his Father was sitting in the driver's seat, staring straight ahead. Noah thumped the roof. Hard.

As he drove towards the exit, Noah smiled to himself at the sight of his parents' car. It bounced and rocked on the spot – the elderly, overweight Duncan was hurling himself from one side of the back seat to the other, barking loudly. Noah could still hear the dog's deep, unfamiliar woofs as he pulled out of the hotel car park and drove away.

twenty-two

Sitting on his desk, Noah swung his legs backwards and forwards making contact with the metal wastepaper bin every now and then. He looked at his watch. It was nearly seven in the morning. 'Where's Hell, for fuck's sake? She knows I come in early. What with meeting these new women and the worst bloody family reunion ever, she must know I need to talk.' He kicked the grey bin again. A clanging sound rang through the empty office. Noah looked at his watch. 'I can't sit about here all fucking day. I've got to do something.' He jumped off the desk, kicked the bin hard and sent it scudding across the floor. It came to rest against the base of a swivel chair and rolled noisily on its side.

Noah rang Helen's number and waited impatiently for her to pick up the phone. She didn't. He banged the receiver down. He pulled at his tie, loosened the knot, and unbuttoned his shirt collar. 'Got to *do* something.'

He sat down, his head in his hands, and scanned the tidy desk, the neat arrangement of pencils in one corner and the square block of white notepaper in the other. Then he sat upright and with a poise he didn't feel, dialled the Soul Mates number. He jabbed irritably at buttons on the phone until he reached Grace's recorded message. As he listened, he pictured her sitting in front of him, her hair under the palm of his hand. When she stopped talking, he put the phone down. Then he dialled again.

He rang repeatedly for nearly an hour, each time trying harder to hear something significant in what she said. Then he spoke, trying to sound casual. His voice was brittle and high pitched. 'Hi Grace. It's Noah. Hi, hi. Just thought I'd give you a ring. See how you are and everything. Perhaps you could give me a ring, Grace? Be good to hear from you. I, er, I look forward to hearing from you then, Grace. Bye then. Bye. Grace.' He let the phone fall back into its cradle, and slumped in his chair.

'Got to get out of here, got to *do* something.' He left the building. It was only five past eight. 'She'll call me back, course she will,' he said. 'But she only knows my home number … *Of course*, she's probably trying to ring me right now. If I go home, she'll be on the phone, there'll be a message.' *It'll be all right. I know it will.* He ran to his car, his suede shoes making no sound.

Noah saw the trailing telephone cable on the hall carpet as soon as he thumped the front door open. He let out a strangled, choked sound and slammed the door so hard it shook. 'Stupid bastard. Stupid, stupid bastard. She could have been ringing me over and over again. Angela, oh Angela …' He scrambled under the table; sweat piercing through his papery forehead, and pushed the connector into its socket. 'There,' he said. As he straightened himself, he banged his head on the edge of the table. He lashed out angrily, his thin limbs flailed in random sweeps around the hall like a manic tai-chi instructor. His elbow banged against the cupboard door, which opened smoothly and stood ajar. Noah stopped his wild movements, gritted his teeth.

'Just … just calm down,' he said. 'There's nothing in there. He didn't put his lovely boys in there. Got to calm down. What would Angela think?' He glanced at the cupboard door, looked away quickly. *I can't close it*, he thought. *Not going near it. There's nothing in there. Only jackets and stuff. But I'm not going near it.* The letterbox rattled. Noah gasped and his whole body froze.

'What on earth's going on, Noel? You all right, love?' Godfrey stared through the oblong gap.

Noah bent down and stared back at him. 'You made me jump out of my fucking skin,' he said.

'When I heard your door bang like that,' Godfrey said through the letter box, 'well, I didn't know what to think, duck. Worried you'd bin whasnamed, attacked or something. You sure everything's all right, Noel?'

'Fine,' Noah snapped. 'I've got to get back to work, if you don't mind.'

'Have a nice cuppa first. Calm yourself down. You're in a bit of a state, love. Is it that woman again? Let me in, Noel. I'll put the kettle on and you can tell me all about it.'

'I don't want tea. I don't want to talk. All I want is to get out of here ...' Noah put his hand over the letterbox gap so he couldn't see Godfrey's face.

'No need to get all uppity, duck. Only trying to help,' Godfrey said. 'And anyway, I need a word with you about Joey's funeral. But I'll come back tonight, seeing's you're in such a do-dah.'

Noah straightened himself and opened the door.

Godfrey was still trying to ease himself upright. He jumped slightly when he saw Noah. 'See,' he said, 'I knew something was up. Look at you, you're all of a shambles – no tie, your hair's all over the place, and look at them shoes. You don't wear them ones to work. Not normally you don't, do you duck?'

Noah waved his hand impatiently. 'The rest are down there,' he pointed vaguely at the cellar door.

'What you on about, Noel? You *are* in a whasname ... a tizz, aren't you? Why don't you sit down for a bit and I'll make you a drink.' Godfrey moved towards Noah's kitchen.

Noah clenched his fists. 'I don't bloody want a bloody drink.' He had shouted without meaning to. 'Look, if you really want to do me a favour,' he kept his voice low 'you can close that door for me.'

'What ...?' Godfrey smiled fleetingly. Then he wrung the corner of his apron busily.

'Just do it,' Noah said. 'Just close that bloody door. Just close it.' He backed out of the front door. His voice trailed away as he ran up the path.

twenty three

Helen carried a bundle of post to her desk. She held a crumpled raincoat over her arm, the belt trailing on the newly-cleaned office floor. Noah pushed from his mind the images of Hell's kitchen, the mess of spilled food. He ran up behind her, treading on her belt. Helen turned sharply. 'Careful, mind my new … Noah, what's up? You look awful, what's happened?'

'I can't go back. And she's only got my home number. I had the bloody phone unplugged. She's probably given up. Bet she thinks I didn't want to hear from her, bet she thinks …'

Helen put down the envelopes and coat. 'Hold on, slow down,' she said. 'Come and sit in here.' She led Noah into an empty office. There was nothing but a desk in the middle of the room, and a dead pot-plant on the windowsill. 'Still haven't replaced old Stan, have they? Come on, no-one's going to mind us being in here. Sit down, Noah.'

He slid down against the wall, and sat with his knees drawn up tightly to his chest. He buried his face between his pointed kneecaps.

Helen perched on the edge of the desk and strained to hear the muffled words as Noah spoke. 'It's no good,' she said, 'I can't make out what you're saying. You'll have to come out of there.' She leaned forward. 'You're all folded up like a little umbrella.'

Noah wiped his eyes, tipped his head back until it hit the wall. His Adam's apple rose and fell rapidly as if trying to find its way out. His hair stuck up in wispy spires, as fine as dandelion clocks. A thin string of snot hung from the end of his nose.

Helen bent down in front of him, pulled a tissue from her sleeve, tucked it into his hand, and then guided his hand to his face.

Noah jerked his head away. The snot string broke, landed on his shirt. 'I can manage,' he said through his tears. He waved the tissue. 'This been used?'

'Never mind that,' she said, 'just tell me what's wrong.'

He described the meeting with Grace, referring to her all the time as Angela. He spoke quickly, his breathing was rapid. Luminous white lumps shone on his knuckles as he gripped his knees tightly.

'That's good though isn't it, Noah?' Helen said. 'You met her, it went well – she even came back to yours. What happened then? Has she said something?'

He banged his head against the wall as he spoke. 'How could she say anything? I left the fucking phone unplugged, didn't I? All that time. She might have been ringing and ringing, needing to talk to me again. And I left it un-fucking-plugged.'

Helen put her hand on his shoulder. 'Stop banging your head, you'll hurt yourself.' She waited until he was still. 'Now listen, it's not as if it's been a long time, is it? She might not even have tried to ring yet – and if she did, well, she'll try again. If she wants to. I think you're worrying about nothing. Well, not nothing … you know, I mean, worrying about things that might not have happened.'

He hit his head again. 'It's not just that though, Hell. It's my bloody Father, the house, the cupboard. The things … all the things I told you about. You don't know what it's like. I can't go back. I can't.'

Helen prised one of Noah's fingers from his knee. She held it tightly, shaking it as she spoke. 'Now, just slow down a minute. I can't do much about your Dad, but tell me what you mean about the other things – about the house. What's happened? Tell me slowly, Noah, and if I can help, I will.'

'It's my house, there's … oh God, Hell. I told you. There's something … I can't stand it. It's just not right. I've tried, I really have, but …' He rubbed his eyes, then squeezed them shut.

Helen looked surprised. 'But you *love* your house, all that dusting and cleaning and having everything in order – I don't know where you get the energy. I hardly bother with mine. So why don't you want to go back? What's changed?'

'*Me*. I've changed. I can't take it anymore. There's always been something, I've just pushed it away, been kidding myself. Then the door came open again. I couldn't close it, I just couldn't. I told *him*, the bloke next door but one, to do it.' Noah sniffed. 'The last thing I need is to go home and find him curled up in the corner, gibbering like a lunatic. Had enough of that myself.' He blew his nose on Helen's tissue. 'Course, he's *bound* to find them. He's always wanted to get in and have a poke about. Oh, God, what am I going to do?'

Helen squeezed his finger, shook it again. She spoke softly. 'Listen, Noah, I don't know what's happened – you're not making a lot of sense, me dear.' She gave a little laugh. 'But something's obviously upset you. Why don't you take the day off? I can tell Personnel you're not well – they don't need to know the ins and outs. Then you just go home and get some rest. I can run you home, it's —'

Noah snatched his finger from Helen's grasp. He banged his head hard against the wall. 'You bloody deaf or what? I *can't* ... I'm not going back, I've already told you. How would you like it if the cupboard under *your* stairs had —' He swiped at his nose, struggled to his feet.

Helen stopped him. 'All right, all right, I'm sorry. Stay where you are. We'll sort something out. I'm going to get you a nice strong cup of tea, a box of tissues, and then we'll think about what to do. You said your neighbour's there?'

Noah nodded. 'I only asked him to shut the cupboard door, Hell. But I bet he'll go nosing about. God help him if he does – you never know what'll be in that cupboard.' He slumped down in a crouched position. 'I couldn't close the door. I couldn't even close the bloody door.' He cradled his head in his arms, and clasped the back of his tiny skull. 'And all my shoes are still in the bloody cellar. I just can't go down there, Hell. I can't.' He rocked himself backwards and forwards.

Noah heard Helen come back into the office and looked briefly over his shoulder. He saw her put two mugs on the dusty desk. Then she closed the door. Noah turned away again, continued to stand and stare out of the window. He said nothing.

'I've got this,' Helen said, edging her way in front of him. She took a toilet roll from under her arm and held it out to him. 'Best I could do, I'm afraid.'

Noah stared silently ahead.

Helen placed the hard, greyish roll by his feet. 'No teabags left either. I've made you a coffee instead, Noah. Made us both one. Fancy sitting down with me and drinking it?'

Noah remained motionless.

Helen stood in his line of vision, her face close to his. 'Don't know what's so interesting out there today – it's not much to look at is it, the roof tops of other offices?'

Noah didn't reply.

'I suppose there's the odd pigeon as well, to add to the interest.' She touched Noah's arm.

He didn't respond, continuing to stare straight ahead. He ignored Helen as she stood inches away from him. He had the feeling of being remote, of looking inwards rather than really seeing what was right in front of him.

'What is it, Noah?' Helen's voice had a thread of worry woven through its usual calm sound. 'You can talk to me, you know.'

For several minutes Noah stood like a statue of himself, barely breathing, silent and still, his fixed eyes blinking in slow motion. His face was pale and drawn, with charcoal dents under his eyes. Teary dampness clung to his chin, otherwise his face was dry again. Dry and grey like ash.

Helen got the mugs of coffee, held them in front of Noah. 'Come on you, drink this. You're making me nervous just standing there like that.'

And Noah came back to himself. He took a deep breath, his eyes stopped looking through Helen and instead he focused directly on her. He nodded. Took the mug and drank the cool coffee in one go then handed the mug back like an obedient child taking medicine.

'You say I can talk to you, Hell,' he said.

'Oh, you did hear me then. I thought you'd gone into a trance or something.' Helen attempted to laugh but it came out forced and sounded like she'd choked on something.

'Thing is, do you really want to hear?' Noah slumped to the floor and sat cross-legged, his head dropped forward on his chest.

Helen struggled to join him, grunting slightly as she got herself into a kneeling position, then, adjusting her clothes, she let herself tip to one side and landed softly on her hip and bottom. Her arms went out instinctively to balance this manoeuvre. 'I know, I know', she said, 'lose some bloody weight, stop eating bloody cakes, get up off my fat —'

Noah shook his bowed head. 'That's right Hell,' he said, 'change the subject. You tell me to talk and then you start going on about yourself. How huge your arse is and how massive and bloated your belly is and how you can't stop stuffing cream cakes down your fucking throat. And how you can't sit in a chair properly because —'

Helen slapped her palm on the wiry office carpet. 'Stop it. Just stop right there, Noah.' She swiped the back of her hand roughly across her eyes, slicing off budding tears before they fell, and sighed deeply. 'Listen to me a minute, Noah. I know you're in some sort of pain here. I don't know exactly what's going on, but I'm willing to listen – and yes I do mean it, I do want to hear what you've got to say.'

Noah lifted his head, was about to speak.

Helen held up her hand to stop him. 'No, you wait. Let me finish.' She took a deep breath and carried on. 'I will listen to you. I always do. And if I can help, I will – you know that. But you've got to realise how bloody hard you make it sometimes.'

Noah tugged at the hair in front of his left ear. 'You don't understand how it is for me, I —'

Helen interrupted. Her face was flushed with red blotches. 'Actually Noah, I think I understand you pretty well by now. You're right that there are things I don't understand. I'm not psychic. But you don't have to be so unkind. That's what makes it hard to be there for you. You go off into some ranting rage about me being the size of a house — and yes I know I'm a fat cow — all because, well, because we weren't talking about you for one second. At least I think that's why. I don't really know …' Her voice trailed away, like the fade-out ending of a sad song. She lifted her hands to shoulder height in a questioning gesture, then let them fall heavily beside her. 'I just don't know,' she said again.

'All right', Noah said, 'I'm sorry, okay?' He tugged again at his hair, his bony fingers plucking and twisting. 'It's just that I wanted to talk to you. I mean really talk to you, Hell — stuff I can't even make sense of myself; my fucking family and all the things going on at home, and the, you know, the way it's been going with these women and everything — and I thought you were avoiding it. Like people do — you know, they ask you how you are but what they really mean is for God's sake don't tell me. They ask you how you are, then they tell you about themselves for three-and-a-half fucking hours. Or they keep telling you how much worse it was for them. Do you know what I mean?'

'Oh, I know what you mean, Noah. I know exactly what you mean,' she said.

Noah caught the irony of this but felt too exhausted to acknowledge it. He rubbed his eyes.

Helen also seemed tired and deflated from the encounter in the empty office.

I don't think she'll lecture me any more today, Noah thought. *Even if she is right.* 'Look,' he said, 'perhaps we can talk another time? I have got things I need to tell you but I think I'd rather leave it for now. I don't think I've got it in me to talk anymore now, Hell. I'm too … you know, just too sick of it all. I just don't know what to do, Hell.'

twenty-four

'Yes? Can I help you?' Godfrey spoke like an old-fashioned receptionist. He sounded out of breath.

'Oh, hello,' Helen said. 'Is that Noah's neighbour? I'm, er, I'm just trying to find out if everything's all right. I'm a friend from work. My name's Helen.'

'Yes, this is Noel's neighbour speaking. Well, next door but one. The poor old chap next door's just passed away. I expect Noel's said …? Anyway, what can I do for you Helen, love? It's Godfrey here, by the way.'

'Hello, Godfrey. No, Noah hasn't mentioned anything about his neighbour, er, passing away. But that might explain things. Noah's a bit, well he's a bit upset at work this morning. I just wondered if you might know what's the —'

Godfrey interrupted; his breathing had started to slow. 'You're telling me 'e's upset, love. He was in such a to-do here earlier,' he said. 'Phew – s'cuse me, love. I've just run up his cellar stairs and I'm all whasnamed. All puffed out. Anyway, I told him to hang on and calm hisself down, but would he listen? Would he whasname … cocoa. I knew there was something up. He had the wrong shoes on and everything. Still, I've got all his best ones out the cellar now. You send him home, duck. I'll get a nice bit of dinner ready for him, then I can sit with him for the afternoon. We can watch one of them quiz shows.'

Helen twisted a loose thread on her cardigan sleeve. 'The thing is,' she said, 'he's saying he doesn't want to come home. Something about the house has upset him. Do you know anything about his, er, his cupboard?'

'Oh, don't you worry about that, duck. Noel gets hisself all worked up. You tell him the door's shut, and it's whasname in there … ammaculate; all his little coats hanging up nice and everything.' Godfrey coughed. 'Well, the whole house is the same. I thought he'd like me to have a tidy round, you know, make it nice to come home to. But Noel's so house-proud. Keeps the place like a palace, he does. Is what I have done though, duck, is, I've given his clocks an extra bit of a wind. Why he wants so many is beyond me though. Oh, and his shoes, of course. They're all stacked nicely on their little rack in the cupboard under the stairs, and … oh, I'm going on a bit love, where was I?'

'No, it's okay,' Helen said. 'What you told me about Noah's next door neighbour – that's probably what it's all about. It must have got to him, I suppose, must have upset him more than he realised. Had the poor man been ill?'

'Joey? He'd been in a home for ever such a long time, love. Me and Noel were there with him when he passed on, bless him. P'raps Noel's been whasname … broody over it.' He coughed again. 'What with that and all these women he's been getting tangled up with. No wonder he's in a state. He really ought to come home, Helen, duck. Want me to come and get him?'

'No, no, don't you worry,' Helen said. 'I'll go and have another word with him. See if I can persuade him to let me bring him home. Thanks ever so much, Godfrey, you've been very helpful. We'll be there soon, with a bit of luck.'

twenty-five

Noah pointed as they reached the turning to his road. 'This one,' he said.

'It's okay, I know the way,' Helen said. 'Soon have you home.' She glanced at Noah, smiled and turned to look at the road again. 'How you doing, me dear?'

'I'm fine. I er … I just got a bit uptight, that's all. I've had a lot on my mind lately, you know, what with one thing and another. Thanks for listening and all that.' He rubbed the back of his neck. 'D'you … er, d'you think Angela will be at mine when we get there? Possibly?'

Helen changed gear before she replied. 'Well, she'll probably be at work, won't she? Can't really say for sure. Your nice neighbour – Godfrey – he'll be there though.'

'I don't want him poking his nose in.' Noah scowled. 'I must've been mad, leaving him there on his own in the first place. Can't believe he touched my clocks – if he's caused any damage, I'll kill him.'

'Well, it was good of him to bother, if you ask me. He seems really kind. You're lucky to have a neighbour like him.' Helen paused, touched Noah's knee. 'I'm very sorry to hear about your other neighbour though, Noah. That must have been, well, it must have upset you.'

'What other neighbour? Oh, *him*. I didn't really know him.' He rubbed his temple with his finger. *Don't even want to think about that old bastard. Not ever again.*

'Oh, I thought – well, Godfrey said – well, that you were both with him when he … when the poor old chap died.' Helen frowned. 'Anyway, I'm sorry.'

The subject of Joseph Pepper's death hung in the air, as potent and cloying as the swaying air freshener dangling from Helen's mirror. *She thinks I'm deeply disturbed*, Noah thought. *Thinks I'm in shock because I was there when that murderous old bastard gasped his last breath. Good riddance, I say. After what he did … all those old rumours, more or less admitted it, he did. The boys, the lovely boys.* 'No,' Noah shouted.

Helen stamped hard on the brake. She turned her head rapidly from side to side, scanning the road. '*What?*'

'It's … sorry, it's nothing. I was just, you know, thinking out loud.' Noah tapped the dashboard. 'Keep going, you're blocking the traffic.'

The gears screeched as Helen pulled away. 'I thought you'd *seen* something,' she said. Her face was white. 'Someone in the road or something. Christ, my legs are all shaky. The sooner we get back to yours the better. I need some tea even if you don't. With lots of sugar.'

Noah fumbled for his key. His pocket was stuffed with the tissues and toilet paper Helen had given him. Godfrey opened the door as Noah pulled a soggy white bundle from his trousers.

'Oh, look at you. Just like one of them magicians with doves up their whasname … up their jumper,' he said. 'Come on Noel, darlin', get yourself inside. You as well, duck – Helen, isn't it? – in you come.' Godfrey ushered Helen in with his hand on her shoulder. 'Now, I've got you both a nice bit of something to eat. Didn't know how long you'd be, so I didn't make anything too fancy. If I'd known you'd be all this time, I could of made a few cakes. I bet you're fond of a nice cake, aren't you Helen, duck?' He looked at Noah. 'I know he is, aren't you, Noel?'

'Why don't you just leave things alone?' Noah said. 'What d'you think you're doing anyway, messing about in my kitchen, my house …? Just leave things alone.'

'Only trying to help, duck.' Godfrey said. 'P'raps Helen would like to go and fetch the things from the kitchen, then. It's all on a tray, love, covered with a cloth.' He sat down and brushed his plain white apron. 'No need to worry, Noel, I've left everything just as it should be. Your kitchen's spotless, love – eat off the floor you could. All I did do though, was chuck that fruit away. Gone all rotten, hadn't it?'

Noah refused all the food Godfrey offered him, but accepted a cup of tea, which he left to cool by his side.

'Drink up, Noel. Got to get something inside you. You sure you won't have a little sarnie?'

Noah shook his head. He picked up the tea and sipped grudgingly. He spluttered and grimaced. 'You've put milk in it,' he said. '*And* it's nearly cold.'

Godfrey laughed. 'I *thought* it had a bit of a twang. You know what I've done, don't you duck? I've gone and made it with one of your posh tins of tea. Lord Sheraton or something like that. Oh, I'm a silly old whatsit,' he chuckled, 'aren't I, Helen? Want some proper tea, love? Something to get rid of the —'

Noah interrupted, '*Earl Grey.* It's Earl Grey tea. You shouldn't be messing about in my kitchen.' *Why does he always have to poke his bloody nose in?*

Helen smiled, 'Mmmm, please,' she said, holding out her teacup. She reached for another triangular sandwich. 'Come on, Noah, Godfrey's only trying to help.'

'Won't be a jiffy,' Godfrey said as he gathered up the cups. 'Tastes just like the scent my old Mum used to wear, that does.'

When he returned, Helen held a finger to her lips and pointed at Noah, who was folded up small, asleep on the sofa. His shirt had come untucked. It hung over the edge of the seat, rising and falling slightly with his breathing.

'Bless him,' Godfrey whispered, 'best thing for him, a bit of shut-eye. Never seen him scruffy like this though, have you? Like a dog's dinner, look at him.' He offered Helen a plate of biscuits, sat down next to her, his hunched shoulder touching hers. 'Now,' he said in a whisper, 'what we going to do with him? I s'pect you've got to get back to work, haven't you, duck?'

'No. It's a bit late now,' she said, 'and anyway I told them I might not be back. I can stay here with him. I told him I would. Course, he might not want me to …'

'Don't be daft,' Godfrey said, spraying biscuit crumbs as he spoke. 'He'd be pleased as whasname … pleased as Punch. What with all them other women he's bin chasing, I bet he won't be able to believe his luck.'

'Oh, no, it's nothing like that.' She blushed. 'Noah's not interested in me like that … we're, you know, we're just friends. How long's he been getting himself all worked up like this? I mean as bad as this?'

Godfrey leaned against Helen. 'It's since he's got hisself involved with all these women, if you ask me, duck. I mean, he's always been a bit highly strung, you know what he's like, but now … *and* there's more of them on his answering thingy. I don't think it's doing him no good at all.'

'I know what you mean. He does get stressed about it all, but he seems to be set on this idea.' Helen fiddled with her sleeve. 'Maybe it'll work out for him. If he meets the right person.' She bit into a white chocolate biscuit and watched Noah's narrow outline on the sofa. 'I wouldn't want to see him get hurt again. He's really gone overboard about this latest woman. I haven't seen him this bad before. Perhaps it's her on the answer machine?'

Godfrey smoothed his apron over his knees. The flabby tyre of his stomach, his squashy erection and the dusters in his pocket formed a series of padded mounds in his lap as his posture became more hunched. His breath whistled faintly through his nostrils. 'No good asking me, Helen, love. They all sound the same. At least that one he met in the café won't be bothering him again – Sparkle, I think her name was – needed a good hose down, that one did.'

Helen smiled. 'Noah can be a bit on the critical side. I felt a bit sorry for that woman,' she said.

'Oh, so did I, duck. She'd of been all right with a good bath and some nice clean clothes. But young Noel didn't take to her. Course, he'd got hisself all keen on this other one by then, this little angel he keeps going on about, so I helped him get it all sorted out. Just so everyone knew where they stood.' He nodded towards Noah. 'I'll go and get him a blanket, love. Tell you what, why don't you have a listen to them messages? See what you think. I've got half a mind to swipe them all off. It's not doing him no good at all.'

'lo, Noah. Ss'me again. You are a busy little bee, aren't you? You mustn't work too hard, you know. All work and no play makes Noah a dull boy, and we don't want that, do we? Sspeak to you soon, and lots of —'

Helen pushed the stop button. She twisted the thread on her sleeve again. It started to unravel. She crept back to Noah's sitting room and ate three more biscuits, and then pulled again at the thread on her sleeve. A springy line of kinked wool came free. Biscuit crumbs caught in the back of her throat and Helen coughed. Noah moved his head but slept on, a hibernating stick insect. Helen reached the kitchen just as she began to cough convulsively. 'Teach me to be greedy,' she said. Her eyes streamed.

Godfrey peered round the door, a fluffy, turquoise blanket under his arm. 'Thought I heard you in here. What's up, love – is he awake, what's he said?'

Helen shook her head. 'No, I'm not crying,' she said.

'Was it them women on the phone? All that lovey-dovey business? You don't want to take no notice, Helen, love; you're better than any of them. Now, come on, take my hanky – clean out of me drawer this morning – and we'll have a brew. Proper tea. Not one of his fancy ones. You pop the kettle on. I'll just go and cover him up.'

Godfrey and Helen sat at Noah's kitchen table for the rest of the afternoon. They talked about Noah in hushed, concerned voices, like worried parents. Godfrey collected a fruitcake and some more biscuits from his own kitchen. Helen made tea and washed up the cups and plates as they used them.

'I'm terrified of breaking something,' she said.

'Don't you worry, duck, I won't say nothing if you don't.'

'Knowing him, though, he's probably got everything numbered or labelled or something.' They both laughed, then stopped to listen in case they had woken Noah. There was no sound other than the constant background of ticking and periodic chimes.

'What you gone and done here?' Godfrey said, picking up the loose thread on Helen's sleeve. 'Look, you've snagged your cardy. Want me to give it a quick mend, duck? – I'm not too bad with a needle and thread, if I do say so meself.'

Helen tucked the wavy end of her sleeve inside itself. She laughed weakly. 'No, honestly, it's not new. Thanks, though.' She smiled. 'Something I've been wondering – what happened earlier, all the upset at work and everything – what was it, d'you think, that Noah was so scared about? All that about the cupboard, the house? It really seems to bother him, doesn't it – has he ever mentioned it to you?

'Oh I don't know what he's on about, duck. I've bin round, winding his clocks and what not, and it all seems right as sixpence to me. I reckon he's just got hisself all hot and bothered over these women. That, and poor old Joey popping his clogs the way he did. I just don't think he can cope with the emotional tur … turbulation of it all.'

Helen smiled. 'You're probably right. Funny though, when I mentioned it, he said he hadn't really known him – erm, Joey, I mean.'

Godfrey chuckled. 'No, love, he's having you on. We used to go and visit Joe every week. Once I got him there, he was all right – I think it upset him seeing the poor old bugger in a place like that – you know, he didn't like to stay too long or anything. Nice that we had each other to go with, specially the night poor old Joey got taken, God rest his whasname … his soul. Trying to tell us something at the end, he was – how much he thought of us and that sort of thing.' Godfrey's eyes filled with tears. 'Poor old bugger was all on his own. Lived here years, he did. Never had no family or nothing. There was a lot of talk years back about him being a bit … you know, bit peculiar and that. And some of 'em even used to say he'd got a liking for little boys, but I don't pay no attention to that sort of thing. He never did me no harm. He always kept hisself to hisself. Rattling about all on his own in that house next door …'

'Sorry. I didn't mean to upset you,' Helen said.

'Tell you what, duck, it's Joey's funeral next week. Having one of them council ones, they are. Nothing fancy, Matron said, but at least they give 'em a nice send off. Why don't you come? Keep me and Noel company? You know him; he's bound to be in a state. He could do with you being there. Bit of mortal support.'

'Oh. I don't know what to say.'

'Go on, love. He needs a bit of looking after. And he won't get much of that from the likes of Sparkle and that lot, will he?' Godfrey winked at Helen.

'I'll think about it. Perhaps have a word with Noah tomorrow. If he'd rather I didn't —' She stopped abruptly. A thin screech came from above.

Godfrey held his cup just above the table, the tea dangerously tilted to one side. 'Probably outside,' he said. 'One of them motorbikes, they come past here like the wind sometimes.' He hunched over the table again to drink his tea.

'Oh, right,' Helen said. 'Sounded like it came from – I don't know – difficult to say, I suppose.'

'Tell you what, Helen, duck, I'll go and have a peep at Noel. Make sure it didn't wake him up.' Godfrey patted Helen on the shoulder as he left the kitchen.

The screech sliced through the kitchen again. This time it definitely came from above. For several seconds, Helen sat still, staring at the ceiling. Then she shook herself. 'Oh, for God's sake,' she said. 'Let's go and have a look.'

As Helen slid carefully round the half-open kitchen door, she collided softly at chest level with Godfrey. They both gasped. Helen put her hands up to her throat. Godfrey clutched the edge of his apron. Then they both giggled.

Godfrey shoved Helen back inside the kitchen. He shut the door behind them. 'Gordon do-dah,' he said, giggling, 'I nearly wet meself. You didn't half give me a fright Helen, love.' His bulging apron wobbled and shook with his laughter.

'Me too,' Helen managed to say between her giggles. She pressed her hands over her cheeks. 'Where were you?'

'Oh, it's him, love – I went to check on Noel – you'll never guess what he's gone and done,' Godfrey said.

'Oh my God, what? What's wrong?' Helen's colour drained. The fingerprints stood out on each side of her face.

'Gone and took hisself off to bed, hasn't he? Fast asleep, he is. Found him up there just now. Them stairs give you the whasnames … the willies, don't they love? He ought to get them seen to.'

twenty-six

Helen plumped the sofa cushions and tidied away all traces of her night in Noah's sitting room, except for Godfrey's turquoise blanket, which she left folded on a chair. She said goodbye to Noah as he washed up the breakfast things. 'See you later,' they said simultaneously, and gave each other feeble smiles. *At least I didn't wake up clutching her like an octopus this time*, Noah thought.

When Helen had gone, Noah sat on the hall carpet and listened to his messages. He erased Esther's voice after her first few words. He did the same with his Mother's message. Then he paused for a few seconds, willed himself to breathe calmly, and pressed for the next message. He felt certain it would be Angela, but feared what she might say. It was Esther again.

'lo, Noah, you there? S'me … still trying to get —' Noah erased her voice. *It'll be her this time*, he thought. Again, Esther spilled into the hall. And again, Noah pressed the button to erase her. He could tell from the intake of breath, that the next message was also Esther, though he cut her off before she managed to complete 'lo.' He kept his finger held over the erase button, ready to chop off the first syllable of her next message. But it wasn't her. For a fragment of time, Noah didn't recognise Grace's voice. He knew only that it wasn't Esther.

'Hello, it's Grace. I got your message. I'll try another time. Hope you're okay. Bye for now.'

Noah played the message again and again. Through repetition, it became both meaningless, just a collection of words, a pattern of sounds, and loaded with significance. Noah read so much into these few short words. Without noticing, he joined in, muttering the words unconsciously. He repeated the chant softly to himself throughout the day, his lips barely moving as he shaped the words.

At work, Noah was calm yet preoccupied. Although he managed to focus on what needed to be done, his mind was always filled with Grace's message. He paid detailed attention to his work, making up for time previously lost on his personal anxieties. He finished outstanding graphs, flow-charts and diagrams. And Grace's words ran through his mind continuously, like a fragment from a pop song. He had favourite segments – *I'll try another time. Hope you're okay –* which he said to himself most of the time, but he still memorised the whole message, and repeated it to himself hundreds of times.

At home, Noah listened to the real message. And waited. He cleaned his kitchen, removed invisible traces of Helen and Godfrey, and carefully polished all the clocks. He made small meals for himself, counted out pasta or vegetables, cooked them and then ate even smaller portions than he'd made. He inspected his face in minute detail, with a powerful torch shone into a magnifying mirror. He picked and prodded at the bumps and craters, changing the lunar landscape of his face to the uneven red glow of Mars. He returned the turquoise blanket to Godfrey, and promised to go with him to the funeral at the end of the week. All the time, he chanted Grace's message.

On Wednesday, Noah decided to ring Esther. She had left at least one, sometimes two messages for him every day since the weekend. She showed no sign of giving up. 'I'll be kind,' he said to himself. He played her most recent message, made a note of the number, even though he felt it was probably forever branded on the convoluted surface of his brain. He wrote it down, small silvery pencil marks on a white page, sat on the hall floor and rang her.

'I know you've left millions of messages, and I'm sorry not to get back before now, but —'

'*Noah*, oh, you'll never guess – I was just going to ring you,' she said. 'What a lovely surprise. Sso nice to hear from you. You been busy? Course you have, silly question. S'pect you haven't had a minute to yourself. Mustn't work too hard, you know, ss'not good for you. All that stresss and everything. Fancy a drink? Take your mind off things? Or shall I come round and see you? Perhaps you'd rather come round here, I could make us a nice dinner. Now, what d'you fancy? Oooh, as if I didn't know the answer to that one.' Her high-pitched laughter filled Noah's ear.

'Look, just … just hold on a minute,' he said. 'I don't want, I can't, I didn't ring to … it's just that, all those messages you've left me. I thought, well, I wanted to explain.'

Esther interrupted. 'S'alright, Noah. There's no need to explain. Now, why don't you —'

Noah mouthed the word *fuck,* banged his fist on the floor. 'No, why don't y*ou* … why don't you just listen? Just stop for a second and listen. The reason I rang was to ask you not to leave any more messages. Please.'

'How am I s'posed to get in touch then?' Esther said.

'Look, you won't need to. That's why I'm ringing. I just wanted to … well, to say that I don't think this can work. And I … I just want to leave it at that.' *Got the message now, you stupid fat cow?*

'You going all shy on me again, Noah?' she said. 'I know a good cure for —'

'There's someone else,' he said, his voice cold. 'All right? I've met someone else. We're very happy. Now, will you *please* stop ringing me?' He waited for Esther to speak. He heard only the whistling sound of her breathing. He added in a softer tone, 'It wouldn't be right, would it? Surely you understand. I hope things work out for you. I'd better go now. Bye.' He put the phone down before she could speak again.

When the phone rang immediately, he let the answer machine pick it up and listened for Esther's voice, her anger, her hurt feelings. When Grace spoke, he grabbed the phone quickly. 'Yes, I'm here, it's me. I forgot the answerphone was on – sorry. It's really good to … I'm so glad you … thanks for ringing. I …' He clambered to his feet. His mouth was dry.

'Hello Noah.' Grace sounded flat. 'Sorry I haven't been in touch before. I, well, to be honest, I kept putting it off. Then when I got your message on the dating link thing, I realised it was only fair to ring you.'

'Oh. Is … is everything okay?' Noah said, his stomach tightening.
'Yes, fine,' she said. 'Well … no it isn't. Not really.'

'Do you want to tell me?' Noah sank to the carpet, heavy with dread.

'I just wanted to say that I'd like to leave things as they are. I, well, I don't want anything else to come of this, and I thought it best to make that clear.'

'But we talked. You *really talked* to me. We got on well, didn't we? Can't we give it a bit longer? Have a think about it. Please.' *Don't do this Angela. Please don't do this to me. I can't let you go now.*

'I've been thinking about that, Noah,' she said. 'Talking to you really did help. It made me realise that was what I'd needed to do. I'm very grateful for that.'

Noah curled into a small ball. 'So that's it then? You don't want me. Don't want me to look after you or anything? Not your type, I suppose.'

'It's not that – I enjoyed talking to you, I really did —'

Noah interrupted, 'So why can't we *keep* talking, then? Doesn't make sense to stop doing something if you like it, does it? I'd look after you, Angela, I really would.'

'My name isn't Angela.' The phone went dead.

Noah listened to the thrumming purr as he bit the back of his hand. He rocked himself backwards and forwards. 'Grace not Angela, Grace not Angela,' he said quietly.

An hour later, in a numb, trance-like state, Noah picked up the piece of paper with faint silvery numbers. He rang Esther. As he expected, she talked enough not to notice his monosyllabic input. He agreed to accept her offer of dinner, took directions of where she lived, and drove to her house. Numbness saturated him.

'Okay, Angela, if you don't want me … perhaps this'll make you change your mind.' He paused. 'Grace. Grace not Angela. Got to get it right.'

twenty-seven

'Now, you come and get comfy, and I'll get us a nice drink,' Esther said. 'We're having a takeaway – is that all right? I thought it would give uss more time together.' She hugged him tightly, and then led him into the small sitting room. 'Ssit yourself down,' she said, pushing Noah's shoulder.

He fought the urge to resist her firm pressure, and sat heavily against the frilled cushions.

'Aaah, look at you,' she said. 'No need to be nervous, you know. I know you've been frightened of getting involved, but it's going to be all right now.' She lifted her shoulders high, to give Noah a reassuring smile, then left the room.

Noah closed his eyes, whispered, 'See what you've made me do, Angela?' He scanned the room. Display units held arrangements of cute animal ornaments. There were several vases filled with large, colourful silk flowers – oranges and yellows, with unconvincing gold foliage. A teddy bear wedding was taking place on a small table, with stunted ceramic figures dressed in top hats, waistcoats and pastel-coloured dresses. Noah sneered and closed his eyes again. He felt tired. The disappointment and anger that had driven him to Esther's house began to seep away. *Now she'll see how serious I am. See she's hurt me so badly I had to turn to someone else for comfort. All the big love stories have that, don't they? Jealousy and passion and people realising that they do love you after all.* These thoughts encouraged Noah, but he couldn't shake off the blanket of fatigue weighting him against Esther's cushions. When she came back with two glasses of wine, he didn't move.

'Aaah, that's better, you look all nice and relaxed now.' She handed him the drink and squeezed next to him on the sofa. 'Cheers then, here's to uss,' she said, holding up her glass.

'Er, yes. Cheers,' he said.

Esther swallowed her wine quickly and put the glass down. She took Noah's free hand, lifted it to her mouth and pressed a wet kiss on the back. 'Sso glad you changed your mind. You won't regret it, you know. All that nonsense about there being someone else – I knew you were just trying to make excuses.'

Noah sat forward, started to speak, but she put her fingers on his lips.

'We're going to have a lovely time, you and me, aren't we?' She stroked his leg. 'First things first though – let me get this meal sorted out. Ss'all in the oven, heating through. You could do with a bit of fattening up, look at you – all bone and baggy trousers.' She rocked his knee from side to side, before struggling to her feet.

'Ha.' Noah made his mouth lift at the edges. When she had gone, he grimaced. *I did try to tell her*, he thought, *tried to explain about Angela*. He felt detached, almost indifferent. Her size, her simpering manner bothered him less now. She was just a pawn in his plan to win Angela back. *All's fair in love and war*, he thought. He remained in the same slumped position, the glass of wine still in his hand. 'Let's get this over with,' he said to himself.

They ate the meal at Esther's cluttered, candle-lit dining table. Her pudgy knee pressed harder against Noah's leg as they made their way through the aromatic portions of Chinese food. Esther chewed, swallowed, smiled and talked throughout. She seemed unaware that Noah had eaten little and said even less. He twisted and rearranged noodles around his multi-coloured patterned plate, nodded and periodically gave taut, twitchy smiles.

'S'nice, isn't it?' She stroked the back of his hand quickly, then spooned more rice onto her plate. 'Want ssome more Noah?'

'No, no, really, I'm full. Thanks.'

'Aaah, have some wine, then. Here, let me top you up.' She reached for the bottle across the densely-covered table. Her arm brushed the silk petals of a tangerine-coloured flower, tipping over the top-heavy arrangement.

'Careful,' Noah said. It came out sharply but Esther smiled at him.

'Doesn't matter, there's no water or anything.' She stood the vase up. 'They're not even real.'

'Really? You surprise me,' Noah said. *I could say anything to her*, he thought. As Esther held the wine bottle over Noah's glass, he shook his head. 'I'd rather have water,' he said.

'Aaah, not worried about driving, are you? You're sstaying here with me tonight, aren't you?' She stood behind his chair, wrapped her arms around his chest, and buried her head against his neck. She mumbled, 'I'm not letting you escape again, you know. You're sstaying right here, you are.'

Noah didn't move. Staring ahead, he said, 'Yes. I know I am.'

He allowed himself to be dragged back to the sofa. The sense of detachment still enveloped him. He had the sensation of watching himself and Esther from a distance. Looking down, he saw Esther ease him back against the cushions, saw himself pinned between the plump upholstery of the sofa and her large, soft breasts. She moved her hands over him, stroked his face, his hair, his shoulders and down the length of his thighs. Then she repeated the swift movements. This time Noah caught her by the wrist and jerked her hand away from his head.

'Did I mess your hair up?' she said. 'Aaah, come here, let me make it nice again.' She tried to free her hand but Noah held her tight. She laughed, said, 'S'all right, I won't touch it if you don't want me to.'

He released her wrist, but sat with his head angled away from her, his jaws clenched. Esther snuggled closer. She drew her feet up onto the sofa, leaned into Noah, her head on his shoulder. She stared up at him, grinning.

'Not used to this, are you? Me neither. We can learn together. S'all right, you know. God meant for uss to love one another.'

Noah groaned.

'Oh, come here,' she said, and clutched him tightly.

He watched from his aloof place as she kissed him. He felt nothing. Saw her unbutton his shirt. Just as with the meal earlier, her appetite was undiminished by his abstinence. She spread herself over him, her upper body crushing his chest, her legs flattening his. He imagined the view from his disembodied place, his body no longer visible beneath Esther's wobbling folds of flesh. He lifted his feet off the floor to prove to himself that he could still move.

'Oohh, that's it, Noah. Let your body move. I can feel you letting go now,' she said.

Noah lifted his feet, locked his knees and held his legs out straight. He counted to ten, then let his feet fall to the floor again.

Esther pressed herself harder into his lap. She was breathing fast. She rubbed her hands over him again and again, making his skin tender where his clothes chafed.

Noah repeated his leg exercises at regular intervals. He despised her for the increased urgency of her response. He thought of Angela. *Wouldn't need to do knee bends to make her think I was getting in the mood.* He visualised Angela sitting on his floor, his hand hovering above her hair, feeling the heat of her in his palm. And then he *was* moving. Moving towards Angela, pushing his bony hips upwards to find closer contact with her.

The heaving, panting Esther enthusiastically received these unconscious responses to the image in his mind. She struggled out of the top part of her dress, and unhooked her bra. It flopped into Noah's lap, the huge moulded nylon cups like matching sugar bowls. Noah didn't want to see the contents of the bowls. He kept his head down, his eyes closed, and reassembled the image of Angela. *My hand*, he told himself, *my hand is over her head, and she leans back and I bend to kiss her neck, and ...*

Esther pulled his head to her breasts. The cool, slightly damp skin smothered his face, absorbed the sharp outlines of his nose and cheeks. He stopped breathing; afraid he would choke on inhaled lungfuls of her pulpy, suffocating flesh.

She sits in front of me, I kiss her neck and she leans back to pull me closer and I reach down to stroke her breasts and she ...

Noah was drowning, felt desperate for air. He dug his head back into the sofa but the soft, unset putty of Esther's breasts poured over him, moulding to the shape of him.

She presses her mouth hard onto mine and we kiss, really deeply, and her tongue pushes and I can hardly breathe and I stroke her hair, but she twists at my clothes, pulls and claws and snatches to get them out of the way, and I slide onto the floor with her, and we're still kissing, and making noises as we gasp for air but can't stop kissing, and then she's on top of me and she slides herself onto me, and I feel air on my face as she leans back, and I can breathe but my mouth feels empty and I find her small, hard nipple because I want to suck and taste and bite ...

As he drew Esther's nipple into his mouth, Noah squeezed his eyes shut.

She's moving fast on me, on my stick, and it's a big stick now and it's in her, my stick is inside her, inside Angela, but she's doing it too fast and I want to say slow down but I can't stop and she can't stop, and it's going to happen, I can't help it, it's ... uuhhh, uh, Angela.

'Angela.' Noah's orgasm jerked itself out of his system, snatching away all traces of his fantasy. He waited, his eyes closed.

Esther tried to heave herself off Noah. Her left knee was trapped between the cushion and the arm of the sofa. Her dress was caught under Noah's leg. She tugged and struggled as tears ran down her face, dripped onto her large white breasts.

'Sorry, I ... well, I'm sorry ...' Noah still had his eyes closed. He fumbled with his trousers, tucked in his shirt, and zipped away his shrivelled penis. Something wedged in his zip. He looked down. The strap of Esther's bra was tucked in with his shirt. He pulled it free. 'You better put this on,' he said, holding it out to her.

Esther snatched the bra from him, still trying to free herself from Noah's lap. Her breasts swayed and shook as she sobbed.

'Don't,' he said. 'Please don't cry. Come on, let me help you.' He pulled at her dress, caught underneath him. He couldn't free it. 'Look, if you lift up a bit.'

She didn't move, didn't seem to hear him.

'Can you just ...' Noah still gripped a handful of the dress.

'Oh, I don't care about that,' she said, her voice thick with tears. She slapped at his hand, missing him and hitting her own leg. 'Look at you. It's not even as if you're good-looking or anything, is it? Didn't think a man like you would – well, do that ssort of thing.'

Noah released the fistful of fabric and slumped into the sofa. He looked at Esther. *Didn't mean to upset her,* he thought. *Never meant to make her cry.* He watched Esther's miserable face as he spoke, and she became real to him. For a brief moment, he glimpsed his own behaviour. He felt ashamed. 'I've hurt you haven't I?'

'Course you have,' she said. After several attempts to choke back her tears, she asked, 'Who is she? This Angela?'

'Well, she's not anyone, not really. Not any more,' he said.

Esther took a deep breath and dabbed at her wet cheeks with the back of her hand. Then she started to cry again. 'S'no point lying now, is there? You've said her name and everything – you could at least tell me who she is.'

'Well, it's not her name. She's not really ... She's someone who, well, I was in love with her,' he closed his eyes, 'but she didn't love me.'

Esther blinked hard and dabbed at her eyes with her pudgy fingers. 'What, you mean you're not together now? She's someone you *used* to be with?' She paused. Her tears stopped. 'And you've split up? And when you said her name, it was a mistake, in the heat of the moment, wasn't it? P'raps I reminded you of her, did I?' She looked hopeful.

Noah shook his head as he listened to Esther's version. His thoughts raced. *She thinks it's all in the past. I can't tell her any different, I've already hurt her enough. Can't make things even worse. Can't tell her that I only came here to get back at Angela, make her realise that she does want me. And I want her about as much as I* don't *want this poor wobbly bitch sitting here looking all desperate and pleading.*

'No. No,' he said. 'You didn't remind me of her, but what you said is right – it was a mistake. A great big mistake, and I'm sorry. I wish it hadn't happened.' Noah was filled with regret and shame and couldn't redirect these unfamiliar feelings onto someone else. He wished he hadn't come to Esther's house. Wished he hadn't intended from the moment he'd rang her, to use her like this. *I shouldn't have hurt her. I really wish I hadn't hurt her.*

'Well, I s'pose if you didn't mean it …' Esther said.

Don't, thought Noah. *Don't be so bloody forgiving. Don't, don't, don't.*

Later, in the stillness of the early hours, Noah lay awake in Esther's bed, listening to her breathing. He stared into the darkness, going over and over the events of the evening. It took him until daylight to absolve himself of the responsibility for hurting Esther. *She shouldn't have thrown herself at me*, he thought. *She shouldn't have said that about me either. I can't help the way I look. I never said anything about how fat she is, or about that stupid grin she keeps doing. Wish I hadn't come here at all. If Angela hadn't told me it was all over, I wouldn't have had to come here. She made it turn out like this, really. If she'd let it be the way it was supposed to, no one would have got hurt. And I wouldn't have been stuck here all night, waiting to escape.*

He looked at the shape of Esther, curled on her side, facing him. He could just make out the paleness of her face but her features were not clear. He imagined her smiling broadly, her cheeks pushed up, her eyebrows raised high, and everything supported by her shoulders, hunched up to her ears.

I preferred it when she was blubbing, he thought, but then immediately changed his mind as he recalled Esther's face, collapsed and heavy with misery. He wanted to leave, go quickly and quietly while Esther still slept. *Surely,* he thought, *she'd get the message then – wouldn't keep pestering me with phone calls every five minutes.* But he was unconvinced by what he told himself, and made no effort to leave his edge of the bed, where he lay still as death, staring into the dark space of the room. Sleep eventually claimed him, giving an hour and a half of unconsciousness that halted Noah's thoughts and eased his face at the jaw and temples.

He awoke abruptly as Esther was getting out of bed. 'What …?'

'S'all right. S'only me,' she said. 'Just popping to the loo, then I'll make us some nice breakfast. Won't be long.' Her puffy face inflated into a smile. Her filmy, lilac nightdress, its creases stuck to her left thigh, only slightly obscured her naked body.

Noah could see the springy dark nest of her pubic hair, the chunky shape of her legs, her weighty breasts. 'Aren't you cold in just that?' he said.

'Aaah, ss'all right, I'll pop my dressing gown on. S'in the bathroom. Sleep well?'

'No,' he said, then seeing her face drop, added, 'No problems. Thanks.'

Esther shrugged him another smile and hurried out of the room.

Noah pulled the quilt to his chin and curled himself into a ball. *Better stay half an hour, I suppose*, he thought.

Esther kicked the bedroom door as she came back, startling Noah out of a light doze. Brightly coloured cups, bowls and plates rattled against each other on the tray she carried. Her dressing gown was the same fabric as her lilac nightdress, and Noah could still see the hazy outlines of her body.

He looked away and busied himself with propping up the pillows. 'I don't usually eat much for breakfast,' he said.

'Aaah, be a nice treat then, won't it? You need ssomeone to feed you up, look after you, that's what I think. Now, come on, what would you like first? There's toast and cereal and fruit juice, and a nice pot of tea.'

The mention of tea made him think of Angela. *She came back with me*, he thought. *She actually came to my house and had tea with me. Sat on the floor and drank tea. We got that far. I had her in my house — oh God, why didn't it stay like that? Why did it have to go wrong?* He shook his head rapidly. 'I don't want any tea, thank you. I only drink it on special occasions. Definitely no tea.'

'S'no problem, I can go and make some coffee. That be better?' She started to get off the bed.

'No. I won't, thanks,' he said. 'I'll have some orange juice, that'll be fine.' Noah reached for a glass.

'Oh, it's pineapple. Ssorry, let me go and see if there's some orange in the cupboard.'

'No look, just leave it, will you? This will be fine. Actually, it's all I want. I'm really not hungry.' He swallowed the sweet, sticky juice and felt it seep through him. *All I really want is tea with Angela. Tea and talk and looking into her eyes, listening to her voice, holding my hand over her hair.*

'Oh, ssurely you can manage a little bite?' Esther said. 'Here, at least have half a slice, then we can —'

Noah interrupted, 'Then I've got to be on my way. Mustn't be late for work.'

'S'ever so early, though. I thought we could have a bit of lie-in. You know, a nice ssnuggle up?' She lifted her shoulders high in a broad grin, the ribbon and lace on her dressing gown merged with her hair as she handed him a plate.

Christ, thought Noah, *I've been here all night. What more does she expect?* He ripped a corner of the toast with his teeth and chewed quickly. It lodged, dry and hard in his throat, as he tried to swallow. He forced down the rest of the slice and flung back his side of the quilt. His penis stood erect in his lap, red and swollen against the bony whiteness of his pelvis and thighs. *Fuck, fuck, fuck*, he said inside his head.

'Looks like part of you isn't too keen to rush off to work, doesn't it?' Esther said, staring at his penis. She stretched her hand towards him. As her fingers touched his hip, Noah twisted his feet round to the floor and stood up. With his back to her, he pulled on his clothes.

'Really must go,' he said, balancing on one leg to tie his shoelace.

'All right then, Noah.' She sat back against the pillows and sighed, a resigned, sad expression on her face. 'I'm sorry I got all upset last night. I'd built my hopes up. Ssilly, isn't it? You tell yourself you won't, then you go and think all sorts of things, make plans in your head and everything. And you go and forget about the other person – about how they might not ssee things the same way. When you ssaid that name, I – well, you know what happened. I just hadn't put that in any of my plans about how it would be.' She took a deep breath and let it out slowly. She looked tired, her face was sad, all traces of her readily-available grin had disappeared. She seemed lost. 'I didn't even mind you not being, well, you know …'

'Not being what?' Noah said.

'Well, you're different, aren't you? That's all I mean. You're just a bit different – a funny old stick. But I don't mind. I don't think that's important. We got on so well on the phone. And we're all God's children, He —'

Noah cut her off. 'What do you mean, *different?*' he said.

'Ss'not important, Noah. Surely what matters is how we get on and what we feel about each other. I told you, I don't mind.'

'Well, thanks very much, that's all right then, isn't it? Long as you don't mind.' He walked towards the door.

Esther sank further into her pillows. 'Ssorry. Can't seem to get anything right. Everything I ssay comes out wrong. I never meant to offend you or anything. I'm ssorry.' She was looking at the tray, still balanced on the bed in front of her.

Why can't I just walk out and slam the door? I ought to, after the things she's come out with. He stood in the doorway of the bedroom, watching her. 'Look, I'd better go,' he said. 'I'll give you a ring though. If you want me to.'

Esther smiled. It was a weak, polite smile, and it faded fast. Noah thought it looked more natural than the huge grin she usually forced onto her face. This smile touched him.

'You don't have to,' Esther said, quietly.

I do, thought Noah. Guilt still encased him, though more loosely, like a skin he was starting to shed. 'No, I will,' he said.

twenty-eight

Noah shut his front door quietly and leaned against it, his eyes closed. Hot, prickly tears pushed between his eyelids. He made no sound as he cried. He felt weary, his clothes were creased and stale, but he had no energy to get himself bathed and changed. All he wanted was to be in his bed, removed from the reality of his night with Esther. He dragged himself up the stairs, wiping his eyes on his sleeve. He curled into a ball, still dressed, still wearing his shoes, and covered himself with the quilt. He fell asleep within minutes and slept for the rest of the morning, and into the early afternoon. At times, his body twitched and jerked, but mostly he remained still.

In his dream, Noah opened his front door to Joseph Pepper and stood aside as the old man walked in. Noah felt obliged to offer him something to eat and drink, but knew he was doing this only to distract. 'Have some fruit,' he said, but as he held the bowl towards Joseph Pepper, he noticed how bloated and rotten the fruit was. Grey fur blanketed the pears and apples, the bananas had turned black and a blue-tinged mould spread over the oranges.

Joseph Pepper waved his large hand over the bowl. 'Not for me, thank you,' he said, 'I've come for the lovely —'

Noah cut in quickly. 'How about a nice cup of tea? There's Lord Sheraton, if you'd like. I know you're a bit of a tea addict.'

'I can't stop for tea,' said Joseph Pepper. 'I've come to see if they're still safe. I made sure they were put away, nice and safe. Let me see.' He moved towards the hall cupboard.

Noah stood in his way. 'Cake,' he said, 'what about some cake?' He felt his heel press against the cupboard door. He put one hand on the doorframe. Joseph Pepper shuffled and mumbled to himself. He rubbed his hollow cheek. Noah heard the rasp of stubble against his bony fingers. He watched the old man's hand as he lowered it to his side. Then he noticed Joseph Pepper's clothes. He was dressed in white, but it was a smeared and dirty white. His loose cotton trousers were smudged with rusty brown stains. His sleeves, rolled back to his gnarled elbows, were streaked with the same colour. He wore a long apron with a large pocket. Noah could see it was meant to be white, but it was almost covered in different shades of brownish red. 'You're a butcher,' he said.

'Knew that, didn't you?' Joseph Pepper said. 'Always knew there was something, didn't you?'

'But you didn't look like a butcher when I let you in.'

'Weren't paying attention, were you? Know what happens if you don't pay attention, don't you?'

Noah swallowed hard. 'What?'

The old man raised his right hand high above his head, then brought it down fast, slicing through the air in front of Noah's face. 'Have your fingers off, that's what. In my line of work, you would.' The effort seemed to strain him. He breathed hard, and his colour paled.

'I'm not hanging about waiting for you to breathe your last breath,' Noah said. He laughed and put his hand up to cover his face.

'Not paying attention again, see?' said Joseph Pepper.

'What? What do you mean?' Noah was no longer laughing.

'Already have. Knew that as well, didn't you? Already breathed my last breath. Now, let me see my —'

'What about some chocolate? A sandwich? Fairy cakes, biscuits, a piece of toast?' Noah spread his feet and placed his other hand on the cupboard doorframe. His dream gave him the knowledge that Joseph Pepper couldn't move him, but that didn't stop the old man coming close. Noah could smell his foul breath.

'I'll go on my own, then. Find them myself, see?' He turned slowly and walked towards the cellar, mumbling as he went. Noah caught the words '…and find my lovely …' He shuffled away. The backs of his trousers were whiter than the front.

'Don't go down there.' Noah shouted. 'My shoes are down there. That's where I clean them – you might, well, you might trip over them, or …'

Joseph Pepper turned his head stiffly, to look back at Noah. 'Or what?'

Noah's mouth pulled against the words he tried to shape. His lips trembled and twitched. 'The plaster,' he said. 'It's not dry yet. That wall where the … where the damp got in.'

'Nice and soft, was it?' The old man looked away and continued his slow progress towards the cellar. 'Better have a look, then. Used to do odd jobs here, see. Bit of this, bit of that – anythink what needed doing, I'd do it, see? If people wanted repairs done, they'd come to the butcher. Know my way around, I do.' He opened the door to the cellar and shuffled through, leaving it ajar behind him.

As Noah lurched forward in his dream, to close the door, his body convulsed him violently awake. The confusion of this abrupt awakening made him mistake the moist darkness surrounding him for that of the cellar. He clutched his limbs tighter to his body, fearing contact with what might be buried in the walls. As his senses adjusted, he realised where he was, and lay for a long time without moving, while the dream receded. Then he peeled away the quilt and squinted in the warm afternoon light that filled his bedroom.

'Oh no, the time …' He shivered, even though the room was warm and fuggy. He pulled his bathrobe over his crumpled clothes, and went downstairs. When he peered nervously at the cellar door, it was shut. He sat on the hall floor, his back against the wall, and balanced the telephone on his outstretched legs. 'What am I going to say? Can't tell them I had the day off because of a bad dream, can I? Can't say I stayed awake all night, next to some fat woman I hardly know, just because I felt guilty.'

He held his fist against the side of his head, an imaginary phone, 'Oh hello,' he said, 'it's Noah Quince here, from Graphics. Just ringing to let you know that I couldn't get into work today because of a dream about a dead butcher, come to check on the remains of the boys he sliced up when he used to live next door.' He inclined his head, as if listening. 'Yes, yes, I hope to back at work tomorrow – as long as there isn't another visit from the odd-job butcher, of course, or chopped up boys hanging in the coat cupboard, or piles of hands at the bottom of the wardrobe. You know, the usual things going round this time of year.'

He pressed his palms hard against his eyes; saw white sparks behind his eyelids. His knees jerked and the phone tipped to the floor. 'Oh, fuck it. Let them think what they like. I can't talk to them now. I'm hardly ever off work anyway. I always stay late, and get in early. They can do without me for one day. I'll be back tomorrow.' He wanted to sound angry, but his voice was feeble, like a child pretending not to be scared of the dark.

A tinny voice told him to hang up and try again. Noah stood up. He left the nagging telephone where it was, and went to the front door to pick up his mail. There were three envelopes and a small piece of paper with a frilly edge where it had been torn from a notepad. He placed the envelopes on the pew and read the note:

> Been trying to knock you up but no reply.
> Hope you are not ill in there. You need anything you give me a call.
> Will keep popping round.
> Doing some sausage rolls for Joe's funeral tomorrow.
> See you in a bit.
> Love Godfrey xx

Noah folded the paper again and again, until it was a small white cube. He held it between his fingers, and pinched hard to try and stop the folds springing undone. He started to cry, swiping roughly at his tears. 'Can't even have a lazy day at home without people interfering. Don't want *him* round here, making a fuss and trying to take over.' He put the cube of paper on his outstretched palm and flicked it hard. It struck the face of a clock, bounced off and landed in front of the hall cupboard. Noah pulled his bathrobe closer to his body and tied the belt tightly over his shirt and trousers. He still felt cold.

Forgot about that bloody funeral. I thought he said the end of the week, anyway. I can't go if it's tomorrow – not now I've had today off. He'll have to go on his own. I'll go and tell him.' He snatched his keys off the hall table, pushed his hands deep inside the towelling pockets and with his head down, walked briskly to Godfrey's house.

'Oh, Gordon whatsit.' Godfrey opened the door as Noah was about to knock. 'I was just on me way round. Bin so worried, I have. Whatever's up, duck?'

'Nothing. Overslept, that's all,' Noah said. 'Just wanted to let you know I won't be coming to the funeral.' He turned to leave.

'Hang on,' Godfrey said, 'what d'you mean, not coming? You said you was. It's all arranged now, love. Got a car to pick us up and everything. You not well, Noel? Come on, come and have a sit down, you don't look too whasname ... too perky.' Godfrey put his hand on Noah's shoulder to guide him inside. 'You haven't got that virus going round, have you, duck? Look at you, big dark circles under your eyes, and your face all sunk in. P'raps we ought to get the doctor out?'

Noah shook his head. 'There's nothing wrong. I told you, I overslept, that's all.'

'What, till gone two in the afternoon?' Godfrey was filling the kettle. He looked over his rounded shoulder at Noah. 'I banged and banged on your door – enough to wake poor old Joey, it was, so you must of bin deeper asleep than normal. That's a sign of being ill that is, duck.'

'I'm not bloody ill, all right?'

'All right, all right, if you say so,' Godfrey said. 'Why aren't you coming to the funeral then?'

'I can't get the time off work. You said it wasn't until Friday. Anyway, it's not as if I knew him, is it?'

Godfrey took a clean, folded hanky from the pocket of his blue and white striped apron. He shook it open, held it out to Noah. 'It's Friday *tomorrow,* you silly bugger. Got yourself all upset, haven't you? Here, duck, have a good old blow. All this business has got you right mixed up, hasn't it? You have a good old cry while I make the tea.'

'I'm *not* crying,' Noah said, and put his hand to his face. It was wet. He pressed the hanky hard against his eyes. *Oh fuck. Now I'm blubbing without even realising. It's love. This is what it does to you, isn't it? Angela's got no idea what she's done.*

'Nice hot cuppa, Noel.' Godfrey put two steaming china mugs on the table, and sat opposite Noah. 'That'll make you feel better. Now, let's get this funeral sorted out.'

Noah sat in a daze, sipping the hot tea. He listened to Godfrey without registering his words, and shivered. Snatches of the evening with Esther flashed into his thoughts, and were mixed with memories of the dream. His head ached.

'Anyway, duck, that's just about it,' Godfrey said.

Noah stared at him. 'What?'

Godfrey patted Noah's hand. 'You're not yourself, are you, lovey? Look at you, sitting there all hunched up and cold as whasname … cold as ice-cubes. I think the best thing for you is to get yourself back to bed. Soon as I've got these bits out of the oven, I'll come round and sit with you.'

Noah stared down at Godfrey's hand, covering his own. Large wet spots landed on Godfrey's warm, floury skin. 'All right,' was all Noah could say through his tears.

Godfrey helped him to the door, his bulging apron brushed against Noah's thigh as they jostled along the hallway. Noah remained silent. He didn't look back when Godfrey called out for him to leave his front door unlocked.

twenty-nine

Noah propped up his pillows and sat back to wait for Godfrey. *I'm not going to sleep this time*, he thought. *No more butcher dreams, thank you very much indeed.* He felt safer in his bed, and pushed away memories of what had happened with Esther. Now it seemed like a story he'd heard, and he could smile about it from this distance of pretence. He grafted his own experience onto an unknown person. *They* had fucked Esther, not him. *They* had used her to spite the woman they loved, to make her jealous and remorseful – not him. *They* had hurt Esther, then felt so guilty and ashamed they'd stayed all night, clinging to the edge of her bed. Not him.

He smoothed the quilt and ran his hands across his hair, leaned back against the pillows and waited. The clocks chimed the hour at three. Noah made a note to himself to adjust some of the slower ones – the grandfather clock sounded nearly five minutes faster than the others. The house seemed too quiet when the clocks had finished chiming. Noah coughed, just to add noise to the ticking background. 'Where's he got to?' he said. 'No good saying you'll come round then leave people to sit waiting for ages. Especially with me being ill. Anything could happen.'

He tried the cough again, this time making it louder and more prolonged. He pulled the quilt up higher, closed his eyes and thought of Angela. He imagined her in the park, sitting at the small table, opposite him – and the way she'd looked at him. What had it meant, that look? Noah hadn't been able to read it then, and now, thinking back, he was still puzzled. *She probably thought what an ugly bastard I was*, he thought. *But she did sit and talk to me. And she actually came back here. So I can't be that bad.* He replayed every moment of the time he'd spent with Angela. *Got to get her back*, he thought. *I mean, she was here with me. That must count for something. I can't lose her now. Just a bit of time, that's what she needs, to get this Bri bloke out of her system. And once she knows there's the chance of losing me ... once she knows she's not the only one with a Bri in the background, then she might change her mind. All I've got to do is let her know. Somehow.*

The sound of the doorknocker broke into Noah's thoughts – three sharp taps followed immediately by Godfrey's voice, calling through the letterbox. Noah rushed downstairs to let him in. 'Thought you'd got lost,' he said.

'Sorry, love. Had a little visit. Olive Fitch from up the road. She popped round with some flowers for tomorrow, bless her. They look like she's had them on her windowsill for a fortnight, but it's nice of her to bother. Used to get her chops in his butcher's shop, I s'pect duck. No one else round here has done anything for him. Mind you, that's not surprising is it? Anyway Noel, how you feeling now? You look a bit brighter. I've brought you a few nibbles, look.' Godfrey folded back the white cloth that covered a plate of sausage rolls, sandwiches and plain fairy cakes.

'Didn't think it was right to ice them, not for a funeral. What d'you think Noel – these be all right?' He went into the kitchen, filled Noah's kettle then returned to the hall. ''ere duck, your phone's off the whasname ... you know, the hook. You want to put that back on.'

Noah sighed and replaced the receiver. 'Make yourself at home, won't you?' he said.

'Well, you want looking after, don't you?' Godfrey said. 'Get stuck in with that food. Then you can tell me if it'll do for tomorrow.'

Noah picked up a sausage roll. Flakes of puff pastry fell on the table as he bit into it. 'I don't know why you've made all this food,' he said. 'There'll only be you and the Matron to eat it.'

'Now Noel, don't start all that again. *You're* coming as well. It's only right and proper. We was both there when the poor old bugger kicked the do-dah. The bucket. Least we can do is make sure he gets a bit of a send off.' The telephone rang and Noah's answer machine clicked on. Both men stopped to listen. Helen's voice filtered through from the hall.

'That's your lovely Helen,' Godfrey said. 'Aren't you going to pick it up, duck?'

'Can't leave anything alone, can you?' Noah sighed and pushed past Godfrey. He stood for a second, listening to Helen's message, then picked up the phone. 'It's okay,' he said. 'I am here.'

Godfrey called from the kitchen doorway, 'Helen, love, tell him he's got to go to Joey's funeral tomorrow.'

'For Christ's sake,' said Noah, glaring at Godfrey. 'Sorry about that,' he said to Helen. 'I've had the day in bed – not felt too good. I'm all right now though. I was going to ring in, but I just didn't feel up to it, Hell.'

'Never mind, just as long as you're okay,' Helen said. 'I was getting worried. I've been ringing and ringing. I was going to come round after work if I couldn't get hold of you this time. See if you wanted me to come with you to the funeral tomorrow, but if you're not well …'

Noah slumped against the wall. He rubbed his eyes, and let his hand remain over his face, like a mask. 'Yes,' he said, 'all right. Thanks.' He held the phone out and waved it towards the kitchen, then went back to sit at the table.

Godfrey finished the conversation with Helen and then joined Noah in his kitchen. 'She's coming round at eleven, Noel. Said to let you know she'll tell them at work that you'll be back on Monday. All right, duck?' He patted Noah's shoulders as he squeezed past his chair and continued with making the tea. Noah stared at the plate of funeral food in front of him.

When Godfrey had gone, Noah took his mail off the pew. He ripped the envelopes in half, then in half again, and let the thick slices of paper fall to the floor. 'More bloody junk mail,' he said. 'Double glazing and bloody insurance companies, as usual, I suppose.' He sat down heavily on the hall pew, and cried. His spine tapped the hard shiny wood behind him.

He pushed the torn envelopes with his foot and bent to pick them up. There was black handwriting on one of the frayed sections. He parted the soft edges of the white envelope, and carefully pulled out the folded contents. He didn't recognise the looped handwriting, and scanned the words quickly for clues. The last word seemed huge and darker than the rest. Grace.

Noah inhaled a sharp, whistling breath. He fumbled for the other sections of the letter, and read rapidly, trying to hold the pieces together in his shaking hands. 'God. Oh God,' he said, as he read the letter again and again. 'She's sorry. Didn't mean to hurt me. Hopes I understand. Oh, my little angel. Course I understand, course I do. Oh, Angela, Angela.' He took the letter to the kitchen, laid it on the table, and read the page again. Then he found his reel of sticky tape in the drawer and carefully joined the pieces together. 'There,' he said, patting the paper. 'All right now, my little angel, all mended now.'

He took the letter to the telephone table. 'I'll ring her. Right now. Ring her and tell her everything's all right.' There was no telephone number under the four lines of Grace's address. Noah turned the page over, searching for a string of numbers. He read the letter again. 'She's forgotten to put it,' he said.

He dragged the Yellow Pages off his shelf, snatched at the thin pages, and found the section for florists. He rang the first local one he found. A woman told him the shop was just about to close. He banged down the receiver, shouted, "Well, fuck you then,' and dragged his finger down the column of shops until he found another one. They took his order. It would be delivered the next morning, they told him, some time between ten and eleven.

That evening Noah made some phone calls. He rang Helen to confirm arrangements for the funeral. 'You sound a lot brighter,' she said.

Noah told her he felt better. 'I'm a bit excited, actually. About tomorrow.'

'Don't say things like that. That's horrible, that is.'

'No, not that. I mean ... well, I'll tell you when I see you. Don't forget, wear something black, Hell.'

Next, he rang his Mother.

Noah could hear the surprise in her voice, his call must have caught her off guard. She sounded momentarily flustered. 'Noah … oh, is something wrong? What's the —'

Noah cut in, 'No, Mother, nothing wrong,' he said, 'I just thought we could go through the list now, this evening.'

'What do you mean, Noah. What list are you talking about?'

Noah sighed. 'Well Mother, it goes like this. Every Saturday you ring me and ask me if I've been shopping, ask me what I've bought, then you ask me if I've eaten any fruit this week and if there's any left in my fruit bowl – in case it goes off. And then you tell me what I should have bought. And then you tell me what to eat. And then you tell me what offers there are at the shop. And then you say the dog needs a walk and you have to go.'

'Well, dogs have to be taken out for exercise, Noah. Duncan can't go out on his own, can he? He's got no road sense whatsoever. And your Father never has the time to take him, so I end up doing it. Still I don't mind, it means I get a bit of —'

Again, Noah cut into his Mother's torrent of words. At first she seemed not to hear him and carried on talking about the dog. 'Yes, very interesting,' he said, 'but the point I'm making is not really about the dog. In fact it has bugger all to do with that fat oily creature.'

'Noah, don't talk about poor Duncan like that. He's a lovely old —'

'Never mind him,' Noah said, aching with impatience. 'The point I'm trying to make is that you always ring. Same time every Saturday. And you always say the same things, week after week. So I thought I'd change the routine for once. And what I'd like to know is this. What business is it of yours what I eat, when I go shopping, whether my apples have gone mouldy, or anything else for that matter?' He slapped the wall in frustration.

'Well, I don't know what's got into you today, Noah. I really don't. I always ring you; you know I do. Just to see how everything is. And you *do* let the fruit go rotten – I was saying to your Father only the other day, when we were watching the news, what a waste of good food it is with you having a big bowl of fruit every week and hardly touching it. Some of those poor little children in the hot countries could do with —'

'Go off even quicker there, wouldn't it? In the heat?'

'Noah, don't be sarcastic, you know what I mean. Now listen, I don't know what this is all about but you seem to be in one of your moods today. Is it something at work? You're not ill, are you?'

'No, there's nothing wrong with me. Well, nothing out of the ordinary anyway. Just the normal, everyday effects of being locked in the cupboard under the stairs.'

His Mother made a snorting laugh. 'What on earth are —'

Noah interrupted her again, his eyes wide with anger. 'You! You used to lock me in there. Make me sit in the dark for ages. I only remembered it the other night. Just came back to me, out of nowhere. And now, now I want to know what you've got to say about it. Actually. Because to tell you the truth, I'm pretty bloody unhappy about it.' He wiped spittle from his mouth.

There was silence at the other end of the phone.

Noah waited a while, his erratic breathing making his ribs expand and deflate rapidly. 'Well? Are you still there? Bit more difficult to talk about than decaying fruit isn't it?'

'Noah ... I ... you've got this wrong. I think you must have, well, I mean it's all such a long time ago now, isn't it? Memory can play tricks, can't it? I know I often think of things from my childhood and then I'm not sure if it happened or if it was just something I was told – some family story that gets passed on, so in the end no one really knows when it happened. Or if it ever did. I mean, you're a grown man now, perhaps you just —'

'What, imagined it? Made it up after all this time? Why would I do that, for Christ's sake? And if it's a family story, Mother, well ... you tell me, is it a family story?' Again there was a long pause, the tension between them almost audible in the fizzing silence on the line. 'Come on, Mother. This isn't like you. You usually do all the talking.' He heard his Mother draw in a sharp breath, and pictured her disapproving face, the lips a tight line, her nostrils flared and her cold eyes giving him that superior look. But when she spoke, the image altered. There was something in her voice that made him visualise her instead as smaller, less sure of herself.

'You were a difficult little boy, Noah,' she said. 'A very difficult boy. I didn't always know how to deal with you. I … it was, I did some things that perhaps I shouldn't have done. I was … we were both young and a bit, well, worried.'

'So you locked me in the fucking cupboard?' He heard his Mother protest about his language but ignored her and carried on. 'You're telling me that you were worried about your child so you put him in the cupboard under the stairs and locked him in the dark all on his own? And all these years later, all you can talk to me about is rotten bloody fruit.' He looked down at his fingers. He was holding a tuft of his own hair. 'No wonder I've got the sort of problems I have now,' he said.

'Noah, you've always had problems. You … I tried to do the best for you but I never really understood what you wanted. There weren't all these child experts in those days. Psychologists and the like. And people didn't talk so openly. Not like they do now. On the telly, in the papers and goodness knows what else. You just had to get on with things as best you could. And we always kept ourselves to ourselves. Your Father didn't like …' she trailed off, her voice faint and shaking.

That bastard, thought Noah. *He's even worse.* 'What about him?' he said. 'What little delights have you got to tell me about him? I already know he hates me, he made that clear enough at the family bloody reunion. Mind you, I've always known he hates me so don't waste time on that one. Couldn't wait to have a go, could he?'

'Noah, your Father doesn't, well, he doesn't hate you. It's just … well, he found things a bit difficult. We both did. No, your Father made sure you had a good home, went to school properly and that you had all the things you needed.'

Noah scowled. Memories of time spent with his Father were spiked with unease at the very least, and more often with fear, anxiety, humiliation. He had dreaded being alone under the silent, mocking gaze of the man. He used to search frantically through his young mind for something to say just to break the frightening silence.

Once, when his Mother had gone shopping and left Noah with his Father more than an hour had passed without his Father saying a word. Noah was at the table, drawing in a book. He liked to have his pencil very sharp, so every time after he'd drawn a few neat lines, he sharpened it to a point, placing the curled shavings on a sheet of plain paper kept specially for the purpose. His Father sat in his armchair reading the newspaper. Each time he turned the pages, he shook the paper violently, slapped the middle and cleared his throat in an irritated manner. Noah tried to guess whether he was the cause of the irritation, or if it was the newspaper. And if it was the newspaper, was it something his Father had read or the fact that he had difficulty turning the pages?

He'd wanted desperately to talk to his Father, make a joke or chat about nothing in particular just to lift the heavy blanket of silence that shrouded them. But fear prevented him from saying a word. Everything his racing mind conjured up as a possible topic he rejected, anxious that it would be wrong. Eventually his Father slapped the paper down on the floor beside his chair. Noah waited with tense shoulders for him to leave the room. But his Father stayed where he was, tapping the arms of his chair impatiently, clearing his throat. And sighing. Hard, exaggerated, annoyed sighs that left his chest with force. Noah fought for something to say, the responsibility for the prolonged silence all his, but his mind went blank.

He dared not look at his Father or even in his direction, and concentrated on his drawing so hard that it became his whole world. The rough surface of the thick cream-coloured paper so close to his face he could smell it. The sharp pencil marks – the colour of mercury. All he could see, hear and smell was the scratchy grey world of his drawing, but all he could sense was the huge, looming, presence of his Father. He *had* to say something. It was a test. That was why his Father was so annoyed, waiting and waiting for his son to come out with something useful, worthwhile, interesting, clever.

His head hurt. His chest was tight. He needed to go to the toilet. But he couldn't move until he had proved himself to his impatient Father. *He's waiting, he's getting angry, he thinks I'm stupid.*

Noah's careful drawing had turned into a chaotic scribble. His usual neat lines had disappeared underneath jagged, random zigzags scuffed over the paper. There was a frayed hole in one place where he had pressed too hard. *He's still waiting. It's been too long. I've got to say something. I've got to.* He ripped the page out of his drawing book, held it up. 'Look, Dad, look what I've drawn,' he said in a rush. The sudden movement disturbed his collection of pencil shavings. The sheet of paper they had been arranged on took flight and sailed like a small magic carpet to the floor. Coils of red-edged pencil shavings lay scattered on the floor around Noah's feet.

'Oh for God's sake.' His Father spat out the words. He stood up. 'Can't you even let me have a few minutes' shut-eye?' He held his wrist, inspected his watch, sighed. 'Where's your Mother got to?'

Noah shook his head. He was still holding out the drawing.

His Father looked at the floor next to the table. 'Look at that bloody mess down there.' He bent down and grabbed his newspaper, scrunching it in his fist. Looking at Noah, he shook his head, closed his eyes for a few seconds, then marched out of the room. As he passed the table he said, 'You bloody little weakling.'

'Noah?' His Mother's voice again. 'You're not going to talk to your Father about this are you? He … it might be best to, well, to leave things as they are. After all this time.'

'Oh, but that doesn't seem very fair, does it? Why shouldn't he have the chance to stroll down memory lane as well? I'm sure he's got a few happy stories he could add; what do you think? You know, all those fond recollections of family life in the Quince household.'

'He was a good Father to you, Noah.'

'Of course he was. All those relaxed times we spent together, the way he'd get down on the floor, join in playing with my toy cars, the dens he helped me build in the garden, the easygoing chatter between the two of us.' He slapped his palm against the wall to emphasise his words. 'No wait a minute, I think I've got that wrong – wasn't it more like the way he used to take the piss out of everything I did? Sit there criticising and mocking, raising his eyes up to the ceiling. Wasn't that more like it, Mother? And the one time I did make a den in the garden, he went mad, ripped it all down, all the deckchairs and old sheets I'd arranged so carefully - he knocked it all down. Or don't you remember that either?' He slapped the wall again and the vibrations shivered up his forearm. His hand stung.

'Look, this isn't going to do any good, Noah. All families have their ... well, their difficulties. And your Father wasn't, well he didn't know how to ... he's not a very tolerant man, Noah. You know that. But he's not a bad man. And I tried to talk to him, explain how you had to have things ... well, you were better if you could have things a certain way. But your Father didn't like the idea. He thought you should do as you were told. I didn't know how to keep you both happy. That's what it was, you see. I mean, I was caught in the middle.' She sighed. 'I'm going to have to go in a minute, Noah.'

'Got to take that bloody dog for a walk? Is he more important than —'

'No, it's just that I'm a bit upset. This has all been a bit, well, you know ...'

'And me? Don't you think I'm upset as well? Just tell me again, before you go – just so I know for sure. You did used to lock me in the cupboard under the stairs, didn't you?'

'You wouldn't eat, Noah,' she said. 'You'd go for days and days without eating a thing. I tried everything to get food inside you. But you just shut your mouth as tight as you could and that was it. I was sick with worry. You were so thin. God knows what people thought. And you wouldn't speak. I couldn't get anything out of you about what was wrong, nothing. You just, well it felt like you just shut me out. Me and your Father. You were so ... I don't know, so cut off, in your own little world. And all I wanted was to look after you. But you wouldn't let me. I didn't know what else to —'

'So you shut me in the fucking cupboard?'

'Please. Don't use that language, Noah.' There was a long pause.

Then she added, 'Yes. I did do that. I did put you in the cupboard. It was a terrible thing to do. But I was in such a state – you were screaming for hours. Every time I tried to talk to you, or if I even looked at you, you just screamed and went as stiff as a board. I got so upset, Noah. I don't think I really knew what I was doing. I just wanted you to be quiet for a little while. That was all. And then you were, when I put you … when I, you know, the cupboard. You went quiet and I … well, I got myself sorted out, calmed down. Ready to cope again. I've never really forgiven myself either, for doing such a terrible thing. I promised you when you were asleep that I'd never do it again. And I never did, Noah. But the way you went so quiet that time I did … well, the time I did put you in there … and me just leaving you like that, it, well it played on my mind. Still does.' She let out a long breath.

'But it wasn't only the once, was it, Mother? I remember it happening several times, I can see it —'

His Mother interrupted. 'That's the worst part of it, Noah. I blame myself. You used to …oh dear … you used to take yourself in there.'

Noah put his hand over his eyes. *No*, he thought. *No, don't let it be true*. But part of him knew that it was. *I don't want this to be real*. He could hear his Mother talking but couldn't take in her words. He put his forehead against the wall and turned his head from side to side. *I used to get in the fucking cupboard on my own. What sort of kid does that?* He opened the door to his own cupboard and stared at the darkness. He reached inside, switched the light on and the brightness in the cupboard made the hall seem gloomy and dim. *Perhaps they should have had a light fitted in there for me.* He tried to laugh.

'Noah, can you still hear me?'

He snapped off the cupboard light and closed the door. He was shivering. 'Well,' he said, 'nice to talk to you, Mother. But I must go now. I'm sure it's time for you to take the dog for a walk, isn't it?' As he replaced the receiver, he could hear his Mother's voice.

'Noah, wait. Noah —' He unplugged the phone.

So, the Mother-parent used to lock me in the cupboard under the stairs, he thought. *Just her little way of getting a bit of quality time to herself. Bit of a break from bringing up baby. Well, I suppose they all used to do it in those days. No need to feel bad about it, Mother, it was probably just a trend in parental skills. Like not letting babies sleep on their stomachs and that sort of thing.* He laughed, tugged at his hair. *And of course, it's done me the fucking world of good, hasn't it? Still, can't let these things get in the way, can we?*

He plugged the phone back in and rang Esther. 'Said I'd ring, didn't I?'

'I half expected you not to, if I'm honest,' she said. 'S'lovely to hear from you, Noah. I've been thinking – why don't I come round to you … now that, well, now everything's all right?'

'What? When? What for?' *No thank you very much indeed*, he thought.

'Right now, if you wanted me to. But I thought p'raps tomorrow? Or Ssaturday? Ssometime over the weekend?'

God, I only bloody rang because I said I would. Thought we'd got all this sorted out. 'Well, I'm not really feeling up to much,' he said. 'Just had some, er, some news from my Mother, and … er, I've got to go to a funeral in the morning as well. Tell you what, I'll give you another ring. That'll be after the weekend, though. Okay?'

'Oh, I'm ever so ssorry, Noah. It's not your Dad, is it? Course it's all right if you don't ring. Aaah, you poor thing – s'there anything I can do?' Esther sounded genuinely sorry.

'No, it's not my bloody Father, but fingers crossed …' he said. He inhaled, held his breath for a few seconds and then released it in a long sigh. His irritation lessened as he breathed out, gave way to a softer and more lenient feeling. Noah was touched by her kindness. He also still felt guilty. 'No, no, there's nothing you can do. But thanks. What about you – you, er, you all right?' *She hardly knows me, yet she's being so bloody nice.*

'I am now you've called, Noah. I did ssay a couple of little prayers for you to ring me. I'll ssay ssome more now, to help you through the weekend.' Her words were threaded together by a slight wheeze.

'Yes, well, anyway, got to go.' *Be easier if she just told me to piss off or something,* Noah thought. He went to bed early, still wearing his clothes, but not his bathrobe, which he hung on the back of the door. Although he had slept much of the day, he still felt tired, and soon fell into a deep and dreamless sleep. He kept Grace's letter, shiny with tape, under his pillow.

thirty

When Helen arrived, Noah was dressed and waiting. His black suit contrasted starkly with the papery whiteness of his face.

'Sure you're up to this?' Helen said. She laid her hand on his arm.

'Be all right once it's all over and done with,' he said. 'You look ... well, different.'

'Is it okay?' Helen brushed the front and sides of her dress. 'Only worn it once, to an evening do, years ago.' The dress was slightly too tight over her upper body and the flared skirt just skimmed her knees. The shiny, synthetic fabric clung to Helen's legs as she moved, which made her look as if she was wearing short black trousers. There were black and purple sequins around the neck, which had already caused a thin pink rash on her throat.

'Never mind,' Noah said. 'It's not as if there'll be anyone there to see it.'

'Very funny.'

'Anyway, don't worry about that,' he said. 'Listen, I've sent some flowers. They should get there about now. What do you think?'

'Bit of a turnaround for you, isn't it?' Helen said. 'Thought you didn't know him. Still, it's a nice thing to do – it's what you're supposed to do at funerals, isn't it?'

Noah shook his head rapidly. 'No, not for *that*, not for the funeral, I mean I've sent *her* flowers – Angela.'

'Oh, so it's all hunky dory again now, is it?' Helen peeled her dress away from her legs. Full of static electricity, it crackled and flew straight back.

'Well, I hope so,' Noah said. 'She sent me a letter. I reckon she's had second thoughts, Hell.'

'Is that what she said, in this letter?'

Noah picked a fibre off his collar. 'Not in so many words, but ...' He released the fibre and it floated in the air, a transparent thread catching the light.

'But what?' Helen said. She waved the drifting fibre to one side. It swooped, caught in the angry slipstream of her hand. 'Don't go reading things into it that aren't there, Noah. You know you'll only get disappointed.'

'But she said she was sorry for hurting me, that she never meant to upset me, and that she really liked talking to me. Anyway, it's done now, the flowers are on their way.' Noah sighed and rubbed his eyes.

'Oh, come here, you,' Helen said, as she wrapped her arms round him. They stood together, gently rocking from side to side for some minutes.

Noah felt safe, just as he had in his bed, buried under the quilt.

Helen spoke into the side of his head. 'I sometimes wonder why I bother with you, you know.' She gave a weak, muffled laugh.

'Because I give you such good advice about your clothes, perhaps?' he said.

Helen pulled away. She pretended to hit each side of his face. 'Cheeky sod,' she said. 'Come on, let's go and get Godfrey. Time's getting on.'

'Just one thing, Hell,' he said. 'You couldn't go and get my shoes for me could you? They're in the cellar. I can't wear these suede ones with a black suit.'

'What, you're not worried about who might *see* them, are you?' She laughed, but then stopped when Noah didn't join in. 'Yes, course I will. You go and get Godfrey.'

Godfrey came to his door carrying a foil-covered tray. He handed it to Noah and scurried back to his kitchen. 'There's two more of them to take Noel, and a couple of tins of cakes. That be enough, d'you think?'

'Don't know who you think'll eat all this,' Noah said. 'There's only us going.'

'Well, we don't want people going hungry, do we duck? There's his friends at the home, and the Matron. P'raps some of the other staff will come in just out of respect. I've done sandwiches, sausage rolls, a few little cheesy tarts, then there's crisps —'

Never mind the fucking crisps,' Noah said. 'You coming or what?'

'Oi, don't you take your nerves out on me, Noel. We're all on edge this morning, duck.' Godfrey stacked and balanced the tins and lumpy, silver trays, and held the pile steady with his chin. 'Right, off we go then, love.'

'You going in that?' Noah nodded at the yellow gingham apron tied over Godfrey's suit jacket.

'Oh, silly bugger, I am,' Godfrey said. ' 'ere, give us a hand, Noel, and undo me, will you? Save me putting this lot down.' Noah pushed his tray across Godfrey's worktop, making it skid against the tiled wall. He sighed and grabbed at the apron ties, pulled sharply. Godfrey toppled backwards slightly, then overcompensated to find his balance and tipped forward, breaking his fall against the edge of the cooker.

'Whoopsy daisy. You'll have us both on the floor if you're not more careful, duck.'

'Well, just stand still, then.' Noah snatched at the knot, which was now smaller and tighter. 'It's no good, I can't undo this,' he said. 'Why d'you have to do it up so bloody tightly in the first place? Come on, we've got to go. Hell can sort it out for you.'

A large maroon car was parked outside Godfrey's house. The driver was looking down at a clipboard, writing.

'Oh, Gordon bloody whasname,' said Godfrey. The minicab's here. Noel, that's our minicab. Quick, go and tell him, before he drives off.'

'All right, don't wet yourself,' Noah said. 'He's not going to drive off, is he? – he's only just got here.'

Godfrey nudged his way past Noah and hurried towards the car. 'Coo-eee,' he called. 'We're on our way.' He opened the back door of the car and laid his trays carefully on the seat. 'Be all right there, won't they?'

The driver nodded. 'Are they ready? Half ten, I've got it down for. If you want to give them a quick shout …'

'Who?' Godfrey looked up and down the street from his hunched position. Then he laughed and patted the driver's shoulder. 'No, it's us, duck. We're the ones you're picking up. I'll just go and get Helen. Won't be a tick.'

Godfrey and Noah hurried to Noah's front door. Godfrey knocked and called Helen's name at the same time. Standing beside him, Noah said, 'All right, all right, let's get inside first – we don't want the whole fucking street to hear. Take this bloody tray, can you?' He shoved the foil-covered tray into Godfrey's chest, unlocked the door and both men squeezed through together. The tray banged against the wall. There was no sign of Helen. The cellar door was open and cold air percolated into the hall.

'Hell, you down there?' Noah called from the hall.

Godfrey slapped Noah's arm. 'Course she's not, don't be so daft, duck. What would she be doing down your do-dah? Your cellar? She's probably gone upstairs to spend a whasname … a penny. No lavs at them crematoriums, is there?'

'She's looking for my black shoes down there. Actually,' Noah said. 'I asked her to. Give her another shout, will you?' The top of Helen's head came into view then, as she came up the cellar stairs. Godfrey held out his hand to her, the tray wedged against his side and caught under the stretched arc of his other arm.

'Up you come, Helen. Minicab's here, love. He's outside with his engine running.' He braced himself to take the strain as Helen heaved herself up the steep stairs. 'Look at you, all done up smart. What d'you want to go scrambling about down there for, love? And you in your nice outfit as well. I mean there's not —'

Noah interrupted from the front doorway. 'Er, excuse me,' he said. 'My cellar is perfectly clean and tidy. Actually.'

'Well you're right about that,' Helen said. 'It's more like an operating theatre than a cellar.'

'What do you mean? Why, what did you see?' Noah said. He tugged at the knot of his tie. *Please don't say you saw dead bodies coming out of the fucking walls.*

'Not his shoes, for a start, did you duck?' Godfrey held out the tray for Helen to take.

'No, not a trace,' she said. 'Looked everywhere —'

Godfrey cut in, 'That's because they're in here,' he said. 'Got them all up the other day, I did. Remember, Helen love? Puffed me out something whasname it did ... something lawful. ' He opened the hall cupboard and bent down, dragged out two pairs of shoes. 'Which ones d'you want, Noel?'

'*Black*. The black ones,' Noah said. 'I didn't know you'd been moving my shoes all over the place. And who said you could go poking about in my cupboard?'

Helen lifted the tray in front of her. The foil crackled. 'Now, now, you two. Godfrey was trying to help, and I forgot about the cupboard, I ... oh, can't we sort this out later? Shouldn't we just get ourselves in that minicab? Noah, quick, put the shoes on.'

Noah sat on the floor to change his shoes. There was a tap on the front door. It was the minicab driver. 'Sorry, ladies and gents, but if we don't make tracks sharpish, I'll have to leave you to find your own way.' He clapped his hands and rubbed his palms impatiently.

'Do beg your pardon,' said Godfrey. 'We're coming right now, aren't we?'

Noah stood up, a suede shoe on each hand. He glared at Godfrey. 'Right then,' he said, 'let's go, shall we? If you're *finally* ready.'

Helen followed the driver to the car. Black tubes of clingy fabric outlined her stout legs, as tight as a wetsuit. Godfrey offered Noah his arm.

'Just get in the car,' Noah said. 'And take that fucking apron off.'

'Oh, bugger the apron. I'll tuck it in, no one'll see. Come on, duck.'

The journey was rapid and uncomfortable. The car tilted and swayed around corners, and jerked abruptly to sickening halts, too close to other vehicles. Noah flexed himself against anticipated accidents, his legs strained with the effort of pushing hard onto imaginary brake pedals.

'I could have done without sitting next to this food,' Helen said. 'I'm not a good traveller at the best of times.' She held the door handle with one hand, and tried to steady the trays and tins with the other.

'Nearly there, love,' said Godfrey. 'When we get out, Helen, would you have a go at me pinny? Only me and Noel couldn't get it undone. If not, I'm going to have to stuff it down me whasnames … I don't want to show you two up. What with you both looking so smart.'

Helen smiled faintly and nodded. She pulled the dress away from her legs. It crackled.

Hushed, reedy music filtered into the warm, stuffy air of the crematorium chapel. Every now and then it wavered dramatically, as if a lump of chewing gum was stuck to the tape. Then it receded again, a drone in the background.

A man stood near the entrance, his head bowed. He wore a dark grey suit, too tight for him. His fat neck rolled over the collar of his white shirt and settled half way down, making an airtight seal. He held out his hand, gestured to the long, shiny wooden seats, which were all empty.

Helen, the first to enter, nodded her thanks. 'Shall we sit at the front?' she asked Noah and Godfrey, over her shoulder.

'That's for whasname … for family, isn't it, duck?' Godfrey hovered in the doorway. His gingham apron wafted slightly with the breeze from outside.

'Well, there isn't any bloody family, is there?' Noah said, also in the doorway. He beckoned at Helen with a frantic fanning gesture. 'Get this bloody thing off him, can you?' He tugged hard at the hem of Godfrey's apron. Helen tried to undo the knot but it wouldn't loosen.

'Don't want to budge, does it, love?' said Godfrey. 'Never mind, you've done your best.' He turned to face Helen and gave her hands a squeeze. 'Hang on, we'll soon get this sorted out.' He lifted the hem of his jacket and held it awkwardly under his chin. Then he tucked the apron into his trousers and smoothed the jacket down again. 'There, never know would you? Is what worries me though, duck, is where to put this food.'

'Just leave it there,' Helen said. 'We can't really do anything else with it, can we? Come on, we ought to go in.' She guided them both with her hands on their shoulders.

As they went through the door, leaving the food in the entrance lobby, Godfrey glanced back. He stopped and spoke to the man in the tight suit. 'S'cuse me, duck, will that be all right out there? Won't be in the way or anything, will it?'

The man nodded and smiled. He spoke in a whisper. 'Be fine, sir,' he said. 'Please take a seat.'

Godfrey gave the man a thumbs-up sign and hurried to join Noah and Helen, in the second row. He negotiated the narrow space carefully, his hunched, bulky shape moved sideways in a crab-like waltz. The bulge of his apron looked like a roll of fat, slipped much further down than his collar. For once, the outline of his erection was not obvious.

'Hurry up and sit down,' Noah said.

There was movement at the door. The fat man gestured with his hand again, keeping his head bowed. His neck looked redder, and vibrated slightly when he moved. The Matron appeared, walking slowly. She nodded at Godfrey then turned her attention to an elderly woman holding her arm. The two women sat at the end of the front row, nearest the door. Another lump of chewing gum distorted the music, and then the tape came to an abrupt end.

The fat man straightened himself and turned to face the entrance. Then he stepped quickly aside, and inclined his head in a deeper bow. A swish of fabric broke the silence as the vicar swept briskly into view. Behind him, four men walked carefully in time, the coffin on their shoulders. They placed it on the draped plinth next to the vicar and walked away, out of sight.

Noah clutched Helen's hand. She turned and gave him a reassuring smile, squeezed his hand, then faced the front again. The vicar talked loudly to the back of the room. He spoke quickly and with a matter-of-fact tone. Noah thought it was like an uneventful weather forecast, which he found vaguely comforting. *Glad he's not coming out with all that crap about what a wonderful person Joseph Pepper was*, he thought. *That would be a bit hard to take – Joseph Pepper, the odd-job butcher man who specialised in young boys. What could the vicar say about him? 'Dearly beloved, we are gathered here to mourn the passing of a man who devoted his life to that of slicing up others …'*

'You're cutting off my blood supply,' Helen said, leaning close to him.

Noah loosened his grip but he was agitated, and jigged his legs up and down rapidly, as if he was shivering. He saw Godfrey peering at him from the other side of Helen, but wouldn't make eye contact with him.

'*Noel*,' Godfrey whispered. 'You all right, Noel? Want a hanky, love?'

'Shush,' Helen said. She tapped Godfrey's knee and squeezed Noah's hand. 'I think it's nearly finished now.'

As her whisper faded, it was replaced by the whirring sound of the curtain being opened behind the coffin. Joseph Pepper was transported slowly backwards in his standard-issue coffin. The fake brass handles looked too shiny and new to be burned.

Noah stared intently. *Go on, burn in hell*, he thought. *The world will be better without you.* Mine *will be, anyway. Perhaps you'll leave me alone now. Stay out of my house. Out of my dreams. Just leave me alone. Go and turn to cinders. And those stinking butcher's clothes as well. Burn, you bastard. Go on, burn to a crisp. Nice and slowly. One bit at a time. All raw and bubbling. Lifting up off the bone. Then bursting into flame*. 'Done to a turn. Sizzling.' Noah stood up. '*Then* you'll have to leave me alone. Just leave me alone, leave —'

'Noah!' Helen said. 'Noah – stop it.' She shook his arm. 'What's wrong? Are you all right? Come on, let's get you outside.' She pushed Noah to the end of the long shiny bench, then walked him quickly towards the back of the chapel and across to the other side. The vicar, the Matron, the elderly woman, the man in the tight suit and Godfrey all watched in silence as Noah, a reluctant groom being dragged by his determined bride, was hauled rapidly down the side aisle and out of the door.

Godfrey struggled to get up, but toppled back down onto the bench. Apart from the swaying curtain closing over the coffin, everything was quiet. The taped music jerked back to life as Helen guided Noah through to the entrance lobby.

When Noah realised that he'd actually said some of what he'd been thinking, he felt disorientated, just like he did after a bad dream. 'Wha …?' he said.

'Sit down,' Helen said. She patted a chair in the lobby, then sat next to Noah and held his hand. 'It's all right, Noah,' she said. 'It's all over now. We'll just sit here for a while, okay?'

'I didn't mean to *say* anything,' Noah said. He shook his head to clear it, then stared straight in front of him. His face was blank. Again, he shook his head, hard. Then he stood up suddenly. 'I meant it, though,' he said. 'I bloody meant it.'

Helen stood up and tried to put her arm round him. 'Come on, Noah, calm down.'

He shrugged her arm away. 'Calm down? Would you be calm if he'd tucked all his handiwork away in *your* house? Would you be calm if he'd come lurking about in your cellar to check up on his little treasures? And if you found chopped up bodies all over the place when you were looking for something to wear?' Noah was shouting now. He lashed out, hitting a tray of food. Sausage rolls scattered to the floor, the pastry separating away from the bullets of greyish-pink filling.

The vicar left as briskly as he'd arrived. He shot an irritated glance at Noah and Helen, but did not stop to speak. Another car arrived outside, and the fat man at the door indicated with more arm movements that it was time for the next funeral group to gather.

'Don't waste any time in here, do they?' Godfrey said. 'Hardly got me seat warmed up.' He joined them in the lobby, wiping at the corner of each eye with a large white handkerchief. Then he slapped Noah's arm with the back of his hand. ' 'ere, what was all that fuss about Noel? I couldn't make out what you was on about, all that shouting and whasname … all that carrying on. That's not how you're meant to behave at a time like this, duck.'

Helen, scrambling on her hands and knees to pick up the scattered food, patted Noah's left shoe. 'He just got a bit upset, didn't you?' she said. 'This sort of thing affects everyone differently, doesn't it?'

Godfrey joined her on the floor. 'S'pose you're right, Helen love – 'spect they're used to it here, ay?' He gave Noah's ankle a shake and smiled up at him. 'Sooner we get you home the better.'

Noah stared straight ahead.

'I'm just going to have a quick word with Matron,' Godfrey said as he pulled himself up from the floor. He scuttled over to the two women. The Matron was waiting for the elderly woman to stand up.

'Lovely service, Matron, wasn't it?' he said. 'Poor old Joey …' He wiped his eyes again, and added, 'Nice of you both to come. He would of liked that, old Joey would.' He held out his hand to introduce himself to the elderly woman.

'You still at the bank, Dennis?' she said.

'This isn't Dennis, Ruby,' the Matron said. 'This is one of Joseph's friends, Mr …?'

'Godfrey, duck. But you call me what you like.' He held the old woman's hand.

'Mr Godfrey used to come and see Joseph. Remember?' the Matron said.

The old woman stared at Godfrey. Her watery grey eyes flickered. 'Joseph?' she said.

'Never mind, Ruby,' said the Matron, smiling at Godfrey. 'We've got to get you back to the car. Ready? Hold my arm.'

Godfrey took the old woman's other arm and walked slowly

out to their car. While the Matron unlocked the door, he stood with the woman's arm linked through his own and patted her hand. 'We were going to come back with you,' he said. 'I done a bit of food for everyone, but … well, young Noel's got a bit, you know, a bit histrionical.'

'Yes. Yes indeed.' The Matron glanced back at the lobby. 'Well, never mind. We weren't expecting anything after the service in any case. Ruby has an appointment for a blood test. Then we're off to buy her a new pair of slippers, aren't we Ruby?'

'P'raps you could take the food back for the old folk, then?' Godfrey said. 'Just so it don't go to waste.' He bent over to help Ruby into the car.

'Goodnight Dennis,' the old woman said. 'Don't go working too late.'

'Well, I suppose —' The Matron stopped abruptly. The doors of the waiting car opened. Three young women and an older man got out. Grief hung in the air around them. Talking was no longer possible. The Matron gave Godfrey a sharp nod, got in her car and drove away. The old woman waved. Godfrey waved back.

'Better make ourselves scarce, duck,' Godfrey said to Helen.

'Let's get this food out of the way.' Helen nodded towards the sombre group. 'The last thing they want to see when they walk in is a picnic.'

The minicab pulled into the gravelled driveway. Godfrey carried the food over. Helen checked they had cleared everything from the lobby. Noah walked in silence, his face still blank. A long, narrow strip of yellow gingham fluttered through the vent at the back of Godfrey's jacket.

'What, this lot going back again now, is it?' the driver said.

In the minicab, Godfrey and Noah argued over their destination.

'We could always head for the bloody circus,' the driver muttered.

'They weren't expecting us,' Noah said, 'otherwise they wouldn't be going off on a fucking shopping spree, would they?'

'But there's still all them others, duck,' Godfrey said. 'All them other poor old dears stuck in that place, they won't turn their noses up at a nice bit of tea, will they? A few little sausage-rolls and cakes; it'll be a real treat for them, won't it? Anyway, the poor old buggers will be missing Joey. This'll cheer them all up a bit.'

'What, a heap of squashed sausage rolls?' Noah said. 'Anyway, most of them don't even know what day it is. D'you really think they'll notice that old bast —'

Helen cut in. 'Hold on, hold on,' she said. I think the day's got to all of us – we're all upset. Perhaps it would be best if we gave the home a miss? Godfrey?'

The driver sighed. 'Once you've made up your minds, ladies and gents – we haven't got all day, you know.' He tapped his watch. 'Only at this rate, we might as well book ourselves a plot each and pay the vicar in advance.'

Godfrey blew his nose, stuffed the hanky back in his pocket. 'All right, Helen love. S'pose you're right, duck. But you'll come back to mine for a cuppa, won't you?'

'Thank Christ for that,' Noah said. He slapped the back of the driver's seat. 'Back where you picked us up, please.'

'Circus it is, then,' the driver said as he started the car.

thirty-one

' 'nother cake, Helen?' Godfrey said, holding the tin in front of her.

'Well, just one more,' she said, reaching into the tin. 'This is a lovely spread you've done. Must have taken you ages.'

'Oh, I love a bit of a session in the kitchen, don't I, Noel?'

'Apparently,' said Noah. He stood up. 'I'm going home. Get this suit off. I'll be back later.'

'Sure you're all right, Noah?' Helen said. She looked concerned. She walked to the door with him, put her hand on his shoulder. 'Wasn't *too* bad today, was it?'

'Oh, no,' he said. 'Fucking wonderful. Never had such a nice time.' He rubbed his forehead. 'Least it was quick. I'd had visions of him grabbing me by the ankle as he was lowered into some dark, gaping hole in the ground. I'm glad they cooked him instead.' Noah stared into the street. 'Perhaps he'll leave me alone now.'

'Noah?' Helen rubbed his forearm.

'I'll ... I'll be back in a bit.' He walked away, staring ahead.

Noah took off his shoes. He pressed the button on his answer machine. There was a message from Grace. He listened in a trance-like state. Her words seemed to float around him, were hard to catch and comprehend. He pressed the button again. Still, he felt that he was dreaming. He pulled off his tie, rubbed his eyes. Once more, he played the message, and tried hard to concentrate on what Grace said.

'I wanted to say thank you for the flowers,' she said. 'They're really beautiful. But you shouldn't have sent them. I didn't expect anything like this. It ... I don't know, it makes things harder.' There was a pause. Then her voice again, shakily, 'I shouldn't have got involved in any of this. I've made such a mess of things —'

Noah listened again. *Sounds like she was crying,* he thought. *I could make her feel better. If only she'd let me. I wonder ...* He dialled 1471. Grace hadn't withheld her number. *Can't believe it*, he thought, *just can't bloody believe it – this was meant to be*. He wrote the number down quickly and rang her immediately. She answered after three rings.

Noah cut in. 'Can I come and see you?' His last two words were overlapped by Grace's recorded voice. He realised he was talking to her answer machine. He put the phone down. *Not leaving messages*, he thought. *Far too risky. I'll try her again later. I'll keep on trying. I'm not giving up now.*

In his bedroom, Noah took off his suit and hung it back in the wardrobe. A faint rasping sound came from the behind the clothes. Noah shut the door hard. The wardrobe creaked with the movement. He pulled on a pair of clean, pressed jeans and a long-sleeved, charcoal grey teeshirt, and hurried out of the bedroom. He tried Grace's number and got the answer machine again. Then he returned to Godfrey and Helen.

'We've just bin talking about the funeral, duck,' Godfrey said. 'Here, have a nice little sarnie.' He held out one of the trays. He had taken off his jacket and untucked the apron, which was now spread, crumpled, over his lap. 'We thought it was all a bit quick, didn't we Helen, love?'

Noah waved away the tray of sandwiches, and sat down opposite Helen at the dining table. 'If you ask me,' he said 'they should have just dumped him in a landfill site.'

Helen kicked him under the table. 'Don't be nasty, Noah,' she said. 'I think it's sad when old people die and there's no one to send them on their way. I wouldn't like to end up like that. And I bet you wouldn't either.'

'She's right, Noel,' Godfrey said. 'We all like to think we've got somebody who'll make the effort when we kick the mop-bucket, don't we? I want more than a few quick words from the vicar before he lifts his dress up and runs off as if he's late for the London do-dah. London marathon.' Godfrey took a bite of his sausage roll, and a gulp of tea. 'At least we were there for poor old Joey.'

'We won't all end up like that though, will we?' Noah said. 'I've got no intention of being on my own when I die.'

A fleeting look passed between Helen and Godfrey.

Noah sat up straight. 'I've, er, I've just been playing my messages. Actually. You know, friends worried about me and everything. Ringing to see if I was all right —'

Helen interrupted. 'She got the flowers then, did she?'

Godfrey shoved the last piece of a sausage roll in his mouth and swallowed hard. 'What flowers?' he said. 'Who you bin sending flowers to, Noel – not that grubby girl in the café, was it?'

Noah glared at Helen. 'Thanks, Hell. I never said you could tell everyone, did I?'

Godfrey peered at Noah from his hunched position. He tapped the table in front of him. 'I'm not everyone though, am I duck? Helen only mentioned it. You know you can tell me anything.' Godfrey continued to stare at Noah, an expectant smile on his face.

'*What?*' said Noah. *For Christ's sake, it's like being in a fucking aquarium with these two sitting there gawping at me and discussing all my business about Angela,* he thought.

'Well come on, then,' Godfrey said. 'Put us out of our mystery, duck.'

Noah took a deep breath. 'Angela,' he said. 'Okay? It was Angela. And she rang to thank me. She, er, she wants me to go and see her.' He rubbed the back of his neck, settled his shoulders against the chair. 'Yes, she wants to see if we can, you know, sort things out and ... well, see how it goes.'

Godfrey reached forward and squeezed Noah's arm. 'Oh that's lovely, Noel. She's the one you were sweet on, isn't she? Oh, we're so pleased for you, aren't we Helen?'

Helen looked straight at Noah. Her face was blank. 'Of course,' she said.

Godfrey left the room to make more tea, after telling Noah and Helen to eat the remaining food.

Helen did as she was told, and began to cram small sandwiches into her mouth in quick succession. She pushed the trays towards Noah. 'Go on,' she said through a muffled mouthful, 'eat up. After all, you're going to need all your strength now, aren't you? Now the woman of your dreams has changed her mind.'

Noah pushed the tray away. 'What d'you mean? You are pleased for me, aren't you? I mean, after everything I've been through and …'

Helen peeled the paper case from a fairy cake and poked it, whole, into her mouth. She peeled another one as she ate. She smiled at Noah, and although the bulging cake distorted her face, he could still make out her sarcastic expression. When she had gulped the mouthful down, she said. 'Yes, chuffed to bits. Best thing I've heard for ages. Just what we all need, isn't it, after a funeral? Some lovely romantic news. I mean, what could be better?' Crumbs puffed into the air as she spoke. She slapped the second fairy cake into her mouth.

'Hell?' Noah stretched his hand across the table.

Helen did not put her hand out to meet his. She sat looking down at her plate, chewing rapidly.

Noah tapped his fingers lightly on the table and said her name again.

Helen looked up. Her face was tight, somehow closed. She stared at Noah with her eyebrows raised.

'Hell, why are you being like this?'

Helen slumped slightly, dropping the sandwich she'd just picked up back onto her plate. 'Oh, I don't know,' she said, then sighed. 'Take no notice. It's just, well, I just don't want you to get hurt again. You've been so upset lately – all this stuff with these women, and the other day at work, and you being worried about your house and everything. I worry about you, Noah.'

'But it'll be better this time,' he said. 'Angela, she's … well, she's special.'

'But that's part of the problem, Noah. Women aren't really like you want them to be. You get this perfect vision in your mind of how bloody wonderful everything's going to be, then it all goes wrong and you come back to earth with a great big thud – it's not good for you. No one can live up to what you want.'

'Oh, but she can. Angela can. You should see her, Hell. She's gentle and kind and soft. All she needed was a bit of time. She's been hurt. Needs looking after.'

'Don't we all?' Helen's voice was cold. 'But you're not the sort of man that —'

Noah stood up. 'What? Not the sort of man that can look after a woman? Not the sort of man women want? Not the sort of man women want any-fucking-thing to do with?'

Helen held up her palms. 'No. I didn't mean … look, all I meant was that it's one thing for women to want someone to look after them – listen to them, buy them presents and do things for them, all of that – but it's something altogether different for a women to, well, to want anything more, anything deeper than that.'

'Oh, what, you mean like sex and love and closeness and that sort of thing? Well, how come one of them can't keep her hands off me, then? How come I spent the night with her? *She* didn't want me to put shelves up, mend her car, buy her expensive presents or take her out to dinner. Nothing like that.' Noah's face was red, his lips drawn back from his teeth. 'She just wanted me to fuck her brains out. And I did. I actually did. So how do you explain that?'

'Noel!' Godfrey put the tea tray on the table. 'Don't talk like that in front of Helen. She don't want to know about your personal whasnames … carryings-on. Do you, Helen, love?' He smoothed his apron, cleared his throat. 'Shall I be Mother?' he said.

Helen stood up. She pushed the chair neatly under the table. 'Not for me, thank you,' she said to Godfrey, then laid her hand on his forearm. 'Thanks for all you've done today. But I've got to go now.' She turned her head in Noah's direction but did not look at his face. 'Bye then,' she said.

'Wait a second, duck,' Godfrey said as he scurried after Helen.

'I'll get your coat. Oh, and Helen, take some of this food home with you, love – look there's masses left. Hang on, I'll do you a whatsit … a doggie bag.'

Helen accepted obediently and kissed Godfrey's cheek.

'Don't you worry about him in there,' Godfrey said, gesturing over his shoulder. 'He says things he don't mean sometimes. You should hear what he comes out with to me. Take it all with a pinch of salt, love.'

Helen gave a tired smile and left.

Noah caught up with her when she was a short distance along the road. He tugged at her arm. 'Don't storm off,' he said.

Helen stopped walking. 'Hardly storming, am I?'

'Yes, but you're all angry and upset with me, aren't you?'

'Well, to be honest, I don't know how I feel. That's why I'm going. I just want to be on my own,' she said. The carrier bag swayed heavily against her legs.

Noah shifted his weight from foot to foot. 'I don't want you to go, though.'

Helen shrugged. 'It's always about what you want, isn't it? Not that I mind – don't think that. No one has pinned my arm up behind my back and forced me to be there for you, Noah. But it would be so nice sometimes if you could just see things from my side.'

Noah twiddled with his hair. 'What do you mean?' he said. There was a whine in his voice.

'Well, like today, for instance,' Helen said. 'I mean, I came along to support you at a funeral you didn't want to go to. And all you did was criticise and complain. You didn't really need me there at all, did you? Then on top of all that, you go and announce that you've been – well, getting up to all sorts with these women.' She searched in her pocket for a tissue. 'And all the time, you've been going on to me about how difficult it's been.' She blew her nose. Her eyes shone with tears. 'I thought, I really thought, when you sat talking to me all those times, that you … I just had no idea that all the time you were off with other women. Not, you know, like that. Not after we woke up together and you had your arms round me and … well, I suppose I couldn't help thinking …'

'It wasn't like that,' Noah said. He twisted his hair in tighter spirals 'I … well, it wasn't like you said, Hell. I only did it because Angela didn't want me. Well, I *thought* she didn't. I never even wanted to do it. That Esther woman made me. And I felt sorry for her. And —'

Helen scraped tears off her face with the soggy, scrunched-up tissue. 'I don't believe I'm hearing this, I really don't. I'm going home.'

Noah watched as Helen walked away from him. The carrier bag of leftovers rustled as it bumped against her legs. He called out, 'I did need you today. I did.'

Helen kept on walking.

Noah said, in a quiet voice, 'I did need you, Hell.'

Godfrey stood on his front door step, his arms folded. 'Coming back in, duck?'

'No. I'm going home now.'

'Don't s'pose *you'll* have a doggie bag?' Godfrey sounded tired. 'Tell you what though, Noel, you ought to take more care of Helen. Loves you to bits, she does.'

'Yeah.' Noah tapped the toe of his shoe on the pavement. 'She likes looking after me.'

'And why d'you think that is, you silly sod? You shouldn't of said what you did, Noel. About that other woman. Even if it was true, you shouldn't of said it.'

'It *is* true. Why shouldn't it be —'

'I don't want to hear about it, duck.' Godfrey swiped his apron as it billowed up towards his chest. 'That's your business, that is. All I know is that you've hurt poor Helen. Really upset her, you have.'

Noah kicked harder at the pavement. 'Well, you're right about one thing – it *is* my business. And no one asked you to stick your nose in. So just stop bloody interfering.'

'I'm only trying to be a friend, Noel. Do a little bit of mismatching for a couple of silly buggers who can't see —'

Noah interrupted. 'You don't know what you're talking about.' He turned, started walking towards his house. 'Just … just mind your own fucking business' he called over his shoulder.

thirty-two

Noah rang Grace again when he got indoors. Again, her recorded voice greeted him. He dropped the receiver heavily back into its cradle. 'Bet she's there. Just doesn't want to talk to me. I'm not giving up though, not now.' He tried the number again, but it was still the answer machine. He rang Esther instead.

The lisping sound of her voice filled him with gloom until he realised that this was also an answer machine. 'Well, well,' he said, 'even the fat one's out. One miserable little funeral and the whole bloody world disappears.'

He stalked his empty rooms, increasingly frustrated and unsettled. 'What now? What are you supposed to do after a day like today – just go home and sit in front of the fucking telly?' Noah sat down on the edge of the sofa, got up immediately, and paced in and out between the hall and the sitting room. He tensed and released his fingers; the bones clicking like knitting needles. 'I'll have a bath. Then I'll try Angela again, later on. Catch her off guard.'

He shut the bathroom door, turned on the taps, and pulled off his clothes. His foot caught in the leg of his tiny underpants and toppled him off balance. 'Fuck.' He spat out the word as he tugged at the fabric caught round his ankle. The elastic catapulted the underpants off his foot and they settled on the surface of the bath water. Noah grabbed them, slopping water on the floor. He twisted them violently until his wrists hurt. 'You fucking …' His face was purple and distorted. He plucked and snatched at the wet material, turning round on the spot, as if fighting an invisible opponent. With each hand holding a bunched fistful of the wet fabric, he wrenched as hard as he could, to tear it. The sound of snapping stitches was his only reward, as the fabric stretched but did not separate.

'Fucking, fucking bastard,' he shouted. 'Break. Rip to shreds. Come on, split open, you bastard. Die. Fucking die. Die, die, die —' Noah bit savagely at the misshapen material, locked his teeth and strained his head backwards. Nothing gave. He heard a dull squealing sound inside his head as the cotton slid through his clenched teeth. He was panting hard. 'Okay, you bastard. Okay.' He bent over and thrashed about wildly, trying to loop his foot into the strained wet fabric. Finally, he found a hold, dug his heel into the carpet and pulled upwards. His whole body shook. His face was dark and sweating. Knotted veins stood out on his head and the backs of his hands, ready to burst through his skin. He held his breath and pulled harder, the room fading to blackness around him.

Finally the material gave way, slowly, reluctantly and with hardly any sound. It parted as if in slow motion, a quiet separation away from the elastic waistband then down through the damp white material to the left leg opening. Noah let out a grunting, moaning noise and slapped the ruined garment again and again on the floor and the walls.

Eventually, exhausted, he let it fall in a ragged heap, and sank to his knees. The carpet was soggy. The bath water had spilled over the edge and soaked a large patch of the bathroom floor. He struggled to his feet and pulled the plug out. With the taps still running, Noah lay on the floor and sank into an exhausted sleep.

The sound of running water woke Noah in the early hours of the next morning. He was cold and stiff. He struggled to his feet and turned off the bath taps. He pulled towels out of the cupboard and spread them over the floor, treading on them to soak up water from the carpet. Drowsy disorientation slurred his thoughts and actions like a hangover. He could recall the events of the funeral, the strained time spent with Helen and Godfrey afterwards, and his attempts to ring Grace when he returned home. After that, everything was distant and hazy. He picked up the ragged underpants and examined them as if for the first time. 'What the fuck?'

Quickly, he bunched up the fabric into a ball and stuffed it deep into his laundry basket, then covered it with wet towels from the floor. His head ached, his body shivered. 'Think I must be coming down with something.' He trod into more towels, to mop up as much water as he could from the dark circle of carpet around the bath. 'That's what it is, I'm not well. Fever or something. It's made me all confused. I probably collapsed and laid here all night.'

Noah's whole body shook. He draped a large dry towel around his shoulders and clutched it to his chest. 'That'll have to do for now,' he said, dropping another towel to the floor and treading lightly on the edge. He shuffled out of the bathroom, and went to bed. He was asleep within seconds, the towel still wrapped around his cold, shaking frame.

thirty-three

Noah woke abruptly from his short sleep. The house was silent. He looked at his bedside clock. It was still early – only half-past seven. *Thought it was later than that.* He stared into the morning gloom of his bedroom, trying to hear what had woken him. He felt weak and tired. His head ached. 'Nothing there,' he said as he struggled to clear his mind, which felt foggy and slow. 'He won't be back again, not now they've burnt him.' His voice sounded thin and rasping. He was aware of a sour tang in his mouth as he spoke. 'Christ, I feel rough,' he said. 'Probably eaten something dodgy. One of those sausage fucking rolls, I bet. Wouldn't be surprised if some of the ones on the floor found their way back to Godfrey's bloody tea party.'

He dragged himself to the edge of the bed and sat up. The towel bunched into uncomfortable ridges as he moved. Noah tugged at it and dropped it on the floor, puzzled but too exhausted to wonder what it was doing in his bed. He pulled on his bathrobe and crept stiffly downstairs, holding his head as still as possible to keep the thudding pain at bay.

In the kitchen, he poured himself a glass of water and swallowed two paracetamol tablets. They lodged in his dry throat, bitter and chalky, and would not shift with more water. Noah could taste the acrid substance as the tablets dissolved. Grimacing, he walked to the telephone and dialled Grace's number. The ringing tone thrummed in his ear for a long while, hurting his head.

Then Grace spoke. 'Hello,' she said. 'Hello?'

Noah was too surprised to answer straight away. 'Oh, you're there,' he said after hesitating, his voice cracked and faded. He cleared his throat, choking back the rising taste of the tablets. 'Sorry, I was just going to put the phone down. It's me, Noah. I, er, I wondered if I could come and see you?'

'Oh,' Grace said. 'Noah. I thought it was – well, I didn't know what to think – you know, when the phone goes at a funny time ... Anyway, are you all right?'

'Yes. Well, no not really.' Noah swallowed hard, making a dry click 'But it's going to be okay now. You won't need to rush off again. Not now he's gone.'

'I'm not sure ... What d'you mean? Are you sure you're all right?'

Noah held the phone away as he was overtaken by a coughing fit. He hunched himself over, the effort of coughing making his head scream with pain. Thick paracetamol paste coated his tongue. He could hear Grace's voice, distant and tinny, coming from the receiver, but couldn't make out what she said. He waited for the cough to ease and took a deep breath. He couldn't think clearly.

'Sorry about that,' he said. 'Where was I?'

'Look, Noah,' she said, 'you really don't sound too well. Perhaps you should go and rest or something.'

Noah shook his head. Searing ribbons of light darted behind his eyes. 'No,' he said, 'I need to come and see you. I need to talk to you. Actually.'

'Why don't we talk another time?' Grace said. 'You're obviously not well. And it *is* quite early. You could give me a ring later on if you like ... if you feel better. And thank you for the flowers. They were —'

Noah cut in. 'No. I need to come and see you. I'm not giving up. You were *here*. You came here. And now he's gone ... now they've burnt him, you'll come back, I know you will. I'm not giving up, Angela, not now.'

'Look,' her voice had gone cold, 'my name is not Angela. I don't know what you're talking about. And I don't want to know. I have no idea who Angela is, but I do know it's not me. Now will you please leave me alone?'

'Oh, I'm sorry, I'm sorry. I didn't mean ... it's what I call you. I ...' The line was dead. Noah coughed weakly, then said into the purring receiver, 'I'm not giving up. Not now.'

Hunched and shivering, Noah rocked himself backwards and forwards on the spot. He touched the telephone with his shaking fingers, and smiled. 'It'll be all right when I see her,' he said. 'I'll explain it all. Everything. She'll understand then. I'll sit on the floor and talk. Just like she did.' He wrapped the bathrobe tighter around him, and hugged himself to try and get warm. He felt slightly dizzy and leaned against the wall to keep his balance. After a few moments, he lifted the receiver and rang Esther.

''lo?' Her voice transmitted a smile.

'Thought I'd tell you everything's going to be all right now,' he said.

'*Noah*. I've been thinking about you ... wondering how you are,' Esther said. 'You okay? How did it go?'

'Well, not too good. Actually. It's my fault, I keep saying the name wrong.'

'Aaah, I'm ssure nobody noticed, though,' she said. 'Was it a big funeral?'

'No, not that, not the funeral,' Noah said. 'Oh, that's the least of my worries. All over and forgotten, that is. Done and dusted. Actually. Well, dusty ... definitely dusty.' *He won't be coming back now he's been burnt to a cinder.*

'Ssorry?' Esther said.

'Dust,' he said, 'that's what he is now. You know ... ashes to ashes, dust to dust.'

'But —'

Noah interrupted. He started to talk but was convulsed by another coughing fit. Finally, he managed to splutter, 'I wasn't talking about the funeral.'

'Oh,' Esther paused, then added, 'but what you said, about the dust and ashes. I thought —'

'Never mind all that,' he interrupted again. 'The thing is, all I did was say the wrong name. That's not the end of the world, is it? Anyone can make a mistake, can't they?' He rocked himself gently, his shoulders hitting the wall.

'You're not still worried about that are you, you ssilly old thing?' Esther said. 'Like you explained to me, Noah, that was just a mistake.'

'What, could *you* forget something like that then?' Noah rubbed his neck. His throat felt swollen and gritty, his eyes watered from the coughing.

Esther laughed. 'Not worth letting it sstand in the way, is it?' she said. 'Not now we've got it all cleared up and everything.'

'No, that's just what I think. See, if I can just get that across —' His words disappeared into another rasping cough. 'I think the best way to sort it out is face to face … explain the whole thing properly.' Noah glanced at the cupboard. *And I'll do something about that as well,* he thought.

'All right, then,' Esther said. 'You come round anytime you like Noah. I'll make us ssome breakfast, shall I?'

Noah shook his head furiously, and mouthed to himself, *'What?'* He tried to retrace their conversation to work out how Esther had got to this point. His mind was muddled and he felt too exhausted to think straight. *She probably just wants to help*, he thought. *She's the type. Like Hell. They all want to help me get the woman I love.* He wiped the corner of his mouth with the back of his hand and transferred a milky smear of saliva onto his bathrobe.

'Noah? You sstill there?' Esther said.

Noah nodded. He stared ahead, his eyes fixed but not focused. Esther's voice was clear, and very close. It seemed to come from inside him, while his own thoughts felt like speech, external and exposed, for anyone to hear. His reply formed inside his head. He could almost see it throbbing in time with his headache, a dull red pulse. *Look after me. Look after me.*

'Hello? Are you there, Noah?' Esther said again. 'Can you hear me? There's nothing thiss end. Noah? Hello. Hello?'

Her words vibrated in Noah's head, each one setting off a series of piercing lights behind his eyes. *Why can't you listen?* he thought. *Just look after me. Just help me get Angela back.* He coughed again, more feebly this time, renewing the bitter taste in his mouth. He wanted to spit. Instead, he made a puffing, breathy, smacking sound, like a baby refusing a spoonful of food. 'Beauhhhh.'

Esther responded immediately, 'Oh, you *are* there. I thought there was ssomething wrong with the phone. I couldn't hear you. You all right Noah? That ssounds like a nasty cough you've got there. What about if I come over? Bring you some medicine; make sure you've got everything you need? You don't want to be coming out if you're not feeling well, do you? Go on, let me come and ssee you. Mmmm? Noah? What d'you think?'

Noah nodded. *Yes, yes, just shut up*, he thought. But she carried on, her lisping voice like a snake hissing through his head.

'Sshall I, then?' she said. 'You'll have to tell me how to get there. Noah? Won't take me long. Just give me a tick to get ready. All I need is a quick sshower. I'll pop in the chemists on the way; get you some nice bits and pieces to make you all better. Aaah. Noah? I'll come then. Sshall I? Noah? *Noah?*'

'Yes,' He shouted the word, making his head sing with pain. 'Yes. I said yes. How many more times?' He gave Esther directions, stumbling over familiar road names and struggling to remember which turnings to take. Then he told her that he was going to lie down, or he thought he told her. She was still talking inside his head, but Noah could no longer follow what she said, so he put the phone down, and shuffled into the sitting room.

He let himself collapse onto the sofa, bent himself awkwardly into a foetal position and closed his eyes. He was too cold to sleep, and his head was pounding harder than ever, but lying down did at least ease the dizzy feeling. He thought of the earlier conversation with Grace. He smiled. *She knows I call her Angela. My little angel. She'll get used to it. Suits her more than Grace anyway. Once she realises how special it is, she'll love it. Be my secret name for her. She'll let me call her Angela all the time. Angela my angel.*

He swallowed hard to stifle threatening tears. Unconsciously, he ground his teeth in time with the thudding beat of his headache. 'Angela my angel, Angela my angel,' he repeated to himself. It became a single line, one nonsense word, flickering like a faulty neon sign, its thin green glow leaving an eerie image imprinted on his mind.

thirty-four

Noah heard the car door slam. He pushed himself up on his elbow; saw Esther tottering along his path. She carried a large bunch of flowers, a carrier bag and a teddy bear, which was wedged under her left arm. She looked flushed but, as ever, was smiling broadly. Noah heaved himself off the sofa and went to the door before she could knock. She looked startled when he opened it, and tried to pat her chest to show her breathless surprise, but the flowers got in the way. Noah held his bathrobe tight against his neck, and stood aside, gesturing for her to come in.

'You do look pale, you poor thing. How are you feeling now?' she asked.

Noah didn't answer. He stood shivering in the hall, clutching at his robe. *They're a bit fucking bright*, he thought, squinting at the gaudy pink and yellow flowers.

Esther thrust them at him. 'These are to cheer you up,' she said. The collar of stiff cellophane circling the flowers quivered near his face.

Gingerly, he took the bouquet and held it at a distance. He nodded. 'Yes,' he said, 'not sure if I've got a vase that'll suit these.'

Esther raised her shoulders in a smile. With a sudden movement, she swung the carrier bag forward with one hand and held out the teddy with the other. 'For you,' she said. 'A few bits and pieces to make you feel better.'

Noah took the bag with his fingertips, glanced quickly inside, then put it on the floor beside him. He let his eyes skim past the teddy bear, and stared at Esther. She smiled again and danced the bear up and down in her hand. It was dressed in a navy blue tee shirt with *Get Well* printed across the front in glittery silver lettering.

'Teddy wants a cuddle,' she said, and shuffled closer to Noah. He backed away. The carrier bag rustled as he brushed it with his shin.

'Put it in there for now,' he said, indicating the bag with a nod.

'Aaah, come on, you take him,' she said. 'Look, he wants to be with you.' She waved the toy from side to side. 'Everyone needs a teddy to look after them when they're not well —'

'I said put it in there.' Noah snatched the bear and shoved it in the bag. He walked into the sitting room and wedged himself into one end of the sofa, then crossed his arms.

Esther followed him with the carrier bag. She put it down next to his feet and sat on the opposite sofa. She still smiled, but with an edge of nervousness. She twitched her fingers on the arm of the sofa, and looked round the room. Pink blotches erupted on her cheeks and neck. 'Sssory Noah, not in the mood, are you? You must be really under the weather, you poor thing. What can I get you? How about a nice cup of tea? A bit of ssomething to eat?'

'Nothing. I don't want anything. Actually,' he said. Then added, 'But thank you anyway.'

'Well, what about some medicine then?' she said. 'Have a look at what I've got you. Must be ssomething in there to make you feel better. Is it your head? Your tummy? Have you got a ssore throat? I didn't like the ssound of that cough – you have to be careful, you know. Come on, let's find you some nice cough mixture.' She reached across and pulled the carrier bag towards her, then lifted out several small packages and laid them on the floor between herself and Noah. There were painkillers, throat pastilles, vapour rub, powders for a cold, cough syrup, and a bottle of Lucozade. Then she tugged at something larger. 'Look, I've even brought you a hot water bottle in case you were cold.' Finally, she pulled out the teddy and propped it against her chair. 'Mustn't forget him, must we? Now, sshall I go and fill the hotty for you?'

'No,' Noah said. He shivered. 'Well, I suppose I am a bit cold. Actually.' Staring at nothing, he continued inside his head. *I don't care what you do, just get on with it. Then help me sort things out with Angela.*

'Aaah, you're all muddled up, aren't you?' Esther said. 'Let's get you nice and warm, give you ssome medicine, then perhaps you can have a little doze.' She gathered up the packets and bottles and took them to the kitchen.

Noah could hear her banging cupboard doors and drawers. *Clumsy cow*, he thought, and pulled a face at the teddy. He inhaled ready to call out for her not to break anything, but was seized by a violent bout of coughing. It made his ribs ache and his chest feel tight. His throat was raw. The coughing sapped his remaining energy, and he slumped back against the sofa, eyes watering and his head screaming with pain. He closed his eyes against the light.

When he opened them again, Godfrey was hunched in front of him. His apron draped low, hiding his trousers, so that he appeared to be wearing a long pink skirt. His face was screwed up as he peered closely at Noah.

'Oh no,' Noah said. 'Not you. How did you get in? You didn't knock.' His voice croaked.

'You was busy coughing your guts up, duck, otherwise you'd of heard me knocking. Anyway, your young lady let me in. I saw her arrive earlier and thought it was Helen, so I popped round to say you know, to say hello. Then off I go calling her Helen as soon as she opens the door, only it's not Helen, is it?' Godfrey lowered his voice in an exaggerated whisper. 'Is this the one?'

'What one?' Noah said.

'You know, Noel, your special one. What did you call her? Your little do-dah ... your little fairy, wasn't it?'

'*Angel.* She's an angel,' Noah said. 'You're the fucking fairy —'

Esther came back into the room carrying the hot water bottle, cough mixture and a spoon. Glugging sounds came from the red rubber bottle as she bent over Noah to tuck it against his chest.

He gripped the slurping bottle, holding it like a shield. Warmth penetrated through his bathrobe, and a strong smell of rubber radiated around him.

'Well, someone likes playing whasnames ... playing nurses, don't they?' Godfrey said. He sat next to Noah. 'What's up with you, duck? You didn't sound too clever, hacking away like that. You going down with something?'

Noah shrugged. He let his head fall forward and rested his chin lightly on the rubber bottle stopper.

Godfrey bent to try and look at him but Noah stared at his knees. 'S'pose he told you he wasn't well on the phone, did he duck?' Godfrey said to Esther. 'Got you all the way over here on a Saturday morning, to come and look after him, did he?'

Esther smiled. She was shaking the bottle of medicine. 'I don't mind. S'no trouble, I —'

Godfrey interrupted, 'Only there's no need, see. I usually take care of him. I know what he likes and what he don't. And anyway it's nicer, isn't it duck? You know, what with him not being well ... nicer for him to have a man doing things for him. You just leave him to me, love. You go off and do a bit of shopping or something. He'll be all right with me.'

Esther shook the medicine bottle harder. 'S'all right, really. I came specially, didn't I Noah?'

Godfrey edged closer to Noah on the sofa and patted his knee. 'Very kind of you it is as well, duck,' he said to Esther, 'but he don't really want you seeing him like this, does he?'

'No,' she said and a short silence followed her firm announcement. She continued quickly with a fluttery laugh, 'No, it's fine, really. We'll be perfectly all right. I've got him lots of nice things to make him better, and —'

Godfrey interrupted her again. 'He's very pacific about what he'll take and what he won't. You don't want to go giving him all sorts. I know you're his whasname... you know, his little angel and everything, but —'

Noah raised a hand, then let it flop back against the water bottle. 'Can you two stop bloody talking about me as if I wasn't here?' His voice was fractured.

'Beg your pardon, Noel. Thought you'd nodded off, love. I was only saying to your whasname ... your angel friend here that you won't want her seeing you in a state like this. Will you. Ay?'

Noah pushed himself to the edge of the sofa, still holding the rubber bottle. 'She's *not* my angel,' he said. 'She's ... this is Esther.' He rocked backwards and forwards, stared at the floor and muttered to himself, 'I've got to go and tell her. It's just what I call her, that's all. She'll understand, if I go and tell her ...' His voice trailed away.

'You're not going nowhere, you're not.' Godfrey put his hand on Noah's back.

Esther shook the bottle of medicine furiously. She squatted in front of Noah. 'Here you are, Noah, take some of this.' She twisted the top, straining to make it turn. Her face glowed.

Godfrey made circular rubbing movements on Noah's back, like he was winding a baby. 'Don't want it, do you Noel?' he said.

Esther held her breath and forced the bottle top again, pushing against her breasts with her white-knuckled fists. She panted then started twisting again. 'The other night I was Angela,' she said. 'Today I'm Helen. And now I'm *not* an angel.' She struggled with the bottle. 'I don't understand any of it.'

Noah continued to rock, his gaze fixed on the carpet.

Esther huffed deeply. 'Who's Helen?' she said. 'And why do you keep calling me different names? Who are these other women? And what about —' Her wrist suddenly gave, the lid came off in her hand, and she lunged forward as she lost her balance, toppling into Noah. Lapping sounds came from the hot water bottle. Esther laughed, her breasts squashed against Noah's knees. 'Whoops,' she said, and raised her shoulders in a huge, stupid grin.

Noah still rocked to and fro, but did not speak. Rigid veins throbbed on his forehead.

'Oi, you be careful now,' Godfrey said. 'You'll do him a whasname, you will. A misprint. Throwing yourself all over him like that.'

'S'all right,' she said, giggling. 'Noah doesn't mind, do you?' She patted Noah's leg. 'Aaah, he's all tired, aren't you? Come on, have some medicine, then you can get a bit of ssleep.' She held out the spoon and tipped the bottle. Her tongue protruded from the corner of her mouth as she concentrated.

Noah's body lurched forward, gripped by a spasm of coughing.

As he fought to take in breath, his body buckled in the middle and his head jutted forward, knocking the spoon, the bottle and its glutinous contents out of Esther's hands.

'Ah. Nnn —' Esther flapped her hands frantically to try and catch the bottle. She slapped against Godfrey's hands as he joined in. 'Quick, quick,' she said. The slow motion spillage took a matter of seconds, and they all watched as the cough syrup rolled itself onto Noah's bathrobe.

'Clumsy cow,' Noah said. 'Look what you've done.' He stood up, the medicine dripped off the bottom of his robe and landed in thick splatters on his feet and the carpet.

Esther snatched at the robe's hem, lifting it to stop the dripping. 'Oh Noah, I'm ever sso ssorry. Oh dear, look, let me hold this up and we can stop the worst of it getting on the carpet. You need to take if off. Quick.'

Noah yanked at the place she was holding. His fingers slid on the sticky liquid. He glared down at her. 'Let go. Just let fucking go.' His voice was hoarse and cold.

Godfrey pulled off his apron and wiped at the glistening brown spillage. 'He don't mean it,' he said to Esther, 'but he don't want you going near his do-dah. His ... you know. You should of listened duck. You should of let me look after him.'

Noah pushed Godfrey away. 'You can fuck off as well,' he said. 'Both of you. Leave me alone. Just go away, go on, get out.'

'But Noah, you're not well —' Esther started to say. She was crying.

Godfrey cut in. 'Come on, Noelly. You need a hand, duck. Just to get all this mess cleared up and everything. Want me to run you a bath?'

Noah made a grunting, moaning sound. He stared maniacally around the room, his fists clenched tight. He inhaled deeply, then let out a long wailing sound, 'Nnnnnnnnnoooooooooooo ...'

'All right, all right,' Godfrey said. 'You mustn't go getting yourself all wound up like that, duck. We'll go, won't we Helen? I mean, er ... whasname. We'll go, ay?'

Esther nodded. Large tears slid down her cheeks. 'I'm sssorry, Noah, I'm really ssorry. Will you be all right? Shall I ring you later? Tomorrow perhaps – or in a day or two? Sso ssorry.'

Noah stood perfectly still. He snapped his fingers. They slipped silently instead of clicking impatiently.

thirty-five

Noah took off the bathrobe and gathered it into a ball. He grabbed Godfrey's apron off the floor, shoved it into the blue towelling bundle, and carried the heap into the kitchen. 'Why should *I* fucking wash it?' he screamed, and walked back into the hall. He opened the cupboard and threw the sticky clothes inside. When he tried to slam the door, it thudded softly against the belt of his robe. Noah ripped the door open again and kicked at the tangled pile. 'Bastard,' he said. His voice had almost gone. Fragments of words came out as he tried in vain to shout. '...'king ...'stard.'

He kicked harder and harder. He could hear bones and tendons in his leg click as he thrust it out again and again. Sharp, fluorescent pain burned upwards from his right foot as his toes smashed into the doorframe. His other leg buckled and Noah fell to the floor. He let out a high-pitched humming sound from the back of his throat, as if he'd forgotten the words to some tuneless song. Naked and trembling, he sat on the hall floor, cradling his foot.

Twisted, looping thoughts made him feel light-headed. Somehow, he felt detached from the pain in his foot. Numbness rubberised his body while his mind simmered and flashed with images and snatches of conversation. Momentary glimpses of Esther, sitting on top of him; his hand above Angela's head; the coffin sliding backwards; Godfrey asking him if he wanted more cake; the red light on his answer machine flicking on and off – all this whirled inside his head for an unregistered period of time.

Then, as if a switch had been flicked, his mind cleared. Noah knew exactly what to do. 'Right,' he said, pushing himself up off the floor, paying no attention to the throbbing tenderness in his foot, or his pounding head. 'I said I wouldn't give up. And I won't.' He made it to the top of the stairs without stopping, dressed himself quickly, pulled Grace's letter from under his pillow, and went back downstairs. 'Now, have I got everything?' He patted his pockets. 'Wallet.' He said. 'Where's my wallet?'

In the sitting room, Noah lifted cushions and moved books. He ignored the Velcro noises his socks made on the sticky patches of carpet. Turning round on the spot, he checked the room for his wallet, looking in the same places two or three times. Then he noticed the teddy bear. 'You still here?' he said, and picked it up. With his face stretched into a taut smile, Noah pulled the teddy's arms off. The body fell to the floor, the empty sleeves flopping at its sides. Noah opened the glass door of the pendulum clock on the back wall, and placed the arms inside, beside the large brass key. When he closed the door, he smiled at his reflection.

He patted his pockets again. The wallet made a flat, square shape, its button pressed out a circle in the denim of his back pocket. 'Hah.' Noah slid the wallet free, 'There all the time.' Automatically, he opened it, closed it straight away and shoved it firmly back in his pocket. 'Right then,' he said as he put his shoes on, leaving the laces undone on his swollen foot. Smears of sticky cough mixture transferred to everything he touched. He shrugged his jacket on, slipped the letter in his pocket, closed the front door quietly and walked to his car.

As he manoeuvred the car out of its tight space at the kerb, Noah laughed loudly. 'On my way now. Not giving up now.' He stretched to see his reflection in the rear view mirror, and laughed again. 'Whoo, wait till she sees me standing on her doorstep. What a surprise. No more messing about. No more playing games with bloody phone messages. Oh no, not any more, thank you very much indeed. Now it's time for some action. Actually.' He slapped out a fast drum-roll with his palms against the steering wheel. 'And I'm on my way.'

Snatching regular glimpses of his reflection in the mirror, Noah drove towards the outskirts of town. After four or five miles, he pulled over and stopped the car. 'Where the fuck am I?' he said and checked Grace's letter for her address. He scrambled through his glove compartment for a local map, and searched for her street. The map was unused, given free with petrol, months ago. Adverts for shops, taxi firms, builders and hairdressers were printed round the edge.

Noah left brown smudges and fingerprints on the glossy, ink-scented paper, like an erratic trail of footsteps leading through the streets. Finally, he found Grace's street and set off again. 'Won't be long now, Angela,' he said, his face fixed in a grin. Every few minutes he snatched the map off the passenger seat and spread it roughly on his lap, glancing at it to try and get his bearings. At the same time, he tried to concentrate on the unfamiliar roundabouts, traffic lights and road signs ahead of him. After he'd passed the same pub three times, he pulled into a side road and looked more carefully at the map. 'Okay, he said, 'this is where I am, and that …' he dragged his sticky index finger across the paper, '… is where I want to be. So, if I go down here, along there, and … no wait a minute, that bit's one way.' He sighed and started again, tracing different roads to join up the distance between him and Grace. Finally, he folded the area he needed into a rectangle and held it in his left hand as he drove. But he immediately got lost again.

'Not funny any more,' he said, and stopped the car next to a newsagents shop. A woman rushed along the pavement with a miniature dog. It looked like a guinea pig; long, wavy fur sticking out at all angles. When Noah wound down the car window, the dog stopped pulling on its lead and barked up at him. It growled, showed its tiny teeth, and jumped frantically up and down, trying to reach Noah. It yapped a piercing, gruff little noise without pausing. The sound vibrated in time with Noah's headache. He tried to shout above the barking, but the woman didn't hear him, and with an indulgent smile at the dog, she pulled its lead and rushed on her way.

A teenage boy who had just come out of the newsagents, wandered towards Noah's car. He pushed a bicycle with one hand, and held a sports magazine with the other. Noah got as far as saying, 'Excuse me, you don't know where —' when the boy got on his bicycle and rode away. Noah stuck his middle finger up, and with a twisting action, waved the boy on his way. *Doesn't bother me*, he thought, *I'll still find it. Won't give up now.* He looked at the map again, then noticed someone else coming out of the newsagents.

Noah got out of his car and walked quickly over to the young woman. She was trying to steer a pushchair through the door, which she held open with her foot. Her straggly hair hung in her face. When she looked up at Noah, he was reminded of the dog, and half expected her to growl at him. Instead she simply stared. From the pushchair, a young child stared too.

'Wondered if you could tell me how to get to ...' He looked at the letter. 'Griffin Road?'

The young woman narrowed her eyes in thought and looked into the distance. Then she clicked into life. 'Yep, got it. Now, hang on ... yeah, what you need to do is —' She described the route, slicing through the air with curving hand movements, all the time leaning away from Noah.

Noah repeated what she had told him, thanked her, and left her to negotiate the shop door on her own. As he walked to his car, he heard the child say, 'Mummy, I don't like that man. He makes me frightened, Mummy.'

Noah talked himself through the short journey. Each time he came to a landmark, he began chanting the next one the woman had told him to look for.

'Now, petrol station on the left, petrol station, petrol station ... ah, *petrol station*. There it is. Almost there now. Mini-roundabout, past the telephone box, and ... there we are. Griffin Road. Made it!' He parked the car and for a few seconds, he sat beating the palms of his hands together in a frenzied burst of applause.

He found Grace's house easily, a short distance from where he'd parked. He rang the bell and listened, trying to hear movements inside. His features were set in a rigid grin.

The door opened without any warning sounds from inside. Grace drew in a sharp breath. She froze, eyes wide, one hand raised halfway to her face.

'Said I needed to see you,' Noah said.

'I ...' Grace shuddered. She put her hand up to her head, where she had a white towel, wrapped like a turban. She wore a long, white dressing gown. It was thick and fluffy, and looked like snow before it's been walked on. 'I'm not dressed,' she said.

'That's okay. I mean, I don't mind.' Noah coughed and shifted his weight from side to side. 'You didn't know what time I'd get here, did you?'

'I didn't know you were coming at all, actually,' Grace said, her voice cold. 'I think that would be nearer the truth, don't you?' She edged behind the door and held it in front of her. A narrow strip of white dressing gown remained visible.

'Yes, I'm sorry, but I really do need to talk to you. I —'

Grace interrupted him. 'Like I just said, I'm not dressed.'

'It doesn't matter, honestly —'

'It matters to *me*,' she said. 'I think you'd better go.'

'No, please, just listen,' Noah said. 'Don't send me away. You know what it's like ... I mean you know what it's like to be hurt. You know how it keeps going round and round in your head, over and over, so you can't think about anything else. Don't tell me to go, please. I only want to talk to you. We talked before, we —'

'Hush, keep your voice down,' she said. A faint smile touched her face. She added, 'What will the neighbours think?'

Noah clapped his hand to his face, then mouthed an apology.

Grace smiled again, briefly.

'What if I go away and come back in an hour, give you time to get dressed and everything?' He felt the blood pounding at his temples. He was smiling so hard, his skin felt as if it might split and release his ecstatic, grinning skull.

'Well, I don't really know ...' Grace said.

'Please,' he said. 'What harm can it do? I just want to talk to you, I need to explain, I can't leave things like this.'

Grace said nothing. She looked at the ground. The ice-cream swirl of towel on her head tilted towards Noah.

'I'm not giving up, you know. I won't go away.' He forced a laugh, tried to sound like he was joking. 'I'll camp on your doorstep. You'll get sick of seeing me.' His voice started to rise again.

'Shh.' Grace waved her hand for him to be quiet. She sighed deeply, then slumped her shoulders. 'All right. But not for long. *Really*, not for long. I have things to do.'

'An hour,' he said. 'I'll be back in an hour.' He stepped towards the front door. It clicked shut. He went back to his car with a bouncing stride, despite the sharp pain in his foot and the dull thud of his persistent headache. This constant discomfort had become oddly comforting, and intermittently, he provoked the pain by grinding his teeth or bunching up his toes. 'Right,' he said as he got in his car, 'let's go and find a flower shop.'

thirty-six

He headed back to the petrol station. Black rubber buckets, filled with garish flowers, were lined up in front of the forecourt shop. Noah scooped up one bouquet after another, until his arms were full. Water dripped from the stems onto his jeans and shoes. He took the crackling armful of flowers to the checkout and laid them on the counter. The bored-looking young man made no comment. He simply counted the bunches of flowers – seven – and told Noah how much they cost.

'Can you wrap them?' Noah asked.

'Already wrapped, int they?' The young man shook the stiff transparent paper.

'Yes, but haven't you got some …' Noah held his arms apart, '… you know, some sheets of wrapping paper? To put round the whole lot.'

'We don't do that.' The young man sniffed and wiped his nose with the back of his hand. He held the same hand out for Noah's money. Noah placed it on the counter.

Outside the shop, he stopped to gather the separate bunches tighter together so they would be more manageable to carry. They slipped against each other. He dropped one bunch and as he bent to pick it up, another began to slide from his grip. *Fuck's sake*, he thought. *There won't be any bloody petals left on them at this rate.* He noticed the row of black buckets. *I'll have one of those. If they can't be bothered to supply wrapping paper, they've only got themselves to blame.* He dumped the flowers in the end bucket, carried it quickly to his car and, looking round to see if anyone was watching, tipped the small amount of water on the ground. *Let's get out of here*, he thought as he shoved the bucket and flowers in the passenger door and slammed it shut. As he drove off, he shouted, 'Next time, get some fucking wrapping paper.'

The car was filled with the bitter smell of chrysanthemums. There was an undertone of something else, a stagnant, pond-water sort of smell. Noah drove half-way to Grace's house, pulled into a quiet cul-de-sac of bungalows, and lifted the flowers off the passenger seat. Each bouquet consisted of a mixture of blooms and colours. Spindly pink and red carnations, floppy yellow and rust-coloured chrysanthemums, and sprigs of tired foliage with yellowing, waterlogged stems. A sickly red rose hid in the centre of each arrangement.

Noah poked and rustled through the heap of flowers. 'They're crap,' he said. 'I can't give her these.' He looked at his watch. 'Don't want to be late getting back though. Or get lost again. What if I just —' He took the flowers out of their wavy-edged wrappers, kneeled on his seat, and leaned over to lay them along the back seat. He sorted them into piles of matching colours – all the yellows in one pile, the reds in another and the sickly mauve and faded pink ones in yet another. 'These bloody brown ones look like they've been dead for weeks,' he said, grouping the russet-coloured chrysanthemums together. 'Just have to do for now, I suppose.'

He re-wrapped the new arrangements, leaving out several stems that had no flower heads, and held a bunch at arms length, turning it to check his efforts. 'That's a bit better. Not that they're anywhere near good enough for Angela. I'll get her some special ones next time, from a proper florist, white and delicate, with ribbon. Or a great big bunch of red roses —'

He was motionless for a few seconds, lost in thought. Then, grabbing the red bunch that contained the roses, he twisted himself back in his seat and pushed the flowers between his knees to hold them steady.

'This,' he said, 'is more like it. Much more fucking like it.' He ripped the roses out and tossed the remaining red flowers from that bunch into the passenger foot-well. Then he plucked the limp petals. 'She loves me, she loves me not, she loves me —' The front of the car was scattered with rose petals.

Noah parked outside Grace's house and waited. There were twenty minutes to go. He watched her windows. The top left one. The top right one. The downstairs window, the front door, then up again to the top windows. It was a hypnotic vigil. Noah barely blinked. At times he thought he caught a glimpse of movement, but when he stared harder he couldn't be sure if he had imagined it. The only time he looked away was to check his watch. 'I'll be in there with you soon, Angela,' he said. He coughed hard, and banged his throbbing head against the car window, still watching Grace's house. Two minutes before the hour was up, he got out of his car and gathered up the flowers. Balancing them in the crook of one arm, he bent back inside the car and picked up a folded carrier bag from the passenger seat. He pushed it carefully into his jeans pocket and locked the car.

Grace opened the door straight away. She was dressed and her dry hair was shiny. Her eyes widened when she saw Noah holding the flowers, but her face showed no other expression. 'You didn't need … I mean, it really wasn't necessary —'

Noah interrupted. 'No, but I wanted to,' he said. 'They're not exactly wonderful, I didn't know where to go for decent ones, but, well, just as a way of saying sorry.'

'Look, you'd better come in.' She moved to one side.

Noah smelled her newly-washed hair as he stepped into the light hallway. He waited for her to close the door, then followed, limping slightly, to a small sitting room with neutral coloured walls and furnishings.

'Well, sit down,' Grace said. 'I'll go and find a vase for these.' She rubbed her fingers together, 'There's something sticky …' She started to back out of the room, holding the armful of flowers awkwardly in front of her.

Noah stepped quickly towards her. 'Hang on,' he said as he reached out to touch her. 'They can wait.'

Grace stiffened, clutched the flowers tighter to her body. Her shoulder knocked against the doorframe.

'Steady,' Noah said, 'I didn't mean to make you jump.'

Grace said nothing, just gave a small nod.

'Why don't you sit down for a minute?' Noah said. He was standing very close to her. 'I said I wouldn't keep you long, and I won't.'

Grace looked at him over the flowers and made a face to show she was trapped.

Noah stepped away, but watched her closely as she laid the flowers on a pine chest next to an armchair. Once she had sat down, he seated himself on the plump cream sofa opposite.

Grace seemed nervous. She shifted her gaze often, looking around the room as if it were unfamiliar to her.

She's probably trying not to look at me, just a bit shy, Noah thought. *She's still gorgeous though.* 'It's probably best if I just say this, you know, directly,' he said. 'Better than going all round the houses.' He took a deep breath. 'The thing is, I had to come and see you. I can't stop thinking about you. I know I got your name wrong but —'

Grace leaned forward. She said, 'It's not just that. It's ...'

Noah quickly filled the space she left. 'You see, it's really important that you understand. There isn't anyone else. I'm not really getting your name wrong at all. It's you — Angela is *you*.' He sat back slightly, relieved.

'I haven't got a clue what you mean,' she said. 'My name is not Angela. I've got a name of my own. It's Grace. It's Grace now and it always has been. Maybe you're mixing me up with someone else? Perhaps I remind you of someone? Perhaps you've just got a bad memory for names. I don't know. All I do know is that I am *not* Angela. Okay?' Her face was white and pinched. She looked angry.

'No,' Noah said, 'look, all I mean is that I've called you Angela since we first talked. I think of you as Angela. I say it without even realising, because ... well, because that's who you are ... in a way.' He watched as she twisted her hands in her lap.

'It might be best if we just forget all about it,' she said. '*I* know who I am. If you want to think of me as someone else, that's up to you. I don't want to keep going over it.' She stood up. 'Now ...' she shrugged her shoulders to finish the conversation. She looked determined but uneasy.

Noah caught hold of her left wrist. 'I don't think of you as someone else,' he said. 'It's *you* I'm thinking of. *All the time.* Actually. Angela this and Angela that. I wonder what Angela's doing now? Can't you see? I'm in love with you. *You*, not someone else.' His voice cracked.

'Please, don't. Just don't.' She pulled her hand away and rubbed the wrist. 'Oh, more sticky ... it's on you as well ...' she sighed. 'I'm really sorry things haven't worked out the way you hoped. I should never have come to the park that day. Shouldn't have got involved in anything like this. I'm sorry.'

Noah shook his head. The movement made him feel dizzy. 'No,' he said. 'No, don't say that. That day in the park was one of the best things that's ever happened to me. And when you came back to mine ... you talked and talked. And I stroked your hair. You don't *really* believe that shouldn't have happened, do you?' He tried to take her hand again, but she moved away sharply.

'This is all, well, it's just got out of hand,' she said. 'I've explained and apologised about coming back to your house. I was in a state. I shouldn't have done it, any of it. Now, I don't like this, I don't like it at all. I just want you to go.' She was shaking.

Noah sat down. He put his head in his hands and rocked backwards and forwards a few times, then held his hands in front of him, palms open. 'But I *love* you,' he said. 'You can't just send me away. I'm in love with you.'

'You don't know me,' Grace said. 'You can't —'

Noah cut in, his hands waving now. 'I know enough. I love you. That's all there is to it.'

Still standing, Grace folded her arms tightly across her chest.

When she spoke again, her voice was kind, but she repeated the same things, apologising to Noah for getting involved, saying that she hadn't meant to hurt him.

Noah interpreted her words inside his head, and smiled to himself as things began to make sense. *She's struggling with this,* he thought. *She didn't expect this to happen. Now she feels guilty. All that moping about for months over that fucking Brian bloke, now she's gone and fallen head over heels in love with me, and she's trying to deny it. It's obvious.* He stood up, put his hands on her shoulders, and stretched to hold himself as tall as possible.

'It's all right,' he said, gently rubbing her upper arms. 'I understand how difficult this is for you.'

Grace stiffened and leaned away from him. She smiled, a stiff twitching of her mouth, then she looked away quickly. 'Do you?' she said.

'Of course I do,' Noah said. 'All this has caught you off guard. It'll take time. You're still making big adjustments, aren't you?' He continued to rub her arms and shoulders, in a light and friendly way.

She held herself rigid. 'I'm glad you understand. I thought ... well, never mind. It's just good that we've got things sorted out.' She shrugged free and moved quickly away, hugging herself where Noah's hands had been. 'I'll go and get that vase —' She stood still, rubbing harder at her sleeves. 'This sticky stuff is everywhere. What ...?' she held her hands to her nose. 'What is it?'

Noah wiped his hands on his jeans, picking up more stickiness. 'Sorry, I forgot about that,' he said. 'Don't worry, it's only cough syrup.'

'I *thought* I recognised that smell,' Grace said. 'I er ... I'll go and do the flowers.' She scraped her hands hard against each other, then lifted the bouquets, trying to hold them with her fingertips.

Noah watched her leave the room, then sighed deeply and let his shoulders slump. His head was banging now, a harsh drumming sensation nearer to sound than pain. His foot felt too big. It was hot and soft like a baked apple, the skin stretched tight over the puffy flesh. Grinning hard, he ignored his pains and called out to Grace, 'Would you like a hand?'

'No thanks. I've nearly done now,' she called back from her kitchen.

Noah patted his pocket. It rustled. He looked round the room, taking in the neat, calm atmosphere. *Just how I imagined it*, he thought, *all pale and relaxing*. His hand went back to his hip and he rubbed the bulging pocket again. Grace came in with two vases of flowers. She looked at his hand, diverted her eyes away immediately, and busied herself with placing the vases.

Noah coughed and clasped his hands together. 'You've made them look really nice, much better than they were.' He nodded at the flowers. 'There's not a lot of choice at petrol stations, is there? Anyway, I didn't know what sort of flowers you like.'

Grace brushed her hair away from her face in a matter-of-fact way. 'These are fine. Thanks.' She looked at her watch. 'I'm really going to have to make a move. It's just that …'

'Don't worry. I'm off now,' Noah said. He jangled his car keys and smiled. 'You wouldn't mind if I er, just popped up to use your bathroom, would you?'

'No, of course, it's …' She moved to the doorway and pointed upstairs, '… just on the left, there.'

'Right,' said Noah. 'Thanks. Won't be a tick.' He made his way upstairs.

'Your shoelace is undone,' she called after him.

'Yes,' he said.

In Grace's bathroom, Noah locked the door and leaned against it. He prised the carrier bag slowly out of his pocket. 'Sshhhhh,' he said to himself in a whisper as the bag unfolded with a crackling noise. In the silence of the white bathroom, the sound seemed loud and echoing.

He knelt on the floor, his right leg held out awkwardly to take pressure off his foot. Carefully, he tipped the bag upside down and gave it a little shake. The rose petals fell out in a damp clump. *Shit*, he mouthed. He rolled the carrier bag into a ball and crammed it back in his pocket, then poked the heap of bruised red petals. Some of them separated and lay on the white carpet, limp and torn. 'Look more like used fucking plasters than rose petals,' he said, 'she'll think I've cut myself.' He stirred the pile with his fingers, making more petals come loose. A sour smell tainted the air. 'Right,' he whispered to himself, 'better get a move on. She'll wonder what I'm doing up here.'

He scattered small clusters of petals around the bathroom, on the floor, in the gleaming white bath, along the windowsill, and inside the pocket of Grace's white dressing gown, which hung on the back of the door. Then he flushed the toilet and ran the hot tap for a few seconds.

He opened the door noisily and coughed. As he was about to make his way back downstairs, he noticed an open door along the landing. *Bet that's her bedroom*, he thought. He called downstairs, 'Must do this shoelace up before I come down, in case I trip over it.' His voice sounded false and high-pitched. Grace came to the bottom of the stairs and looked up at him.

'Oh. Right,' she said.

Noah stood and looked back at her, then he moved as if to sit on the top stair. He waited until Grace disappeared out of sight, then he straightened himself and went back into the bathroom. He grabbed a handful of petals off the carpet and rushed to Grace's bedroom. He drew in a sharp breath as he entered the room. A huge brass bed, draped in white cotton took up most of the space. *Oh, I can't wait to be in there with her*, he thought. Then he pulled back the white quilt, opened his hand and let the rose petals fall onto the clean cotton sheet. Some stuck to his fingers, and he scraped them off, crushing them even more. His hands were stained. Colour bled onto the sheet. He tugged the quilt back in place. 'Right, let's get out of here,' he said to himself, and hurried back downstairs.

Grace sat on the edge of the pine chest. She looked up as Noah came back into the room, and gave a tight smile.

'Okay then, I'll let you get on,' he said. 'It was lovely to see you. Thank you for letting me explain.'

'Oh, well …' Her voice trailed away. She looked at the floor.

'It *will* all work out,' he said. 'You'll see.' He wanted to kiss her. *No*, he thought, *not this time*. He turned and walked towards the front door. Grace followed to let him out. 'Your lace is undone again,' she said.

thirty-seven

Noah was so excited on the drive home that he had to stop the car for a while. He pulled into a lay-by. 'Yes!' he shouted. 'Yes, yes, yes.' He banged his fist several times on the passenger seat, laughing and stamping his good foot. The car rocked. He watched two strutting magpies on the dusty, litter-strewn patch of grass that separated his car from the road. 'Two for joy,' he said, and wound down the window. 'Two for fucking joy.' The magpies jumped slightly, then continued their proprietorial search. Deep, iridescent greens and blues glinted in the blackness of their wing feathers. 'You're like a pair of bent coppers, you two,' Noah called to the birds. 'All done up in your uniforms, but crooked as conmen.' He laughed. The magpies ignored him. 'You know what, though? I don't give a fuck. There's two of you, that's what counts. No more of that "one for sorrow" stuff, thank you very much indeed. What we've got ourselves here is very definitely two for joy. Me and Angela. If that isn't two for joy, I don't know what is.'

He let his arm hang over the open window and banged his hand against the outside of the door. The magpies hopped away, towards a bin, began tugging at the overspilling rubbish. Noah raised his voice, 'Don't walk away when I'm talking to you.' His harsh laugh erupted into a cough. 'You haven't heard the best bit yet. *Rose petals*. That's what I've just delivered to the woman I love. Actual red rose petals. Now, Chief Inspector Fucking Magpie, is that romantic or what?' He made a questioning gesture with his hand. 'I mean, how many men are going to do something like that? And how many women dream of it happening, hmmm?' He jerked his head quickly from side to side, rubbing the back of his neck. His head, neck and shoulders felt as if they had fused together. Electric currents of pain shot through his contracted muscles. 'You think about it. What woman is going to find real rose petals scattered in her bed and *not* fall madly in love?'

I can just imagine it, he thought. *First she'll find the ones in her bathroom. She'll think how lovely they are. They'll have had time to unfold by then. Be like little red hearts all over the floor. She'll get down on her hands and knees and pick them up, every last one. I bet she'll keep them, in a special little box or something.*

The birds were stabbing at cartons and balls of screwed-up paper. Noah put his hands either side of his head and pressed hard. He could feel the pounding thud of his pulse. He felt vaguely sick, but pushed the sensation away and forced a tight smile to his face. 'But that's not all,' he called to the birds again. 'Oh no. Later on, when she goes to bed – what do you think she'll find?' He ripped a strip of paper off the map, rolled it into a ball and threw it at the magpies. They lifted off the ground, settled again immediately and carried on vandalising the contents of the litter-bin. 'You listening to me?' Noah shouted. 'I said what do you think she'll find? More rose petals, that's what. And do you know what? She'll be so happy I bet she'll cry. But the main thing, the really important thing, is that everything will fall into place. She'll realise she loves me. It will hit her like a ton of bricks.' He jerked his head. 'She'll get straight in her car and drive round to mine.' He stared into space for a while, his mouth stretched by a faint smile, his watery eyes blank and unblinking.

Eventually Noah snapped out of his meditation, and started the engine. The magpies took no notice as he drove past. He wound the car window up as he shouted at them. 'Two for jo-oy.' The birds ignored him.

thirty-eight

Before he went home, Noah drove to the local supermarket. Inside, the effort of pushing the trolley made him feel dizzy and he stopped frequently to rest, leaning on the cold metal handle. He couldn't concentrate. His mind kept wandering to his image of Angela finding the rose petals. *More roses*, he thought, *must get her some more*, and steered his way to the flowers. He chose a large bunch of deep crimson roses, with tight velvety buds and long, thornless stems. He stood them in the corner of his trolley, then made his way to the shelves of toiletries.

Got to get rid of the smell of this cough mixture, he thought. He stared at the rows of shower gel and deodorant, all of them in black, blue or silver containers. He took two of each colour. They rolled against each other as he moved through the store. Next, he went to the wine aisle and chose three bottles of champagne. *Wonder what sort of things she likes to eat?* The chinking bottles and rattling cans in his trolley distracted him briefly, but then the sounds receded. The bustling noise of the supermarket ebbed away, and Noah drifted along the colourful corridors with his thoughts turned inward. He touched the roses with his fingers and smiled. *I'll have these waiting for her when she comes to mine*, he thought.

A disembodied voice made a muffled announcement. Noah could not make out the words, but thought vaguely that the message was for him. He stopped and listened as the indistinct boom was repeated.

'What did she say?' he said to himself. He pulled a loaf of bread from the shelf, put it in his trolley and carried on, his head on one side to catch any further messages. Sounds seemed distant. He could hear the squeaking wheels of his trolley, a child crying, faint music, and the voices of other shoppers, but all of it was remote, as if from the far end of a tunnel. Then another announcement. Noah strained to understand the words, but the voice seemed to be talking through a wad of cotton wool. He was no longer sure if it was male or female. But he was certain now that the message was for him. He headed for the nearest checkout.

'What did they say?' he said.

'Sorry?' said the large, friendly-looking woman. She had jet-black hair with a white parting where a quarter-inch of roots showed through.

'That message just now,' Noah said. 'It might be important. I didn't catch it.'

'Tell you the truth, dear, neither did I,' the woman said. 'You switch off after a while. Probably today's special. Or the reduced stuff in aisle three.'

Noah looked around, but there was no one else to ask. 'No,' he said, 'it was definitely for me. It might be about Angela. I need to find out.'

The woman frowned. 'You all right, dear? Want me to call someone?' She continued to speak, but Noah could not hear the words.

He watched her mouth moving for a few seconds. Then he dragged the trolley away, between the high walls of tins, jars and packets. He tipped biscuits, crackers, cakes and boxes of chocolates in with the rest of his shopping. All the time he was listening for another announcement, but there were no more.

At the checkout, he stood in a dream while a different woman, with pencilled eyebrows, swiped his purchases and sent them down the conveyer belt. Every third or fourth item, she paused to look at Noah. She had an expression of surprise from her eyebrows being drawn too high. Her face also showed distaste. Eventually, she said, 'There's no-one to pack this lot, if that's what you're waiting for.'

Noah shook himself and limped to the end of the belt. He tried to put things into carrier bags but his hands were slow and clumsy, so he transferred everything back into the trolley. He paid the woman.

She asked him several questions but he could not grasp what she was saying, so he just shook his head in response. She gave up in the end and finished the transaction in silence. Her thin lips made a straight line, contrasting with her arched eyebrows.

In the car park, Noah stood muttering to himself as he tried to remember where he had parked his car. 'Where did I put the bloody thing?' he said. People glanced at him as they manoeuvred round him, their unruly trolleys heaped high with food. Noah wandered up and down, lost in thought. His foot hurt. His head pulsed with pain. *I just want to get home*, he thought. *Get home and wait for my angel.* When he spotted his car, tears of relief filled his eyes and he limped towards it as fast as he could, his key held ready to unlock the door. Aching to sit down, Noah almost fell into the driver's seat and sat with his eyes closed for a while. Then he rubbed his forehead, turned the ignition key and pulled out of his parking space. His trolley of shopping stood abandoned at the edge of the car park.

thirty-nine

Godfrey came out to greet Noah when he arrived home. 'Wondered where you'd got to, duck. I've bin keeping an eye out to catch you. Your Mum came round earlier.'

'What?' Noah scowled at Godfrey. He wanted to be indoors on his own.

'Well, I thought you'd want to know, duck. She said she was sorry to miss you, but she had to get on. "Tell him I'm ever so sorry," she said, Noel.'

'You spoke to her?' Noah said. 'Can't you keep your bloody nose out of anything?'

'Only being neighbourly, Noel. I did offer her a cuppa, but she had to rush off. Seemed a bit down in the dumps she did, if you ask me, love. I 'spect she worries about you, ay?' Godfrey folded his arms across his chest. 'You look tired, duck,' he said. He wore a plain white apron, the corner of a duster poking out of the pocket. 'Why don't you come round for a bit?'

'No,' Noah said. 'All I want to do is get inside and have a sit down. On my own.'

'Suit yourself love. I'm here if you need anything, don't forget. How's your cough? You had me worried earlier, getting yourself in a state like that.'

Noah clenched his hands tightly. His keys dug into his palm. 'I wasn't in a state,' he said. 'I was just fed up with people interfering, that's all.'

'Well, I know what you mean, duck. That Esme girl ... a bit pushy, weren't she? I told her you wouldn't like her making a whasname ... a fuss and everything —'

Noah coughed as he tried to interrupt. He held up his hand to stop

Godfrey. 'Look, I don't want to talk about it. Anyway, everything's going to be all right after today. Now, I've got to get some shopping put away and get myself ready.' He turned to go inside.

'Want a hand with your bags, love?' Godfrey said. 'And what's up with your leg? You're walking with a whasname ... a limp.'

Noah continued to move towards his front door, ignoring Godfrey. He put the key in the lock, pushed the door open and almost collapsed inside. Godfrey caught him under one arm and helped him to the pew. 'You sit there a minute, Noel. You're worn out, aren't you? Completely knackered. Good job your Mum didn't see you like this, ay? Now, you sit there for a bit, and I'll go and get your shopping out the car.' He held out his hand for Noah's keys. 'Then you can get settled down, put your feet up and re ... recouperfy.'

Reluctantly, Noah handed over the keys. His limbs felt floppy with tiredness. He stared after Godfrey as he went through the door, and didn't move. *Angela*, he thought, *Angela, everything will work out. I'm just a bit tired, that's all.* He wept softly, barely aware of the tears on his dry face.

Godfrey came rushing back. 'I've bin right through your boot, duck. There's no shopping nowhere in that car.'

Noah tried to heave himself off the pew, but the walls swayed in front of him and he sat back down, exhausted. 'You haven't looked properly,' he said. 'There's champagne and shower gel and everything in there.'

'No there's not, love,' Godfrey said. 'All I could find was some dead flowers on the floor, and a bucket.'

Noah held onto the arm of the pew to try and stop the spinning motion behind his eyes. 'You're sticking your bloody nose in again, aren't you?' he said.

'What you on about now, duck?' Godfrey pulled the duster out of his pocket and patted his forehead with it. Yellow fluff stuck to his hair.

'*You*. You've taken it, haven't you?' Noah coughed weakly.

'Come on, Noel,' said Godfrey. 'Come and sit on your nice comfy sofa. You've got yourself in a right old whasname ... picadilly, haven't you?' He guided Noah to the sitting room and sat him gently on the sofa. '*I'm* looking after you this time. We'll soon get you back on your feet and right as fourpence.'

'What about the things for Angela?' Noah said. 'I chose it all specially. She'll be round later.' Noah rubbed his eyes. 'I –'

Godfrey ran his hand over Noah's hair, then rubbed his fingers against his thumb. 'Dear oh dear,' he said, 'you've got that linctus do-dah all in your hair, duck. You do need looking after, don't you?'

Noah dragged his hand heavily across his scalp, a grimace on his face. 'But what about my shopping?'

'Tell you what, love,' Godfrey said. 'I'll take you shopping later on, when you're feeling better. How's that? Ay? But for now, I'm going to run you a nice hot bath. Get you out of those sticky old clothes.'

'I've already been shopping,' Noah said. 'I told you …'

Godfrey shook the duster, folded it and put it back in his apron pocket. 'P'raps you meant to go, love. I do things like that all the time. I get halfway up the stairs and then forget what I'm going up for. *And* you're tired, Noel, that doesn't help. You've had a lot on your plate in the last few weeks, haven't you? What with all them women, then poor old Joey popping off like that. Not surprising you're a bit forgetful, is it duck?' He walked towards the door. 'I'll run that bath.'

Noah said nothing. He leaned to one side and pulled his legs up onto the sofa, then lay staring towards the window. *I'll just wait till he goes*, he thought. *Then I'll get everything ready*. He could hear the sound of gushing water and Godfrey singing an unidentifiable song. *Interfering bastard*, he thought, and then fell into a light doze.

A string of saliva connected Noah's face to the cushion when Godfrey shook him awake. He allowed Godfrey to take his weight and almost lift him off the sofa.

'Up you come, duck,' Godfrey said, as he pushed his arm around Noah's waist.

Noah's feet dragged as the two men made their way to the stairs, and he leaned against Godfrey without saying a word. Carefully,

Godfrey managed to get Noah up the stairs by standing close behind him, bending Noah's legs to take each step. By the time they got to the top, Godfrey was panting and his face was shiny with sweat. 'Phew,' he said. 'Wouldn't fancy that after a full English breakfast. Now, here we are, a nice hot bath. You can have a good old soak'.

Noah stood in the bathroom doorway, swaying slightly. His face was white, his eyes sunken in dark hollows. 'I don't want that butcher to come back,' he said in a faint voice.

'You what, Noel? You still on about that shopping? Never mind that now. Come on, in the bath. Mind that bit of floor there though,' he pointed, 'it's all wet down there.'

Noah stood looking at the foaming bath water. He ached all over, and felt immensely tired. When he turned and saw Godfrey standing beside him he was surprised, and strained hard to understand what Godfrey was saying. His legs trembled and buckled, he sank halfway to the floor.

Godfrey caught him again. 'Whoops, up you come, duck.' Godfrey propped Noah against the wall, raised his arms and pulled his top over his head. 'Right, that's that one,' he said, still supporting Noah with his arm and shoulder. 'Now, let's have them sticky old jeans off.' He started to unzip Noah's jeans.

'No.' Noah put his hand over Godfrey's. He had no strength.

Godfrey straightened his hunched body and looked at Noah. 'It's all right, duck. All boys together now, aren't we? Not like that chubby friend of yours catching sight of your whasname, is it? Come on, let's pop these off and we can have you in them nice suds. Warm you up, that will.'

Noah gave in, too tired to argue. He stared straight ahead as Godfrey pulled the jeans down his legs, and stepped out one foot at a time, balancing himself by holding onto Godfrey's back.

Suddenly Godfrey gave a loud gasp.

Noah cupped his hands over his genitals.

'Gordon whatsit, Noel. Look at the state of your foot. It's black as your do-dah ... your hat. What on earth you done, duck?'

Noah looked down at his bruised foot. The skin looked puffed and shiny, and was mottled purple and blue. It seemed to darken as he watched. Now his shoe was off, the swelling increased and his foot grew to twice its normal size. He inspected it in a detached way. If it hadn't been so painful, he would have thought it had nothing to do with him.

Godfrey rolled up the sleeves of his shirt, got down on his knees and examined the foot more closely. 'No wonder you forgot to go shopping, duck. Your poor foot's come up like a whasname ... like a balloon. Don't know what you've gone and done to it, Noel, but you can't go walking round on that.'

Noah could feel Godfrey's breath on his swollen skin. He flinched as Godfrey moved to stand up.

'Don't you worry, duck, I won't touch it,' Godfrey said. He stood up and guided Noah gently to the bath. Noah hobbled, using the heel of his right foot. He sat on the edge of the bath. Godfrey swung his legs slowly over the side and into the water, while Noah clung to Godfrey's shirt. Finally, Noah felt the bubbling water surround him with warmth, and his tense muscles began to relax. He closed his eyes and rested his head against the cool enamel of the bath. The beating thud of his pulse thrummed in his head and his foot, the rest of his body seemed to melt in the water. He moaned softly.

'That's right, duck, you let yourself go. Make you feel a lot better, this will.' Godfrey held his duster under the cold tap of the basin, then wrung it out. 'Here, give me that foot.' He knelt beside the bath and held his hand over the side. 'Let's see what we can do to get the swelling down.' He laughed and patted his apron. 'Oh, listen to me, not that *I'm* much of an expert, ay duck?'

Noah lifted his right leg to the surface; his pointed knee broke through the suds.

Godfrey scooped his hand underneath Noah's stringy calf and cradled the leg. With his other hand, he laid the cold yellow duster across Noah's foot. It felt cool and soothing.

'Hope that's clean,' Noah said. His voice was filled with relief.

'Cheeky bugger, course it is,' said Godfrey. He shuffled himself from side to side. 'Tell you what though, Noel, I'm getting me knees all whasnamed down here ... all soaked to the skin. You bin splashing in the bath, or what?'

Noah didn't reply. He tried to remember why the carpet was wet, but nothing came to him. He let his thoughts wander. Every so often, Godfrey ran the duster under the cold tap again, then returned it, cool and damp, to ease the throbbing foot.

Suddenly, Noah heard the telephone ringing. He jolted upright, taking the duster under the water with his foot. 'That'll be her,' he said. His eyes were wide and startled. 'I've got to get that.'

'Hold your horses, Noel,' Godfrey said. 'You can't go nowhere, you can't. Not in your condition.'

Noah pulled himself more upright. The fine hairs on his arms were swept backwards, flat against his skin. His elbows were pale blue. He struggled to get himself up, but the effort was too much for him. He slid back down into the water. 'You get it then,' he said. 'Quick. Don't let her ring off.'

Godfrey looked puzzled. He didn't move.

'Well, go on for Christ's sake' Noah said. 'Get a fucking move on.' The duster floated over his thighs.

Godfrey grunted as he pushed himself up from the floor, and hurried to the top of the stairs. 'Gordon bloody thingamajig, I'll give meself a coronet, at this rate,' he said.

Noah listened to the ringing telephone, willing Godfrey to reach it in time. *Hurry up and answer it*, he thought. The ringing continued. *Oh, hold on Angela, please hold on*. He shouted after Godfrey, 'And don't you go saying anything, will you?' He could hear the thump of Godfrey's feet going down the stairs, and then his muffled voice. He strained to listen but it was impossible to make out what was being said. After a while he heard Godfrey laughing. Then there was more muffled talking followed by another, longer laugh. *Come on*, thought Noah, *stop pissing about. Just get up here and tell me what she said. Don't want him making stupid conversation with Angela, or asking her loads of bloody questions*. He clenched his hands under the water, making the yellow duster ripple and curve under the bath foam. It looked like a large fried egg, with the yolk broken.

'Co-ee, I'm on me way back up, Noel.' Godfrey stomped heavily up the stairs and appeared, red-faced, in the doorway.

'Well?' Noah said, 'what did she say?'

Godfrey lifted his apron and wiped his sweaty face. A rounded lump bulged in his trousers. He took a deep breath. 'How d'you know it was her?' he said.

'Just fucking tell me what she said, will you?' Noah's face was twisted.

'Give us a chance, duck. Let me get me breath back.' He paused, breathing hard. 'Phew! Now – she said she hopes you feel better and would you like her to come round to see you or do you want to wait a couple of days? Then we had a bit of a laugh, Noel, because I told her about me wet knees and your sticky trousers and —'

Noah hit the water with the palm of his hand. Bits of foam flew upwards, landing on his face and shoulders. 'You mean you told Angela you were giving me a fucking bath?'

Godfrey laughed and brushed his apron flat. 'It weren't no Angela, duck. It was Helen.'

Noah let out a long sigh and slid deeper into the water, until froth circled his neck, like a fur collar. 'Hell,' he said quietly.

'She's a lovely girl, that one,' Godfrey said. 'Why don't we get you out of there, get some nice clean clothes on, then you can give her a little whasname ... a little tinkle, tell her to pop round?' Godfrey stood with his hands on his hips. Splashes had soaked into his apron, like watermarks in white paper. The knees of his trousers were dark and wet from the floor. His face was still flushed. He bent forward and caught the duster, wrung it in the basin. 'Noel?'

Noah stared back for a few seconds. 'You look a right bloody mess,' he said.

'Oi, you, you're not no oil whasname ... no oil painting yourself. Look like one of them birds, laying there like that. You know, one of them whasname birds. A voucher.'

Noah sneered. 'You going to give me a hand getting out of here or what?'

Godfrey pushed his sleeves up higher. He reached into the bath for the plug. The water swirled and gurgled away, while he helped Noah get out of the bath. He wrapped a large towel round his shivering frame, then supported him as he limped to his bedroom.

Noah sat on the end of his bed. He felt slightly dizzy from the effort of walking, but his foot was less painful now, and his headache had receded to a dull thrum.

'Shall I help you get your clothes on, Noel?'

'I think I can manage to dress myself,' he said. 'Actually.' He flapped his hand at Godfrey. 'Once I've got a bit of privacy, that is.'

'Oh pardon me, duck. Just thought you could do with me, you know pulling you up and tucking you in. But I'll go and give the bath a swish round. Let you get on with it.'

Noah dragged on a pair of loose jogging trousers that his Mother had bought him years ago. They were for doing odd jobs around the house, she'd told him, but Noah had tucked them at the back of a drawer. He had only worn them once before, in the garden. *Look like a fucking Sunday morning shopper*, he thought. But the light material felt comfortable. He eased a sweatshirt over his head and walked out onto the landing.

Godfrey came out of the bathroom, a towel flung over one shoulder. Without speaking, he went down the first few stairs, then turned to look back up at Noah, his hands held out. Together, they made careful progress down the stairs. Godfrey led Noah to the sofa, drew up a footstool, and lifted his leg onto it gently. Then he scurried away to the kitchen to make tea.

Noah sat still, pleased that the ordeal of the bath was over, and surprised at how much better he felt. *Not long now*, he thought, *I'll just let him fuss about a bit more, then he can bugger off and I'll be ready for Angela*. He plucked at the fabric of his navy blue trousers. *Get these off before she comes round though, that's for sure*.

'Noel, d'you fancy a bit of something to eat now?' Godfrey called from the kitchen. 'Or shall we wait till Helen gets here?' Noah didn't answer and after a while Godfrey returned to the sitting room. 'I said did you want —'

Noah stopped him by saying, 'I heard what you said. Who said anything about Hell coming round?'

'Well, I thought, you know, because she rang, I just thought it'd be nice if … I'll give her a quick ring now, shall I?' Godfrey turned to leave the room.

'No,' Noah said. 'If I want to invite anyone round, I'll do it myself. Actually.' He angled his foot from side to side on the stool.

'But Noel, she'd love to come and see how you are. She really cares about you, you know duck. Let her come round for a couple of hours, ay? Be a chance for you two to make up … you know, after the funeral and all that, won't it?'

Noah glared at Godfrey, shaking his head. 'I said no. I'm too tired to have people round.' He forced a yawn. 'I could do with some time on my own now. Actually. Have a sleep, like you suggested.'

'All right then, duck, if that's what you need. I'll just sit over here and keep an eye on you while you have a little doze. Want me to get you a nice blanket, keep your feet warm?'

'No.' Noah said it harshly. He sighed and rubbed his temple. 'Look, just go home and let me have a bit of peace, will you? I don't want any more fuss.'

'All right,' Godfrey said. 'You don't have to get all irrigated, Noel. P'raps a sleep would do you good, duck. I'll pop back later then. Ay?' Godfrey gave repeated instructions for Noah to ring if he needed help, offered to make a flask of coffee, enquired how Noah would manage getting to the toilet, before he finally left to go home.

Noah sat back and smiled to himself. He looked at his foot and tried to wiggle the fat toes. There was only slight movement, but less pain now. 'Definitely on the mend,' he said. 'And at least I don't stink of cough medicine any more. All I need now is for Angela to get in her car and come round. And she will, I know she will.' His thoughts followed her impending visit, going over different versions of how it would be, who would say what. In all the scenarios he pictured, she was happy, crying tears of joy, and declaring her love for him.

Several hours passed as Noah sat in this state of reverie. The light began to change. Clocks had chimed during his daydreaming, but Noah had taken no notice of the time. Now he realised that the evening was slipping by. He pressed his bladder and nodded to himself. 'Thought so,' he said. 'Time for a piss.' His body was stiff when he moved to get himself up off the sofa, but after a few steps he became freer, and tackled the stairs confidently.

Before leaving the bathroom he paused to stare at his face in the mirror. He wanted to smile but his reflection remained blank. His face looked elongated. The deep lines that ran from his nose to his mouth made him look like a puppet – a ventriloquist's dummy. He turned away, still unable to smile. He went to his bedroom and rummaged in a drawer for his thickest pair of socks. He rolled both of these over his swollen right foot, and put a normal sock on his good foot.

Back downstairs, he felt round the edge of the hall cupboard for his soft suede shoes and put the left one on. He sat on the edge of the sofa for a long time, his ears primed to catch the first ring of the telephone. *Any time now*, he kept telling himself, *she'll ring any time now*. But the phone didn't ring. The last of the fading light shrank to darkness.

Noah rang Godfrey, who answered immediately. 'I'm going to bed now,' he said. 'Don't come round, all right?' He gave Godfrey no chance to reply before he put the phone down. He hobbled to the pew and picked up his car keys, opened the front door and looked up and down the road before stepping outside.

forty

She can't have found the roses in her bed yet, Noah thought, *otherwise she'd have been in touch. Or perhaps she's so overcome that she's in no fit state to drive.* As he drove past the newsagents he yapped like the dog from earlier, and laughed out loud. He continued on to the petrol station and pulled in. He topped up his almost full tank and went inside to pay. Two people were queuing at the checkout, and Noah walked to the back of the shop before joining them. He picked a can off the shelf and shook it, then put it back and took a different one. After rolling it thoughtfully in his hand for a moment, he nodded and took it to the checkout. He paid and went back to his car.

Outside Grace's house, Noah sat and watched the windows in sequence. The light was on downstairs and twice, a faint light showed through the upstairs window. 'She's spending a penny,' he said. He sat in his car for hours. The night air was cool and still. He watched as lights went off in houses, saw moisture form on car windscreens, and all the time kept guard on Grace's house. He changed his position every now and then to ease his stiff muscles but was determined not to let his injured foot distract him. It was still very tender and occasional sharp pains ran through the arch, making it twitch, but Noah tried hard to ignore it.

It was four-thirty in the morning when he started to shake the can of spray paint – softly at first, afraid that it might wake people, but then more vigorously, so that the metal beads rattled. All the houses were in darkness. Grace had gone to bed just before midnight. Noah opened his car door and took his time getting out, knowing that he would be stiff. He stretched and walked up and down the pavement.

Then he leaned over the car parked in front of his, held the can of red paint at arms length and pressed the button. A hazy circle of paint appeared on the bonnet. Noah stopped. He looked closely, straining to see his artwork in the orange glow of street lamps. Then he pushed himself against the side of the car and held his arm as far as he could across the roof.

'Shit,' he said. Even standing on tiptoe and with his arm at full stretch, Noah could not reach far enough across the car roof. He stood back and looked at the other cars. *Why do they need to make them all so fucking high?* He shook the spray can hard, making the beads rattle furiously. *Suppose I could climb up on the bonnet and* ... He tried to assess the best way to get himself up onto the car's bonnet without making a noise and without knocking his foot. *But what if someone drives past? Might be a bit difficult to explain ...*

His foot felt hot against the cold pavement and was throbbing inside the thick socks. Beads of sweat pierced Noah's skin and quickly turned to icy prickles on his face. *I'm not giving up now I've got this far*, he thought, and gave the paint can another fierce shake. *Right, I'll just have to do it then. It'll be worth it. Anything for my angel.* He limped to the front of the car and looked up and down the street. As he leaned forward and put his hand on the cold metal of the bonnet, he suddenly jolted upright as if he'd touched an electrified fence.

'Yes,' he said, too loudly. 'Why didn't I think of it before?' A dog barked. Noah froze, waiting for it to stop. When it did, he moved carefully to his own car and opened the passenger door. 'The bucket,' he said. 'The fucking bucket. Obvious, isn't it?'

Balanced on the petrol station bucket, Noah resumed his work with the spray paint. His body pressed against the side of the car to keep himself in place, he stretched his arm as far as he could across the roof. He sprayed each letter slowly, stopping to check it before doing the next one. Under the glow of the street lights, he couldn't make out the exact colour of the car, a murky, mid-blue or green perhaps, but was satisfied that his message was easy to see.

My Angel stood out in large clear letters. His arm ached when he had finished, so he rested before moving on to the next car. It was white. Noah put his bucket in place and got to work. He sprayed a large heart on the roof before filling it with his message: *Noah Loves Angela*. He sprayed three kisses on the bonnet, then he moved along to the next car. It was silver and looked as if it had just been polished. The chemical smell of the paint hung in the damp air, and Noah thought he could feel the fine mist settling on the back of his hand. He wrote *I Love You* then underlined it.

He walked backwards and leaned against Grace's garden wall, facing the cars. *She'll love this*, he thought. He assessed the distance of the next three cars in front of the ones he'd already decorated, and decided they would be visible from her bedroom window. He picked up the black bucket, shook the spray can and limped towards the first car. He spelled out the word *Good* on the roof. On the second car, he put *Morning*. Then he realised that the third car was red. 'Fuck,' he said, spitting the word into the silent street.

A dog barked further along the road; stopped after a few half-hearted woofs. Noah passed the red car and sprayed *Angela* on the next one, a beige Mini. He moved the bucket away from the cars and stood on it again to check his handiwork, frowning at the gap made by the red car. 'I know what will help,' he said. He sprayed an arrow along the side windows of the red car. *Now she'll see it easily*, he thought, pleased with his idea. The black bucket stood upside-down on the pavement. A temporary bollard for that morning's pedestrians.

As he drove home, Noah felt deeply tired. Each time he tried to reflect on his artistic endeavours, the memory slipped away, and his mind became numb. By the time he was back indoors, he could recapture only fragments of what he had done. Aware of a cold tingling on the pad of his right forefinger, he climbed slowly upstairs and held his hand under the hot tap for a while, then went to bed. Dreams saturated him immediately.

forty-one

Dull, thudding sounds came from the hall cupboard, but Noah knew not to open the door. He crouched outside the cupboard, naked except for his right foot, which was bound in a great wad of white, bloodstained cloth. In the dream, he could see through the door, even though it was still solid.

In the cupboard, Joseph Pepper was at work. He raised his cleaver carefully above an unidentifiable, waxy-looking carcass, then brought it down in a controlled arc. As he moved, grey ash rose from his skin like puffs of talcum powder. He looked up and saw Noah watching him.

'Bit cramped in here,' the butcher said. 'Not enough room to swing a cat. I'd get on better, see, with a bit more space.'

Noah pushed against the door with his shoulder. The rhythmic thudding continued.

'Think I didn't know you was there, did you?' Joseph Pepper said.

Noah screwed his eyes tight and shook his head. He wanted to run but couldn't leave the cupboard door.

'Who d'you think sorted your foot out for you? Know all about the body, butcher's do. Surgeons we was in times gone by, see. Come on, let me out.' Joseph Pepper sounded breathless. He wheezed heavily.

Noah pushed himself harder against the door, snatching at the discoloured rag wrapped around his right foot. It wouldn't come off. Clouds of ash rose from the surface of the fabric. Bloodstains darkened the deeper layers, as the butcher's apron bunched on his foot began to ooze blood. Noah watched his penis quiver slightly as urine trickled onto his legs.

'Natural reaction, that is,' said Joseph Pepper. 'Pigs do it all the time. There's piss everywhere by the end of the day. But it's all part of the job, see. The lovely boys – they did it as well. You get used to it in my line of work.' He laughed, a dry rasping noise. Regular thudding sounds continued to vibrate in the walls.

Noah ripped frantically at the binding on his foot as it changed colour from rust to almost black. He looked at his hands. Only his right forefinger was marked with the blood. He held it out, pointing at nothing. A different sound came from behind the door – a clean snapping like celery being broken. Then Noah heard his jackets swaying, the swish of nylon as the zipped protectors rubbed against each other.

'That's it,' said Joseph Pepper, 'all done for now and hung up to drain.'

Noah hit the door with his fist. 'Why d'you do this?' he shouted. 'Why?'

'Gets them nice and white, see,' the butcher said. 'All pale and lovely.' There was a smile in his voice.

Noah banged the door again. 'No, no, no, no,' he said, 'why d'you do *this*? Why do you keep coming back here? Why can't you leave me alone? You're dead now, you're gone, burnt to fucking cinders —'

'Call it a bit of overtime,' said Joseph Pepper. Puffs of ash wafted from the gap under the door. He added, 'A craftsman like me, see – don't like to leave his work unfinished. And there's them lovely boys to see to. I'm not going to leave them lying about, now am I?'

'You can't keep coming back, you're dead.' Noah was laughing but he didn't know why.

'Not going to let that stop me, am I?' said Joseph Pepper through the cupboard door, which bent and buckled as the butcher struck against the inside. The wood bowed out in the middle, taking on cartoon qualities. The hinges became elastic as the door stretched away from, then snapped back into its frame.

High-pitched laughter squealed in Noah's ears. He knew it was his own but had no sense of making the sound. It carried on, straining and warbling until it woke him. And became a ringing telephone.

forty-two

Noah nearly fell down the second half of the stairs, his heels scudding over the carpeted edges. He saved himself by grabbing the banister. His injured foot burned with pain from being knocked. He clutched at the receiver. 'Why don't you leave me alone?'

'Noah?' It was Helen.

Noah made a moaning, grunting sound at the back of his throat, words trapped under a bubble too thick to burst. Then he began to cry, spluttering and snorting into the phone.

'Hey, come on,' Helen said.

Noah cried harder at the kindness in her voice. Large sobs made him shudder and gasp. Tears mingled with flakes of dry skin, ran over his chin and down his neck. Extracts of the dream replayed in his mind, like a trailer for a film. As he rubbed away tears, new ones welled up and blurred his vision. Looking down at his naked body made him think of the carcass in his dream. His white legs were mottled with purple. Blue veins threaded just below the surface. The smell of stale urine clung to him.

'Noah, I'll come over,' Helen said. 'Okay?'

'I, I, I …' Words lodged in his throat.

'It's all right, Noah. Go and sit down. I won't be long.' Helen rang off.

Noah dragged himself upstairs, unreeled a long scarf of toilet paper and blew his nose. He pulled on his limp, stale clothes from yesterday, barely noticing the smell of paint. The trailing paper got caught inside his jogging trousers and protruded from the cuff of the left leg. The sobbing began to retreat. He was unaware of making a low, grizzling noise as he went downstairs to wait for Helen. She arrived about ten minutes after her phone call, and knocked on the door while Noah was blowing his nose again.

'Oh, look at you,' Helen said from the doorstep, reaching out her hand to stroke Noah's shoulder. He burst into tears again, and half fell into her arms. Easing him gently away, she held his hand while she stepped inside and closed the front door. She leaned against the wall and opened her arms to encircle him. He clung to her, crying into her shoulder and neck, as she rocked him from side to side.

Noah squeezed his eyes shut but tears still forced through the lids, and images of Joseph Pepper still darted across his vision. He could feel Helen stroking his back and his hair, and he knew that she was muttering something against the side of his head. He caught odd words.

'Poor you,' she said, and '... funny old thing.'

Eventually, Noah became calm. He leaned away from Helen and rubbed his eyes, took a deep breath. 'I can't stand it any more, Hell,' he said.

'Come with me,' Helen said. She took his hand and led him to the sitting room, sat him on the sofa. 'Tell me all about it.'

Noah twisted a wisp of hair at his temple. 'He's still here,' he said. 'He hasn't gone. And he'll keep on coming back now, I know he will. Oh Jesus, Hell.'

'All right, all right,' she said. 'Now just slow down. Who are we talking about?' She brushed the side of Noah's face with the back of her hand.

Noah shook his head. He was making the grizzling noise again. 'Him, it's *him*. Joseph fucking Pepper.'

'Noah, he's dead now.' She cupped his face, turned it towards her own. 'He's dead. You know that really, don't you? We watched his coffin disappear behind the curtains, didn't we? Hmm?'

Noah jerked his head away. He patted his pockets, looking for his length of toilet paper. His nose was beginning to run. 'He won't let that stop him,' he said, waving his hands as if to cast a spell on his leaking nose. 'I've got a tissue somewhere.'

Helen tugged lightly at the paper sticking out of his left trouser leg.

'Funny place to keep it,' she said smiling, 'but I didn't like to say.' Then she noticed his other foot. 'Oh God, what have you been doing to yourself?'

'Bit of an accident, that's all,' Noah said, and pulled the tissue free. He tucked his bruised right foot behind his left one. *Not bothered about that*, he thought, *I'd rather be covered in bruises than have that fucking butcher creeping about here all the time.* He blew his nose, dropped the crumpled ball of toilet paper on the floor.

'I thought it was going to be something about one of your ... well, one of these women you're seeing,' Helen said. 'But that funeral has really got to you, hasn't it?' She stroked his hand.

'It's not the funeral. It's *him*. He comes here, Hell. He's got things stored here, things he comes back to check. I knew before, because I kept finding them – in the cupboard, in the cellar, inside the clocks. Then when he died, it got worse. There's the dreams, he —'

Helen put her fingers up to Noah's mouth. 'Shush, shush,' she said. 'Don't get yourself upset again. Just think about it for a minute, Noah. You've just said it yourself. It was a bad dream. You don't believe in ghosts, you don't believe in life after death. In fact, I'd say you're one of the most sceptical people around, right?'

Noah nodded. He was about to speak but Helen carried on.

'So what's all this about then? Some old man you hardly knew, walking about in your house, checking on things he's got stored away in your cellar. And as if that wasn't bad enough, this particular old man is dead. Now, in my book that makes him more than just a nosy old so and so, trespassing on your property. That sounds more like a screenplay for a horror film.' She paused. 'Or just a really bad dream. Wouldn't you say?' She held Noah's hand and smiled.

She thinks I'm crazy, he thought. *The way she's talking, being so kind and everything, but really she thinks I'm a complete nutter.* He nodded and disappeared further into his own thoughts as Helen sat beside him, stroking his hand and talking softly. Noah had no idea what she was saying but found her voice comforting. *Can't stay here any more,* he thought. *I've got to get away. Just get a few things together and go. Perhaps I could stay with Hell? Or even him with the apron. Just for a few days. Not the*

Mother-parent though. Couldn't stand her being so jolly. Anyway, don't want to be near that stinking dog. And she might shut me in the cupboard again. Suddenly Noah sat up very straight. 'Angela,' he said. 'I can stay with Angela. Of course —'

'What? What d'you mean?' Helen said.

'Well, I can't stay here, can I? I know you don't believe me, and that's all right. The thing is, Hell, I've just got to get away. And Angela ... well, she's probably going to ask me to move in soon anyway.'

Helen sat very still, looking at Noah. After a while, she stood up. 'So it *is* about those women, after all,' she said.

'It's, no ... I told you. It's my dead fucking neighbour. But if the only solution is for me to get out of here, well, it would make sense, wouldn't it, for me to go to hers?' He untangled another section of toilet paper and wiped his nose, which was red at the tip.

Helen walked to the window and stood in front of it, facing Noah. Lit from behind, her face was in darkness. When she spoke, her voice quavered. 'You don't have to go to all this trouble, you know,' she said.

Noah strained to see her expression. 'What trouble?' he said.

'All this stuff about things going bump in the night, when all you really want to do is tell me that you're setting up home with some woman out of the paper.' She fiddled with the sleeve of her jumper. 'Does she even *know* about this, Noah?'

'No. And I don't want her to either. I mean, if she finds out, she might never come here again.'

Helen brushed something off the front of her jumper. 'No, I mean does she know about you moving in with her?'

Noah laughed. A wet, bubbling sound came from his nose and he quickly swiped at his nostrils with the tissue. 'Well, put it this way,' he said, 'when she looks out of her window this morning, she's going to have a pretty good idea about it.'

'I can't make sense of anything you're saying Noah. Just tell me what's going on,' Helen said. Her voice was thick. She flicked at each side of her face with the back of her hand.

Noah realised she was crying. 'You blubbing?' he said, peering at her shadowed face.

'Never mind me. Just tell me what's going on, because to be honest, Noah, I can't keep doing this.' She sniffed and searched her sleeve for a hanky. 'And yes, I am *blubbing*. Of course I'm bloody blubbing.'

Noah stretched forward and dangled a piece of toilet paper in front of Helen. He still couldn't see her face properly. *What do I do now?* he thought. *She comes here to listen to me, and now she's bloody crying as well.* He sighed. 'Well, I wanted to make myself clear ... let her know exactly how things are. So I left her a few messages last night.'

'On her answer phone, you mean?'

Noah shook his head and laughed again. 'No,' he said. 'I got sick of all that. I went round there, Hell.'

'And?' Helen said.

Noah saw images of his artwork in his mind – the large red heart, the messages and the kisses. He smiled to himself. *Wish I could have seen her face*, he thought. He pressed the tip of his forefinger against his thumb. It still felt slightly numb. Unconsciously, he lifted his hand to his nose and sniffed. A faint trace of the car paint was ingrained in the swirls of his fingerprint. He smiled again. Then he jumped, coming back to his surroundings as *Helen* clapped her hands sharply in front of him.

'Christ's sake —' he said.

Helen eased herself down onto the floor and knelt in front of him. 'You listening to me?' she said. 'I mean *really* listening? Not off on another daydream?'

Noah nodded. *Just look after me, Hell*, he thought. *You're good at that. I don't want any lectures.*

Helen shuffled her position so that she was sitting down, her legs tucked to one side. Her knees cracked as she moved. 'Got to spell it out for you, haven't I?'

Here we go, thought Noah. He folded his arms across his chest and waited. He thought of Angela, when she'd sat here, his hand hovering over her hair.

'I'd hoped you'd work it out for yourself, but ...' She looked at the carpet.

'Work what out?' He sounded sullen and impatient.

Helen lifted her head and raised her eyes to the ceiling. She took a deep breath and spoke to the clock on the wall behind Noah. 'Why I'm here,' she said, 'why I'm always here.'

Noah watched her eyes following the pendulum. Her face, always filled with kindness, looked sad and tired. 'You're being a friend,' he said. 'And I *am* grateful, honestly I am, Hell.' As he said it, he knew that he really meant it. He leaned forward slightly and patted Helen's upper arm.

She let out a sound, half-sigh, half-laughter. 'Yeah, a friend. That's right. That's me. Good old Helen, everybody's friend,' she said.

Noah felt nervous, uncertain what to do or say. *This is the wrong way round*, he thought. *I'm not supposed to be the one doing the listening.* 'Come on, Hell,' he said, and forced a laugh. 'I need you to be my agony aunt.'

Helen's shoulders slumped and she looked back down at the carpet. She gave a deep sigh. 'Well, I can't,' she said quietly. 'Not any more.'

Noah sat forward on the sofa. 'But you've always listened to me. You're good at it, you —'

Helen cut in, 'But not good at wearing the right clothes, am I? Or good at being thin and stunningly beautiful. Not good at having a soft little voice. And of course, now you've discovered my disgusting little secret – my little food problem – that doesn't exactly put me up there with the dream woman does it? I'm not good at fitting in with your idea of the perfect, ideal, one hundred per cent bloody wonderful dream woman.'

Noah grabbed a tuft of hair at the nape of his neck and twisted hard. His pulse was racing. His thoughts swirled like some mad fairground ride gone out of control. *We had a deal,* he thought. *She looks after me. She likes it. Now she wants all that to change.* He tried to smile. His face felt tight. 'Come on Hell, you know what I'm like – you know me better than anyone, I —'

'Oh I *know* you. I've sat and listened to you, I've cheered you up, supported you, covered for you at work, *defended* you at work, stood up for you against people who can't stand the sight of you. I've taken all your little digs and jibes about my clothes and my weight. God, I've even peered down your neck to look at your spots ...' She brushed tears off her cheeks.

Noah was about to stand up but Helen put her hand on his knee.

'No, hang on a minute,' she said. 'You're right, I do know you. But what do I get back in return? What? Shall I tell you?'

Noah leaned back stiffly, pushing himself into the sofa. *Don't need this*, he thought. *After the night I've had, I really don't fucking need this*. He clutched his arms tightly round his ribs, and pressed his lips firmly together.

'What I get in return,' Helen said, 'is you taking the mickey, you making unkind comments, you letting me right inside your life, but staying on the very edge of mine. You're selfish, Noah. You're so wrapped up in yourself, you wouldn't notice if my head fell off and rolled across the floor.' She stopped to blow her nose.

Noah blinked hard. 'That's not fair,' he said. 'You're just not being fair.' He wanted to get up, leave the room, but Helen sat too close for him to move.

'No,' she said, 'I'll tell you what's not fair, Noah. It's not fair that you've let me give so much, and given nothing back. You've let me get close to you. You've let me care about you, then you've thrown it all back in my face by getting hitched up with some woman out of the small ads. That,' she brushed tears off her face, 'is what's not fair.'

Noah twitched his left leg up and down. His right foot throbbed. The carousel in his head rotated in slow, distorted circles. He thought about his painted messages, about the dream, about Godfrey helping him in the bath. Everything slurred together and spread across his view of Helen, sitting in front of him. 'I've ... I've got to go,' he said.

'Go where, Noah? Go and see one of your women? Or go and look for dead neighbours lurking about in the cellar? I suppose anything would be better than staying here with me, wouldn't it?'

Noah struggled forward. He tried to stand, but Helen stayed

too close to his legs. He half-stood, bent at the knees, trying not to topple backwards onto the sofa. *Get out of the way*, *please just get out of the way*, he thought. But she didn't move, and Noah sat back down. They waited in silence, the room filled with the static charge of their tension. Noah stared at Helen. She looked at the floor, the clocks, the window – anywhere but at him. *I've got to get out of here*, Noah thought. *Got to get to Angela's. She might even be on her way here. That's all I need – if she turns up and finds another woman sitting on the floor . . .*

He watched Helen's eyes, red and puffy, as they moved from one part of the room to another. Her face looked miserable. Noah continued to stare, scrutinising the rest of her. *At least she's got a decent pair of jeans on*, he thought. *Not three sizes too small for a change. And that jumper, it looks new. Actually suits her.* 'You look nice,' he said.

Helen laughed, a small dismissive puffing sound. 'Oh right, here it comes,' she said. 'The criticism of my clothes.'

'No, really,' he said. 'You do look nice.'

'Well that's quite something, coming from you. But it's not enough is it? I mean, you've made your mind up, haven't you? There's only one woman for you. I could be wearing a designer ball gown and a bloody tiara, and you'd still be off after yet another woman who doesn't want to know. Wouldn't you Noah?'

Noah twisted his hair. 'But she does want to know. That's what I've been telling you, Hell. This one's different.'

Helen shrugged. 'Oh, they're always different, Noah. You don't want to think about that though, do you?' Her knees made loud popping noises again as she shifted her weight and heaved herself up off the floor.

Noah stood up immediately.

'You go,' Helen said. 'Go and see how different your special woman is, Noah. And don't forget to tell her about your friendly neighbourhood dead man, will you? And the news about you moving in with her. I mean, she'll need to know, won't she? Go on, go and tell her all the things you've sat and told me. Get her to have a look at your acne, ask her what your dandruff's like, the hairs up your nose – everything. See how different, how special she is then.'

Noah bit his lip. 'Why you being like this, Hell?' he said. He stood near the doorway, the baggy jogging trousers bunched at his knees.

'Why?' she said. 'You really don't know, do you?' She shook her head. . 'Well, could it have something to do with the fact that I care about you? D'you think that could be it?'

Noah stared at her. 'But ...' He moved back to the sofa and sat on its arm.

'Yes, I know,' she said. 'Doesn't make any sense, does it? I mean, you're cruel, self-centred, you use people, you're ...' she wiped her eyes and blew her nose, '... just my type, in other words.'

'I'm not ... what d'you mean?' Noah tugged at his ear lobe.

'Oh, you know – I go for people who don't give a toss. The more they walk over me, the more I want them. Comes from having a mad Mother. I've always looked after her, and she's always treated me as though I'm invisible. Same thing with men, I always go for the ones that can't wait to walk in the opposite direction. Then you come along, all needy and neurotic, and hey presto, I turn straight back into a doormat.'

'*I'm* not neurotic.' Noah said. 'And I never asked you to help —'

Helen interrupted. 'Oh but you did, Noah. All the time. "Tell me what to wear, Hell," "Tell me how I look, Hell." And anyway, I can't help myself. I'm probably programmed to do it or something.' She dabbed at her eyes again, with the soggy tissue. Her face was blotchy.

Noah felt a rising panic in his stomach as he watched her. *Too much going on*, he thought. *Need to get out of here*. He laced his fingers at the back of his neck, closed his eyes and pulled his head down towards his chest. *Got to clear my head, got to try and get this all straight.* When he looked up, Helen was standing in the hallway, facing back into the room. Light from the window highlighted her puffy, red face. Noah saw that she was still crying.

'I'd better go,' she said.

Noah nodded.

'I'm sorry,' she smiled at him. 'It's what you wanted isn't it? But not who you wanted it from, hmm? I suppose we don't always get to choose, you know ... who loves us, do we?' She closed the door softly as she left.

forty-three

Noah sat staring into space. Helen's face kept coming to him, pained and wet with tears. A knot tightened in his stomach, he felt hot but his skin was covered in cold sweat. He tried to think clearly but his mind felt clogged and slow. *I'll go to Angela's*, he decided, and picked up his car keys.

On the way to his car he felt light as air, as if he was hovering above the pavement. He rubbed his hand over his concave stomach. *Haven't had anything to eat since ...* He couldn't remember. He was pleased. The light-headed feeling and the hollow sensation made him feel slightly drunk. *Mustn't tell the Mother-parent*, he thought, and smiled. *Don't want her coming round to force-feed me. Or lock me in the cupboard.*

He got in his car and drove away, distracted by snatches of broken thought, and pleasantly numbed by his inability to follow them. He got to Grace's road without noticing the journey, and parked at the far end, on the other side from her house. From where he sat, he could see her upstairs windows but not her front door.

Bit busier here than it was last night, he thought. He watched as three police officers – two male and one female – walked back to their parked car. Two little boys with bicycles were looking at the police car, and the youngest policeman bent down to speak to them, then he got in the car and it pulled away.

'It's them bloody magpies again,' Noah said, and ran through the song in his head. *One for sorrow, two for joy, three for a girl ...*

'Three for a girl, well, they've got that right – three for *my* girl.' A small group of people was starting to disperse away from the cars that Noah had sprayed. Some of them wandered back to their houses. Noah saw two elderly black Labradors, cajoled up from their lopsided resting places, and led away by their owner. Two men and three women remained by the cars. As if he was watching television, Noah observed them through his windscreen. He thought they looked excited, with all their hand gestures, head shaking and nodding. One of the women slapped the roof of the silver car. Her face was flushed and her mouth moved quickly, although Noah could not hear what she said. He wanted them all to go. *Can't walk up to Angela's door with that lot standing there, can I?*

He sat looking at the five people as they moved round the cars, rubbed at the paint, talked to each other. 'Actually, they should feel honoured,' he said. 'Being part of something so romantic, helping me and Angela get together.' He rubbed his hands then clasped them between his knees. *Soon as everyone's gone*, he thought, *I'll go and see her.*

He sank down in his seat and watched until the last of the gathering – a short man with a huge, pregnant-sized belly, had waddled back to his house. Noah hooked his fingers through the door catch, but didn't open the door. He froze, suddenly afraid, his heart beating fast. *What about the police? They're bound to be back.*

He fiddled with the bunch of keys, rattling them from side to side, unsure whether or not to drive away. Then he grabbed them, flung open the door and walked across the road to Grace's house.

He smiled as he passed the cars, but when he got to Grace's path, he stopped. Fear paralysed him again. For several seconds, he stood fixed in place, his body tensed against some imminent attack. Then he turned and ran back to his car, ignoring the slicing pain in his foot as it struck against the surface of the road.

He had to grip the steering wheel hard to stop his hands shaking. He drove past the red-sprayed cars without looking at them.

forty-four

Noah found a telephone box and parked next to it. He rang Grace.

She picked up the phone and said a bright hello.

'It's me,' Noah said.

'Oh,' she said. 'You. What do you want?' Her voice had changed, become heavy and flat.

'Listen, I did it because of how I feel for you. I didn't mean to cause any problems —'

'Well, I really wish you hadn't,' she said. 'Such a stupid thing to do.' Her voice was cold. 'It was quite a shock, you know. All that red on my sheets, I didn't know what on earth —'

Noah cut in, 'It wasn't meant to shock you, honestly. And as for the police and everything, well, I didn't think you'd take it like that —'

'Oh, don't think it wasn't in my mind,' she said. 'And if you ever come here again, I will, I mean it, I *will* go to the police.'

Noah closed his eyes and held his breath for a while. He felt dizzy. 'But they've been. I saw them, not long ago. I mean, the cars ...'

'What cars?' she said. 'I've only just got up. Believe it or not, I couldn't sleep last night — what with you prowling about in my bedroom. I don't ever want you here again. Is that clear enough for you? Not ever. You're a horrible little man, you give me the creeps. I did feel sorry for you, but you gave me the creeps right from the start. I try not to judge by appearance and all that sort of thing, but I should have followed my instincts. I tried to be friendly but look where that's got me ...' Her voice rose and trembled. 'I was so stupid to have anything to do with you.'

'But, I told you — I love you, Angela, you know I do.' He

twisted the telephone cable round his wrist. 'Leave me alone,' she said it quietly and slowly. Then she repeated herself, shouting this time, 'Leave me alone, you creep. Leave me *alone*.' The phone went dead.

Noah leaned heavily against the thick glass wall. The receiver purred in his hand. He wanted to cry but no tears would come. He felt empty. The word 'creep' was trapped inside the telephone box. He couldn't stop hearing it. *How could she? How could she say that to me when she knows how I feel about her? How could she be so hurtful? I only wanted to love her.* He dropped the receiver and let it dangle, then pushed hard against the stiff door and stumbled to his car. Sitting inside, he gazed ahead, seeing nothing. 'How could she?' he kept repeating to himself.

forty-five

Noah drove to Esther's house. He watched the traffic carefully, looking for police cars, expecting at any moment to hear sirens, see flashing blue lights. 'Can't go home,' he told himself. 'They'll be waiting for me. Thanks to bloody Angela.' He brushed away a film of sweat on his forehead and wiped it on his jeans. 'I never thought she'd do this to me.'

When he parked outside Esther's house, Noah felt his stomach turning over in sickening somersaults. *At least I'll be all right with her*, he thought. *Though Christ knows I don't want to be here.*

He forced himself to walk to her front door, rang the bell and waited. The churning in his stomach speeded up, and a watery fluid filled his mouth. He clenched his teeth tightly, pressed his hand against his mouth, and made a low moaning sound. After a few seconds, the certainty that he was going to be sick receded, and Noah's stomach settled. He pressed the bell again.

'Come on,' he said, and stepped backwards to look at the upstairs windows. The house was still and quiet. He pressed the bell again, this time leaving his finger on the button for a long time. 'Stupid cow can't be out,' he said. 'She just *can't* be.' He glared down at the cheerful flower tubs either side of the front door, then jabbed at the bell several times with his finger. 'Open the door. Come on, open the fucking door.' He was shouting now, and thumping his fist against Esther's front door.

The sound of a voice, muffled at first, came from the neighbouring house. Noah heard locks being pulled back, a chain rattling, and then a man stepped out onto the path.

'What's going on?' His stern face was spattered with shaving foam. 'What's your game, mate? What the bloody hell d'you think you're up to?' He stood with his fists on his hips.

'Obvious, isn't it?' Noah said, 'I'm trying to get an answer.' He gave the man a quick look then turned back to face Esther's door.

'Yeah? From the whole street, by the sounds of it. Not in, is she?' He crossed his arms and stepped closer to his side of the garden fence. 'Now, I suggest you try again another time.' He stared at Noah. 'You got that?'

Noah turned and walked back to his car. He muttered under his breath, 'Mind your own fucking business' He didn't look back but knew that the man was watching him as he got in his car.

Inside, Noah locked the door and sat back hard against the seat. He felt sick again, but fought it with his anger at Esther's neighbour, who was still standing on his path. 'Interfering bastard,' Noah said, and was gripped by a convulsion that tilted him forward. He leaned towards the passenger seat, as hot vomit pumped up his throat. It hit the seat and floor, instantly changing the dark upholstery to a glistening beige colour.

Looking at the spreading heap made Noah sick again. He dragged his hand over his mouth and sat back, his head leaning on the headrest. He kept his eyes closed for a while. The stench of fresh vomit filled the car. Noah felt for the handle and wound his window down three inches. *I should have hung on to that bloody bucket*, he thought.

The speed of his recovery surprised him – his head and stomach felt calm and settled. He opened his eyes and glanced at the house next to Esther's. The man had gone. 'Fucking good job,' he said. A lump of something soft was stuck to his bottom lip, and he wiped it away many times after it had gone.

He sat outside Esther's house for nearly two hours, drifting in and out of a light, restless doze. People walking past made no attempt to hide their curiosity, and looked through his side window. Noah cut himself off by refusing to return their looks, and kept his gaze inside the car. He had become used to the stink of the vomit. He'd covered the biggest heap, on the floor, with his road atlas. He felt vaguely annoyed at Esther for taking so long to come home, but he grew increasingly detached from the outside world and everything that had happened. He felt safe in the cocoon of his car, and content to stay there, waiting.

When Esther tapped on his window, Noah saw her as if in a dream. He watched as she smiled broadly and mouthed words at him. He felt no need to respond from his distant observation place.

Esther became more animated as he sat unmoving and barely blinking, looking at her. Eventually she realised that the window was slightly open and angled her head to talk through the gap.

'Can you hear me, Noah? You coming in?' She waggled her fingers over the top of the glass.

Noah still stared at her.

'S'ever so nice to see you. I've been thinking about you a lot. Ssaid lots of little prayers for you, sso you'd get better. Aaah, come in and have a drink.' She smiled, her breath making a faint mist on the window.

Look at her, Noah thought. *That stupid grin. That fat body. And she's clumsy as Coco the fucking clown. But ...*

'Noah?'

But she's bothered about me. At least she cares about me. Wants *me, even.* He placed his hands on the steering wheel and laid his head gently on top of them. He was crying softly, tears sliding down his cheeks and onto his hands.

'Come on Noah,' she said. 'You come in with me. I'll look after you.'

When he looked at Esther's face, he saw how kind her expression was, saw the concern in her eyes. *She really does care*, he thought. *Wants to help. And I've been ...*

'Open the door Noah.'

I've been so fucking rotten to her. Used her. Treated her like shit.

'What about if I get in and ssit with you, then?' Esther waved her fingers again. Her smile had gone. She looked worried.

Noah lifted his head off the steering wheel and pressed his knuckles against his eye sockets for a few seconds. Then he shook his head and wound the window down fully. He felt weak and deeply tired. He was still crying, but paid no attention to his tears or wet face. He saw the concern on Esther's face change. Now she looked wary.

'What?' she said. She was crouching beside his car.

Noah reached out and put his hand on her forearm. He looked into her eyes. 'I'm sorry,' he said. 'I'm really sorry.'

'Oh, don't be ssilly, you've got nothing to be sss —' Her face beamed with a huge smile again, her shoulders lifted up to her ears.

Noah squeezed her arm. 'No, no, please, don't say anything. I can't, I'm not … this isn't right for me.' He saw her smile disappear. 'But you've done nothing wrong. You deserve better.' He gave her arm another squeeze. 'I won't be in contact again. But I wanted to say thank you. Thank you and sorry, Esther.' He looked in her eyes for a few more seconds, then drew his hand in and closed the window. He started the car and drove away. His hand slid down the gear stick, on the slimy coating of cold sick.

forty-six

Noah saw the flashing red light on his answer phone as soon as he stepped inside his hall. As he held his finger over the button ready to play the messages, there was a knock on the door.

'Three guesses,' he said quietly, 'who that is.' He opened the door and let Godfrey in.

'Good job I popped round, duck. Only came for a quick word, but the state of your car ... I *knew* you wasn't well. You look terrible, white as a whasname ... a pillowslip. You should of let me stay and look after you.'

Noah shook his head.

'I would've, Noel.' Godfrey brushed the front of his dark green apron.

'I know you would,' Noah said. He gave a faint smile, and put his hand against the wall to steady himself. *And I'd have let you. Then I'd have told you to fuck off.*

'You go and sit yourself down, Noel, and I'll pop home and get me bucket and sponge. Have that front seat good as new in a whasname ... in a tick, we will.'

Noah shook his head again. 'You know what it is, do you?'

'Well, it's not rice puddin', is it duck?' Godfrey said. 'I'm not worried about a bit of old sick. Never hurt nobody, that hasn't.' Godfrey pulled his apron straight. 'Anyway, I've got me gloves, haven't I?'

Noah watched Godfrey fiddle with the door latch. He felt a great surge of affection spread through his stomach and chest, and then lodge itself in his throat. He waited until he was sure he wouldn't cry. He pointed at Godfrey's apron. 'That suits you, that dark green.'

'Oh thanks very much, love. Special whasname, it was. Special offer. Two for the price of three. Got a dark blue one and a couple like this. Lovely bit of cloth, it is.' He adjusted the hem with a quick tug.

'Looks better than those bloody frilly ones,' Noah said.

Godfrey slapped Noah's arm with the back of his hand. 'Cheeky bugger,' he said. 'I can tell you're on the mend. Now, do as you're told, duck. Go and sit down while I give that car of yours a good going over.' He opened the door and stood in a slice of bright light, making a dark, squat shadow on the hall floor.

'What did you come round for?' Noah asked. 'You said you wanted a word.'

Godfrey looked back over his hunched shoulder. 'Oh, it's about Helen's leaving do, duck. I thought we could —'

Noah cut in. '*What* leaving do? What fucking leaving do?'

Godfrey turned to face Noah. 'Oh, Gordon do-dah, I hope I haven't gone and put my whasname in it. I thought you knew, duck.'

'Knew what?' Noah said. He gripped the edge of the wall, his fingers like locked claws. 'And how do *you* know anyway?'

'Well, Helen popped round to see me, Noel. Must have been, oh …' Godfrey looked at the nearest clock. 'Probably about —'

'Never mind what fucking time it was,' Noah said. 'Just tell me what she said.'

'Well, it was while you was out anyway – she'd made her mind up, she said, duck. Wanted a fresh do-dah … a fresh start. Said she wasn't getting nowhere with it, so she was giving up before she wasted too many more years.'

'*What?*' Noah said. 'Getting nowhere with what?' He could feel a fluttering sensation in his stomach. His legs shook at the knees. *Butterflies in my stomach again*, he thought. *Different fucking butterflies this time though.*

'Well, work I suppose, Noel.' Godfrey turned away and stepped out onto the path. 'Right, I'm just going to get this sick mopped up, duck.' He disappeared out of Noah's view.

Can't fucking help himself, can he? Noah thought. *Can't stop being a busybody, always looking after someone – after me.* He sighed deeply. *And*

I can't stop throwing it back in his face, can I? He leaned into the wall. Coolness seeped through his arm. 'Hell's leaving me,' he said in a whisper. 'I've lost her. And I still need her. I always have. I shouldn't have let her go. That night when I held onto her – should have kept holding her tight.' He stared at the grandfather clock and realised that it had stopped. 'It can stay like that now,' he said. 'They all can. No point going round and round forever. And staying the fucking same.' He eased the shoe off his left foot and swung it across the hall with his toes.

forty-seven

Noah pressed the button to play his messages. His Mother spoke first, telling him she had called round to see him. Then he heard Grace's voice. He cringed, expecting anger and coldness. As he listened, tears blurred his vision, and he slumped against the wall. 'She's not going to tell them, at least that shows she's still got some feelings for me,' he said. He pressed the button and listened to her message again. Her voice was clipped and formal but not filled with the ice he'd expected.

'Noah, this is Grace,' she said. 'I've seen the cars now. I can't believe ... well anyway, I've seen the damage now. The funny thing is, my car was further down the road. I couldn't get a space any closer. No one knows it's got anything to do with me. It's not my name, of course ... I thought you ought to know I won't be contacting the police. I actually feel sorry for you. You're obviously not well. If there's anything else like this, I *will* report it. *Really*. All I can say is —'

Her message was cut short by the machine. Noah played it twice more. 'Wonder what she was going to say,' he said. 'Not how much she loved me, was it?' He forced a feeble laugh. The sound stretched and lingered. He laughed again. Then he couldn't stop. He laughed harder and louder, gasping for enough air to fuel continuous explosions of joyless, raucous noise. He hugged his birdcage ribs and spewed out a raw, rasping cackle.

'After —' he was overcome by the jagged laughter again. 'After all the planning and meetings and ...' he snorted as he stared to giggle again, 'phone calls and fucking messages and ...' He made a high whooping sound, slapped his thigh theatrically. 'After all that, and I *still* haven't found —'

Several minutes later, the heaving laughter began to subside.

Noah struggled to regain control over his breathing, which was interrupted by random outbursts of giggling. When he had finally calmed himself, he sat down wearily on the pew. 'So,' he said. 'That's it then.' He sat listening.

The house ticked and clicked and whirred with the sounds of the clocks, counting out their final hours. Noah had never noticed how intrusive the sound was. It seemed to eat into him, peck and chip at his skin.

'Should have made do with what I already had, shouldn't I?' He looked round the hall. His face was twisted with misery. 'I mean, there's plenty of lovely boys here to keep me company. Cupboards full of them. *They* won't go away and leave me will they?'

He stood up, walked to the hall cupboard and opened the door. The blue bathrobe was coiled on the floor. Noah knelt down, lifted an edge and pulled it over himself as he curled into a ball on the cupboard floor. The smell of cough medicine comforted him. A thin line of saliva unwound itself from the corner of his mouth. He lay in the dimness of the half-closed cupboard, and stared up.

The swaying shapes above him hung in a neat row. In the order they were killed.